# Ditch Weed

ISBN # 978-1-940189-33-8



Cover design by Babski Creative Studios
Cover image courtesy of iStock photos

Printed in United States

Twisted Road Publications

# Ditch Weed

a novel by
## Rhett DeVane

Dedicated to the people in my life who have
helped me learn to channel my inner ditch weed.

# Acknowledgements

I wish to take a deep bow of gratitude to the following folks:

my dedicated editor/publisher Joan Leggitt, for her talent, patience, and guidance.

my ever-expanding clan of fellow writers, especially critique group members, past and present: Donna Meredith, Susan Womble, Gina Edwards, Peggy Kassees, Pat Spears, and Lynne Bryant.

longtime friends Susan Mary Malone and Cherry Weiner, the two people who first believed in me as a fiction writer.

heart-family members Denise Fletcher, Jerry Johnson, and Scott Lee. Denise and Jerry, for their input on deer hunting, Scott for his knowledge of Florida waterway laws.

high school creative writing teacher Sharon Lasseter, for lighting that torch under me all those years ago.

my cousin Audrey Dees and her late husband Robert Dees for sharing their knowledge of vintage cricket buckets.

the Tallahassee water aerobics gang. There was no end to the ideas that popped to mind as we joked, splashed, and managed not to drown.

Chattahoochee, Florida, for being a special and interesting place to grow up, truly a town where everyone knew everyone and looked out for each other.

Dorris and Theresa DeVane, the best parents a girl could ever have, for instilling a deep reverence and respect for the North Florida forests, wildlife, and waterways.

my readers, who continue to inspire me.

And finally, to the universal, all-knowing essence that graced me with the desire and ability to create settings and characters and bring them to life on the page.

# Foreword

**Ala-dang-bamer, Summer of 2018**

**M**ama called me Danae the Ditch Weed. Said that wasn't a put down. It was a compliment, a tribute to my stubborn nature.

A ditch weed will grow anywhere, anytime. It'll send up flowers even when everything else bakes to brown. Besides, a weed is just a plant growing in a place you don't want it to grow. And low and behold, if ditch weeds aren't looked upon favorably these days. Now, they're native wildflowers. People take their pictures and make maps on what roadsides or swamps to find them. Carloads of eco-tourists roam in SUVs, ready to check off the ones they spot.

Ditch weed. Wildflower. Guess I'm both.

I am wild, or I was. And I have produced one flower in my life: Stella. Named after my mama Estelle. With my sister Mouse's name tagged on: Marie.

My fingers twitch. My skin prickles. I can feel every nerve on edge. A joint would make this situation, this place, tolerable, but I don't smoke now, legal or otherwise. Haven't in years, after I found out Stella was growing in my belly. Quit drinking then, too.

My daughter runs up and screeches to a halt, holds up her hand.

I admire the insect resting in her open palm. "That's what we called a Georgia Thumper. Pretty, huh?"

Stella nods. In her hand, the black grasshopper with yellow racing stripes perches with no sign of distress. Good thing, too. They can hiss and vomit a nasty dark goo the locals call tobacco spit. Like my sister Mouse, Stella has a way with creatures. Will Stella be like Mouse when she grows older? Mouse, who never got that chance. But by God, my daughter will.

"Farmers hate 'em," I say. "They're destructive to crops, but I always thought they were pretty. In a few weeks, that little 'hopper will grow to over three inches long."

Stella holds her lips in an O. She squats and urges the insect to launch from her palm. Like Mouse in that way too. My sister would never trap anything, never hurt anything. Mouse wouldn't even capture lightning bugs in a canning jar, regardless of the fact Mama had punched air holes in the screw-off top.

"Can we go into the house, Mama?"

"No, Bug. The floorboards are rotten in too many places. No telling what kind of critters are living in there."

I have no desire to set foot one inside. Next time I happen by here, which I never plan to do anyway, this old shack will be nothing but a ghost. The new owners can raze it, or burn it.

"You lived here when you were little like me?" Stella's gaze roams from the covered porch with its buckling wood, to the curls of paint hanging from the clapboard, then up to where the storms have rolled up the tin roof like the lid of a sardine can.

"I did. Until after your grandmama passed. Then I lived with Aunt Sylvia. She passed before you were born."

"Did I have a granddaddy too?"

"Yes. You did. He lived here." With Gary and his two cousins, and Malcolm and his father Jerome, reliable men have been a force in Stella's life. Unlike mine.

I dig in my pocket for the cell phone. Where is that realtor?

"Can we come back here sometime?" Stella bounces from one foot to the other. Her pigtails swing.

The woods call to her. I understand. We have parks in Chattahoochee, and plenty of trees. But Stella hasn't yet ventured into the North Florida backwoods. I vow to take her, next time Malcolm and I go scouting for the best spots to hunt deer. I'm not sure if I'll introduce her to guns and hunting. Maybe hiking.

Unlike me, Stella's slight of build, like Mama and my sister Mouse. Her eyes favor her daddy's, but the rest of her speaks of the Wilson women. Her size doesn't mean she's weak, or timid. The child ain't afraid of nothing. For that, I am both proud and a little anxious.

Reckon Gary deserves credit, too. The father of my child is gentle and patient. Heck, he can get Stella to mind better than me or anyone else.

A maroon sedan pulls into the driveway. Ruddy dirt clouds rise and settle in its wake. The next owners should pave it. A woman steps out, papers in hand.

Today, the house and the ten acres it sits on go onto the market. Land ain't worth squat here in rural south Ala-dang-bamer. I'll price it right and take the first offer, just to be rid of it. Most of the money will go into Stella's college fund. Mama would like that: her granddaughter, the first to get so far along with an education. Stella leans toward veterinary medicine. She also plans to be a professional dancer. Or maybe a queen, or an astronaut. She keeps her options open.

"Are we going home after this?" Stella asks.

"Yes. Mama Mevlyn is cooking your favorite, chicken 'n' dumplings."

"Umm!" My daughter spins, her arms held like propellers.

"Run on and play while I speak to this lady."

"I'm going to find that sugar-plum tree!" Her words come out in twirly bits, high and low as she rotates.

I smile, remembering her, and my, favorite poem from childhood, The Sugar-Plum Tree—one my mama shared with me, then I shared with my daughter. Mental note: find an appropriate shrub in Miz Mevlyn's yard and make Stella a magical sugar-plum tree loaded with candy and confections—keep the tradition alive. It'll be a good birthday theme. "Don't go past where the grass stops," I call out, "and steer clear of the briar thicket in the back yard."

"How come?" The spinning stops. She holds her arms akimbo, sassy-like.

Because bad things happened in that corner.

Because I will shield you from them.

Because it's not weeds growing there. It's vines. And they will snare you.

"Snakes. Snakes might be in there." What a lame answer. Kid deserves the truth. One day. When she's older.

"But—"

"I know you aren't scared of them, Bug. Humor me, will you? I don't want to rush you to the hospital this morning because you tangled with a rattlesnake, and besides, there're dumplings waiting, back at Mama Mevlyn's."

My daughter lets out a whoop, twirls a few times more.

"We have one quick stop to make, then home."

"Where to, Mama?"

"To the place some of your family rests."

She looks at me funny, her eyebrows scrunched.

To the tiny cemetery in the woods next to a deserted church, to pay respects to Uncle Bully and Aunt Sylvia. And to the people who used to be my family.

Stella takes off. Her pigtails wave like twin banners.

"She's a cutie." The realtor stands a few feet away, watching Stella fly. "Too bad you can't stay here and build a new house. It's a lovely place."

One

## Chattahoochee, Florida, May 2010

"They ought to sell underthings in dadgum gray-blue," Mevlyn Jenson mumbles. She watches a young gal load indigo jeans with a handful of white T-shirts and underwear. "They gonna end up that shade anyhow."

Sonny, the terrier/mutt mix, spots the newcomer and doesn't bark. A good sign. Sonny is a spot-on judge of questionable character. Still, Mevlyn notes how the little dog yawns, stretches, and glances toward her for confirmation.

The woman—not much more than a girl really—fits what Mevlyn calls "P.R. People." Not Public Relations, but Purty-much Ruined. This one has P.R. etched all over her, as clear as if it had been printed in permanent marker. The way she keeps her eyes aimed down like she'll blend into the fake pine paneling if she can. The way her stick-skinny shoulders curl forward and her hair looks like it tangled with a weed-whacker. But there's a bra line and no skin tight pants with the top of thong underwear showing. Mevlyn chalks the gal a few points for that.

Mevlyn tosses a dryer-warmed sheet onto the folding table and crosses the Wash-Away Laundromat. Sonny's nails click-clack on the stained dark green linoleum behind her. They both stop and stand beside the woman, Mevlyn with her arms propped on her ample hips, Sonny sniffing the air. "Honey, didn't your mama teach you about washing clothes?" Mevlyn pops an air bubble from a thick wad of gum for emphasis. Sonny steps closer, snuffles the young woman's feet.

She looks from the dog, then up to Mevlyn. "Ma'am?"

So much pain echoes from inside those brown eyes, Mevlyn feels a wave of weakness threaten her balance. Give the gal a few more points for being polite. "Darks in one load and lights in another, lest your drawers get a good dose of cast-off dye."

The young woman digs in her ratty shorts pocket and produces three quarters, a dime, and a handful of lint. Mevlyn's black-painted eyebrows ripple. Her husband of going on sixty years tells her they look like wooly worms auditioning for a hoochie-coochie show, or at least he did before he got eat up with cancer so bad he doesn't have the energy to care much about nothing anymore. "You're new to this, ain't cha?"

The woman's gaze drops to those Dollar Store flip-flops. Sonny tips his head from one side to the other, assessing the stranger, listening for cues.

"I can't stand by and watch your pure ruination." Mevlyn pokes through the soiled laundry, selecting the pale-shaded clothes. So many years of touching other folks' human soil makes her impervious to the threat of bodily fluids. "I'll help you out this once, but I aim for you to pay close attention, hear?"

Mevlyn trundles back to her supplies, then returns and measures a cup of soap powder into the second washer, loads the coin tray, and gives it a hearty shove. "From now on, you bring more in here than a pocket full of lint. You ain't got enough money there for one load, much less two and a dryer. And extra soap powder. Can't do without that."

She dials the water temperature and allows the basin to fill. "Run your water in, first off. That way, you don't end up with clumps of soap on your clothes. Cold for colors. Warm or hot for whites or lights."

Mevlyn mashes the T-shirts and underwear into the water. "And don't go cramming them all in on one side, neither. Makes the washer off-balance. Lordy, if I had a nickel for every washer tore up by that practice, I could rent the Riviera and invite half of this town. Even out your load like I'm doing." Mevlyn studies the gal for a moment through thick false lashes. "Reckon you can recall all that?"

"Yes 'um."

"It's a smart person knows when to ask for help," Mevlyn says. She slams the washer lid and calls back over her shoulder as she turns away, "fools let on like they know it all."

Sonny snorts, then gives a half-hearted woof! before turning around and tip-tapping back to his bed of towels beneath the front counter. If Mevlyn had to supply what her little watchdog meant by his comment, she would guess "uh-huh, fool."

Mevlyn scans the room, checking the status of her two reserved dryers, glancing down the scuffed tile for signs of leaking water or cast-off trash. The joint might be old and near worn out, like her, but by God, she will keep it presentable.

The Wash-Away Laundromat has seen over fifty-five years of service. Mevlyn often ponders, if all the socks she has washed over those years lined up top to toe, would they stretch to London or Moscow? Or maybe around the world? If she had internet, she could look it up. Someone somewhere had figured the answer, or said they did.

One sure fact about the business of keeping clean: people's soiled laundry reveals epistles about their lives. The preacher of one Baptist church has a passion for dark chocolate, from the looks of the smudged icing stains on his Sunday dress shirts. He drinks red wine, not the watered down grape juice used for communion. And across the years, Mevlyn has seen enough lipstick-tattooed collars from supposed happily married men to start a gossip column for the Twin City News. Lord knows, she doesn't like to think about what dapples the sheets.

Intimate apparel provides the most intriguing and revealing tidbits. Mevlyn makes her way across the room, chuckling in spite of the pain in her left hip. She drags a damp comforter from the maws of the triple-loader, heavy-duty, upright washer. Amazing, how many men don't wear briefs at all! When that fact crosses her mind, she can barely contain a smile thinking about some of Chattahoochee's most upright and uptight citizens flying commando.

Her infirm husband Sam has gotten terribly lax about personal hygiene. Mevlyn counts the pairs of boxers in the hamper at the end of a week to assure Sam has worn a fresh pair every day. "Ain't done nothing but sit around," Sam answers her persistent nagging the same way every time, "no need in messing up a clean pair for that."

Heaven help the man. If he could get away with turning a pair inside out to get an extra day's wear, he would. At least he can still control his body functions. Who knows for how long.

"No sense to it, Sam. You're just being plain-out sorry. We own a business full of washers and dryers. I'll not have you smelling like a stinky old man."

Men are a foreign country and she still doesn't understand their language, maybe never will. But cancer and morphine do strange things to a person, too. The fastidious Sam she had married would've hair-lipped Hell before appearing anything but hygienic and dapper.

Mevlyn forces herself to not think about the once-proud man who withers away in the cramped ranch-style house not more than sixty feet from where she stands. She allows her comic memories to coat her bad reality like fabric softener over burlap.

Funniest intimate apparel incident had been when Elvina Houston's washer broke down and she dropped off a couple of loads for the wash, dry, and fold, One-Day Super Service. Mevlyn vividly remembers holding the skimpy flesh-toned, thong-style panties up in disbelief. Elvina Houston, Queen of the Little Old Lady Hotline and surely in her early seventies, wearing such? Mevlyn had pondered on that for some time, 'til she found out through one of her many sources that Elvina had worn the pitiful scrap of cloth for some kind of radio station charity drive dare. And it wasn't the first time Elvina wore such, neither. Years back, when the panties were called G-strings, Elvina and a bunch of women ordered some from the Fredericks of Hollywood catalog and gave their honest evaluations of the fashion. Lawd, what some folks do for entertainment.

Thong panties are one fashion invention Mevlyn can't fathom. Why bother to wear them at all? She threw panties in the trash when they began to crack-creep. Certainly, she wouldn't buy them to start out that way. Women talked about how they didn't leave a visible panty line. That was understandable; naked buttocks couldn't leave a mark. Except hers, with the minefield of little fat dimples. Thick cotton is best for concealing unfortunate imperfections, she thinks.

Her discovery of Bessie Brister's Goodwill trade-in practice had been rich, too. Mevlyn had once commented to the old woman after noting her varied wardrobe, "Miz Bess. I swannee. I've never seen you in the same dress twice. Your closets must be full to busting."

Bessie had craned her stooped neck to see if anyone was in earshot before replying in a low voice, "I buy them at one of the three Goodwill Stores in Tallahassee, then take them back for a money return, and use that to buy new used ones, after I wear them once to church. End up paying close to nothing at all."

Might not have been the most miserly thing in the world, but it was the most miserly thing she had ever heard. Bessie—sweaty rolls of money stuck in her drooping bosom and, if rumors were to be trusted, in mason jars filled with greenbacks in the dirt under her azaleas—had stood there in Mevlyn's laundromat and commenced to poor-mouth about her sad, sad life. Some folks ought to be taken out behind the barn and slapped silly. Just making a mental list of folks bound for correction helps Mevlyn cope.

Sonny settles into a cat-chasing dream, his feet jerking in rhythm. Mevlyn casts a furtive glance back to the young woman. She sits crumpled in one of the orange molded plastic chairs and picks at her cuticles. Purty-much Ruined.


**D**anae watches the woman with the dyed black hair and that bizarre painted-on mole above her lip that looks like a tick. With all of those deep wrinkles and that poofy hair style, she has to be pretty old, somebody's grandma. Even when she isn't looking, Danae gets the creepy feeling she—and even that scruffy dog—can see every move. Some people have that way about them, like her daddy. Do something wrong and be ready to have your head slapped across the room by a thick hairy arm you never saw coming. Just pray he'd had a couple, or three or five, so his aim wasn't dead-on.

The room feels warm and close, and reeks of fake mountain-spring air. Too much heat radiates from the machines, though many aren't in use this time of the day. Given a few more weeks, the June temperatures will be soul-crushing, inside and out. Danae leans to feel the wind from the struggling window air conditioner, barely cool on the pearls of sweat peppering her temples. A couple of large room fans might make a difference.

Then again, maybe not. Stirring bad air doesn't make it less bad.

TWO

**M**evlyn grows accustomed to seeing P.R. gal once a week, when she comes in with a box of cheap soap powder and a dingy pillowcase of dirty clothing. Since the initial in-service training, the gal carefully separates the lights from darks, often catching Mevlyn's eye and nodding with a shy smile, as if to say See? I remembered.

Mevlyn figures the little gal has no transportation. She arrives on foot with the makeshift bag slung over one shoulder like Santa's Southern backwoods helper.

"You got a name?" Mevlyn stops by washer number four, one of the machines the gal favors. "Not that I'm trying to pry into your business. I just like to speak to my regulars."

The gal swings the packed pillowcase to the floor. "Danae."

"Danae. Strong name." Mevlyn extends her hand. "Mevlyn Jenson. Pleased to make your acquaintance."

The grip is firm, but Mevlyn notes how the gal doesn't crush her hand. Danae's palms are rough and calloused, and the fingernails show a scrim of dark.

"You from around here?"

Danae shoves one hand deep into her pocket and extracts a few coins. "No'um. Dothan, Alabama."

Mevlyn takes note of the way she finger-counts the quarters. No freeloader, this one. Since that first day, she's brought enough to pay and never so much as asked for change. Yet, something about how the gal doesn't meet her eyes tells Mevlyn she's spinning a story. "Dothan, eh? Husband's got kin up around those parts. Your folks still thereabouts?"

Danae's brown eyelashes flicker. "Daddy . . . Daddy still lives there."

"Well, now. How'd you end up here in Chattahoochee?"

Danae shrugs, seems to sink farther into herself. "Good 'a place as any."

What kind of an answer is that, for such a young gal who looks barely old enough to vote, or drink? This gal's going to be a hard nut to crack. The phone rings. Mevlyn nods and shuffles back to the front counter. The bunion on her left foot scrubs against the seam of her shoe. If she had the money, she'd have the extra skin scraped off, after the hip replacement she's needed for a few years.

No need to beat that dead horse until it can be used for a wall hanging. Sam's chemo and pain medicines have sucked the money pit dry. Not that it was ever full.


When she leaves the car repair shop to pick up a lunch order, Danae sees a woman step from the Wild Rose Diner. The woman clutches a brown paper takeout bag in one hand. Both arms lace across her chest, close like a cadaver cradled in a coffin. Danae notes how she keeps her head down and clings to the far right of the sidewalk, though no one challenges her for space. Like Mouse used to move.

The lunch orders can wait. Mr. Hal won't mind his sandwich cold. Her new boss is laid back. The BLT is for Danae and her appetite has dried up. Danae darts across West Washington Street, jaywalks, but what the heck. Only a couple of cops in this town, and she bets they wouldn't bother to harass her. Danae slows her pace to match the woman's.

Mouse? Could it be?

In a blink, Danae turns into the baby sister. Her protector, her guardian, walks feet from her. In the same town where Danae had ended up. Carrying takeout from the same restaurant. On the same sidewalk.

It's a struggle not to bolt to her.

The familiar ache starts in her center, the same way it had felt when they'd discovered Mouse missing. Sure, Mouse had left her daddy and mama, too, and Uncle Buck and Aunt Sylvia, but Danae always thought of it as the day Mouse had left her.

Danae's chest constricts. Breathing becomes shallow, the way Mouse had taught her. A stillness, barely alive, a trick to blend into a wall, a chair, a bed, until the scary things stopped. Mouse could manage it better. As Danae walks, aware only of keeping the petite woman in sight, she hears the ghost echo of her older sister's voice. "You are such a wiggle butt. You must learn how to be perfectly still, Little Bit."

Little Bit. Mouse had called her that, those years ago. If Danae ran to her now, wrapped her in a tight hug, would Mouse even know her—tall, with big feet and big hands and a big voice.

Danae slows her pace. Mouse had not been someone to corner. She'd draw into herself like a gopher turtle sucking into its shell. After Mouse left, years of living around Daddy had taught Danae: observe first, then come out swinging only if you had to. Or run.

After two blocks, the woman turns right, still hugging the sidewalk's edge. Danae sucks in a deep breath and walks faster. She stops at the corner, leaning to view the side street. The woman slips through a doorway midway down and disappears.

Danae takes a few steps. Stops. Questions crowd her mind like cattle bound for a loading chute. Is it really Mouse? What is she doing in Chattahoochee? Has her sister been here all this time and how did she survive alone?

The ancient question—why did she leave?—Danae no longer entertains. Now she's older and understands. Mouse moved to stay alive. Same reason Danae did. First to Aunt Sylvia's when the second stroke claimed her mama. Then completely out of the area, after the old man tried to beat Danae senseless.

"You won't lay a hand on me ever again, you sombitch." The familiar burn starts in Danae's stomach. She clenches her fists until the jagged nails dig into her palms. Next time, she'll do more than leave the old man in a pool of blood, out cold. A taste coats her tongue, tinny like a piece of foil. Aunt Sylvia has to put up with Daddy now. But she can, and will, protect her own piece of dirt. Too bad Mama hadn't inherited that same brand of gristle.

Danae walks to within a few feet of the business storefront where the woman had entered, close enough to read the looping script on the sign: Dr. Ben Johnson, Veterinary Medicine. Makes sense. Mouse was always good with animals.

For a moment, Danae toys with the idea of pushing through the door.

But no. She taps off a mantra on three fingertips: Watch. Plan. Act.

Mouse would be so proud of her, how she'd come up with that on her own, to help curb her tendency to fire on impulse. Not that it would always work, if she actually remembered to use it.

Danae spins around and heads in the opposite direction. Back to work and her boss's waiting lunch order.

Her lips curl up and she whistles a tune. Maybe it truly is like Aunt Sylvia says. Fate puts a person right where she needs to be.


Mevlyn lifts a platter of homemade butterscotch chip oatmeal cookies from a shelf beneath the front counter and walks to washer number four. Danae looks up from sorting clothes.

"Tried out a new recipe yesterday. I'd love it if you'd sample one or two and give me an opinion."

Danae slips a cookie from the chipped ceramic plate. "Thanks."

"Go get you a soda pop from the cooler, if you want something to wash it down with." She notes the gal's hesitation. "Go on. Just call it payment for being my guinea pig."

Mevlyn watches Danae wolf down five more cookies, stopping only for a gulp of cola. "Either I'm a hell of a cook, or you're a hell of an eater."

Danae swipes crumbs from her lips with the back of a hand and looks at her a little sheepish. "Guess I was hungry. Sorry."

"Don't be. I'm flattered. Since Sam got sick, I don't get the opportunity to cook much for someone. My husband barely eats enough to keep a housefly alive. And sweets make him nauseous. Left to my own, I'd as soon order out or open a can of soup."

Mevlyn glances toward the small color television beside the front counter. "My show's on." She sets the cookie plate down, shuffles to a duct tape-patched, faux leather rolling chair, and settles in with the remote control in one hand and a cold can of diet cola in the other.

The first cluster of commercials provides Mevlyn an opportunity for a quick bathroom break. She transfers three washed loads to the reserved dryers before returning to her post.

"My aunt used to watch this stuff," Danae says as she pushes a wheeled basket of wet laundry toward the bank of dryers. "Never got how anyone could get so wrapped up in it all."

Dryer number four. Wonder why the little gal favors that number? Mevlyn holds one finger to her lips and leans in to catch a scene. She waits until the show pauses for a station break before answering. "It's simple. Ain't no way on heaven and earth that I could ever have as screwed-up a life as the folks on my shows. Not a one of 'em stays married for more'n a few months before taking off with someone else's wife or husband. Half of 'em have slept with and had younguns with the other half. Small wonder all the kids don't end up with their eyes set too close together and dumb as a stick, what with all that mixing.

"Way I see it, these soap box dramas help me see how good I got it. No one's showing up pregnant and in tears on my front stoop, and I can rest assured that some long-lost cousin won't come back from the dead to make my life a living hell."

Danae throws her load into dryer four. "I never much got into them myself." Mevlyn hears the metallic clank of change.

"You spent a lot of time with your aunt, then?" Mevlyn forces her voice to remain neutral, calm. Like a trainer approaching a wild horse with a bridle.

"Lived with her, for a while."

Mevlyn swigs the cola. Wipes the foam from her lips. Belches. "Which show did she favor?"

"All I remember is her talking about some guy named Victor. He was filthy rich and always telling everyone what to do."

Mevlyn hammers her palms on the padded armrests. "That would be The Young and the Restless. 12:30 every weekday on the CBS channel out of Tallahassee. I've been watching that one for years. When I can't find anything to start up a conversation over, I can always comment on it. You'd be surprised how many male-folks around here tune in, too."

She motions to one of the molded plastic chairs. "Drag one of them over and watch with me, Danae. You have to wait on your clothes anyways."

Three

**M**evlyn nods good morning to a Chattahoochee police officer as he passes by the front counter toward washer number twelve. No magic in predicting that. The law enforcement people—what the local kids call the "Po-Po"—always select one of the machines on the side directly across from the back wall of dryers. Numbers ten through twelve are the laundromat's version of the gunfighter's seat in a saloon. Back against the wall, eyes ahead to scout for potential danger, side door two steps away.

Laundromat numerology is an overlooked science, as worthy of study as head lumps and astrological charts. The harried mothers pick the first machines as they enter the double glass front doors. They choose the closest dryers too, immediately past her reserved machines. Having kids to chase makes a woman conserve energy where she can, though Mevlyn lost her one chance to experience motherhood years ago.

Used to be, everyone made time for the weekly trip to the laundromat. More and more, homes had private machines; most, better quality than the Wash-Away's. Pity. That luxury robbed folks of one more place to slow down long enough to interact. And now with cell phones and the internet and a choice of a jillion TV stations, will people get to the point where they can't recall how to politely pass the time with each other?

A red paisley bandana twirls and tumbles inside reserved dryer number one. Caught up with a jeans' pant leg, then free, shoved behind a towel, then flipping into sight again. The circular dance lulls her into a peaceful drowsiness.

"Mevlyn?"

The voice snaps her eyes wide open. Her hand flitters to her chest.

"Sorry to startle you, dear." Elvina Houston studies her, a folded quilt cradled in her arms.

Mevlyn rocks the chair forward to its upright position. "Wasn't asleep. Just resting my eyes."

"I catch a few winks at the Triple C's front desk myself from time to time," Elvina says. She drops the quilt onto the counter.

"I don't get much chance to nap, what with caring for Sam and all." Mevlyn picks up the quilt and judges the weight. "Don't see many of these anymore. Ones nowadays are light as dust."

"That belonged to my dear friend Piddie Longman. It's a genuine antique. But I still like to use it. Can't fathom having something just to look at." Elvina sniffs as if she smells something foul. "But it's heavy, too much for summer. I like to clean and store it properly, and my machine won't handle the bulk."

"My triple-loader will. Sure you don't want to take it to the dry cleaners?"

"That'd cost a small fortune. Nope, it's 100% cotton and I'm happy with just a wash, dry, and fold."

"All righty." Mevlyn scribbles a ticket. "I'll have it ready for you by this time tomorrow." She considers. Might as well take advantage of the Hotline Queen, though Elvina sometimes makes her uneasy. Best not to alert the old woman's radar.

Some secrets need to stay that way, and Mevlyn certainly doesn't want Elvina starting an inquisition.

"Anything new?" Mevlyn keeps her voice casual. Elvina can sniff controversy from two counties away.

Elvina deposits the claim ticket in her straw purse. "Mr. Hal's hired a drifter over at the auto shop. A girl."

"That so?"

Elvina's smartphone plays a little gospel tune and she taps the screen. "Law's busted another meth lab across the river." She slides the phone into a belt holster. "I get text alerts for all the surrounding counties."

"Technology is a marvel."

"Surprised you don't have a cell phone, Mevlyn, what with Sam so sick."

Mevlyn points to the bright yellow device lying next to the TV remote. "I use Sam's old walkie-talkies. Don't cost me a fortune and they fit my needs. Not like I live across town."

Elvina harrumphs. "Where was I . . ." She taps one red-shellacked nail on her lip. "So I told Mr. Hal he shouldn't hire a complete stranger without a thorough background check. I even offered to research for him on the internet. But that's his business, I suppose. And get this, he's even letting the girl sleep on a cot in the back of the shop." Elvina's eyes narrow to slits. "You seen her?"

A sense of protectiveness slips over Mevlyn. "She's come in to do laundry a couple of times."

Elvina leans in. "Oh?"

"Keeps to herself." Elvina will want more, so Mevlyn adds, "seems nice enough."

"Ted Bundy was nice. And that didn't turn out so well for all those murdered women. Women can be serial killers too."


**M**evlyn takes a breath of fresh air and watches Sonny lift his leg and dribble urine, always on the same three bushes, before he sniffs out the proper place to complete his evening constitutional. Sniff, walk a few steps, sniff, walk, sniff, twirl in a circle, hunker down. Then pop up, turn to inspect, and use his back legs to scratch a flurry of dirt and dried grass over the pile.

Mevlyn whistles. Sonny makes a second sweep of the three bushes, hiking his leg, though symbolically this time. When she slides open the patio door, he dashes inside ahead of her.

The scent hits her, one she associates with disease, decay, death. A sickly, almost sweet, odor reminiscent of lilies past their prime, turning to torpid goo. The cinnamon butterscotch aroma of baked cookies has retreated like a spooked fox tailed by hounds.

She grabs the economy-sized can of linen-fresh spray and fogs the narrow foyer, through the den, into the kitchen. The cologne of cancer retreats a few inches. "I'll have to burn this damn house down to be rid of that smell, after it's all said and done," Mevlyn says to Sonny in a voice so low, the dog pricks his ears and turns his head.

She fills the dog bowl with kibble and glances from the narrow window over the sink. Birdfeeders are empty. Again. Careful to make as little noise as possible, she takes a bag of mixed seed and slips from the patio sliding glass door. A cardinal—a flash of red in the gloaming—swoops to land in the dogwood by the patio and watches her service both feeders. The finches and chickadees will be close-by, peeking through the slender branches of the hedges. The doves will show up later.

The grass needs mowing. The ligustrum hedge needs clipping. The flowerbeds are doomed. Who has the time for such flippant hobbies as flowers. Mevlyn mentally tabs her extra cash; enough to hire that neighbor boy for a few hours of labor?

"This yard looks like no one lives here." Not far from the truth. The thought flushes guilt over her skin.

A wren perches on the fence, chattering. Mevlyn turns, reenters the house, and sits in the chair with a view. From behind the glass door, she watches birds flock to the filled feeders. The noisy wren first, with his long beak jabbing, pitching seeds to the ground as if he's dissatisfied with her charity. Like some people. Except for Danae.

Then, the cardinal. The bright scarlet crested male is joined by his frumpy, brown female. Mevlyn and her husband often make fun of this aspect of nature, how the male birds wear all the color and flash, but in humans, the females take that role.

A chickadee lands on one feeder and selects a single seed, then flies to perch on the dogwood. It peck, peck, pecks at the husk, over and over. Mevlyn wonders if birds get migraines or at least a little dizzy from the shaking. All that, for a bite or two of food.

In a few minutes, the dinner break ceases. The feeders swing, lonely. Mevlyn glances at the plastic rooster wall clock. Nine fifteen. Predictable as finding Christmas décor on the store shelves before Halloween. The birds come twice a day, 8:00 a.m. and 9:00 p.m. Some days, the pair of mourning doves come, some not.

She stands, grunts her feet and legs into working, and moves to the bedroom to make sure Sam is still breathing.

No matter how often she looks in on him, the worry-fear clenches her chest so hard she might just be the first to die. Can't do that. Who would pull death watch for Sam if she did? Some jobs, she can't pawn off on anyone, and wouldn't even if she could.

# Four

**Monday morning, early.**

**D**anae looks up from her magazine and watches the tall black man enter the laundromat. Broad-shouldered. Handsome. Close-clipped hair. Walks with a slight swagger, his arms held rounded, elbows out: the posture of someone accustomed to a gun belt. He scans the room, his gaze resting on her for a moment before moving on. No doubt, that pause provided all he might need in case he had to pull up her description later: white female; late teens, early twenties; sandy blond hair, cut short; white T-shirt, shorts, flip-flops; appears to be approximately 5'10". He could add her manner of speech, eye color, and distinctive movements later. He'll be observing and listening.

The man carries a dark bag slung over one shoulder, moves to the last washer in the line-up—number twelve, across from the washer she's picked as her favorite—and opens the lid. Danae flicks quick glances his way while keeping up the appearance she's engrossed in the two-year-old *Field and Stream* with half the pages stuck together, or ripped out. Nothing against cops, personally. She's never done anything to warrant their disfavor, unless the last time she fought with her daddy counted. He deserved the punch to his thick head. She should've done the world a favor and killed him.

The wariness stems from constantly hearing how police interfere with a man trying to make a little extra to support his family, have some left for beer and cigarettes, maybe even a quick roll with a two-bit-paid lady friend. If you spotted the Law, you were to look and move the opposite way fast enough so they couldn't draw a bead on you, slow enough as to not snatch their attention straight off. Danae stuffs that time-honed bit of fatherly wisdom down. This man is only here to wash some dirty clothes, not to cause her aggravation.

Surely her daddy didn't report her to the cops. Wasn't like she was a minor who left home, like Mouse did. No, she's legal adult age. Though no one had ever bothered to share exact details of that horrible day when Mouse disappeared, she often wondered if Daddy had been the one who reported it.

Danae shakes off her instant lunge toward fear and calls upon reason. Knowing how Daddy feels about cops, she doubts he would've gotten them involved in this latest business. His pride probably kept him from telling anyone how he had gotten beaten up, this time. Even if he had, she's several counties over, in a different state, and her hair is short and bleached lighter. Should change her name. Paranoid thinking. When Danae can afford one, she'll buy a phone to call her aunt, let her know she's alive and okay, and not to expect her home for a good long while.

Still, she watches the man.

He strides past, glances her way and tips his head once in acknowledgement. Since they're the only two here this early, he turns and asks, "Miz Mevlyn's not around, I reckon?"

Danae fights the urge to offer a snarky reply. The *back in thirty minutes* note Mevlyn left hanging over her folding table is printed on hot pink paper, big as a banner. Even a cross-eyed idiot can see it. Nope, the purpose of his inquiry: to get her to speak.

"She ran over to the house to check on Mr. Sam."

There. He's heard her distinctive Southern drawl, how she called the man *Mr.* in the polite way her mama taught her. Plus, Danae knows Mevlyn well enough to call her husband by name. Two good enough reasons to leave Danae the hell alone.

He opens his wallet. "Well, dadgum." He walks past Danae again, then behind Mevlyn's desk, where he pulls out a small metal box, opens it, throws in several bills, and extracts a handful of quarters. "Shy a dollar or two," he states. "Washer's broken at the house. City'll pay to have my uniforms done, but I don't see sense in that when I'm capable." He gives a little chuckle. "Kid's been in my cash."

"I hear ya." Like he owes Danae, or anyone, an explanation, and besides, she has no clue what it's like to have children snatching her money. Up until a few weeks ago, she had been the one dipping into her aunt's purse or into her daddy's wallet, only if he was dead passed out after a night of carousing, when "God only knew where his money got off to."

This dude has a kind face and easy smile, as if he'd be the sort of father who wouldn't much mind if his daughter, or son, pilfered a buck or three. No, reverse that; he'd have the kind of kids who'd usually ask first, or 'fess up later. It's called "being raised right."

He drops darks into one washer, whites into another. Uniforms, mostly, from the bits of sewn-on patches she catches sight of. And a few camo print pieces. A hunter, like most men in these parts, she surmises. Hunting season's over, it being early summer, but most of the guys Danae knows, or knew, wear camo for any occasion, any time of year. Her daddy's favorite chair has a cushion covered in oak leaf camo print, a Christmas gift from Uncle Bully and Aunt Sylvia.

Danae thinks about camo. That leads to thoughts of pine and oak forests and the loamy scent of decaying leaves. Some look down on shooting game. As if the cello-wrapped cutlets they snap up at the supermarket don't start out as actual living, breathing, and sweet-faced animals. Most folks are so detached from blood and guts reality: unless you're nibbling on a leaf, something died for you to slap that hunk of meat on your four-hundred-dollar grill.

One good-sized whitetail buck processes out as seventy to eighty pounds of ground venison, cube steak, sausage, and tender backstrap. Meat to keep a family of four—three, once Mouse moved—fed for a good number of meals if you stretch it, which Danae's mama and aunt can surely do. Probably the only time Danae heard her daddy halfway praise her mama's cooking—when the backstrap was fried up crisp, with a hoecake of warm cornbread to sop the drippings' gravy. Even then, he would say the meal was *passable*.

The first time Danae shot a deer provides one of the few good memories of her daddy. Danae stares at the magazine page, but her mind wanders to details of that early morning in November.

Something jostled her leg. "Get up, Dannie."

Her father never called her Danae, not since she was a little girl. Unlike what she recalled of her older sister, Danae was rough tumble. No frills, no lace, no gosh-awful pink. She insisted on hair clipped close, jeans, and cowboy boots so worn, the toe leather was thinned white. Tall for eleven, she could kick any boy's ass to Georgia and back, if she had a mind to. Nobody much challenged her. Some felt sorry, as she was the one whose sister went missing three years ago, the one whose older brother J.J. never came back from that fishing trip seven years back. Others, well, she didn't really give a flip as long as they let her be.

She rolled from bed and shuffled to the bathroom to pee. Her jeans, thermal camo shirt, socks, and jacket waited on a chair. She dressed, raked her fingers through her hair, and shoved her feet into the boots. No shower. No brushing of teeth. Deer could smell all that freshness. Better to be day-old human. Even then, you had to stay down wind.

In the kitchen, Big John stood at the stove—the only time he cooked, other than if he was guarding the charcoal grill. Her mama wasn't home from night shift at the nursing home. Even if she had been, Big John wouldn't allow her to prepare the pre-hunt breakfast.

Bacon grease pooled around two eggs. Their yolks, broken on purpose for her daddy's fried egg sandwiches. He turned off the burner, then scooped them up, shook off the excess grease, and transferred them both to split day-old biscuits slathered thick with mayonnaise. He slapped on slices of cold ham and cheddar and wrapped the loaded biscuits in paper towels. A thermos filled with strong coffee stood on the table. He poured two tall Styrofoam cups for the road. His coffee was black. Danae doctored hers with whole milk and three heaping teaspoons of sugar.

"Get your coat." He motioned to the camo print insulated jacket slung across the back of one kitchen chair. Not new, and not hers, but a hand-me-down from some friend's son. No mind that it was so big it fell well below her knees and she had to roll up the sleeves; it would keep her from freezing her butt off in the predawn air.

Two shotguns, a rifle, and ammo went into the truck along with the thermos and the brown bag already shiny with grease. They pulled around to the back of the property where dogs yipped in their pen, ready to run. Danae hopped out and helped her daddy load up four: a blue tick hound and a redbone hound—the two lead trackers—and two tan and white curs from different litters. Uncle Bully's three hounds would round out this morning's pack. Those deer didn't stand a chance.

On the way, Daddy sucked down coffee. Danae drank hers too. He shoved the bag her way and she doled out the fried egg sandwiches. One bite and the grease went down so good. No talking. Only chewing and slurping. One day, maybe she could tolerate coffee black. But now it was warm. And sweet.

"Miss, I believe your washer's stopped."

The man's voice jerks her from a memory she's gnawed on so often, she could go back to the exact spot where she had raised the shotgun, pick out every tree, every leaf, and describe the smell of that first blood.

"Ah. Yeah." Danae drops the magazine onto a nicked, pressed-board table and stands. Her load is small, and she's mixed white and dark this time. Good darn thing Mevlyn didn't witness that. Heck, why pay for two machines when she doesn't even own enough clothing to fill one?

"I should be back before Miz Mevlyn, but if she comes in, let her know I'll square up with her. Reckon she'll be seeing a lot of me until I get my washer fixed." He nods, checks his watch, and heads toward the door.

Why does he feel as if he has to explain to her? The answer pops up. He's a black man. She's white. So naturally he would worry she'd assume he might steal. The realization settles on her shoulders, weighing heavy.

Danae sits, alone once more, with only the churn of his washers and the click-click of some button or snap hitting the inside of the dryer's metal cylinder. The cop dude probably has a to-do list, this being his day off. Something for the kid he spoke of. Maybe some yard work. Says a lot about the town, how he'd leave his clothes unattended. Anyone could come take them, right? But Chattahoochee's small and folks watch out for each other. Good thing fate landed her—and Mouse?—in such a place, since few people in their lives had watched out for them. The racial issues are another matter. If this town is anything like the one she escaped, being different isn't covered by community compassion.

The Wash-Away rings hollow without the chatter of people. If she had anywhere to be, she'd leave her stuff in the dryer. Maybe hop the Yamaha and ride up toward Lake Seminole. Pretty up there. Nothing but a couple of tennis courts, a few picnic shelters, and a wide view of the lake. The place creeps her out a bit, given its history. Mr. Hal relayed the story of how one of the locals, a gay florist, had been nearly beaten to death not far from the main lake landing, a few years back. Put the town on the map for something other than having a state mental institution on the main drag. Bad things could happen in the woods, and those things had nothing to do with the wild animals.

Not like she needs to go home and clean some house or apartment. Home for now is a barren and borrowed room barely large enough for a cot, with one cracked and fogged window, and a corner sink and toilet. A prison cell might be more appealing. But hey, at least she's inside out of the elements and it's free, thanks to the generosity of her employer.

Danae picks up the magazine and flips to an article on big bass lures. When she finally talks to Mouse, they can find a place, move in, and maybe buy some fishing gear. With the Apalachicola River less than a mile away, there's bound to be plenty of spots to cast a line from the bank. Lake Seminole's out. It's across the Georgia line; getting a license in two states is too dang expensive.

Mouse refused to hunt—a fact their daddy threw in her older sister's face. Danae can't recall if her sister ever fished.

Danae flips the page, shifting to an ad for boat motors.

She'd been barely eight when Mouse left.

What kid that age remembers anything to amount to much?

Five

The second Mevlyn steps into the house, intuition alerts her; something's amiss. The air holds the taint of things gone bad. Sonny brushes past her and heads toward the back of the house.

She pitches the keys onto the kitchen counter and trundles to the second of two bedrooms. The master bedroom used to be theirs. Now, Mevlyn sleeps alone in the king-sized bed they bought a year ago; my, how things can change in such a short time. The guest bedroom is Sam's world, set up with a hospital bed with side rails, a small television, radio, oxygen tanks, and a bedside table so filled with medical trappings the wood barely peeks through.

"Sam? Sam?" she calls out, heading down the narrow hallway. "Honey?"

No answer. Dear God.

Sonny appears at the bedroom's threshold, twirls in circles the way he does when he senses life's gone crossways. She enters the room. The rumpled bed is empty. Sonny yips once, crosses the floor, stops, loops back, and looks up to her with a high-pitched whine.

Mevlyn takes the same route. Sam slumps on the floor, his back to the wall. His legs splay out in front of him. His head lolls forward.

Her chest squeezes. Is he . . . dead?

Mevlyn lowers herself to a painful squat. Her hips scream. "Sam?"

He moans and coughs. She hears the rattle of deep phlegm and releases a relieved sigh. The tang of urine lifts from his saturated pajama bottoms.

Now what.

Had this been a couple of years ago, she could've grabbed him underneath the arms and dragged him up and back onto the bed, where she could bathe him and put on a fresh adult diaper and dry pajama bottoms.

Should've pushed the bed flush to the wall. But she had to be able to reach Sam from either side, and there's the problem in a nutshell. The rail's down. Did she leave it that way this morning?

"I'm going to get us some help." She rests one hand on his lower left leg. "Don't you worry none."

As if he could. The drugs keep him so doped, he rarely opens his eyes.

Mevlyn uses the side of the bed to pull herself to her feet. Sonny watches with round moist eyes. "What'll we do, huh?" she asks the dog. "Those first responder folks been here three times already this month."

There's probably some law she doesn't know about, a mandate that says she has to put her husband away in some old folks' home if the emergency calls come too regular. She looks at the phone headset on the nightstand. Not put there for Sam—he wouldn't have the strength to reach for it. Hell, he hasn't even picked up the walkie-talkie in weeks.

What to do?

The answer pops to mind. "I *will* be back with help, Sam. Stay put."

Like he's going to magically come to and get himself out of this mess. Right.

She moves as quickly as her old knees will allow, down the hall. At the door, she blocks Sonny. "Stay here. Watch over your daddy."

She then aims toward the Wash-Away, her thoughts tumbling. Who was there when she left? It takes her half the time as usual to reach the laundromat.

Mevlyn spots the P.R. gal, Danae, her head leaned back to the wall, eyes shut, mouth open. God no. Not another ailing one to worry about. Too young to be dead.

"Hey! Hey!"

The gal's head pops up. She blinks and wipes drool from her lips with the back of a hand. Before she can speak, Mevlyn says, "I need your help right this moment! Follow me!"

Mevlyn moves faster than she can remember in the recent past. Heaven knows, she'll pay for it later. Behind her, she hears the slap of flip-flops. The gal catches up to her, but doesn't fire a hundred and one questions. Good thing too. Mevlyn has no breath to spare for answers.

In the house, she leads the way to Sam's room and to the side of the bed where her husband slumps, pinned between the wall and the bed frame.

"Can you help me get him up?"

Danae pushes past her and takes a beat to access the situation. Mevlyn watches. Danae shoves the bed farther from the wall, helps Sam wiggle forward so he can fully recline, then she positions his bent legs and turns him onto his side, and coaxes him onto his hands and knees. From there, she uses the edge of the bed to help him lift to his feet. He sits on the bed for a moment, moaning insensible words. In one smooth movement, Danae supports his back and swivels his thin body until she can swing first one leg then the other onto the mattress.

"Gal, that was about the darndest thing I believe I've ever seen."

Danae lowers Sam onto the pillows. "It's all about leverage." Danae turns her attention from Sam to Mevlyn. "My mama was a nurse's aide. She showed me some stuff."

"She teach you how to give bed baths?"

Danae nods.

"He's a mess and I could use a hand. He's lost a bunch of weight, but it's still a lot for me to move around."

"Sure."

"I'll round up some clean linens and supplies."

In half the time it would've taken her alone, Mevlyn sees to the cleaning and redressing of her husband. Nothing about the job—the odors, the gray skin, the shriveled man parts—affects the gal. If she and Sam had a daughter, she would be here, helping like this gal Mevlyn barely knows.

Washed and clothed, his thin gray hair combed into ribboned furrows, her husband even looks better. More color flushes his cheeks. His eyes flutter open a couple of times.

"I can't repay you for all you just did," Mevlyn says. "But your next four loads of wash and dry are on the house."

Danae shrugs. "It was nothing."

"It was *everything*." Mevlyn secures both bedrails and yanks on them to assure they're firmly set into place.

Sam moans, a pitch that sounds like a question. He opens his eyes and fixes on Danae, his eyebrows crimped together. "You're surely a big boy." His eyelids lower and his face goes slack.

"First full sentence he's said in weeks." Mevlyn brushes aside a sprig of limp hair that has fallen across his damp forehead. "Sorry about him saying you's a boy. He would never outright insult a person, if he was in his right mind."

"No worries. I get that a lot," Danae says. "Takes more than that to hurt my feelings."

"Well, all the same . . ." Mevlyn tucks the sheets around Sam and kisses his cheek. "He'll sleep now. We best get on back to the shop." She lays the walkie-talkie on the bedside table, within easy reach. Sam can't manage the phone now, but he can push the button on the small radio. Or at least he could, a few days back.

"I have a load in the dryer," Danae states. "Probably stopped by now."

"Well, you better hurry on ahead." Mevlyn leans down to rub the top of Sonny's head. "I hear the old woman who runs the place doesn't cotton to such." She straightens up with a grunt. "I'll be on back in a few minutes. Watch over things for me, if you will."

"**S**hoot." Danae holds up a T-shirt slashed by wrinkles. The rest of the clothes don't matter much. Two towels, a few washcloths, a pair of jeans, a set of twin sheets, and underwear: the sum of her possessions, other than the motorcycle. Mevlyn appears in time to hear Danae's cross comment, a small cooler held in one hand. Sonny taps in behind her.

"Wait right here. I got the fix for that." Mevlyn walks off in the direction of the small bathroom, returning shortly with a wadded-up towel. "Pitch this damp towel in with your load and set it for twenty minutes. It'll steam those wrinkles out."

Danae pulls a quick calculation. If she gets a tuna sandwich and leaves off the tea, and no pie for sure, she can spare the change for the extra minutes. She digs into her pocket.

"This's on me, remember." Mevlyn nods for Danae to throw the towel into the dryer. The old woman snaps the door closed, then deposits three quarters. "That oughta do it. Now, let's have us a snack. All that nursing helped me work up an appetite."

One thing for sure, Danae doesn't argue with Mevlyn. If the woman gets her mind set on something, might as well go along with it. She reminds Danae of Aunt Sylvia that way.

It's not even ten o'clock, but the ham and Swiss on rye goes down easy. And the chess pie, Danae wolfs in less than two bites. Mevlyn provides two chilled colas.

"You're a good eater, that's for sure." Mevlyn hands Danae a napkin. "I got more at the house if you're still hungry."

"No. I'm good. Thank you, Miz Mevlyn." The dryer stops. Danae jumps to her feet and pulls out the load before the wrinkles set in again. It takes less than five minutes to fold the few items.

"You off from work today, are you?" Mevlyn asks when Danae moves toward the front desk.

"We're closed for the day. Mr. Hal has a doctor's appointment in Tallahassee." She's capable of running the shop, a fact Danae pointed out to its owner. He's let her change tires, perform a basic oil change and lube. She's done other things before—brakes, tune-ups, heck, even pulled a transmission once. Mr. Hal may trust her to live in the storage room under his business' roof, but is not ready to go that far. Danae gets it. Trust isn't an easy thing for her either.

Mevlyn studies her with those caterpillar eyebrows rippling. "Reckon I could use a little help, if you're looking to pick up extra work."

"What. Here?"

"Here." Mevlyn tips her head back, indicating the direction of the house. "And there."

"Yeah. Sure."

"My lawn needs mowing. Hedges are so overgrown, my neighbors can't even see me anymore, and my roof needs the leaves blown off."

"Piece of cake."

Mevlyn lowers into her chair and leans back. Sonny circles his bed three times before settling in with a satisfied grunt. "Good. The mower's in the shed out back, if the dang thing'll even crank."

"I can get it running."

The old woman chuckles. "I bet you can."

"Let me take my clothes back to the room and I'll get right on it."

"You got to be at a stopping point by 12:30." Mevlyn's voice is serious.

Danae stalls at the door and swivels. "Huh?"

"Our show's on. We got to see what that Victor's gonna do today. It's Monday. They always leave me hanging by my fingernails on Friday. Can't wait 'til the weekend's past to see how it will all turn out."

Danae grins. Shakes her head.

Then she sees the lady from the vet's office, the one she thinks of as Mouse. The young woman clutches a cloth bag to her chest. Her head tips down, eyes focused on the ground. Danae moves aside to allow her to pass. The woman doesn't acknowledge her or Mevlyn, only moves to the far side of the room, last washer, and flips open the lid.

"She's an odd one," Mevlyn leans over and says in a low voice. "Been coming in here almost a year now, and not so much as a peep to me or anyone else for that matter. She slips in and slips out, sometimes almost without me noticing. Like a ghost."

The business phone jangles. Mevlyn picks it up. "Wash-Away your dirtiest days. How may I help you?"

The word ghost echoes in Danae's head, like the earworm of a hated song. She takes two steps back and lowers onto a chair, and manages enough sense to place the now-clean bag with its scrubbed and scented laundry onto the adjacent seat instead of letting it drop onto the floor.

While Mevlyn trades local gossip with some obviously knowledgeable patron, Danae observes the young woman. How she makes every movement deliberately, as if someone stands in judgement. How she keeps her head aimed down, looking mostly at the immediate area with quick, furtive glances to the room. How her shoulders curl in: a person afraid of taking up too much space.

Had Mouse been this timid? Danae searches memory for an answer. Her older sister had been strong, right? But how could an eight-year-old possibly know that for sure? Danae had been less than strong, too, until she was older and much taller, able to fight back. Plus, Mouse was petite. Danae had secreted one of her older sister's nightgowns deep in the closet. It had been the only thing not cleared away when Daddy gave the order to purge the house.

Danae's spirit wilts. Why didn't she grab it when Aunt Sylvia showed up to take her in? The obvious answer: her mama had just died and Danae wasn't thinking past the next second. In her haste to escape, she hadn't snatched up the shoebox containing the sole relic of her sister.

With Danae now gone, Daddy will pitch all reminders of her, and Mouse's gown, into the landfill. Erased. As if neither one of them existed, or mattered.

The young woman closes the lid on the washer, loads quarters, pushes the loaded coin slide. She gathers her washing powder and empty bags, holds them close to her chest, and slips as quietly as she had entered toward the front door.

A breath before she walks through the door, the woman meets Danae's gaze. The wary, fleeting expression reminds Danae of that first deer.

She stood at the edge of the narrow sandy road. Daddy walked several feet behind, scanning the woods. The cry of the dogs grew closer, more frantic. The pack headed her way, and something bounded ahead of them. Danae stopped. The sound of something heavy parting the brush came from her right. She took the stance Daddy taught her, raised the shotgun and positioned it. The deer could come out anywhere. And it wouldn't take long to cross the road, two hops at best. One chance was all she'd get, Daddy told her. She'd best make good use of it.

Branches snapped. Danae sucked in a breath. The deer! She sighted and squeezed the trigger. Her eardrums rang with the explosion. The deer fell with a thick thud. Its blood mingled with a puddle from the last rainstorm, painting the ditch.

Burned into her mind. Those eyes. Surprise, blind fear, and the basic need to survive. The same look that young woman had held in her eyes.

Six

"**W**ill you just look at that." Mevlyn points to the glass sitting in her kitchen window sill. "I swannee, I cut those off a few days ago and now I already have a fresh crop."

Danae follows the pointy finger to where stalks of scallions rest in paper towels soaked in water. "Pretty cool. My mama used to grow herbs in our kitchen, only in dirt."

When Mevlyn stands, her joints creak and complain. Had to keep moving or she wouldn't, then where would Sam be, with no Mevlyn to watch over him?

"It's the little things like that—free green onions for nothing—that make me happy."

Had to be happy for the small things, since the big things didn't happen so much anymore. Mevlyn helps herself to a coffee refill then holds up the carafe in Danae's direction. "Refresh?"

"Sure. Thanks."

"Your mama sounds like she likes plants. Must be a gardener." Mevlyn casts the bait. Getting information out of this gal is a challenge. Bet Elvina Houston wouldn't even have luck at it.

"Uh-huh." The gal takes her time adding sugar and creamer, stirring her coffee until Mevlyn is tempted to snatch the spoon so it stops the infernal clanging.

Mevlyn waits. When no further information spurts out, she changes tack. "Speaking of gardening, do you reckon you'd be interested in helping me put in a little vegetable plot? Nothing big, mind you. A few tomato bushes, some eggplant, maybe a hill or two of squash."

"Sure."

"I'll pay you, of course." Mevlyn sighs. "I'm late getting it planted this year. Should've had the starts in by end of March, April the latest. But if we ride over to the Walmart in Quincy, there should still be some plants available. Maybe they'll make before the heat sets in too bad."

"Won't hurt to try."

"Settled then. Come Monday after you get off, we'll ride over together. I'll call Elvina about someone to sit at the Wash-Away. She puts in time at the Cut 'n' Curl, but knows women who will jump at the chance to get out of the house for a few hours and look at another set of four walls."

"What about Mr. Sam?"

"I'll set Elvina on that, too. She lives to finagle. All's we need is a sitter for a couple of hours, best. If we don't loiter, we could have time for a quick bite to eat. Maybe Chinese."

Danae carries her empty cup to the sink, rinses it, and puts it into the dishwasher. Whoever raised this gal did some good. She never expects anyone to clean up behind her, a trait Mevlyn finds sorely lacking in people these days.

"I got to take Sonny to the vet for his yearly, too."

Danae spins to face her. "I can do that."

"Now why in the world would you want to do such? Let me tell you, he's a handful. Gets snappish the moment I walk into the clinic. And they nearly have to knock him out to clip his nails."

"I'm good with dogs." The gal squats. As if on cue, Sonny taps over to stand in front of her and she ruffles the hair around his ears. His tongue lolls out to one side.

"Well. I reckon. It'd take a load off me. And I appreciate it." Mevlyn pinches off a hunk of cinnamon roll and pops it into her mouth. "I'll call and see about an appointment."

"I can go on my lunch break. So, any day." Danae lifts to her feet. "Guess I'll get back to those hedges."

Mevlyn nods. The gal lopes to the sliding glass door, opens it, steps out, and closes it behind her. Outside, she dons the dirty sneakers she'd slipped off before Mevlyn summoned her inside for coffee and a hot roll.

Someone has to be missing this good daughter. And if they aren't, well, it's a sad state of affairs.

Danae walks Sonny down the West Washington Street sidewalk, pausing every few feet for the mutt to snuffle and leave two drops of pee. From the Wash-Away corner to the vet's front door would take Danae three minutes tops. Sonny turns the trip into a ten-minute stroll-and-whiz.

After the terrier christens the desiccated shrub outside Dr. Johnson's office—probably the unfortunate last pit stop for every dog—Danae tugs him inside. A perky middle-aged woman greets them, Sonny first, then looks to Danae for her name.

"Miz Mevlyn asked me to bring him in for his shots and stuff." Danae pauses, then snaps her fingers. "And be sure to clip his nails."

"Ah." The woman barely manages a smile. "Good thing for all of us that Carrie's in this morning."

"Carrie." Danae doesn't intend to speak aloud, only to rehearse the name Mouse must be using now. Other than the police investigator who came with his probing questions after Mouse left, Danae can't recall anyone calling her sister by the name Mama gave her at birth, Maria. Mama had loved *The Sound of Music*, so much that Danae had leaned close to softly sing songs from the musical as best as she could, minus a lyric or two, after the first stroke shut Mama down.

"Does Mevlyn need heartworm tabs today?"

"Uh. I'da know."

"I'll call her. No problem." The receptionist motions to a door. "Go on back to exam room one. Carrie and Dr. Johnson will be with y'all shortly."

Danae takes a few steps. The leash grows taut. Behind her, Sonny stands with feet glued, ears back. A few more tugs and Danae gives up, leans down and scoops the defiant dog into her arms. "He's not a fan."

"A fact I remember well." The woman's eyebrows raise and lower. "Doc has a muzzle if we need it today."

Danae carries Sonny into the exam room. The terrier cranks up a low growl.

"Settle, little dude. How bad can this be?"

She considers setting him onto the stainless steel table, then decides not, and sits on the single vinyl-clad chair. Sonny shoves his head beneath her arm and quivers.

Racks of brochures dot the room: flea and tick prevention, heartworms, weight control, diet. Jars of treats and various medical tools line the single cabinet top. A scale sits on one end of the exam table.

Did Daddy take their hunting dogs to a vet? Danae doubts it. At most, he had some buddy give them each a rabies shot. The dogs always looked undernourished and rangy. Made them track better if they were hungry, Big John claimed. They got the cheapest food and a rickety shanty house to shelter from the cold and rain. That was it. No nail spa treatments, no life-prolonging measures. Hell, they were doing good to get names. When one or two died—rarely of old age—more pups appeared from whatever latest litter some other hunter needed to be rid of. Those were the lucky pups. Others ended up tied in a sack of rocks and flung into the nearest lake or river, or left in a cardboard box in front of the grocery store, begging kindness of any passing stranger, or far worse, at the landfill.

The door opens a crack, inches wider. Danae watches. Someone coming in? Or, deciding if they should? She forces herself to look down and remain motionless. Anything to appear nonthreatening.

The vet tech steps inside and idles, waiting. Danae rises to her feet and moves to stand next to the exam table, still not making eye contact. Sonny burrows deeper into the space beneath Danae's left arm.

Danae opens her mouth to speak. Dr. Johnson enters. "Good morning. We'll take Sonny from here."

When she is unsuccessful at dislodging the dog, the veterinarian pries Sonny from Danae's arms. Legs tread air in different directions, scrabbling for grip.

The vet tech rests her hand atop the terrier's head. Sonny calms a notch. Danae breathes in, searching for her sister's scent. That distinct smell should still exist in her memory. She picks up on soap and a medicinal iron smell. Not alien. Not familiar either.

Dr. Johnson hands Sonny off to the tech. The little dog further calms, gazing up at her like he's seen the God of all creation. Mouse used to make Danae feel that way, too, when their daddy raged and Mama cried out and the world heaved upside down.

The vet and tech head for the door.

"Maria," Danae whispers.

The vet tech hesitates. Her shoulders tense. The veterinarian ushers her from the room, leaving Danae to wonder.


Mevlyn offers Sonny a dog biscuit. He sniffs, huffs, and regards her with slit-eyes. "He'll be cross the rest of the day," she says to Danae. The dog steps onto his bed, circles three times, then plops down, his back to both of them. "There you have it."

Danae coils up the leash and hands it over. "He did fine until the nail clipping part. They had to muzzle him, and it took three of us to hold him still."

"My bad little boy, this one." Mevlyn clucks her tongue. The mutt should be more grateful, seeing as how she'd rescued his half-starved butt from the alley behind the Dragonfly Florist. But no, he had more attitude by the day. "No sugar-plums for you tonight, my gingerbread dog."

When Mevlyn turns attention to Danae, the gal wears a dumbstruck expression, a bit whimsical, as if she's seen mystery.

"What . . . um . . . what was that thing you said?"

"Which part?" The rolling chair creaks when Mevlyn leans back. "I said a string of words."

"Sugar-plum. Gingerbread. That."

Mevlyn's lips form into a smile. "From an old poem, *The Sugar-Plum Tree*. It was my mother's favorite children's ditty." She taps her temple. "Used to be able to recite it all, but now only snips and bits remain. Why?"

"No reason."

"My mother had this big red leather book full of poems. *Children's Garden of Verse*. Isn't that a lovely way to put it, garden of verse? It came out in the '50s, best I recall, though the particular poem those words come from is much, much older. My mother loved her books. She passed that particular one on to me, when Sam and I got married. Said I could read it to our kids. Only, me and Sam weren't gifted with children."

Danae looks faraway, like she's in the room but not.

"You heard it before, have you?"

The gal's eyes regain focus. She blinks. "Yeah."

"I've got the book at the house, if you've a mind to read it."

Stormy emotion flashes across the gal's face. For a moment, Mevlyn thinks Danae might cry. Then boom, it's gone and the bland, don't-give-a-crap look takes its place.

Mevlyn crosses her arms and rocks. Digging into an unknown person is like reading a well-written who-done-it book. One hint at a time, a piece here, a snippet there, a few red herrings cast in to throw you off the trail.

Young as she is, this gal holds more intrigue for Mevlyn than anyone she's met in twenty years, maybe longer.

Mevlyn shifts gears. "You off to the shop now?"

"I'd best be. My lunch break is over. Mr. Hal's going to let me help with a tune-up on one of the city cars."

"I put an Irish stew into my Crockpot this morning. Sam may eat a bit of gravy over a potato mashed soft. Sure would be a treat to have someone with a decent appetite help me eat the rest." Mevlyn leans forward and hoochie-coos her eyebrows.

"I get off at six."

Mevlyn bobs her head once to seal the deal. "I'll have the table set by half after six."

Nothing like a home-cooked meal to lure in a victim of a fate she's dying to know all about, her own form of information bartering, Southern-style.

Unless Sam has soiled himself, she may have time to make a pan of biscuits, too.

Danae moves in a fog. The automatic part of her brain steers the way. She crosses West Washington Street between blocks. A truck screeches on brakes and blows its horn. Her eyes look, but don't see. She makes it across and into the auto repair shop.

In the back storage room, she splashes cold water on her face and stares at her reflection in the mirror over the sink.

"The sugar-plum tree." She feels the words on her tongue.

The year she turned four. Before her brother J.J. drowned and everything went from bad to awful.

Seven

**"C**an you close up for me, Danae?" Mr. Hal wipes his hand with the grease-spotted scrap of cloth hanging from his coveralls.

"Sure. No prob."

"Shouldn't be anything new coming in. One of the officers may pick up the cruiser. Give him an invoice. City pays on month's end." Her boss digs in his pocket for his truck keys. "I'm running to the bank, then home. Just cover the phone. All that's needed."

"Yes sir," Danae says.

"Good job on that tune-up. I doubted you—have to tell you that, Danae. But you know more than some of the fellers I've had in here." He chuckles. "And you don't sweat near as bad."

Danae laughs. "I'da know about that."

"Lucky day for me, when you came walking into my shop, yes it was. Your daddy taught you right, for sure." He tips his head, then leaves through the back way, toward the alley.

About the only thing her daddy did right: fix engines. That, and hunt. All the roles J.J. would've fulfilled, pushed off on her. Not like Mouse could've done it. At least Danae has skill at something.

She pulls out the Dollar Store sketch book and flips it open. The paper's cheap, not as smooth as she'd prefer. Guess her daddy would find her others at the house and add them to the burn pile. That's the thing about her leaving fast; she got away with her cycle, a bit of cash, and the clothes on her back.

But she did get away. And she's eighteen. Legal adult. Nobody can force her to go back. Ever.

With a plastic sharpener, Danae files the drawing pencil to a fine tip. She sketches the room in front of her. Double glass doors. Rows of hanging auto thingamajigs. The back of the plastic clock sign announcing *we'll be back at*. One half-dead potted plant. Totally uninspiring.

What to draw? She curls the top sheet over to reveal a fresh page. Allows her hand to draw and shade, draw and shade.

A small tree takes shape, its spiny boughs spread like umbrella spokes. A Chinaberry—junk tree, her daddy called it. He'd saw it down, but Mama insisted it wasn't in anyone's way and provided a bit of shade over that part of the yard. One battle Mama actually won, probably because taking the tree down would mean work. Plus, she didn't confess too much attachment to the tree, otherwise Daddy would've relished hacking it to kindling after a couple of shots of Jack Black. Anything to reinforce his demand for whatever he rallied for at the time; either slamming Mama into fresh bruises, or killing something she loved.

**M**ama was a sucker for birthday parties. Cheap affairs. Nothing catered or fancy. Homemade decorations from found objects, bits of leftover cloth, some cheap balloons. A chocolate cake made from a Dollar Store off-brand mix.

Daddy had gone off somewhere. To the woods. To the pool hall. To some hooch bar. J.J. was there, and Mouse, and Mama, and a few kids she knew.

After the cake and ice cream—Neapolitan, so everyone got a choice of vanilla, strawberry, or chocolate—Mama clapped her hands. Mouse herded them to benches made from concrete blocks and strips of wood.

"We have a very special treat." Mama looked happy, glowing. Beside her, Mouse giggled and clapped. "J.J.," she swung out one arm like a gameshow hostess, "take it away!"

My brother swooped to front and center. Mama's orange story book was in his hand, open like he was getting ready to sing a choir song. He read a poem filled with magic and candy, a gingerbread dog and a chocolate cat. The words danced in Danae's mind.

Mama said, "the most stupendous, amazing thing happened. Just yesterday, we found one of those sugar-plum trees right here, in this very yard!"

I looked to Mouse for answers. Never saw Mama this wacky. Mouse was twitchy, like she could barely sit still.

"Go! All of you, go! Find that sugar-plum tree!" Mama threw up her hands and twirled.

I really wanted to stay and watch Mama being so happy, but the rest of the kids squealed and took off running, so I hopped down from my folding chair and headed after them.

We screeched and dashed around the side of the house, covering ground fast, checking behind shrubs, in Mama's roses, beneath the pecan tree, and finally hauling buggy toward the far end of the property.

I spotted it and pointed, jumping up and down and trying to run at the same time. A small tree stood, prissy-proud with sparkly things swinging from its branches. We stampeded, tearing across the yard. The hunting dogs bayed from their pen. That stirred up the chickens and they carried on, too. We reached the tree and formed a tight circle at its base, looking up, our mouths hanging open.

J.J. pulled up behind us. "Don't just stand there. Get as much candy as you can tote!"

I swiveled to look at my brother. Tall, thin, but athletic. Aunt Sylvia swore he'd be a pro basketball player one day. He was that good. Dark hair, short in back and on the sides, thicker at the top so it swooped over one of his blue eyes. Freckles across the bridge of his narrow nose. How his smile lifted more on the left than the right. The girls loved him. I loved him.

I pivoted to look at Mouse. Her hair hung over her face, a curtain to hide behind.


Danae gazes down, agog at what her hand had transferred to the page. The stunted tree stands, bedecked with candy, wrapped chocolates, and curled ribbons. Children form a circle at its base, reaching up and up. One is taller than the rest—a girl. The profile, so familiar. Why can't Danae's brain bring forth the image of her sister's face?

Aunt Sylvia has a few pictures of Mouse, but she hides them. Big John needs so little reason to erupt. Everyone knows this. Ten years back, not everyone had cell phones to take a selfie at every turn. Her family did good to have a land line. What Danae knew of computers, she learned at school, or at the public library.

When Mouse moved, it was as if the place she once occupied was wiped clean.

Danae holds the page closer. Frowns. On one side, a jagged dark shadow shows beneath the tree. What's up with that? The tree was her and Mouse's hideout, a safe place, the one spot they ran to when Daddy flew into a rage. Maybe the sun was out the day her memory saved this scene, casting shade in ragged shapes; the brain stores everything, she learned in some psychology class. Didn't mean you can access all of it.

"So, you the boss today?"

The deep voice snaps Danae's attention. "Oh." She lays the pad and pencil down.

The man from the laundromat stands in front of the counter, clad in the deep blue of the city's police force. Authority clings to him, a solid aura.

"Hey, we met at the Wash-Away, didn't we?" Before Danae can answer, he's sticking out his hand. She reaches across the counter and he gives her hand a firm shake. "Jerome." He motions behind him. "This here's my boy Malcolm."

"Danae." She starts to add her last name, thinks better of it.

"Pleased to put a name with the face." When he smiles, his teeth glow white against creamy brown skin. Other than her brother, he's the most beautiful man she's ever seen. His son echoes his good looks, down to the twin dimples she hadn't noticed before, the first time she met his father. About her age, a little taller. He eyes Danae with veiled interest.

"Um." She snaps her fingers. "You're here for the cruiser, right?"

"Right."

Danae turns, locates the key fob dangling from the numbered series of nails beneath the counter. "Here you go. She's parked out back. Runs like a charm."

"I believe I might need—"

"Oh. Your invoice. Yeah." Danae shuffles papers, finally extracting the correct one. "Here."

Officer White—his badge proclaims his name in bold lettering—clips the key fob to his belt, then neatly folds the paper and tucks it into a breast pocket. His gun belt leather creaks with every movement. His son stares at Danae, then glances away and feigns interest in a rack of key chains.

"All righty then, Miz Danae. Thank you much. Reckon I'll see you around."

The chimes ring when the door closes behind them. Wow, had she been so out of it that she didn't even hear them when they entered?

*Don't you be like them other women,* her daddy told her more times than she can count, *dreaming their damn lives away. Dreaming's good for nothing except to get you dead one day.*

She pushes aside thoughts of ending up dead and closes up the shop before anything else slips past her defenses.

Eight

"**W**hen you hunt an animal, Dannie," her daddy told her one early November morning, "you gotta learn its ways."

He started calling her *Dannie* after J.J. died. Mama hated it but didn't dare correct him.

"You learn where it feeds, gets a drink of water, the place it wallows out to sleep." He tapped his temple. "You's the hunter. You's the smart one. But don't get so full of yo'self you get to thinking that animal ain't got some smarts, too."

The woods around them echoed with the sound of creatures awakening. He pinched off a plug of Skoal from a flat round tin that was as much a part of his hunting gear as his gun, and positioned it inside his cheek. Danae had tried it once, snuck a bit when he wasn't looking and stuck it in her mouth. Only problem: she didn't spit, she swallowed the thick brown mix of saliva and tobacco. She puked up her ham biscuit and felt green-gilled the rest of the day. Daddy got a huge kick out of that. For once, he didn't rage, slapping her on the back instead, mumbling something about learning lessons the hard way.

**H**umans are animals, Danae reasons, same as deer, turkey, doves, and squirrels. Figuring one out should be as easy as observing and listening. Since her sister clearly isn't a talker—then, or now—and there's little opportunity to interact with her, noticing her ways will have to suffice.

The running shoes are cheap, off-brand, less than thirty bucks, but the best Danae can manage on minimum wage. But who's complaining? Her boss lets her sleep in the back room for nothing—beats hell out of the tarp lean-to she huddled under for those first few nights. Even a lumpy cot's better than hard ground.

The scant cash she had when she escaped her hometown barely stretched for a tank of gas and convenience store food. Even if the cycle hadn't crapped out on the outskirts of Chattahoochee, running out of money would've brought her to a standstill, forced her to turn tail and head back to face God only knows what. But no. She'd finagled her way into a means to make a little change, thanks to Mr. Hal. Then she had spotted Mouse stepping from the Wild Rose Diner. The pieces had fallen into place so easily, ending up here had to be fate tapping her kindly, for once.

The shoes rub her heel, a bit loose. She pulls them off and doubles up on socks. Better. She lashes a bottle of water around her waist with a bungee cord. Not fancy, but it works.

At the discount store, it had come down to a decision: buy either a cheap cell phone or the running shoes, socks, shorts, and another T-shirt. She doesn't talk to anyone, outside of a handful of locals. The phone can wait. Aunt Sylvia is beyond worried sick at this point. Danae feels bad about that. Has the same thing happened to Danae as it had to Mouse? Run off. No word. Diminishing hope. Danae promises herself she'll call the only person she considers family first thing after she gets that phone.

For now, ferreting out Mouse's ways garners the top slot.

Danae stands, bounces a few times to assure her feet no longer slip in the shoes, then stretches her hamstrings and calf muscles. Not one for organized team sports, she had been on the track team in high school. Running seemed a better survival skill than tossing some ball into a net.

Fact is, walkers and runners blend into the background, given a bit of repetition. Happens with anything seen regularly; the brain tucks them into the normal/everyday category, a fact Danae counts on.

Invisible, like a ditch weed. Growing strong and flowering without notice.

Danae leaves the shop, walking first to warm up her muscles, then breaking into a moderate jog. Her body takes over the mindless activity, leaving her mind room to ponder. No wonder so many folks use exercise as meditation.

This is kin to still-hunting, she decides. Sure, she's moving. But she's not actively chasing her prey. Though her daddy scorned doing anything passive, Danae enjoyed still-hunting the handful of times she'd gone with a couple of guys from her senior class. They scattered seed corn and salt licks, starting a month out from hunting season, an all-you-can-eat buffet. The deer drifted in, shy at first, then bolder as nothing alerted their danger radar. That's the problem with accepting an easy meal. Nothing's free. Nothing.

Meanwhile, Danae and her fellow hunters waited in deer blinds or tucked deep in brush, quiet, watching and waiting.

Now, Danae hunts Mouse.

She picks up the pace, easing into her normal running stride. In school, she hadn't been much of a sprinter, but excelled at distance. Down West Washington street, then turning south on Main. A few blocks and a hard right onto a narrow side street that runs behind the veterinarian's office. A battered Jeep Wrangler is the only automobile parked next to the fenced kennel—Dr. Johnson's vehicle. In the three days Danae's been scoping out the office, she's noticed no other means of transport—no motorcycle, no bike.

Point one: Mouse walks to work. Chattahoochee has no bus system. Taxi would be too expensive.

For the next few days, Danae alters her route, purposely leaving earlier each morning. The clinic opens at 7:30 for early drop-offs. On day four, the indoor lights snap on as she passes. No Jeep in the back lot. Has to be Mouse. Danae checks her watch—a Timex field-style with a backlit face and glow-in-the-dark numerals, a graduation gift from Aunt Sylvia, the only acknowledgement she had received.

7:15 a.m.

Good thing she was wearing the watch when she had to leave, or it would've been another thing to buy. The Timex and the second-hand Yamaha cycle Uncle Buddy had bartered for before he died, make up the sum of her assets.

Tomorrow, she'll leave at ten till seven, zigzag the streets, and hope to catch sight of Mouse approaching the office. As soon as she establishes the direction, the quest will simplify. Only a matter of appearing earlier, along the same route, until Danae unravels Mouse's path back to its origin.

Mama claimed Danae had the makings of a detective. How her mind worked with even the tiniest details. How she saw things others missed.

Danae considers this. Her feet accompany her thoughts with rhythmic slaps on the pavement. The shoes offer scant cushion. If she gets a month from them before the soles wear thin . . . She takes her mind off her aching feet, redirecting to Mama's aspirations for her. Who knows, maybe one day she might be a detective. Anything's possible, Aunt Sylvia often reminded her.

Danae harrumphs. Who's she kidding. School costs money.

She halts on the sidewalk near the auto shop. Breathes deep. Allows her pulse to calm. She moves inside, sponges off, and dons work clothes. Coffee pot on, honeybun breakfast in hand. Lights on. Mr. Hal should be walking in shortly.

No time to worry over the future. Only now. And Mouse.

Because when she and Mouse become family again, anything will be possible.


**Y**oung folks think they're the first ones to figure out sex. Mevlyn's read the magazine articles, even a couple of books on the subject. She figures every generation has to feel as if they've pinned down some new facts the old farts never knew.

Mevlyn cradles a coffee mug, tapping her wedding ring against the ceramic in Morse code. She roams mind and memory around the kitchen and den, pausing on the counter, the floor, the sofa, the recliner. Barely one surface escaped her and her husband's lovemaking, if she could call some of it that. Some was animal grunting and grinding. Her recall leads her down the hall, to the bathroom, guest bedroom, master bedroom, and the third cramped room Sam used as an office and she as a sewing room and catch-all for anything that didn't have a rightful place. Every one of this house's walls could tell tales of clothes ripped off and body parts slamming rhythm.

She thumbs through a women's magazine, one in the stack waiting to move to the Wash-Away. Two pages past the recipe insert, an article nabs her attention. Good Lord, what a headline: *Find Your G-Spot and Go There!* She'll have to look that one up, next time she sits at the library's computer.

Sam had no problem figuring out the prime real estate on her lady parts. She found his pretty easy too. Sex was a highlight of being married, right up until Sam fell ill.

Sonny glances up from his chewy toy, his tail wiggles, then he resumes gnawing. True, she and her husband might've had minor disagreements over the years—mainly over his tendency to leave messes in the kitchen—but they shared an almost unholy drive for sex.

Even now, with his oxygen tube strapped on and him so out of it he barely maintains a toe in reality, Sam's man part will stand at full salute a minute or two before it slumps over like a wilted corn stalk. Is he dreaming about her? Mevlyn likes to think he is.

Every morning's the same now. Following nights where she's up four or five times to check on Sam. Bad nights, he calls out, jerking her from restless sleep, her feet thumping the scarred hardwood before she comes fully awake. She's hit the wall a few times, even fallen once and had to crawl like a baby until she could reach the side of Sam's bed to pull herself up. Since then, she has worn a small flashlight on a string around her neck, and does her best to remember to click it on before she takes step one.

If she goes down, who will take care of Sam? Nobody, that's who. They'll both end up in a world of shit. Heck, they could lie here for a good while, wallowing in sweat, pee, and poo, before anyone came looking for them.

No. No matter what, Mevlyn must stay upright and vigilant.

She doles out Sonny's kibble and refreshes his water. The dog licks her hand *thank you* and settles into his meal. Yet another concern: if something happens to her, Sonny'll end up in the pound. He's not handsome by any stretch. Looks aren't everything. But the fact is, the cute, cuddly ones, the puppies and kittens, the ones recognizable as a distinct breed—they are the ones that get the homes.

"Don't you worry none." She leans down and pets Sonny between the ears. He continues to eat, but wags what's left of his tail. It was broken when Mevlyn spotted him in that alley, half-starved and scared of his own shadow. It hung like a branch culled by a wind storm, yet still attached to the tree. The vet cropped it for a reduced surgical fee. He felt sorry for Sonny and Mevlyn, she supposed. Once she rid the terrier of the community of fleas and fattened him up, he looked passable. The orphan possesses an unwavering loyalty most people can't muster.

She leans back against the counter and sips coffee, listening to the sound of his crunching and the calls of morning birds. Outside the window, the feeders bustle with cardinals, chickadees, titmouse, wrens, and doves. Mevlyn likes them all, but favors the smaller birds. The cardinals are bullies. A scarlet male swoops in, scattering the others, content only when he's alone with the abundance.

Survival of the fittest. The meek shall inherit the Earth. Which is the truth? Sure seems those who push and shove get ahead at the expense of everyone else.

The mourning doves arrive. A bonded pair, mated for life. Like her and Sam. Three times larger than the cardinal, they approach the platform feeder as if it's an all-you-can-eat buffet, scooping up seeds until their craws look like neck goiters.

"Enough wasting time." Mevlyn sucks down the rest of her now-cold coffee and rinses out the cup. Sam needs breakfast.

For the past few weeks, all she can get him to eat is oatmeal. One packet of instant oats, mixed with a teaspoon of brown sugar, a little cream, and two mashed sections of a canned peach. Some mornings, he cleans out nearly the entire bowl. Others, Mevlyn does good to coax four or five spoonsful into his tight lips before he falls back to sleep.

While the microwave cooks the oatmeal, she eats her wheat toast with the blackberry jam one of her regular patrons brought by. The deep purple jam tastes of the best part of summer, miles above the mass-produced mess she buys at the grocery store. Mevlyn closes her eyes and enjoys the tart sweetness mixed with real butter.

The microwave dings. She crams in the last bite and wipes crumbs from her lips and hands, and mixes in the butter, cream, sugar, and peaches. Sonny dances by the sliding glass door. She lets him out long enough to do his business, then calls him inside.

The oatmeal cools. She carries a loaded bed tray down the hall. Sonny walks beside her. At the bedroom threshold, Mevlyn pauses. In the scant light filtering through the closed venetian blinds, she can't tell if Sam is alive. Or dead.

She moves closer, watching, holding her own breath until she can pick up on the subtle rise and fall of his sunken chest. She sets the tray atop the bureau and opens the blinds. Lemony early sunlight paints stripes across the floor, bed, and her husband.

"Good morning, my sugar." It's a stretch to coax the cheerful tone into her voice.

Sam emits a low moan. One hand lifts, falls. He knows she's here: the important thing.

No need to sit the bed up for him to eat. The frame is raised to nearly a sitting position to aid his breathing. Mevlyn snaps an oversized adult bib around his neck; she sewed fabric scraps together to save from having to change his pajama top after every meal. More food lands on him than makes it into his stomach.

She takes in the room: sparse, hospital-like. Pictures and excess decoration bother him more and more, as the disease progresses. The only things that continue to bring him pleasure are three mounted prize bass from his tournament days, and his collection of vintage cricket cages and minnow buckets. How he loved to find one of those old galvanized aluminum buckets. If they happened upon an antique or junk store, he'd pull in to check if they might have one he didn't own. Mevlyn runs her gaze down the shelf. Twelve in all, from as early as the turn of the last century, to the '70s. After that, the manufacturers went to cheap plastic. Other than the most battered bucket—his oldest and highly treasured— the rest sport painted logos. The one with the blue spread-wing eagle, the Fenwick Woodstream, is her favorite, though she likes the names of them all: Old Pal, My Buddy, Min-O-Life, Angler's Legacy, Revelation, Stumpy Floater. She chuckles a little to herself at the last one on the shelf, how she'd told Sam that *Stumpy Floater* sounded like the aftereffects of constipation.

Mevlyn sighs and turns from those happy memories to caring for her husband. Marriage is about good times and bad, health and sickness. Says so in the vows.

"I don't want to smell like an old man," Sam told her not long after the cancer diagnosis.

"And I won't have you smelling like one neither," Mevlyn had assured him with a wry smile.

She bathes him at least once a day, and wipes him down and changes his bed clothing two or more times beyond that. Still, the taint of advanced disease covers him like an invisible shell. It matters little to Sam; Mevlyn doubts he can detect his own stench. But she can and she promised. Even if she must do ten loads of laundry a week, she will keep up her part of those better-or-worse wedding vows.

"I fixed your favorite, my sugar." She carries the tray to the bed and settles it across his lap, then spoons up a scant spoon of oatmeal and teases his lower lip. He opens wide like the baby birds in that nest in her camellia bush. She eases the spoon in, uses his upper lip to sweep out the oatmeal, then removes the spoon. His mouth remains open, the oatmeal a gelatinous mound atop his tongue. "Chew it and swallow, sugar. Do it for me."

His mouth moves. His Adam's apple lifts and falls. Four spoonsful and sips of apple juice later, he turns his head away from her. No use trying to force more. After watching him struggle, Mevlyn's done, too.

Sonny whimpers. Mevlyn looks down. "I know. Daddy's not well this morning, is he?"

As if the little dog understands, his tail nub moves side to side once.

Sorrow creeps up and clutches her chest before she can tamp it down. She lifts the tray and carries it back to the kitchen.

Mevlyn stands at the sink and sobs until her cries morph to hiccupped gasps. The gush passes. She takes a shuttering breath and releases it in a long sigh.

"You and me need to get on to the shop," she states to Sonny. He woofs agreement.

Nine

Danae spots the aging pickup truck as soon as it turns onto Satsuma Road. A girl running alone—early or late—no matter if she's big-boned, is like waving a sirloin in front of a junkyard dog.

She slows her pace a tad, checking side to side for possible escape routes in case it's some redneck pervert. The house to her right has a full wooden privacy fence. The one beyond doesn't. She can dart behind that house and take her chances where the truck can't follow.

The pickup accelerates and pulls alongside her. The window is lowered and a brown arm waves her down. Should she hightail it? The danger hairs on her nape aren't standing erect. Yet.

"You seen a couple of dogs?" A voice calls out.

Trust this? Could be a ploy. "Nope."

The driver is young. A black male. Big dude. Her heart rate picks up. She jogs in place to keep her muscles primed in case she needs to pour on the acceleration.

"Pit bulls. Two. One's got a lot of white on her face."

"Pits?" Great. If it's true, now she'll have that to worry over.

"Yeah, but they're friendly. Won't hurt a flea." The hand hanging out of the window lifts and points at her. "You're that girl from the auto shop."

"Uh-huh."

"Met you a couple of days back, with my dad, the cop, remember?"

Danae stops jogging in place. Leans closer to the truck. "Malcolm, right?"

"Yep. Me."

She breathes out. Her pulse calms. "How long've they been missing?"

"Maybe a half hour? I let them out and took a shower. Went to let them in and they were gone. Dug out from the fence."

"I'm pulling a long route today. I'll keep an eye out for them."

"Thanks. Names are Girly—the one with the white face—and the male's Levon." The engine changes pitch. "See ya around."

"Hey, hold up!"

The truck brakes and reverses a couple of feet.

"If I see them, how do I get word to you?"

The engine idles rough. She could tune it up until it purred. "I'll give you my number. Call or text me."

"No phone." Danae lifts her shoulders, lets them fall. Admitting to no phone is like saying you don't have a head. Everyone has a phone.

He looks Danae tip to toe, as if he's viewing an alien. "For real?"

She waves a hand. "Never mind. If I see them, I'll think of something."

Malcolm leans across the cab and digs in the truck's glove compartment. He scribbles on a notepad and hands a slip of paper out to Danae. "Maybe if you spot them, call me from the shop?"

"Sure. I'll do that."

"Thanks, Danae."

"You're welcome."

He looks at her strangely again. Okay, so everybody under forty says *no problem*, but Aunt Sylvia drilled it into her head about that improper response.

Only after he waves again and pulls away does it dawn on her: he remembered her name.

Three turns later, Danae catches sight of the dogs. She slows to a walk, then stops. The white-faced one notices her first and heads her way, with the younger dog in tow. A few feet away, the female dog stops, eyeing Danae with her head tilted.

"Here baby. Here, Girly." She keeps her voice light and calm. "Who's a good girl? Yes you are."

The pit bull hesitates a second longer before walking over and sniffing her. The male dog hangs back. Clearly, the lady is in charge. Danae holds out her hand, palm down. The female sniffs, then slathers the proffered hand with a drippy hello. The male walks over and accepts a head pat. Both tails wag.

Danae considers for a beat, then removes the bungie cord wrapped around her waist. The water bottle, she leaves beside a tree. She'll come back for it later. She loops one end of the cord around Girly's neck and the other around Levon's. The three of them walk the rest of her route back to the shop to phone their owner.

"Good thing you found them," Malcolm says minutes later. "My dad would've killed me." Girly and Levon bound toward him, as if it's been days since they escaped his yard.

"They're good dogs. Maybe one day, I'll have some like them."

"Hey, I'm gonna scoot off down to the river landing Sunday morning. Gonna catch up a few bream. Fry 'em up later if we land enough. Come on down if you'd like."

"No license."

"Don't need one. I fish from the bank, use natural bait, crickets mostly, and no rod and reels. Called the *cane pole exemption*." He hesitates. "I got plenty of extra poles and stuff."

"Might see you." Danae smiles. It would be good to do something besides run the streets or stare at some dumb television rerun. She'd rather hunt, but given it's not season, fishing works. And it's free.

After Malcolm loads Girly and Levon into the bench seat beside him and thanks her a half dozen more times, Danae watches him pull away. Two dog heads lean from the passenger side window, long tongues dripping slobber down the rust-pocked door. She gives him kudos for not pitching them in the truck's back bed like most folks do. Too many get thrown out or jump, and either maimed or killed. Either way, never good for the poor animals.

Danae doubts Malcolm worries much about catching his father's wrath for the dogs' escape. Most folks don't have a daddy who would possibly carry out an idle death threat.

Considering all of the times Danae had prodded Big John's mean side, it's small wonder she's still on this side of the dirt. If she hadn't cold-cocked him and took off the night of her graduation, it might have been her last.

After the dog rescue escapade—and no success with a Mouse sighting—Danae decides to treat herself to a sit-down meal. The thought of one more cellophane-wrapped sweet roll turns her stomach. She had spotted the Wild Rose Diner's sign when she first rounded the corner onto West Washington Street with the tethered dogs loping by her side. Eggs or pancakes today? Either will suffice.

She grabs a twenty from her under-cot stash, more than enough for a hearty breakfast. A few more steps brings her into the diner kitty-corner to the auto shop. The pedestal sign beside the cash register desk announces *Seat Yourself.*

Danae takes a moment to allow the cheerful ambiance to wrap around her. The corner booth positioned with a view from the front and side plate glass windows is perfect. She ambles down the barn plank floor and slides onto the vinyl-cushioned bench. From here, she can watch the entire room. Three other booths along the front window hold patrons. One seats two older women; she's seen one of them at the Wash-Away before. The lady trades gossip with Mevlyn like everyone's business belongs to her alone. The other two booths hold an elderly couple and a middle-aged dude in a business suit. She swivels to take in the three seating areas to her right. Only one is occupied: a group of guys, not much older than her, talking way too loud for first thing in the morning.

Nothing in particular holds her interest, so she looks around the diner. The woman who owns it moved here from Louisiana, Mevlyn told her, so the décor is a wacky blend of down-home country kitsch and Mardi Gras. The comfort of the old South—cathead biscuits, fried chicken and mullet, fresh vegetables, and apple pie—meshes with a fresh attitude and a dash of New Orleans. Even the most hardcore locals clamor for gumbo, jambalaya, and muffaletta. Danae plans to sample everything on the menu, if she stays in town long enough. Maybe she and Mouse will take up permanently here. It's as good a place as any, and a sight better than what she's experienced so far.

Most times, she picks up take-out. Eating inside is a rare luxury, akin to the showers she manages every couple of weeks. Sink baths suffice to keep body stench at bay, but it's worth every cent of the camping fee at the state park across the river to have warm water washing over her head, shoulders, and body.

Julie, the head waitress, stops by her booth, coffee carafe in hand. "Morning, Miz Danae. You meeting anyone this mornin'?"

Danae can count on one hand the number of people she knows in this town. Other than maybe Mevlyn, she can't imagine sitting across from any of them, casually chatting over eggs. "Nope. Just me." Danae flips over the heavy white mug next to her wrapped silverware and nods. Julie decants coffee. Fragrant steam lifts to Danae's nose.

"What for you, this morning, hon?"

"Two eggs over easy, grits, sausage, couple of biscuits." Her mouth waters. The cooks at the Wild Rose make buttermilk biscuits as good as Aunt Sylvia's. Mama tried, but hers usually turned out tough. A little bakery down the street boasts sweet potato biscuits. Danae hasn't had one of them yet; maybe after her next paycheck.

Julie nods. "We just got in some tupelo honey. It was rare to find at a decent price for a good long while, what with the storms blowing the blooms off the tupelo trees. Want some of that with your biscuits?"

"Oh, yes ma'am I do." There's a reason they call the local honey *liquid gold*. Danae could drink the stuff straight out of the bottle. Atop a hot, buttered cathead biscuit—well, it was, as her aunt put it, "good enough to make you want to slap your pappy."

"All righty then. I'll get that order out shortly for you." The server smiles and pours coffee for several more patrons and nods through their orders before pushing backwards through the purple and teal-painted swinging door. A dying art, being able to recall each item without jotting it down.

It'll be a light day at the auto shop. Tuesdays normally are. By midafternoon, she can gather up her sheets, towel, three wash cloths, and the handful of soiled clothing and head to the Wash-Away. It'll be too late to watch the soaps with Mevlyn, but the old woman always catches her up.

The food arrives in less than ten minutes. Julie slides the loaded plate in front of her, along with a saucer piled high with two fat biscuits. She adds a cup filled with butter packets and a plastic honey squeeze bottle shaped like a bear. "Anything else you need to get started off?"

"No ma'am. Thanks." Danae picks up the salt and pepper shakers and gives the eggs and grits a light dusting.

"I can nab you another biscuit or two if that doesn't top off your empty tank." Julie chuckles and moves to deliver dishes to the next booth.

Danae makes a mental note: next time Julie brings her old Chevy in for an oil change, she'll throw in a free vacuum and wash. Her boss won't mind. Mr. Hal knows the value of rewarding good people. If it was her business, she'd do the same. What you put out—good and bad—has a way of doubling back at you.

She digs into the food, relishing every bite. The egg yolks are the right amount of runny. The sausage is done, a bit chewy, but still moist inside. The grits are creamy perfection. Hard to fathom that anyone from around here could screw up grits, but some can. Danae uses one biscuit to sop the plate clean and saves the second for butter and tupelo—breakfast dessert.

One bite is all it takes to send her to a full-on swoon. She closes her eyes. Butter mixes with the honeyed gold, carried by the soft, warm insides of the bread.

The bell attached to the entrance door rings, but Danae disregards it, caught up in the party in her mouth. She swallows and opens her eyes. Mouse stands at the checkout counter, accepting a brown paper bag from Julie. Her sister keeps her head lowered, then takes one glance into the diner. Mouse's gaze rests briefly on Danae before flicking to the booth holding the four guys. The biggest one looks at her overlong, and gives out a dismissive half-laugh, half-huff.

Mouse hangs her head and hands over a couple of bills. She mutters something to Julie. Then she's out of the front door in one quick movement.

Careful not to draw attention, Danae steals glimpses toward the group. If Mouse found them threatening, there has to be a reason. Anger bubbles up inside her. She grits her teeth. The joy of tupelo and butter disappears.

"More coffee, hon?" Julie stands next to her booth.

"No." She reconsiders. "On second thought, maybe one more refill."

The server decants a fresh cup and pitches a handful of sealed creamer pots onto the table. "Anything else?"

"No. Thanks."

Julie slides the ticket face down under the edge of her plate. "Take your time. No rush." She moves to the other booths.

Danae tamps down the urge to jump up and walk over to where the guys sit, fire questions at that big dude. But like stalking prey, sitting back and observing gathers more information than rushing in half-cocked. Her daddy did that, especially after he knocked back a few. Never did him any good, other than encourage a fight.

She moves her empty plate aside and sips slow. Waiting them out. The big dude dominates the conversation, his hands punctuating whatever he finds important. The other three nod, guffaw in spots, jeer in others. She catches names—Rich. Taylor. Jack. Gimp. Danae ferrets tiny details. The big one has a cowlick above his right eye and his lips sag on one side when he smiles or laughs. Beside him, Rich is better dressed, clean cut— his real name, or a title meant to rag on his parents' wealth? The blonde one they call Taylor, sometimes *Tay*, lisps. She can't tell much about the fourth guy, other than the *Gimp* label. Neither he nor Taylor face her and he doesn't add to the conversation enough for Danae to note any speech nuances.

Finally, when Danae has almost given up on them leaving before her, they exit the booth. Big dude leads. The last guy walks with a stiff limp— the one they called *Gimp*. His shoulders slump forward and he keeps his head down, the sure sign he's the omega of this little wolf pack. If he had a tail, it would be tucked tight between his legs.

They're nearly past her booth when the big one, Jack, pulls up short and stands next to her booth. She lifts her eyes to meet his.

"You that gal from the fixit shop, ain't ya?" A taunt.

Without breaking his gaze, she replies, "yep."

He says *uh-huh* deep in his throat without the sound making it into actual words. He studies her a beat too long, then leads the pack away, toward the cash register. One last muttered comment hangs in his wake, one intended for Danae: *Fricking Dyke.*

Other than Mevlyn's gossip partner, none of the other diners pay attention to the brief exchange.

Julie meets them at the desk and accepts their money. The pack exits, jostling and talking loud. The server closes the register drawer and walks to where Danae sits. "Those guys are nothing but trouble with a capital T. They bother you, hon?"

"Nope." Danae balls up her napkin and stuffs it into the empty mug. "Not one bit."

Ten

**M**evlyn plops down on the rolling chair harder than she intends. Something vital gives way. The padded seat rocks side to side and back to front with little urging.

"Well dandy. Another thing to replace."

"Having a bad go this morning, Miz Mevlyn?" Jerome asks. With his loads started in washers eleven and twelve, he leans against a counter reading something on his phone.

"You don't have enough wash time to hear all my tribulations, sir. But I thank you sincerely for your concern."

Danae enters, smiles first at Mevlyn, then pets Sonny, and nods good morning to Jerome before claiming washer number four.

"What would you do if you ever walk in here and that one's taken?" Mevlyn asks. The chair seat whirligigs when she shifts her weight.

"You got a loose screw, Miz Mevlyn?" Danae shoves in the quarter holder and runs water into her washer. "I could probably fix it."

"I got more than one loose screw." Mevlyn chortles at her own joke. "And you probably could fix this here chair. From what I hear, you can fix just about anything, even things I don't know need fixin'."

Jerome laughs. "Heard that, too. Hey, Danae. I owe you big for rounding up my dogs. Those pits are good as gold, but every now and then, Girly likes to instigate a walkabout, and Levon goes along with anything she does."

"Maybe they need more exercise." Danae loads her sheets and towels, shuts the lid.

"Could be. I get them around the block sometimes, and Malcolm takes them. But my schedule doesn't allow any consistency and Malcolm has his studies. I know the dogs get restless."

"I could take them with me. I run early, most days."

"How far?"

"Mile or two. Depends on the weather."

Mevlyn leans back and watches the two exchange words. Nice to see folks talking to each other rather than staring at their dang phones.

"I'd be willing to pay you a little, if you'd be willing." Jerome shoves his phone into his pocket.

"I am all about it."

"Deal then?"

"Deal." Danae takes a step and holds out her hand for a shake. "I like dogs, especially big ones. Anyone seeing me with a pit bull on either side would be plain stupid to bother me."

"You had trouble?" Jerome folds his arms across his chest, his feet planted apart, what Mevlyn thinks of as his police pose.

When Mevlyn stands, the chair seat wiggles like a punch-drunk mushroom. "There you go. Stealing my help."

Danae throws up both hands. "Hey, hey! Plenty of this to go around." She lets her hands fall, then sticks them into her pockets. "I can use the money."

A young male walks past the front door, looks in, then loiters beneath the overhang.

"That one of the Dixon boys?" Mevlyn asks Jerome.

"Yep. The eldest. Jack." Jerome takes his eyes off the boy long enough to ask, "any of them giving you trouble, Miz Mevlyn?"

"Not yet." She frowns. "Been seeing them hanging around lately."

"They bad news?" Danae asks.

"Could be." Mevlyn transfers a load from her triple washer into the first reserved dryer and sets the timer. When she returns to the chair, she settles in slowly, inch by inch to keep the seat from pitching. It does anyway. "This is like riding a rodeo bull."

Danae walks over and stands next to her. "Let me see if I can figure out what's wrong."

With a hand up from Danae, Mevlyn manages to extract herself without landing on the floor. Danae upends the chair. She jerks on first one, then another section of the seat. "Here's your problem. Missing bolt here and the opposite one has worked itself so loose, it's nearly out, too."

She pulls a small multi-tool from her pocket and unfolds it, then uses one attachment to snug the bolt. "That'll help some. I'll see if we have an extra couple of metal bolts lying around the shop. Meanwhile, go easy. These bolts are plastic." She uprights the chair.

"Cheaply made. Like everything else these days." Mevlyn indicates the row of machines with a head tilt. "Couple of them are originals, still plugging along. Rest are different stages of new. The last one I had to replace has already broken down four times."

Jerome looks Danae up and down. "Goodness, girl. What can't you fix?"

"If it has moving parts, I can figure it out. Been tinkering and tearing stuff apart since I was old enough to hold a screwdriver. Got my tail torn up more than once because of that."

Had to be more to the story to get a gal so young to leave home with so little to her name, Mevlyn thinks. She ought to know. Happened to her.

Jerome nods. "You're a good one to have around." He turns focus to Mevlyn. "Now, back to those Dixon boys."

Outside, the big dude leans against the side of the block building. His goons are around somewhere. Mevlyn's seen it all over the years. Cowards run in packs.

"I'll keep an eye out for you, Miz Mevlyn. I'll pass the word on to the other shifts, too."

"Are they a gang or something?" Danae asks.

"Gang wannabes, more like it. Every generation pops them out." Mevlyn points at Jerome. "That one there was a pistol in his day."

Danae regards Jerome, her eyebrows forming twin questions.

"Bad boys go one of two ways," he says. "They either make criminals, or the sharpest police officers."

"How's that work?" Danae flips him a puzzled grin.

"If you did it when you were a snot-nosed little thief, you know how one of them thinks, what to look out for. Times change, sure. But not that much."

"Ah."

Jerome picks up his soap powder box. "On that note, I'll leave you ladies for a bit. Don't fret, Mevlyn. I'll be back to start my dryer."

"You best do that. I got me some connections with the local Po-Po."

Jerome's laugh is full and deep. He gives Mevlyn a thumbs-up and walks out to his truck.

"Nice fellow. No matter what he did as a youngun, he's good seed. Been knowing him since his mama brought him with her, tucked in her laundry basket. His son's a gem, too."

"What's his wife do?"

Mevlyn feels sadness loop her heart. Knowing people means she knows their troubles, too. "She run off. Got herself mixed up in some bad business. Ended up leaving town middle of the night, from what I heard."

"Wow. That sucks."

"Yeah. Shore did. Left Jerome with a young son to raise by hisself. But he's done a fine job of it."

Mevlyn grows quiet for a moment, then says, "You happy with your living arrangements?"

Danae slides onto a chair and crosses one leg over the other, ankle on knee. "Beats sleeping on the ground."

"I got a proposition for you." Mevlyn breathes in and lets the air out in a long sigh. Weariness shoves her shoulders down. Once a thing is said, it's said. "What if you move in with me and Sam?"

"Huh?"

"I got a third room. I can put a secondhand sleeper sofa in there, or a day bed. Or one of them croutons."

"You mean . . . futon?"

"Yeah. One of them. You'd have a bathroom to yourself. I got to move some boxes I have stacked up in the tub." Mevlyn stops, studying the gal's reaction. "What's the catch, you're thinking. Nothing's for free."

"I don't have money for rent."

"Ain't asking for a dime from you."

This time, Mevlyn can't help but chuckle at Danae's expression. "Sam's a handful. You seen yourself how he is. I am about pooped out. If you are there to help me out a little, keep an ear open for him . . . Maybe we could take turns checking on him. I could get a decent night's sleep. Can't recall the last one of them I got." She pauses. "What you say, gal? Want the job? I'll cook some meals, and you and I'll have privacy in our own rooms. I'll even move that little TV from the room Sam's in, set it up for you. He doesn't look at it anymore. The noise bothers him."

"You sure?"

"Danae, I don't know you all-together well. People gonna go crazy when they find out, probably figure you're taking advantage of an old woman and a dying man. But here's the level truth: we ain't got nothing worth stealing. A person would be hard pressed to find a single thing in that house worth more than a plug nickel."

"I don't steal."

"I got a sound feeling that is the truth." Mevlyn holds out her hand. "Want to set a deal with me, like you just did with Jerome?"

"Deal," Danae says, sealing it with a shake.

"When can you move in?"

"Tomorrow after work?"

"All righty then. I'll get busy locating something for you to sleep on." Mevlyn reaches into her cooler and pulls out two colas. "Let's drink to it."

As the two near the end of their celebration, Jerome strides in, his features solemn. "Miz Mevlyn, I found something you need to come look at."

He turns, leaves the building, and waits outside. Mevlyn walks out, Danae behind her. Jerome leads the way to one side of the building shaded by a thatch of young water oaks. Around the steel door, chunks of mortar are missing. Jerome points to chips of concrete littering the ground. "Someone's been working on this door jam. Judging from the size of those marks, I guess a crowbar."

Mevlyn runs her fingers over the exposed concrete. "What in the blue blazes?"

"A little more, and the hinges will give way, no matter if you got it bolted inside."

"What could they be after?" Danae asks, her voice incredulous.

"Coins is all I got. I clean out the machine coffers twice a day, then put the loose change into a bag."

"You carry it home?" Jerome asks.

"Sometimes I do. Others, I put it into a drop safe Sam had installed a few years back. Only a roll or two get left out, easy for me to get to. Folks know where it's at. I've only had a dollar or two go missing over time."

Jerome's lips form a firm line. "You don't carry that bag with you after dark, do you?"

"Oh hell no. I may be old, but I'm not dumb as a stick. People get knocked over the head doing such as that."

Jerome studies the damaged door jam. "I'll get one of the guys to reinforce this for the time being. And we'll keep watch."

Mevlyn shifts her gaze from Jerome to Danae. "Reckon there's any way you could move in tonight? I got a decent sofa in the den."

"Sure," Danae says without hesitation. "Let me tell Mr. Hal and get my things. I'll be back in a flash."

After Danae leaves, Jerome walks Mevlyn back into the Wash-Away. "She's moving in with you?" he asks.

"A swap for the help I need."

"Don't know much about her."

"No. Other than my gut feeling."

"If you'll get her full name, maybe her driver's license number, anything I can use, I will do a little digging."

"I'll see, Jerome. I'll see." Mevlyn settles into the chair with a grunt. "Something about her tells me she's been mishandled. But she's good people."

"I get that same sense. I hope we're both right."

Eleven

**D**anae rides shotgun. Malcolm drives, slow and careful like somebody's ghost grandma. If she knew him better, she'd kid him about how she'd like to get to the river before she turns forty.

She props her right arm on the window ledge, feeling the balmy morning air ripple the fine hairs on her forearm. The truck must've been a spit-shined forest green when new. Beaten by the harsh Florida sun, the paint's faded to a shade that reminds her of milky puke. No matter. It has four wheels—two more than Danae's ever had—and it runs, better since Malcolm let her put in a new set of sparkplugs and adjust the timing.

The process fascinated Malcolm. He sat beside her on a rolling shop stool, firing questions she could answer in her sleep. How could Danae, a girl, know her way around an engine? Vintage vehicles like this one with its antique license tag are a breeze to repair. The newer computer-dictated versions, not so much. She'll need training and experience to conquer them. Maybe one day, she will get the money to take classes.

So, give her daddy some credit, the sombitch. She at least knows how to hunt, fish, and perform basic car repairs. By age six, she'd changed her first tire. Couple of years after Mouse moved, Danae took charge of topping off the fluids, changing the oil, and keeping the tires aired up on her mama's four-door sedan.

Lost in her thoughts, Danae stares at the passing woods—mostly stands of oak and a few cypresses in the wet spots. She never touched Daddy's prized Ford F150. God forbid no. Nobody but Big John was good enough for that. The rattletrap Ranger he kept running for hunting was another matter. It had dents in every panel and the inside had enough crumbs and splattered grease to make a meal.

The pit bulls sit between them on the pickup's ripped bench seat, joyful to be included on whatever adventure the humans have dreamed up. They offer slobbery kisses, as they do every morning when she goes to pick them up for their runs.

Malcolm heads west on Highway 90, then slows, downshifts, and veers south onto River Landing Road, less than a mile out of Chattahoochee. Have to admire anyone who can operate a manual transmission these days, much less a *three-on-the-tree*—her father's mechanic lingo for a shift stick mounted on the steering column.

Danae drums her fingers on the window ledge. The old truck has aged in spades, but is still miles above any of those new growlers with their overblown bodies and fierce grills.

Malcolm hums to himself. No radio. She glances over at him—one of the few people who don't feel the need to fill blank air with words. A definite point in his favor.

The road curves and opens onto a wide paved parking lot. At the end of the twin ramps, the Apalachicola River roils past, the current swift as it comes off the Jim Woodruff Dam. Danae's ridden her cycle to spots above the dam in Georgia, where Lake Seminole collects water from the Chattahoochee and Flint Rivers farther north. Three Rivers, the locals call the area, because the Apalachicola had its start where the lake is now, though Danae imagines it as two waterways joining to become one before rolling onward toward the Gulf of Mexico.

She's been to Chattahoochee Landing numerous times since she hit town, evenings when she sat astride her cycle near the river's edge, listening to the whoosh of water and the crickets and frogs serenading the setting sun.

Miz Mevlyn loves to wax on and on about the Apalachicola, about the long-ago days of the paddlewheel steamboats, and the times when she and Sam were young and crazy. They'd ride a flat bottom fishing skiff thirty miles downriver to overnight on wide sandbars created by the Corp of Engineers' dredgers. Sam once had a box of pot shards and arrow points, prized finds given up by the river's muddy bottom.

"You ever been to a place Mevlyn calls the Bluffs?" Danae asks Malcolm.

"Once or twice, with my dad. It's pretty spectacular." He crosses the parking lot. A few trucks hooked to boat trailers line the periphery, leaving ample access to the loading ramps and floating dock. "You go along for miles, then you round a curve and these cliffs rise up a good five hundred feet. It'll make you stop and stare with your mouth hanging open."

"Mevlyn told me they call it the Garden of Eden, on account of some tree that grows there, like Noah made the Ark out of."

"*Torreya taxifolia*, also known as gopher wood."

"God, you *are* a nerd."

Malcolm laughs. "High praise."

"I figured it was like my aunt used to say, anyone will lay claim to anything that makes their particular neck of the woods holy and graced by God."

"Pretty much. But the tree *is* there. And the gopher wood reference *is* in the Bible."

Danae looks across at him and rolls her eyes. "Whatever." She motions to the parking lot. "Not many people on the river today."

"Only true heathens fish on Sunday morning."

"The others polish their pews and find other ways to rack up sin." Her daddy never set foot in a church, not even for a funeral. Being a hypocrite wasn't on his list of attributes. Give him that. Her mama was the opposite; she went to church every time they opened the doors.

Malcolm steers onto a narrow gravel road barely wide enough for one vehicle.

"Thought we were going to fish the bank." Beside her, Girly and Levon bounce and jostle. Danae loops a protective arm around them.

"We are." He shoots her a look. "What, you thinking I'm dragging you into the woods for some evil purpose?"

"Never crossed my mind." And it hadn't. Even if he was that sort of guy, Danae feels pretty sure she can take him, or at least wound him enough to get away.

"Dad and I have a favorite spot downriver. Water's too swift by the landing." He drives another mile, then parks the truck between two oak saplings. "Here we are."

The hinges groan when they exit the truck. The dogs lunge out of the cab and circle, their tails wagging so hard their backends swing side to side. Malcolm grabs a small ice chest, a bucket, a dip net, and two cane poles from the bed of the truck, and motions for her to carry a second bucket filled with old towels and a plastic basket teeming with live crickets. He leads the way down a path winding between river willows to a small clearing. Danae fills her lungs with the smell of rich, loamy dirt.

"Fish 're bedding nearby, smell them?" Malcolm sets down the cooler. He upends one bucket and motions for Danae to do the same. "True Southern ingenuity, seats that double as carriers."

"I may be small-town, but I'm not stupid." Danae grins.

"Roger that." He folds two of the towels and sets them atop the buckets. "Now, you won't end the day with dents in your butt."

The dogs snuffle the ground and buckets, and nose-bump the cricket basket. They prance around Malcolm's feet, tails held at attention. "Y'all go on and play now. But don't wander too far." He hands over a cane pole to Danae.

Danae releases the hook snagged in the pole's end and unspools the fishing line wrapped around its shaft. She watches Girly and Levon bound through the willows and listens to their gleeful yipped barks, so different from hounds tracking a deer. "Like they're going to do what you tell 'em."

Malcolm unwinds his line. "Don't know what kind of dogs you got where you come from in—"

"Ala-dang-bamer."

"No wonder you left. Had to be even worse being yourself *there* than here."

"Yeah. I guess so." Danae captures a cricket. She holds it between her thumb and index finger and studies the little insect a beat too long.

"What cha waiting on?" Malcolm swings his baited line into the water. The bright orange cork settles and stills. "Need me to do that?"

"I know how to bait a hook, thank you very much." Still, she dislikes spearing the innocent insect. Unless she's willing to eat leaves and shoots—not ready to take that step yet—some creature will die. Have to count the fish she'll consume later, too. Being at the top of the food chain is troubling.

Danae takes a breath and sticks the hook through the cricket's thorax, lengthwise like her daddy taught her. Its legs are still wiggling when she swings the line into the water.

"We catch mostly bream here, good-sized ones. You might luck up on a bass, though not often. Better to use a rod and reel for bass fishing, and most of the deeper holes where the big ones hang out are reached by boat."

"I like bream." Fried up crispy with cheese grits, maybe some coleslaw. Don't know how Malcolm and his dad do their fish, but most folks from the South go for some version of the same.

As if he reads her thoughts, Malcolm says, "Dad's got a propane fish fryer. He said he'll cook up whatever we bring home. I put up bread and butter pickles last summer. That, maybe some home fries or grits. Whatever."

"*You* canned pickles?" Danae takes her eyes off her cork long enough to shoot him an incredulous look.

"Someone had to do something with the nine hundred cukes we got out of the garden, end of the summer."

"Bet your mama loved that."

"Wouldn't know what she loves. She hasn't been around in years."

"Oh. Sorry." Danae chides herself. What a stupid slip, especially after what Miz Mevlyn told her. Not everyone has good memories of their mothers.

He settles onto the bucket and sticks the end of the pole into the soft dirt between his feet. "Don't be. She left when I was little."

Being left behind—something they held in common. "I get that. My sister ran off when I was eight."

They share the silence for a moment. Across the river, an alligator suns on the bank.

Malcolm reminds her of Antoine, back in Ala-dang-bamer. Not so much physically; Antoine is shorter, stocky. More, in the way he makes her feel. Protected. Like nothing can get to her. Bet Antoine feels deserted by her, and Aunt Sylvia. When she gets a phone, she'll call up Antoine, too. No need to explain what went down that night, how the congratulations she gave him nearly got her killed. Antoine knows how things can go bad fast, how sucky her life is.

Danae stares at the cork. Downriver of a bump-out bank, the water here takes on a different personality. Smooth, slower, with deep eddies carving out a hole perfect for bream. A slight breeze sends ripples across the surface of the river causing the cork to jiggle.

"Do you know where she is, your mom?" Danae asks.

"She was in jail down in Liberty County for a while. Drugs, accessory to armed robbery. She got out last year. Don't know where she is now." His shoulders lift, fall. "Couldn't care less."

Danae stuffs down the urge to confide about Mouse, how she's certain her sister is hiding in plain sight, here in Chattahoochee. No, best to hold some things close to the cuff.

"How'd you end up here, Danae, if you don't mind me asking?" Before she has a chance to drum up a good enough story for why anyone shows up in some small town, when they don't know a soul, living or dead, he says, "not an easy place for people like me and you to live."

Now, she's truly puzzled. "People like—?"

He flicks a quick glance toward her. "You don't have to hide, Danae. I'm gay, too."

"Um. *No.* But you . . . are?"

Malcolm pivots his head in her direction. "Wait. You're *not* gay?"

Danae raises her eyebrows, shakes her head.

His mouth hangs open.

"So, what? I drive a cycle, like to hunt and fish, and I'm a tad big-boned." She holds his focus, intent. "Therefore, I'm a lesbian? Jump to conclusions, much?"

Malcolm thumps his chest with a thumb. "I'm a large black dude with incredible muscle definition, drive a pickup, and like to hunt and fish, therefore . . . straight? I'm not the only one jumping to conclusions, sister."

Danae feels her lips lift into a wide grin. She laughs. He laughs.

"We're good. Right?" he asks.

"For sure." She holds up the arm not holding the pole and flexes. "If you'll admit my biceps are just as impressive."

Malcolm's white teeth flash. "I never doubted for one millisecond, that you could stomp me into the mud if necessary."

Danae relaxes her arm. "So, that's settled."

They fall silent. Bream hit both lines, as if someone rang the breakfast alert. In a few minutes, eight fat fish hang from the fish stringer in the water, secured to the bank by a length of nylon twine.

"I can't imagine anyone *not* loving this," Danae comments, threading another doomed cricket onto her hook. "Getting back to me and that whole gay thing—truth be told, the jury's still out."

"Come again?"

"I don't know what I . . . am?"

"You're a virgin?"

She pulls a face. "Ugh. God no." Danae trains her eyes on the bobbing cork, a false alarm this time. "I can't explain it." Really, she could. How can she feel anything for either a male or female, certainly not love. What *is* that, even?

"It's like having an itch you can't scratch," Malcolm offers.

More like itching, but not sure where and what will make it stop. She can't believe she's having this discussion with a guy she barely knows.

"When did you decide for sure?" she asks without meeting his gaze.

"Decide?"

In her peripheral vision, Danae senses his scrutiny. "Yeah."

"It isn't a choice, Danae. That'd be like deciding I have brown eyes. Not like I got gobsmacked one day and decided, oh, I think I'll be gay. Seriously, you believe that?"

"Never really gave it much thought."

"Obvious."

"Does your daddy know?"

"Of course. Other than a stretch back in middle school, I tell him everything. Besides, he's a cop. Not much he can't figure out."

"And he's okay with it?"

Malcolm gives her a hard look. "Why wouldn't he be? He worries. Not about that, so much, as about how narrow some folks can be. He's all about me flying under the radar, not inviting trouble. I don't have anything to hide, but I get it. No need to give people another reason to set me in their crosshairs."

His cork bobs twice, goes under. One snatch sets the hook. The fish plunges for deep water. Malcolm holds fast. The cane bends nearly double. "Big one! Holy cow!"

He allows the line a little slack, then rears back, alternately fighting against the fish's tug and allowing it to run.

"Need me to take over, let me know." Danae sticks the end of her pole into the dirt.

"Get the dip net ready. I don't want to lose this one."

After several more rounds of pull and release, Malcolm guides the line close to shore. They get a brief glimpse of a large fish whipping in the shallows.

"Bass!" Malcolm calls out. "Get ready!"

Danae dunks the dip net into the water near the line. "Do it!"

He gives one last hard pull. The exhausted fish roils to the surface, its tail slapping up muddy water. Danae scoops the dip net below the fish and lifts. On land, the bass opens and closes its wide mouth. Its gills extend and flatten, extend and flatten. Twice, it flaps violently, moving closer to the land's edge. Malcolm crouches and manages to slide two fingers beneath the fish's gills. He holds the fish up and looks it over.

"That's a keeper, for sure." Danae stands with one hand on her hip, the other clutching the dip net like a prop.

"My dad will filet this bad boy up, probably throw it on the grill."

Both of them are so caught up admiring the catch, they don't notice the bushes part behind them.

"Well, now. Ain't. This. Cozy?" A deep male voice says.

They both swivel. Fishing gear in hand, Jack Dixon stands, his malevolent gaze aimed in their direction. The blonde guy Danae remembers from the café steps up beside him. Another person lurks in the shadows, a female. Mouse? What the heck is she doing with these goons?

The girl is silent, her eyes trained on the muddy earth at her feet.

"Too bad our spot is better'n this over-fished hole. I feel bad for y'all."

Malcolm stares hard for a moment then proceeds with the bass. He uses a pair of needle nose pliers to work the hook free from the fish's mouth. He holds the bass in one hand, and takes a couple of steps and lifts the stringer full of bream from the water with the other. When he looks back at Jack, his glare makes a statement.

"C'mon, let's go," Jack says. His nose scrunches. "I can't stomach the *smell* here." He turns. The others swivel and ease down the path toward the road. Over his shoulder, Jack calls back, "If you get ready for some *real* fun, girl, be at Lost Lake Friday night." He barks out a harsh laugh.

The sound of footfall and snapping twigs fades.

"Asshole," Malcolm mutters. He fixes his gaze on Danae. "You don't want any part of that lunatic dude."

"Like I'd *want* a piece of *him?*"

Malcolm tosses the towel cushions aside, then upends one bucket and scoops up a little river water. He lowers the loaded stringer into the bucket. "We have plenty of fish to clean. Let's get out of here." He wraps the line around his pole, crams the towels into the second bucket.

Danae lifts and swings her cane pole toward the bank, captures the line and removes the dead cricket. She wipes her hands on her jeans and winds the line around the pole.

She casts one look in Malcolm's direction, notes the solemn set of his jaw. No use trying to recapture the carefree mood. Malcolm puts two fingers between his pursed lips and emits a sharp, high-pitched whistle. Danae detects no crashing noises from the woods; they'll probably have to go searching for the dogs. Without swapping conversation, they pick up the gear and head back to the parked truck. Girly and Levon sit by the passenger side door, their ears perked. Danae turns her head to make a comment about Malcolm's knack for training dogs. The stone cold expression on his face stalls her.

They load the gear and dogs, then ride in silence to Malcolm's house. Even the dogs sense the chilly atmosphere. As they scale and gut the catch, his mood lightens. His father watches him, but doesn't prod.

Malcolm's version of anger is different from her daddy's. Her new friend tends a controlled, smoldering burn, not a flash fire that scorches, or kills, everything in its path. Danae knows Malcolm's type. Antoine is similar. Both are the sort to wait and watch for an opening to settle a score.

<h1 style="text-align:center">Twelve</h1>

**A** four-year-old girl in pigtails bounds into the Wash-Away and barrels toward where Mevlyn stands. When the child slams into her, Mevlyn steadies her balance on dryer number one's opened door.

"Hey Mama Mevlyn!"

She leans down and hugs the child. "Hey yourself, Miss Prissy."

The girl's mother walks in, lugging three bulging laundry bags. Mevlyn remembers the woman from when she was the same age as her daughter, what seems like just a blink of time ago. "Ginny Beth, don't you be bothering Miz Mevlyn."

"She ain't bothering me one tiny bit." Mevlyn motions to the front desk. "There're some of them oatmeal raisin cookies y'all like so much in that little plastic container."

The girl dances. "Mama?"

"Go ahead on. But no more than two!" She laughs when her daughter jets across the room. "She had no cavities when we went to the dentist yesterday," she directs to Mevlyn. "I want to keep that up." Then, she calls to the child, "make sure you snap the lid shut so those don't get stale!"

Ginny Beth raids the container and darts back to slide up beside Mevlyn. "I got a new toothbrush and four stars for improvement!" She bites off hunks of one cookie and hands the other up to her mother.

Mevlyn pats her on the shoulder. "Good for you. So, you're doing that extra brushing we talked about then?"

"Yep. I do it some with toothpaste, then rinse out the foam and brush with just water." She holds up one hand, the fingers splayed. "Five whole minutes, like you told me."

"Well, goodie goodie!" Mevlyn points to a low table. "I picked up some new coloring books and crayons at the Dollar Store. I'd be pleased if you colored a picture for me. I can take it home so Mr. Sam can enjoy it. Be sure to sign your name on it when you finish. An artist does that."

After the child moves away, her mother says, "that wild child. She listens to you better than she listens to me."

"Your mama said the very same thing about you, as I recall."

The woman flashes a smile, then loads the coin trays on three washers and sets the temperatures. Water dribbles into the tubs. "How's Mr. Sam doing?"

"Not so good, baby. I think he's rounding the home stretch."

"I hate to hear that." She measures liquid soap and dispenses equal amounts into the washers. "How I despise cancer. Mr. Sam doesn't deserve such. *So* unfair."

"Cancer is an equal opportunity disease. It spreads far and wide, with no regard for money, power, age, or how bad, or fine, a person may be."

"If you need me for anything, please call," the woman says.

"I will, honey. But, you got your hands full with a houseful of younguns and besides, there ain't much anyone can do."

"Have you given any more thought to calling in hospice?"

"I did, until I got me some help. Don't you worry. Me and Sam will get by." Before the woman can ask questions or offer up well-intended advice, Mevlyn shuts the door of dryer one and cranks the timer to fifty minutes. "I just now got the new *Woman's Day* in the mail. I'm working on my accounts, so help yourself to it. Looks like it has a good hummingbird cake recipe."

"Thanks. I'll do that." The woman busies herself sorting and loading.

"Of course, there's a lose-ten-pounds-overnight diet in there, too. Small wonder we women aren't crazy as bedbugs." Mevlyn chuckles and moves back to her chair.

At her desk, Mevlyn thinks back to the spring of '47. She and Sam had been married barely a year when they moved to Chattahoochee. Construction on the new hydroelectric dam was getting underway, and the little town showed signs of growing and prospering. The folks were friendly to the point of knowing each other's business, good and bad. But it was the land that captured Mevlyn's heart.

With her accounting papers spread out before her, Mevlyn stares into space, lost in memories of the morning she and Sam rolled into Gadsden County. The Victory Bridge spanning the river floodplain was so narrow, she held her breath nearly the whole expanse from Jackson County on one side, to Gadsden on the opposite. If she reached out her arm, she could surely touch the cement guide wall. The few cars they passed made her squeeze her eyes shut. Didn't bother Sam. He steered the Chevrolet Fleetmaster with both hands on the wheel, chatting about what he knew of the town where they'd be living for a while.

Instead of the palm trees, beaches, and white sands in the magazine pictures she'd poured over for years, back before she caught the bus in Ohio, Mevlyn looked upon a river cupped in rolling hills. And the scent in the air! A blend of rich, wet dirt and things growing.

From the moment the bus carried her away from her miserable life in Ohio, Mevlyn had immersed herself in learning the ways and speech of the Deep South. She met Sam in Montgomery, the place she happened to land. Wasn't the first time a young man fell for his waitress. The job helped her practice her drawl. By the time Sam proposed and they sealed the deal at the Justice of the Peace, Mevlyn could pass as a true belle. She learned to make decent grits and a few basic dishes from one of the short-order cooks.

Her new mother-in-law called her out, no more than a week after Sam took her to meet his family in his hometown of Eufaula, Alabama. Mevlyn charmed his daddy, but his mama watched her like a hungry fox casing a chicken yard. Sam's younger brother Sherman had openly lusted after Mevlyn in a way that made her feel as if she needed to bathe afterward.

It was the phrase *bless your heart* that outed Mevlyn. To this day, she still doesn't fully grasp how a Southern lady can cut you to the bone one minute, then smile and offer up a slice of pie with whipped cream the next. *Bless your heart* wasn't always a compliment. As a former Midwesterner— though Southerners thought of them as Yankees too—Mevlyn vowed to limit her use of the phrase.

Her mother-in-law told her straight up, how she didn't approve of her son up and marrying without so much as a how-do-you-do, and how she was going to be watching every move Mevlyn made. To the woman's credit, she didn't tell anyone else about Mevlyn's ruse, as far as Mevlyn knows.

Moving to Florida took a weight from Mevlyn's shoulders. She could breathe. In Chattahoochee, no one knew her or Sam. She could be the woman she invented as she went along. She laid it on thick, adding big teased hair, fake eyelashes, and flowery dresses.

Their first place was a one-bedroom garage apartment. Not like they needed a lot of room, with no children running about. She took a job waitressing at a small restaurant on West Washington. They lived in the cramped rental until '57, saving up for what Sam referred to as "their next adventure."

That *adventure* turned out to be less than a quarter mile from the first apartment—a nine hundred square-foot, ranch-style house near the main drag, with a falling-down cement block building in its front yard. The house was sound enough, but Mevlyn hated the vine-laced eyesore in front of it. She tried to convince Sam not to buy the place. He did anyway.

Finished up with his part in the ten-year dam construction project, Sam took a job at the state mental institution. She'd failed to become a mother. The lady parts weren't cooperative in that department. Finding a purpose beyond serving up coffee and biscuits took her mind off motherhood.

Mevlyn came up with a plan; she was good at that, according to Sam's mama. Her mother-in-law admired her tenacity, so Sam said, though she would've loved a few grandbabies. Mevlyn would've gladly supplied them, had nature worked things out in her favor.

By the time Mevlyn cajoled the bank into loaning her and Sam the money for her endeavor, the entire town buzzed. That sassy waitress lady planned on opening a self-service washateria, right here in Chattahoochee. Imagine!

Now, years later, Mevlyn looks down the line of washers and remembers how it had all looked when it was new. How the floors shined so much, you could see your reflection. She threw an opening party with punch and cookies, and by that afternoon, the Wash-Away took its place as the social hub of town, second only to the beauty parlor for the women and the hardware store for the men. Plus, all of the kids who walked through the doors became Mevlyn's heart children. Most called her Mama Mevlyn. Some shortened it to *Ma-Mev*. It worked out perfectly—a way to help make a living and a substitute for the babies she never had.

Mevlyn picks up a stack of receipts, puts them down. If it wasn't for the fact the house and loan were paid off, she'd have to close up. My, how she misses those days when people waited their turns for the machines and took the opportunity to swap gossip and recipes.

Ginny Beth stands beside her. "Where's Sonny?"

"He's at the house with Mr. Sam today."

"Oh." Dejected, the little girl shrugs and walks back to her art project.

Seems odd, not having the dog underfoot. For the past couple of weeks, he'd stopped short of the kitchen door, looking up at Mevlyn, then down the hall. "Stay home. I'll be okay," she tells him.

Sometimes, fear clutches her chest and she wrestles it loose. What if Sam takes his last breath and she's not there? If she thought for one second that her husband wanted her by his bedside twenty-four/seven, Mevlyn would shut these glass doors and park her butt in the chair, even pull a cot into the room and leave only to take bathroom breaks and grab a bite to eat.

But not Sam. He'd hate that. She understands.

Dogs sense things humans miss, or rather, things they don't want to admit. She hopes the little dog's presence helps Sam when either she or Danae aren't there.

On the door, the tiny bell rings. Jerome steps inside, carrying his weekly load. "Morning, Miz Mevlyn."

"Morning officer. How's business?"

He sets down the bag. "Booming, hate to say. Been a rash of break-ins. Some vandalism."

"Happens every year after school lets out. Guess it gives the kids something to do."

Jerome shakes his head. "One way to spin it, I suppose."

"I remember you and your friends, back in the day."

"All we did was toilet paper a couple of houses. We didn't use spray paint, or steal."

"Guess the level of play has gone up a notch or two."

"Yes ma'am. Afraid so. At least we don't have the shootings like they have over in Tallahassee."

"Not yet."

Jerome leans over, says in a low voice, "did you manage to get me any information?"

"I feel like a complete sneak, but yes, I did." Mevlyn digs in her bag and hands over a slip of paper. "Alabama driver's license. Name and date of birth. Guess the address is right."

"Eighteen. Huh." He tucks the paper into his pocket. "I got a buddy in that part of Alabama, Houston County Sheriff's Office. If Danae isn't in some database, which I doubt, given she's barely past being a minor, he can probably access more than I can. I'll see what I can find out."

Mevlyn checks out the other patron. The woman's fully engrossed in her magazine. The smaller set of ears belongs to the child, and she's hunkered over the coloring book, baring down so hard, Mevlyn can hear the paper rend. "And you won't share it with anyone else?"

"Nope. Won't. Purely looking out for a friend." He pauses, then adds, "Malcolm's been spending a good deal of time with her, too."

"A father protecting his son is not a bad thing, these days."

<h1 style="text-align:center">Thirteen</h1>

After days of running the streets with Girly and Levon, like punch-drunk rats in a maze, Danae is stunned stupid. Mouse is a phantom. The two times Danae spots her, it's only a glimpse of her backside slipping through the rear entrance to the veterinary clinic.

Maybe she's dug a tunnel. Has to be it. Danae punctuates the theory with a chuckle.

Option A: direct confrontation. Fail.

Option B: stalking. Fail.

Move to Option C? Ferret out details for the next party at Lost Lake, wherever that is, and show up with a six-pack in hand, hoping to see Mouse, the one person Danae never thinks of as a party animal. Her sister likes to read and write. She enjoys her own company and tolerates a little sister to a point. Being at school torments her, not because of the studies—she excels at them. People pain Mouse. Her sister makes herself as invisible as possible without completely disappearing. Until Mouse accomplishes even that.

While Danae's feet pound out rhythm, she amuses herself with metaphors to pass the last few blocks of the two-mile route she runs daily. If Mouse is a buried root that never sees sunlight, Danae is a leaf at the uppermost branch tip, waffled by every passing breeze. Mouse is a submarine at the bottom of a deep trench; Danae is a probe circling Jupiter. Mouse is a hunk of ice while Danae is at a high-rolling boil.

She takes the last turn onto Morgan Avenue and slows her pace for the final few feet. She considers stopping by the Wash-Away for another cup of coffee with Mevlyn, but walks to the house instead. Get some water, shower, then give Mr. Sam his morning wipe down before heading to the auto shop. Mr. Hal is stellar about her late arrivals, given her recent caretaking responsibilities. Most days, she stays late, giving him the opportunity to go home in time for dinner with his wife. The arrangement works for everyone.

Sonny greets Danae when she steps inside. "How's our patient?" she asks the dog. She bends to noodle the scruff under his chin and sucks down chilled water from a jug Mevlyn earmarked for her use only, before heading down the hall to her bathroom. Sonny walks past her into Sam's room.

Such a luxury, a bathroom to herself. Heck, a place to shower, her own tub! Having a dependable routine doesn't suck either.

In a few minutes, Danae enters Sam's room. "Morning, Mr. Sam! Time for your hose down. I've had mine."

He opens his eyes and smiles. Going to be one of his better days. Most mornings, he doesn't interact. She opens the window wide. Fresh air pushes out the stale. The room smells of something spoiled, which, Danae surmises, isn't untrue.

Given a chance, the human body is foul: expelled gasses; sweat tainted by chemicals; urine and feces; sloughed skin stringing dirt pearls in places that touch and rub. Add in disease and altered metabolism and Mr. Sam becomes a cesspool of odor and grime.

Taking care of Mama after her first stroke has given Danae an advantage. She knows how to attend to an altered body and keep her own revulsion to a minimum. If she doesn't pursue auto repair, she could become a nurse.

Nah. She sucks at science. Didn't do overly well at any subject. Though she managed to squeak her way to a high school diploma, college is out of the question, even if the necessary funds magically appear.

Forget inheriting anything from her daddy. By the time he finally keels over, or someone snuffs him out, nothing will remain. The man will sell his soul for a night boozing and screwing. Danae wonders if the last lady he moved into the house is still there. If she's smart, no.

Danae sets down the basin filled with warm water. "Let's get you out of these stinky old pajamas." She rolls him onto first one side then the other, peeling off the sweat-damp material. She removes his adult diaper.

She decants a small dot of baby soap onto a soft, wet rag and starts with his face. His eyes follow her movements.

On many occasions, Danae watched her mama care for her elderly charges, those days when Danae walked from school to the nursing home to wait on Mama to finish work.

Those folks would say all kinds of crazy mess and talk to Mama like she was some long-lost somebody. Mama would smile and nod, and say *uh-huh.*

"Doesn't do either of you a dab of good, to correct what they say," her mama told her. "Unless it's something that could harm them or they're hurting, I play along. If they say the moon's made out of cheese, I tell them I heard they got some good crackers up there to go along with it."

Danae tried her best to remember those words after Mama had the stroke. At barely fourteen, Danae didn't feel like a good enough nurse. Daddy surely wasn't going to sign on for it and Mama needed help while she fought to get better. Danae watched enough bed baths to know what to do. She could change sheets while Mama was still in bed, too, and keep up with when to give medicines.

At first, Mama couldn't form words. What she said came out garbled and all mixed up. Slowly, Danae developed an ear for Mama's altered speech and could make sense of most things. Her mama talked a lot about J.J.—as if her brother was still alive and why wasn't he at least stopping by to say hello? Other times, Mama would get onto the subject of Mouse. She claimed Mouse was hiding in the closet, or under the bed, or even in the weeds outside. Crazy talk.

By nine months, Mama had recovered for the most part. Her balance wasn't perfect, but she was able to return to work a few hours a week. My, how those old folks missed her while she was gone.

Daddy even straightened up for a while. He still came home surrounded by an alcohol-fumed cloud, but he aimed his temper elsewhere. Danae hoped life was taking a turn, that Mouse would catch wind of the changes and come home.

Then, eleven months to the day, Mama suffered the second stroke.

Nobody saw her go down. It was late, around midnight, a time when hardly anyone walked the corridors. One of the aides found Mama facedown, her body already chilling. No amount of help, no matter how fast they could come, could help Estelle Gray.

Her days on this tormented earth were done.

"Feels mighty fine, Cecelia," Mr. Sam says as Danae finishes up.

Mr. Sam calling her by some other name doesn't faze her. She dries off his jaundiced, blood-blistered arms and legs, saying *uh-huh*, offering up a smile every now and then. He's animated this morning. Whoever Cecelia is, she must be important to him. This is grace, him seeing Danae as someone special.

"I have a mystery novel for us today." She clothes him in a dry diaper and clean pajamas, then smooths the fresh sheets over him and pulls up a chair.

She reads to him twice a day, following the morning wipe down and after she finishes eating dinner. He's given up calling her a *big-boned boy*. Danae is accustomed to Cecelia.

Reading aloud calms Mr. Sam. This morning, she opens to the first page of an Agatha Christie mystery. The fast-paced action novels agitate him in ways the mystery stories don't. Danae's never been a fan of the written word. She read only when forced. Mouse is the book hound of the family. Her sister devours at least three library books a week—so she must go to the library branch here in Chattahoochee, too. Danae stores the insight. Did Danae resist books because that belonged to Mouse, some sort of moratorium, her holding out until Mouse came home?

Now, with Mr. Sam, she discovers why her sister likes reading. Danae loses herself in the pages, transports to other places, worlds, and ways of viewing life. Maybe the library can be Option C. The thought of interacting with Jack and his misfits holds less appeal than setting foot in the Chattahoochee branch library, for sure.

"You're getting better and better at your recitation, Cecelia."

"Thank you."

The praise pours over Danae. Nobody ever said good things to her, certainly not her daddy. Mama was too weary, too beaten down. Aunt

Sylvia had tried, but her comments leaned toward pushing Danae to at least finish high school.

Miz Mevlyn supports Danae's commitment. Two bookshelves wait for her to browse: fiction, non-fiction, a set of World Book Encyclopedias, and the Childcraft books, all fifteen! After she ploughs through these, she can get herself a library card, Miz Mevlyn suggests. Danae has a local address to claim, and the price is right: it's free. Mevlyn suggested she could get herself a fishing license too, but that'll have to wait. It's not free.

Mr. Sam falls asleep before the end of chapter one. Danae tucks a sliver of paper inside to mark the place. She watches the old man, then leans down and kisses him softly on the cheek.

In the bathroom, she pours out the water and rinses the basin and cloth, hangs the towel across the shower bar to air dry.

Time to get to work. He'll rest now.

Sonny taps behind her until she reaches the door. She leaves the dog to take his shift and crosses the yard to the Wash-Away.

Mevlyn looks up from her magazine when Danae enters. "How were things this morning?"

"Great. We started *Murder on the Orient Express.*"

"Oh, that's one of his favorites."

"Okay, I'm heading to the shop." Danae takes a step, then turns around and asks, "Who is Cecelia?"

Mevlyn stares at her for a beat. "Why?"

"Mr. Sam's calling me by that name. Just wondered."

"I see."

Danae steps back to the desk and sits across from Mevlyn. The old woman looks down at her clasped hands. Danae waits.

"I didn't fare so well in the motherhood department." Mevlyn looks up. Her eyes water. "We wanted a houseful of kids, planned on having as many as I could pop out. Turned out, my lady parts didn't get the message. I had one miscarriage after another."

Mevlyn stops speaking. Danae settles back into the chair.

"Cecilia was the one that almost made it. She came into this world, but never breathed the first breath. Stillborn. Cord wrapped around her little neck. A perfect little child with a fuzz of dark hair and every finger and toe. I counted them."

"Oh."

"Me and Sam referred to Cecelia as *the one that got away*."

Like fishing, Danae thinks but doesn't say.

"Into every life, a little rain must fall," Mevlyn adds.

Danae notices how a shadow passes across Mevlyn's face. Aunt Sylvia used to resort to the strange old saying when bad things happened and it had a way of making Danae feel even gloomier.

Mevlyn's expression shifts to neutral. "Now, get yourself to work before Mr. Hal comes looking for you."

Fourteen

From the end of June until late September, the Wash-Away is uncomfortable, no matter how low Mevlyn sets the window air conditioning unit's thermostat. She remembers reveling in the heat, for the first few years she lived in the Deep South. Why did folks complain so about it? Let them spend a winter in Ohio, shovel snow until their backs seized up, fight to keep an automobile between the ditches—then they might appreciate the warmth.

Guess she's a true Dixie Belle now; she's earned the right to complain. Being in a room filled with machines churning water and blowing heated air doesn't help.

"My part of the country has two seasons—winter and the Fourth of July," Mevlyn heard one former Michigan resident state. "My husband and I couldn't wait to retire and move south."

Give it a few of north Florida's asphalt-buckling summers, mix in the abundant mosquitoes, and Mevlyn figures even that hardcore fan will wish she had never laid eyes on anything below the Mason/Dixon line. Every place has its own hell. If she gets through until mid-October, the humidity and heat will give way to perfection. Then again, the past few Christmas seasons, she's worn short sleeves. This past winter, only one of her heavier sweaters made it out of the drawer. Say you can't buy into that theory she's heard some folks kicking around, that the Earth is warming? Huh. Don't have to be a genius to figure out things are changing.

Danae walks through the front door wearing cutoff jeans, one of Sam's old T-shirts with the sleeves scissored out, and flip-flops.

"You're dressed for success today, ain't cha?"

The gal ignores the jab. "The hospice nurse is with Mr. Sam. I'm heading to the Apalach with Malcolm."

"Good then. You got sunscreen?" She chuckles. "Never mind answering that. Your face looks as buttered up as corn on the cob. Especially your nose. Might want to smooth that out." Mevlyn smiles. "And I can smell the bug spray from here. I like it when you listen to what I tell you, gal."

Danae sweeps her hand across her face.

"There's some leftover tuna salad in the fridge, if you want to whip up some sandwiches."

"Malcolm's packed up some stuff." Danae idles in place.

"Something else weighing on your mind?"

"Next week." The gal glances around the laundromat. "Malcolm says they're having a thing at the lake."

"They do it every Fourth of July. Big production. Food trucks, music, arts and crafts."

"May I go? I can leave after I give Mr. Sam his bath."

"You don't have to ask my permission, but I appreciate it anyways." This must be how it feels to be a mother, she thinks. "The fireworks are something to see. Before Sam fell ill, we didn't miss it."

"I'll be home to get him ready for the night."

"No, you won't." Mevlyn holds up a stop hand before Danae can offer any sass. "I'll close this place up, it being a national holiday and all. I'll be home with Sam."

"We can take shifts. I'll go for a while, then you can—"

"If I need help, I can call the nurse. Maybe I want to spend the day with Popsie."

Danae stuffs her hands into the shorts' back pockets and rocks back and forth. "Okay. If you're sure."

"I am." She flips her fingers. "Now, get on about your business, and I'll get on about mine." Mevlyn laughs when the gal does the funny head wobble, eye-rolling thing. If Cecelia had lived, Mevlyn bets the child would've had the same fresh attitude.

A blessing, that's what Danae is. Mevlyn doesn't mind at all, that Sam calls her Cee-Cee and Danae calls him Popsie. It's like the two of them have known each other for years, been through all the stages, and come out buddies. No matter that Danae isn't blood kin. Heart kin can be as good, better even.

"Morning, Miz Mevlyn!" Jerome struts in, wearing full police garb.

Mevlyn dabs sweat from her brows. That polyester material has to be hot, not to mention him wearing a bulletproof vest.

She watches him do his usual room eye-sweep. Bet nothing much passes his attention. The shop's full today, with all but two washers in use, and no empty dryers. Everyone's caught up in their own doings, with no mind to her or the police officer standing at her desk. The only one who glances up is Elvina Houston, who's been coming to use the machines for the past few weeks, on days the Triple C Day Spa and Salon is closed. The old busy body must want for entertainment and hot gossip when she's not at her front desk job at the beauty parlor.

"I finally got that information for you," Jerome says. "My friend's been on paid medical leave, for surgery."

"Oh, is he, or she, doing okay?" Doesn't matter that Mevlyn doesn't know the person from Dick's hat band, if someone is a friend of someone you care about, their concerns become yours.

"Rotator cuff repair. He'll be on desk duty for a bit, but he says the surgery helped considerably. Pain is almost gone." Jerome pulls out a notepad. "He did a little digging for me. Turned up some interesting stuff."

She hopes it's nothing to change her opinion of the gal. "Do I need to know?"

"It's nothing bad about her, per se. But it sheds light on a few things."

"Set yourself down. I'll pour you some coffee."

His leather gun belt squeaks when he settles onto the visiting chair. Mevlyn decants him a fresh cup and tops off her own.

"All right." She slides a cup in front of him and sits down with her own. "You have my undivided attention."

Jerome consults his notes. "Mother: Estelle Wilson Gray, deceased four years ago. One brother: John James Gray, Jr., also deceased—boating accident, ruled accidental drowning. One sister: Maria Anne Gray, reported missing at age fourteen."

"Goodness. That's a lot for one family."

"Gets worse. Father, John James Gray, living. Repeated arrests for drunk and disorderly, couple of DUIs. My friend says the officers know that address well. Neighbors have called in noise complaints on numerous occasions, though none in the past couple of months."

"And Danae lived in that." Mevlyn shakes her head.

"Did, until after the mother passed. Records indicate that a Sylvia Wilson Franklin was awarded guardianship of Danae shortly after the mother died." Malcolm flips the page. "Appears Danae attended a local high school and graduated this past May."

"And she showed up in Chattahoochee not long afterwards, with little to her name."

Mevlyn sneaks a peek at Elvina. The woman is engrossed in her copy of the *Twin City News*. She's been on that one page for a while.

Malcolm closes the notepad and tucks it into his shirt pocket. "Lot of baggage for one kid."

Fifteen

## Booster Club Landing, July 4, 2010

Danae stands on the bank of Lake Seminole. Though it is only three miles from Chattahoochee, the lake rests in Georgia. Back in the early '60s, Malcolm tells her, the waterway swarmed with local ski boaters. They grew tired of the stringent Georgia regulations and shifted operations to the sandbars of the Apalachicola River, in Florida. The landing is usually deserted, a beautiful spot with an ample parking lot and a boat ramp only a handful of fishermen use. Now, filled with people and activity, the place feels less ominous. Other than that one time, Danae doesn't venture alone across the state line to the lake. She's kick-butt. But not stupid.

Summer presses down, gifting humidity so high, the air feels soggy. A slight breeze kisses her cheeks. Sweat pools between her breasts and soaks her bra's elastic band. The scent of hot grease and melting funnel cake sugar paints the air. Nothing healthy about any of this food, for sure, unless the slivered tomatoes on the gyros count. Danae plans to cram in as much junk as she can, starting with caramel popcorn and a tall lemonade.

"I like the Madhatter's Festival better," Malcolm states. "They had it last year for the first time, at the Chattahoochee Landing. Went so well, Dad told me the city council is planning to hold it again, toward the end of October. By then, it won't be so gosh awful oppressive," he twists his lips, "in theory. Fall seems to come in late November nowadays." Like her, he stands with arms akimbo, taking in the view across the lake. "They're probably going to move this event to the river landing, too. Lots of grumbling about who has the right to do what, on this piece of dirt."

Danae turns toward the event grounds. "Someone has a ferocious case of patriotism."

Malcolm motions to a thin man who's talking with animated gestures to one of the vendors. He's dressed in red, white, and blue from his top hat to his blue spangled sandals. "That's Jake Witherspoon in action. He owns the florist shop."

Danae takes note of the man's walking cane, red and white-striped with a blue curled handle. "I haven't officially met him, but Mevlyn loves him. He brings her cut flowers to put in Mr. Sam's room, from time to time."

Everyone knows Jake. He's the gay guy who got beaten nearly to death years back, no more than a quarter mile from here at Turkey Point, and on the fourth of July, no less. If that had been her, Danae wouldn't step out of the house on this day, and for sure nowhere near where the assault went down. Says a lot about his courage.

She takes in the decorations. Mevlyn will want to know details.

Tall pines mix with sprawling ancient live oak trees heavy with Spanish moss; the stringy, gray parasitic plant sets the South apart. A stars-and-stripes welcome banner hangs across the road leading to the parking lot at lake's edge. Standing sprays of red, white, and blue carnations adorn a covered performance tent. Flags wave on poles and swing from all of the food and craft booths. Paper maché cutouts of Uncle Sam stand here and there, their outstretched hands providing directions to the festival's points of interest. Danae notes the tallest statue by the stage. One sparkling white glove points north toward the nation's capital; the other points east toward Tallahassee, the state's capital. As Mevlyn might say about this event, *it's clever and cute mixed with mayonnaise.*

Jake spots them and waves, then makes his way toward where she and Malcolm stand.

He and Malcolm greet each other with a slight tip of the head. Danae wonders why they don't hug or something. Then she answers her own musing. Of course they don't. No telling what nutcase might take offense.

She glances from Jake—flamboyant, in-your-face gay—to Malcolm, the last guy anyone would tag as a homosexual. For the first time, she worries. If something happens to Malcolm, like it had to Jake . . .

"Ohmygah, you're Danae, the master dream mechanic everyone's all abuzz about," Jake says. He holds out a hand. Every finger holds a bejeweled ring—rubies, diamonds, and blue sapphires. "Jake Witherspoon."

"Nice to meet cha." She shakes his hand. The grip is firm. Why wouldn't it be? Dear Lord, if she's this narrow in her thinking, how can she expect others to be any better?

"I simply must get Pearl—that's my delivery truck—in for a tune-up. She is positively gasping for attention." Jake points toward Malcolm. "Remind me, will you?" Then, back to Danae. "I hear people are waiting in line for your magic touch, dearie."

Before either she or Malcolm can offer further conversation, Jake flashes a grin. "Gotta scoot. People require direction." He wiggles the fingers on the hand not gripping the cane. "Toodles. Have fun. Don't do anything I wouldn't do." He trundles away, pausing to greet first one person then the next.

"He's kinda—" Danae starts.

"Over the top. I know. We've discussed it. Part of me wishes he'd tone it down a notch or two. The other part cheers him on."

"You're good friends, I guess?"

"Acquaintances." Malcolm jostles her shoulder. "There you go, smearing your assumptions on me again."

"Huh?"

"Are you best friends with every straight person you've met?"

"Of course not."

"But *I* am supposed to be intimate with every gay." Malcolm shakes his head. "We have so much ground to cover, you and I."

"Sorry. Really." It's like Mevlyn says, *assume* is made up of two words, *ass* and *me*. If I assume, it makes an *ass* out of *me*. Danae scolds herself for being that ass.

"Being uninformed is not a slap, Danae. Being ignorant on purpose is. People who genuinely care, learn, then base their thinking on fresh information."

Malcolm walks forward, taking slow steps. Danae bobs beside him. "So, can I ask you a question?"

"Of course. As long as it's not overly creepy." He turns his head long enough to flash her a smile.

"If you see some guy how do you know—"

Malcolm waits for her to catch up. "We have this specialized sense. Gay-dar." He looks upward and holds up one hand, fingers splayed as if it's receiving invisible signals.

Danae stalls. "What the—?" She asks, but he's taken a step beyond her again.

Malcolm doubles back, laughing, and drapes one arm across her shoulders. "The look on your face alone was worth saying that." Several of the festival goers cast disapproving glances in their direction. One, Danae recognizes: Jack Dixon. Malcolm removes his arm from Danae and walks at a fast clip. She catches up.

When they reach a spot where the crowd thins, he halts and says, "I have so many choices for why someone might want to *teach me a lesson.*" Malcolm encloses the last phrase with air quote fingers.

Danae stands with her arms crossed over her chest. Pissed off with nowhere to aim it.

"I can pass for straight, though I don't try *not* to be openly gay," Malcolm adds. "I'm exactly the person I appear. But I can't whitewash myself."

"I don't catch your meaning."

"News flash, Danae. *You* are a white girl. *I* am a black boy. Don't kid yourself. Some of the kind, upstanding citizens in this very crowd would gladly string me up."

His face—normally so pleasant, or at least neutral—melts into a mask of what she's heard Mevlyn refer to as *profound disappointment.* In Mevlyn's view, those judgy sort of people don't have much to recommend them, and Mevlyn is at heart, an optimist.

Malcolm pulls his shoulders back, his posture military straight. "One reason, among many, that I'll hotfoot it out of here as soon as I get my college degree."

Now it's her turn to experience melancholia. Other than Mevlyn, Malcolm is her only friend. By the time he leaves her behind, she'll hopefully have Mouse in her corner. More than ever, she's determined to reconnect with her sister.

"Where will you go?" Danae asks.

Her friend pulls in a chest full of air and releases it with an audible whoosh. "I don't know. I really don't know."


**D**anae chews her way through the remaining daylight hours: two funnel cakes, a cheesy pretzel, a gyro, a tall platter of fried gator tail, and a mound of chili cheese fries.

"Why do I do this to myself?" She holds her stomach.

"I hear you." Malcolm looks as miserable. "I may not eat for a week."

They head for a hillside where people choose spots to watch the fireworks display. Being Malcolm, he has a plastic table cloth, the perfect groundcover, in his backpack.

"Sure you want to sit with me?" Malcolm asks. "I can rip this in half."

"Now who's assuming?" Danae holds two corners of the cheap cloth and helps spread it over the grass. "They can string up both of us."

"Can't believe you just said that." Malcolm chuckles.

"Don't underestimate me."

In the gloaming, people blend into sameness. Skin colors aren't as discernable. Unless someone fires up a cigarette lighter or flashes a handheld light, darkness evens out the lines between races.

On a nearby shore, a second open parcel of land is set up as the staging platform, far enough away for safety, close enough to launch the fireworks over the lake.

"I love this," Malcolm says.

"Did I miss anything?" Someone sits down on the cover beside Malcolm.

Danae hears the squeak of thick leather. Had she not recognized the voice, the sound would've given away the man's identity.

"Nope. Perfect timing. How'd you manage this?"

"I'm on crowd patrol. Can't sit for long. Maybe the first few minutes." Jerome leans forward. "Evening, Miz Danae."

"Hiya, Mr. Jerome."

"Figured Miz Mevlyn would be here," he says, then adds before she can respond, "but I guess she's with Mr. Sam. Understandable." Jerome claps his son on the shoulder. "While I'm thinking about it, why don't you two take the boat out this weekend? I put the trickle charger on the battery, thought I'd have a chance to scare up a bass or two, but one of my buddies needs me to cover his shift. That boat isn't doing anyone any good sitting under the shed. It needs to be run."

"Sure." Malcolm turns toward Danae. "You up for it, maybe Sunday morning before the heat builds?"

"Heck yeah."

"Do you have a fishing license?" Jerome asks Danae.

"No."

"We'll get her one," Jerome says.

Danae adds, "I'll see about it."

A deep sound cracks the air. The murmur of voices quiets. All eyes point toward the lake. The first rocket lifts, explodes, and scatters streaks of golden light. Danae joins the crowd in *oohs* and *ahhs*. Faces around her show only when the sparks light up the night sky. One silhouette catches Danae's attention.

Mouse?

Before the next burst of fireworks illuminates the hill, her sister is gone.


Mevlyn drags a chair next to Sam's bedside and settles in. She watches his chest rise and fall. Thank goodness for days when he rests peacefully. So often lately, he struggles. The pain medications help, but he sleeps more than before. A tradeoff. Still, she's happy with her recent decision to call in hospice. Between Danae's help and their compassionate staff, Mevlyn doesn't feel as alone.

"I know you and Danae like to read your books, so I won't spoil that. I found some other things for us to ponder on today."

Hearing is the one sense the dying retain, from what she reads in the literature. Even when someone's in a coma, they are listening. Or so they say. Mevlyn counts on it.

"I dragged out these old notebooks of mine, you know, the ones where I was in deep training to be Southern?" She holds the first wire-ringed book in a stack five deep. "I need to keep on adding to these. Just when I think I got them all down pat, someone springs a new one on me."

*Southernisms*, the scripted printing on the cover reads. Mevlyn flips to the first page. "Nothing in this part of the country gains meaning unless compared to something else not even remotely similar," she states. "Amazes me to this day."

Mevlyn reads aloud, stopping to chuckle. "Hot as a three-peckered billy goat. Good enough to make you slap your pappy. Running around like a chicken with its head cut off. Stupid as a stick."

She stops and says to Sam, "Don't even get me started on ways to say a person's mentally ill. With the mental institution four blocks down, I guess I'll never hear all of them."

Other Southern ways amuse her. The way they use *slap* to indicate a greater degree of something. *Worn out* versus *slap worn out*. The way words repeated add emphasis. A shirt could be *white*, or *white-white*. If it is so bright it glows like Heaven's Gate, it's *white-white-white*. A day or two off is a *vacation*. A week off where you travel is a *vacation-vacation*.

"I guess if I live to be two hundred, I'll never understand it all, Sam." She flips a couple of pages. "Funeral food and dinners-on-the-ground food are different in the amount of cheese, breading, or grease." The more comfort required, the thicker the layer of melted cheddar baked on top of a casserole. While grilled chicken is fine for a diet, grief or praising God in any fashion necessitates a really crispy-fried crust.

"If coleslaw or potato salad doesn't contain enough mayonnaise to keep a cardiologist in business, the bowl will go untouched." She glances to Sam. "That is the God's honest truth."

She keeps three jars of the white Southern gold—full-fat mayonnaise—in her pantry as definitive proof she hails from the South.

"Plus, the rest of this country is just now figuring out what folks down here have known all along, that bacon is a food group all to itself!"

Sure, she could leave it off and add ten years to her life span, but quality versus quantity applies to years spent on this earth, too.

Mevlyn opens the next book in line. "Goodness. I forgot that I put things in categories. Here're some about temperature." She reads, trailing one finger down the page. "Cold as a frosted frog. Hotter than a two-dollar pistol."

More pages go by. Mevlyn laughs loud. "He's so cheap, he wouldn't give a nickel to see Jesus ridin' a bicycle." She wipes tears from her eyes. "He couldn't find his ass with both hands in his back pockets."

She pauses, her finger hovering over one saying. "I even wrote down this one you told me back in '72: He was so ugly, he'd make a freight train take a dirt road."

Mevlyn tips back her head and chortles. Her ears pick up on a noise from Sam's direction. She snaps her head back to neutral and looks at her husband.

Sam smiles. Those blue eyes she fell for, all those years back, focus on her with tiny humor wrinkles at the corners. Sam never did refer to them as laugh lines.

His lips move. Mevlyn sets the stack of notebooks on the bureau and moves close to Sam, bending low so one ear is directly above his mouth.

"What, my sugar? What do you need?" she asks.

His words come out, barely a whisper. "I love you, Damn Yankee."

Mevlyn turns her head and kisses him. "I love you too, Johnny Rebel."

## Sixteen

"Jeez." Danae stands next to the trailer attached to Malcolm's truck. "I expected some little fishing boat."

"My dad freakin' loves this boat." Malcolm attaches two safety chains between the hitch and trailer. "He wouldn't let me take it out by myself until just recently."

"That's huge." Her daddy wouldn't let her touch his fishing skiff, a flat-bottomed aluminum john boat with a hand-controlled outboard barely powerful enough to create a wake.

When they reach Chattahoochee Landing, they queue up behind four other anglers waiting to launch. Vapor curls and lifts from the banks where the river touches dirt.

"I hear they're hitting good a few miles downriver," Malcolm says. "You want to be in charge of pulling the boat clear or driving the truck?"

"I'll get the bow rope."

"Chicken."

"I can back a trailer as good as anyone. But not with your daddy's fancy boat attached to it, nope."

He depresses the clutch and shifts the truck into reverse. "Okay. I get that."

Danae hops out. She transfers the coolers, rods, tackle, and a dry bag from the truck's bed into the boat, then grabs the thick nylon rope attached to the bow. She walks alongside as Malcolm eases the trailer down the ramp. When the boat floats free of the trailer, she gives him the thumbs up. He drives forward; the empty trailer leaves wet trails on the cement. Danae guides the boat toward the dock and secures the bow and stern ropes to metal cleats.

Malcolm jogs down the dock. "Good job, first mate."

The Suzuki 150 cranks after three tries. It runs rough for a bit before the idle evens out. She unties the bow and stern ropes and gives a shove to push them from the dock. First rule her daddy taught her: make sure your motor works before you get too cocky and have to paddle yourself back to shore. This motor could use a little tune-up—fresh plugs, check the spark plug wires, maybe clean the carburetor.

As if he reads her thoughts, Malcolm says, "she's been sitting for a couple of months." Exhaust lifts from the water when he backs away from the landing. "We'll fish the banks for a while, then we can find a sandbar to have lunch. Sound good?"

"Absolutely." Danae pulls on her new FSU Seminoles baseball cap.

Malcolm hands her an elastic strip with clips at either end. "I suggest using this, unless you want to fish that from the water."

She secures the clips to her shirt and the rim of the cap.

The boat is nicer than any she's ever ridden: a sleek 17-foot Winner, combo ski and fishing rig. Four cushioned white and maroon seats for passengers, with a fifth rotating pedestal seat designed for an avid angler. A walk-through wind shield leads to more cushioned benches on the bow. The paint job and trim are fancy, too. Sparkly garnet and gold, trimmed with teak and shiny bits of chrome. The Seminole-head logo for Florida State University decorates either side of the outboard, which also matches the boat. Danae notes a trolling motor mounted to the bow, and the depth finder, a compass, and a marine radio on the dash. Unlike her daddy's boat, this one has a proper helm, and throttle controls. With the powerful outboard, it will go fast enough to actually lose a cap.

"Got plenty of life preservers if you want to wear one. I don't usually, but they're regulation."

Danae shakes her head.

Malcolm puts the motor in reverse and they pull farther from the dock. She's ready to make comments on the vessel when Malcolm says, "hold on. I'm going to open her up."

He changes gear and pushes the throttle forward. The stern bogs down at first and the bow elevates until they gain speed. He hits the trim lever to change the angle of the motor. The boat responds, lowering to parallel the water's surface, skimming along as if it rides on air. Danae grins until spit wets her lips. She closes them, still smiling. If she didn't think Malcolm would consider her a complete idiot, she'd throw her arms into the air and yell *wheeeee!*

They slow a bit when they pass beneath a concrete train trestle. Danae admires the way Malcolm handles the boat, as easily and carefully as he does his old truck. The outboard hums behind them, still missing a beat every now and then. Danae breathes in the scent of fresh air and mud, a smell so familiar and vital, she wonders how anyone could live without it.

A mile downriver, Malcolm slows the motor, pointing. "Deep banks along here. Let's try our luck."

He pulls parallel to the shoreline, the bow pointed downstream.

"Want me to drop anchor?" Danae asks.

"Let's drift fish for a bit. We can always stop if we luck up on a good hole."

Danae's rusty with a rod and reel. After a few less than stellar casts, she manages to flip the line clear of the overhanging willows and into the dark water.

Fishing requires silence and patience. They cast and reel in, cast and reel in. Malcolm stands on the bow and periodically corrects the boat's drift with the electric trolling motor. Its low whir joins the occasional call of birds and the early morning breeze ruffling the leaves. Other boats pass, cutting back their speed in the unspoken courteous way shared by knowledgeable anglers. Their limited wakes rock the boat and lap the banks, river water music.

The fish don't cooperate for the first hour. Malcolm feels a couple of bumps. Danae gets in practice, but nothing seems to like her attitude. Even the trash fish aren't biting.

"Guess my intel was incorrect," Malcolm says in a low voice.

Danae feels the snatch of her line. "Yah! Got one!"

"Go, girl!"

She wins the battle in less than two minutes and hauls the fish into the boat.

"If it was up to me to feed this crew, we'd go hungry later." Malcolm measures the fish then puts it into the boat's wet well. It's a sound, legal catch, a twelve-inched striped bass. "Sure am glad you got your fishing license."

"Thank Mevlyn for that. She got a tick up her butt about it, yesterday. We went by the county office when we were over in Quincy."

"You could've applied online."

"No internet."

"I have it. I could've done it for you."

"I have a license now, all that matters. Besides, Mevlyn has this thing about getting things for me, like she doesn't want me to be deprived, or something." Danae wipes her hands and takes a swig of the chilled cola Malcolm passes her way. "Like, just last week, she insisted we go and open up checking and savings accounts for me. I only had a few bucks to put in, but no . . . Mevlyn funded both with a hundred dollars." Danae smiles. "She's all about teaching me how to manage my vast fortunes, how to balance a checkbook, even showing me things about her ledgers at the Wash-Away. Miz Mevlyn's good to me. And the way she is with Mr. Sam . . ."

Danae stalls. Such could lead to a conversation about her own twisted family. Malcolm is the kind of friend she feels she can talk to about anything, but not family. She'd rather shove them far back until thoughts fail to rise to the surface. Except for Mouse. Mouse is family she wants to claim, and will.

"Guess you've made huge points with Miz Mevlyn, taking care of Mr. Sam."

"I suppose. But me having a place to live is enough. If people find out about the other things, they'll think I'm trying to, I'da know, take advantage or something."

"So, don't tell anyone. I'm not going to."

Danae shrugs.

"Why don't we go on downriver?" Malcolm reels in his line.

"Okay, but we have to catch at least one more, or hear it from your daddy."

He pivots the trolling motor and lifts it from the water. Danae stores her rod and reel.

Malcolm cranks the outboard and they move slowly into the main channel. "Wanna take the wheel?"

"Like, hellsyeah!"

He stands and allows Danae to slide into the driver's seat. "Okay, Cap'n."

"Never driven one this fancy." She rests her hands on the wheel.

"It's super easy. Not like some of the lakes around here; not much to hit, unless you get too close to the bank."

Danae listens to his coaching. His voice is calm and even. The steering is alien and stiff at first until she gets a feel for it. Her lips hurt from so much grinning.

"Okay, bump it up a little," Malcolm directs. "Let's get her up on plane."

She pushes the throttle. The motor digs in as they pick up speed. The bow lifts.

"Okay, now trim her down like I told you."

Danae pulls on a second lever. The motor tilts up, bringing the propeller closer to the surface. The bow lowers. The engine gains momentum and the boat skims easily across the surface.

"This is fun!" Danae tries to stuff down her enthusiasm. Doesn't work. "Whoo-eeeee!"

Malcolm's laughter competes with the roar of the wind and motor.

"Steer wide of the jetties." Malcolm motions toward three sets of granite rock pilings. Danae follows his instructions. "Let's ride on down so you can see the bluffs. Then we can turn back upstream and hang out on one of the sandbars to eat lunch."

Danae's shoulders relax. Controlling the vessel takes small effort—a different sort of thrill than the motorcycle. Open air skims her face and hair and the sunshine warms her skin. Instead of alerting to every truck and car intent on sending her to intensive care or an early grave, she's far less edgy. The boat is solid beneath her. The cushions comfort and support.

The navigation rules she read over come back to her. Green channel marker buoys—pass them on the right. Like keeping on your side of the highway. In a river as broad as the Apalachicola, she need only watch for the occasional anglers that share space, and keep to the deep channel. Pleasure boaters may appear after church and lunch, but for now, the river belongs to her and Malcolm and this amazing boat.

"How far down to those bluffs?"

"Maybe another twenty minutes, beyond where we pass under the Interstate bridge." He settles back, one arm extended with a hand resting on her seat back, the other arm draped over a padded rest.

Danae's never visited the southern part of Florida, the one people typically envision with its palm trees, white sand beaches, and towering condos, or that middle land where tourists flock to don mouse hats, eat over-priced food, and battle traffic. No, this is what she loves—this swampy, humid, bug-infested and woody expanse similar to parts of lower Ala-dang-bamer. Only, it's better; here she's free to be the person she invents. Not the poor, poor sibling of a drowned brother and runaway sister, or the daughter of a hell-raising redneck who loves pool halls, cheap booze, and even cheaper women.

The river wanders through cypress stands and banks shaded by willows and hardwoods. Their passing disturbs an occasional egret. Malcolm points upward. An osprey rides the thermals. The river narrows as they approach a curve. "Slow up a little," Malcolm says.

She throttles back. The pitch of the motor lowers and the boat loses plane. "Correct your trim a bit," he says.

As if some giant hand pushes the land into a ridge, the riverbanks go from low to over two hundred feet on either side.

"Wow." Her mouth hangs open.

"I told you, amazing. The Apalachicola River Bluffs," Malcolm states. "You might not know this, but this area is part of the foothills of the Appalachian Mountains. Cut her back a bit more."

Danae complies. The outboard calms to a chugging rumble.

"Bring her to the bank. Slow."

"I'da know, Malcolm. Not so sure I—"

"Oh. Okay. Let me."

She stands, still grasping the wheel, then steps aside for Malcolm to regain the helm. He maneuvers the vessel close to the limestone cliff and points to a small stream pouring into the muddy river. "That's a natural spring. Best water you'll ever taste."

He cuts the engine and walks to the bow to prevent the boat from hitting. After jumping onto a small spit of dirt, he secures the bow line to the root of a long-dead tree. "C'mon."

"Sure this will hold?" The current curls in eddies around the side closest to the bank.

"Dad ties up here. So does everyone else. It's all good."

Malcolm holds out his hand for her to jump next to him, then leads her to the source of the stream, a small trickle flowing from inside the limestone rock. He cups his hand, captures water, and drinks.

"Aren't you afraid of catching some disease?" she asks.

"Figure the limestone filters it enough. Hasn't killed me yet." He flashes a broad toothy smile.

Danae gathers a small amount and sips. The water tastes clean, cool, almost sweet. Miles above tap water. "Good. Really good."

"You want to drive us back?" he asks after they board.

"Nah. You can take her for a while." She sinks into the passenger seat.

They head upstream to a long, flat sandbar they had passed earlier. He approaches the shallow water slowly, tilting the motor up as they near. Then he cuts power and hits the switch to completely raise the propeller. Danae watches him jump into water only inches deep. He grabs the rope and one side of the bow and coaxes the boat onto the sand, then uses the bow anchor thrown onto the beach to hold the position.

In minutes, they throw down a ground cloth and dole out pimento cheese sandwiches, chips, and cold drinks.

"Julie at the Wild Rose wrapped me up a couple of pieces of her red velvet cake." Malcolm swipes mayonnaise from his lips. "Hope you like it."

"You're kidding, right?" Danae rolls onto her back, enjoying the shade of an overhead river willow branch. "Later. I'm stuffed right now."

She falls into a drooling sleep and awakens a few minutes later to Malcolm humming some song. She stretches her arms. "This is the most relaxed I've felt in forever. Think I'll have that cake now. Want yours?"

"Sure."

Malcolm looks thoughtful. She's grown used to this expression. He's getting ready to launch into one of his deep discussions. Hope he's not going to ask her about her family. One day, she'll share her own private store of shit-storm stories. Not today. Today is too perfect to spoil. She unwraps both pieces of cake and hands one over. She settles back, content to eat reclining.

"What was it like, your first time?" Malcolm asks.

"First time?" She rolls over to face him. When he meets her gaze, she gets it. "Oh. That."

"Exactly *that.*"

Danae flops onto her back. Above her, blue skies dotted with high white clouds show through the willow leaves. "Not one of my most memorable experiences. Why?"

"Just curious."

She's never talked about it to anyone, not even her best friend Antoine. Certainly not Aunt Sylvia. She would've stroked out, then sent Danae to some church counselor. Mama was gone by that point, and of course, Mouse too.

"It was a lot of sweaty fondling, at first," she says. "The summer before my sophomore year. I was almost sixteen. He was seventeen. It just sort of happened."

"Did you . . . feel anything?"

"Other than uncomfortable during and embarrassed—no, mortified—afterwards, no. Not like he was out to do me any favors." She crams in the last bite of cake and dusts crumbs from her lips and hands.

"And after that time?"

"Twice more. One guy. One girl—sort of."

Malcolm studies her. "Sort of?"

"Touching. Some kissing. Then not. Neither of us were really into it. Or, at least, I wasn't."

"Ever been in love?"

"No," Danae replies without hesitation. "Okay, bad boy. It's your turn. Spill."

"Once, with a girl."

"But, you're—"

"Gay. I know. I am."

Danae waits him out, noting he's barely touched his cake.

"I don't know, Danae. I cared about her. Still do. We keep in touch, though her parents moved them out of town our junior year. We just … *I* just … Something was missing." He blows out a breath. "I felt like I was trying to wear someone else's clothes, walk around in someone else's skin."

When he stops, Danae asks, "but, no boyfriend?"

"Came close. Fell for him. He fell for me. Hard. But his parents caught us making out and that was the end of that." Malcolm brushes his hands together.

"Oh. Wow. What'd they do?"

"Snatched him out of school, our senior year. He was just gone. They stayed in town until a month ago, then they left too. I heard rumors that he'd been farmed out to live with a relative in North Carolina." Malcolm purses his lips. "I never heard from him. I doubt I ever will." Emotion clogs his voice.

"I'm so sorry, Malcolm." Danae reaches over and covers his hand with hers.

"Yeah. Well." He remains silent. Danae doesn't force conversation.

"How are things with Mr. Sam?" he asks when a few minutes have passed.

"Not good for him. Dying isn't easy. But it's a little better for Miz Mevlyn and me since the hospice people came on board. Even with their help, we have to seriously juggle our schedules. I'm there with them in the evenings, nights, and early mornings." She's ready to coax that red velvet cake from him. He catches the lustful gleam in her eyes, then picks it up and devours it in less than three bites. "During the day, when one of the sitters can't be there, Miz Mevlyn and I do our best. Mr. Sam told her after he was diagnosed, that he didn't want to die in some nursing home or hospital. I don't blame him. Still, it's tough. On everyone."

"Does he ever get out of bed?"

Danae shakes her head. "Not lately. He's too weak. Sleeps for the most part. Even so, Miz Mevlyn worries. I do, too."

"What you need is a baby monitor. That way, either one of you can check in on him anytime you want."

"Sounds complicated."

"Not really. I've helped my dad install several security cameras for local business owners. They're trying to nab the person, or persons, breaking into stores on West Washington and Main. Not the same thing, actually, but the idea is similar. If the range is sufficient enough to reach from the house to the laundromat, it could work."

"We have one of those outside security cameras already, but it's not installed. That lady who knows everything—Mevlyn calls her the *town crier*—Evelyn, Evie? I always mess up her name."

"Elvina Houston," Malcolm provides.

"Yeah. That's her."

"Never discredit someone like Elvina. My dad has called on her for intel a few times. He says Elvina learned the trade from a lady named Piddie, who used to be large and in charge. Piddie died years ago, at almost a hundred years old."

"Jeez. That's ancient. So, like I was saying, this Elvina lady stopped by the Wash-Away and gave the equipment to Mevlyn. Said she'd found a system she liked better online, and she didn't want to go to the trouble to return the other one."

"Uh-huh. You buying that?"

"Not for a second." Danae changes direction. "What we really need are cell phones, if Mr. Sam is with it enough to learn to use one. Mevlyn refuses to pay for the service and I don't have enough credit to sign up for an account."

"You need a couple of prepaids," Malcolm says.

"A what?"

"Honestly. Did you grow up in this decade? A prepaid cell phone. You don't need a contract with some expensive provider."

"Oh, like one of those at the discount stores. I know. But don't I still need a way to reload it with money?"

Malcolm doesn't wait for her reply. "I'll get it. You can pay me back sometime. If you don't cruise the internet, you won't run up data charges fast, just checking in on Mr. Sam."

He snaps his fingers. "I could install that security camera at the Wash-Away, too. Aim it toward that back door that looks like where someone's been trying to break in."

"You are beyond awesome." Danae sits up, digs in the cooler for fresh cola. She hands one over to Malcolm, then holds the chilled bottle to her forehead. "I *would* like to get a phone." She removes the cap and takes a deep drink.

"So there you go. It's a done deal. Your next day off, we can ride over to Walmart, pick up a prepaid, and grab a meal."

"I have a little money held back."

"No prob. I know you're good for it." Malcolm smiles.

Back in Ala-dang-bamer, Danae had been one of the few who didn't have a cell phone. People walked around with the devices tethered to them like spoiled, yipping Chihuahuas. Even the dirt-poor kids did something to pay for one—run drugs mostly. Before Mama died, her parents couldn't afford extras. Big John wouldn't have shelled out cash for such a "piss-away" expense.

Later, Aunt Sylvia offered. Danae refused. A roof and food were enough to ask of her aunt, and running shoes. A phone could track a person, allow others to always locate them. Big John didn't need to know her whereabouts. Aunt Sylvia understood. The two of them worked around it; the school and other parents knew how to contact her aunt in emergencies—the old-fashioned, land-line way. Antoine would've figured out a way to get a cell phone for her, but he had the same amount of nothing as Danae.

Once, she heard the term *off the grid,* referring to people not connected to electricity. She's an off-grid kind of person for other reasons, born of necessity.

Danae turns to look at Malcolm. "Nobody's ever done something like that for me."

"Look, you *should* have one. What if your cycle breaks down and you need to call me so I can come get your butt?"

"I can take care of myself."

"Never questioned that for a second." He fist-bumps her arm. "You can be such a hard ass."

*I had to be that way,* she answers in her head. Danae stares across the river. On the far bank, an alligator suns. Why is it so damn hard to trust? Stupid question. She knows that answer.

Malcolm pats her shoulder. The touch says he understands. "We probably should be heading back."

"That's the trouble with good times. They end." Her voice comes out full of longing.

"We'll come again. Lots of good times in our futures."

She turns to him and smiles in spite of the weight pressing down on her chest. "Hope so."

"One more thing," Danae says as they transfer the cooler and picnic supplies to the boat, and gather the trash. "Gotta pee."

"Pick your bush. I promise not to peek. I'll leave my deposit too, after you finish."

Danae slides on her flip flops and heads deeper into the willows. Not like she hasn't pissed in the woods about a million times. Here's where she envies dudes; they have those convenient spouts. No matter how she crouches or how carefully she balances, she always ends up splashing urine on her feet.

Thunder rumbles in the distance. "Good timing, us getting back." Malcolm waits for Danae to board, then pushes the boat away from the shore and moves to the helm. As soon as they are over deeper water, he lowers the prop into the water. The motor cranks, first try.

"Wonder how far off that storm is." Danae turns her head, listening. "Sounds like it's coming from the west."

"Pete's mud hole," Malcolm states. He chuckles at her puzzled reaction. "A saying of my dad's. The worst storms come from the direction of Pete's mud hole, wherever that is."

Malcolm aims the boat upstream. Within a few minutes of reaching plane speed, a high-pitched beeping sounds.

"What's that?" Danae asks.

"Sensor on the motor."

"Better head to shore and let me check it out."

He cuts the power and they move at idle speed. Danae stands and walks to the stern. "Looks like no water's coming from the pilot hole."

"Huh?"

"There's an impeller in the boot that brings in water. The water pump circulates it to cool your engine. That water is expelled here." She points. "No water coming out."

"So, that means . . .?"

"You run this motor without it cooling properly, and you will ruin it."

"What if we go real slow?" Malcolm asks.

"Mr. Hal says this about all engines and I agree. Those warning lights and buzzers aren't called idiot alarms for nothing. Only complete idiots ignore them."

He cuts off the power. The current catches them and they drift downriver.

Danae moves to the bow and lowers the anchor. "There. At least we won't lose ground."

"My dad keeps some tools on board. Can you fix it?"

"Not a water pump. I can, once we're back in town."

"I am *so* screwed." Malcolm leans back his head and blows out a deep exhalation.

"You have a marine radio, and besides, your cell phone. It's not like we'll have to spend the night down here."

"It's not that. I sort of wasn't supposed to come down this far," Malcolm shrugs, "without Dad along."

Danae holds up both hands. "Don't freak. Yet." She moves to the bow and lowers the trolling motor. "We probably have enough battery to get us maybe seven miles upstream."

"You are a genius." Malcolm's expression morphs from glum to hopeful. "That would put us within an okay range. I can call Dad then. He'll get someone to come tow us in."

"Tilt the motor up a bit, but leave enough of the boot in the water. It will act as a rudder so we can keep straight."

"Yes, Cap'n." He raises the motor and Danae starts the trolling motor.

"We won't win any speed contests."

"Wanna fish along the way? It could explain why it will be so late when I call my dad."

"Sound thinking." Danae picks up her rod and they cast and reel, cast and reel.

"If we catch something, we'll need to get it into the boat however we can. If we stop, we'll float downriver."

"Agreed." Danae says.

Four bream and two bass later, they are two miles upstream.

"We should've been doing this all along." Malcolm reels in a plate-sized bream. Between them, they work out a quick system with the dip net. "What a team we make."

"Yeah." Too bad he's gay, Danae thinks. Probably good for her that he is. Sex complicates friendships.

Thunder sounds closer and the intervals between the rumbles lessen. "Let's put up the Bimini." Malcolm sets down his rod and reel and Danae helps him raise the accordion canvas shade. "Have to call Dad soon. He'll be freaking out, with thunderstorms in the area."

"How far do you think we've come?" Danae asks.

"Maybe six miles?"

"Better call him before he calls you." The best defense is a good offense, Miz Mevlyn says.

Malcolm's cell phone trills. "It's him. *Of course* it's him."

"So, you tell him the motor just died. At least we're not sitting at the Bluffs." Danae listens as her friend weaves a convincing story. After he taps the screen to end the call, she says, "Somewhat believable."

"He's going to buzz one of his buddies on the force. It'll take them a bit to get to us. He said to keep coming with the trolling motor until it stops, then to drop anchor and wait. I doubt he'll make it before that storm hits though."

"Meanwhile," Danae picks up her rod and reel, "fish."

In less than fifteen minutes, the trolling motor changes pitch, then stops. They both reel in their lines and set down the fishing gear.

"So much for going farther." Malcolm grabs two paddles and hands one to Danae. "Help me and we'll pull close to the bank."

When they get into a decent position, Danae lowers the bow anchor. On shore, the tree leaves show their lighter undersides and the humidity rises, sure signs of the weather change.

"Storm's close." Danae sits down. Nothing else to do now but wait.

"Boat's coming." Malcolm motions downriver. The roar of a motor, faint at first, increases in pitch and volume.

The vessel rounds the curve at full speed. Danae moves to the bow away from the shelter of the Bimini and waves both arms. The boat slows as it passes them, then the operator hits the throttle.

"So much for flagging down a fellow boater," Malcolm says.

The motor noise fades. Shortly, they hear the motor again, this time heading downstream in their direction. "So much for your *so much*. Looks like he, or she, changed their mind," Danae says.

The vessel roars toward them, slows, circles, and comes alongside. A sleek power boat, white with blue detailing. A Glastron, GTS 205. Ah yes, Danae knows the boat. Between the motor and this particular model, the owner has a good forty grand sunk into it, not counting the trailer.

When the boat nears, Malcolm groans, closes his eyes and shakes his head, then opens them. "Anyone else. Anyone."

Danae sucks in a breath. At the helm sits Rich, Jack's friend. The passenger is the one they call Gimp. He stands and she sees why—from the knee down, his left leg is prosthetic.

"Well, well, well." Rich cuts the engine to idle and pulls alongside. Malcolm helps to keep the two boats from bumping against each other. "Who do we have here?" Danae hears the sneer in his voice.

"Y'all having problems?" Gimp asks. "Can we help?"

"Yep, on both accounts." Danae vows to herself: find out this guy's name. No way she's going to disrespect him for missing part of a leg. Her dislike for the rest of Jack's gang deepens.

Rich stands now, running his gaze from bow to stern. "Where'd you pick up that boat, boy?"

The way he says *boy* sets Danae's teeth on edge. *Boy? Really?* Malcolm fails to buy in.

Danae swivels slightly, enough to see the firm set to her friend's jaw.

"It's my dad's boat."

"Uh-huh." Rich nods. "This one's mine. Graduation present. And *it* actually runs."

Danae props her hands on her hips. "Any motor can fail. Even yours."

Rich throws back his head and laughs. "As if."

Rich. His name suits him. Probably Richard the second or third or some such nonsense. Even without the title, Danae could pick out his type—privileged, self-important. Wealth floats around him like a gilded aura. Bet he's never had to mentally tab purchases at the Dollar Store, then put the least vital item back on the shelf. Heck, his sunglasses cost more than she makes in a month.

When he needs work on *that* vessel, she'll . . . Danae stalls the revenge-think. No, can't risk Mr. Hal's reputation. Besides, the fancy boat's probably under warranty and will go to the dealer shop wherever Dearest Daddy bought it.

Rich caresses the steering wheel as if the boat's a beloved pet. If it was a graduation present, what came his way when he reached legal driving age? A truck, of course. Hope this Glastron matches the truck. Surely it does, down to the custom pin striping.

"Do you need for us to tow you in?" The other boy asks. He looks to Danae. "I'm Gary, by the way."

"Nice to meet you, Gary."

"This is Rich." Gary points to his compatriot. "We're heading back. We can hook y'all onto us."

"Nope," Rich says. "We tow them, it slows us down. We won't beat the storm."

"Seriously, dude?" Gary leans over and says something low into the boat owner's ear. They exchange intense words Danae can't make out.

Legends exist, of wealthy people who wear secondhand clothing and act as if they don't have two nickels to rub together, or others who donate most of their money to charity and world peace. Danae would love to meet one of those, some day. Better luck spotting a unicorn, especially around these parts.

Gary says to Malcolm, "Throw me your bow line."

Part of her wants to stay right here, no matter if the storm to end all summer thunder boomers hits. The smarter part tells her it's a good idea to move.

Rich sighs and rolls his eyes.

Malcolm mumbles under his breath. He breathes in and out, then moves to the bow and gathers the rope and pitches it across. Gary attaches the loose end to one of the metal plates well out of the way of the powerboat's propeller.

Malcolm lifts the trolling motor from the water. "I'll reimburse you for gas."

"Like I *need* your money," Rich condescends to Malcolm. "I'm sure I can come up with a way for you to pay me back." His gaze slides over Danae in a way that makes her skin creep.

Gary scowls at Rich, then looks at Danae with an apology written on his features. If not for Gary, Danae figures Rich wouldn't have bothered doubling back.

A burning question sticks in her mind. Why is Rich lowering himself to hang out with Jack Dixon and his misfits? She does a mental face-palm. Slumming, the excitement of being labeled a bad boy—a *wealthy* bad boy with a father who can bail him out of trouble, and probably already has.

With the extra drag of their boat, the going's slow. Still, they make decent time. Gary looks back periodically, checking and giving a thumbs-up. Rich faces forward.

As they reach the Interstate overpass, another boat heads their way, slowing and circling back.

"That's your dad," Danae states. The man at the helm is another police officer. She's seen him in uniform at the Wild Rose, grabbing coffee and pie.

"Hi boys!" Jerome hails. "Nice of you to get my people closer to home."

Rich smiles wide. "Glad to help out."

If there's one thing Danae despises, it's a stinking hypocrite.

"Mark and I can take it from here," Jerome says. "You two get off this river. The storm is very close."

Gary unties the rope and pitches it to Malcolm's father. Jerome reattaches it to the stern of their boat.

Rich is occupied, carrying on an animated chat with the two off-duty law enforcement officers. What a suck-up. "If you'll drop by the shop, I'll make sure you get gas money," Danae says to Gary.

"No need. Really."

"But—"

"You never leave someone stranded. You just don't."

Danae smiles. She likes this guy more and more. "Still . . ."

"Buy me one of the Wild Rose's burgers sometime." Gary returns the smile.

"I can do that. Stop by any day, except Sunday. I take lunch around one."

Rich salutes them and eases the throttle. The Glastron pulls away slowly, then he digs in and the motor throws a tall rooster tail of spray in its wake. The vessel disappears in moments.

"Ass-wipe," Malcolm states.

The sky is purple, heavy with the promise of rain. Nothing to do but sit back.

"Gary seems okay," Danae says.

"He's basically a good dude."

"Do you know what happened to his leg?"

Malcolm answers, "Tumor, best I recall. Had to get it amputated several years ago."

"Doesn't seem to slow him down."

"Nope." Malcolm watches the sky. "Too bad he's related to Jack Dixon."

"Yeah. Agreed."

Lightning cracks. Thunder rolls.

Danae counts the seconds between the light flash and the sound. "That's only a couple of miles off."

They reach the landing as the first fat drops pelt the river. After tying the boats to the dock, the four dash to their vehicles to wait out the storm. Streaks of lightning pop so close, the flash and thunder occur simultaneously. The tang of ozone fills the air.

Danae watches from the safety of the old truck's cab.

"Hope this doesn't last long. We have a boatload of fish to clean," she says.

Malcolm laughs. She joins him.

## Seventeen

**M**evlyn feels worse than bone tired. She's cell-level tired: the sort of tired where she shoves the dry dog food into the refrigerator and the milk into the cupboard. Her mind's still there, for the most part, but it's tilted, stretched, and plain banged up.

Even with Danae sleeping in the next room, Mevlyn often walks the floors at night—the Southern way of saying *worry-pacing in the wee hours*.

She enters Sam's room and stops to watch him breathe. More and more, he struggles. How much longer until the end? Not for her sake, heavens no. She can't fathom the next second after her husband draws his final sip of air.

Mevlyn loves him fiercely. She wishes for the suffering to end. As soon as that thought solidifies, guilt rides in on its tailcoat. How can she hope for Sam's death? There are things worse than dying. She read that line in some novel and thought, at the time, it was profound. Now, Sam is living it.

A knock sounds at the kitchen door. Sonny woofs. Mevlyn shushes him. She walks from Sam's room and down the hall as fast as she can manage, barely a shuffle. By this time, at the end of the work week, she's overdue time off from the Wash-Away. Time to spend with Sam, though he rarely wakes enough to acknowledge her presence. He knows she's there. Surely.

Mevlyn swings open the door. Elvina Houston stands on the stoop, clad in spandex yoga pants and an athletic tank top crazy with color. A pug dances at the end of a bejeweled leash.

"Me 'n' Juliet were out walking after the rain cooled things down a notch. I just now got some news. Have you heard about the boat breaking down?"

"Now, Elvina. You know I don't much watch TV news."

Sonny squeezes past Mevlyn's legs and the two dogs exchange butt-sniff greetings.

"Not on the television. It's Malcolm and that young gal you've taken in."

"Danae?"

Elvina nods. "Malcolm phoned up Mark Singleton and they took Mark's boat down to the river to tow them in. They should be back," Elvina consults her watch, "about now, I reckon."

"Oh dear."

"Mark's wife texted Mandy at the Triple C and Mandy texted me. I could've called your land line, but I didn't want to risk waking up Sam. If you had a cell phone, I could've texted you straight off. You really should get one, Mevlyn, like I said . . ."

Though she attempts to maintain polite conversation etiquette, Mevlyn's eyes lose focus. Listening to Elvina Houston when she's on a roll is like riding a runaway roller coaster; Mevlyn hangs on and does her best not to scream. Most times, she recalls only about a third of what Elvina says. Now, Mevlyn corrals her brain and ears and tries to make them work together.

Elvina's phone chimes and she taps the screen. "Oh, good. Mandy reports they made it to the landing before the clouds burst open." She slips her phone back into its armband holder. "You and that gal both need phones, what with you taking care of Sam."

Mevlyn hears the rumble of an engine. A motorcycle pulls into the driveway. Elvina glances over one shoulder. "Speaking of the devil . . ." Then, back to Mevlyn. "I've been doing some investigating." Elvina's tone lowers. "I need to fill you in."

"Unless you know more than I already do—she's from Alabama, bad family situation, no priors—you can save your breath for keeping alive." Mevlyn seals the statement with a wry smile. If she could be sure the timing was correct, she might add *bless your heart.*

The not-so-subtle jab is lost on Elvina. "We'll talk later." She tugs on Juliet's leash. "Let me get this little girl home before her two daddies get worried."

The two daddies are Jon "Shug" Presley and Jake Witherspoon, the town's most outspoken gay couple, admired by most. Others who frown on their union can't find enough faults to amount to a hill of beans. Jake's the town florist who creates magnificent arrangements for births, special occasions, funerals, and guilty husbands. Shug is the best hospice nurse in the universe. Mevlyn heard praises for years. Never imagined she or Sam would know him in that capacity.

Mevlyn watches Elvina and Juliet stride away. When they pass Danae, Elvina nods.

"Hey gal." Mevlyn holds open the door. "Heard you had yourself an adventure."

Danae steps inside. Once they're in the kitchen, Mevlyn envelopes Danae in a tight hug.

"I am so glad you're ok. I don't know what I'd do if anything happened to you." Mevlyn holds Danae at arm's length. "You must be starved." Before Danae can respond, Mevlyn moves to the refrigerator. "I made some pasta salad that'll hit the spot. Sit yourself down and I'll spoon you up a bowl."

Eighteen

In the next few days, Mr. Sam grows silent. He opens his eyes a few times when Danae is in the room—a flutter, a short-lived, blank stare—before closing them again. The doctor and hospice nurse tell them, it could be as much as a couple of months or as little as three weeks.

Danae takes extra care to be mindful, further gentling her touch. His skin appears translucent in places. She averts her eyes from those spots. If she studies them too long, will she see his soul? Mama said even the dying, especially the dying, need some speck of privacy and dignity. Along with Danae and Mevlyn and Sonny, the members of the hospice team visit his sanctum. It's good to feel their professional support, but Danae wishes these last few months, days, and hours would belong only to her, Mr. Sam, Miz Mevlyn, and the dog.

Danae discusses dying with the nurse, a kind gay man named Jon (both she and Mevlyn call him by his nickname *Shug*), and with Mevlyn. Everyone seems intent on dissecting the process, as if death can be teased into parts and studied. Danae knows some because of Mama's time at the nursing home, but now understands even more about the human body, how it shuts down, things to expect, signs to watch out for, especially the telltale respiratory pattern that looms in the near future: Cheyne Stokes. Danae finds it reassuring, how death often makes an audible announcement it's on the way. Within twenty-four to seventy-two hours following the commencement of the abnormal breathing pattern, the soul will leave the body.

Mr. Sam isn't there. Yet.

"The lady at the library recommended the book we're starting this morning." Danae picks up the wash basin. Though she hasn't ploughed through all of Miz Mevlyn's books, Danae now haunts the branch library.

At first, she cruised only for a sighting of Mouse. Then, worlds reached out to grab her, aisle after aisle of literary wealth.

"This one's the first in a mystery series by Sue Grafton, enough books to keep us busy for a while if we like how she tells a story."

Her shiny new library card stays with Danae at all times, squeezed between her driver's license and an old school picture of Mouse she had found secreted in one of Aunt Sylvia's bibles a couple of months after Mama died.

Some evenings, Malcolm picks her up and they grab a burger at the Wild Rose, then go together to search for books. He's deep into his online courses, prerequisites for the college classes he'll start in the fall, but he likes to take a break every now and then. Like Danae, he professes a passion for the feel and smell of books. She culls through the stacks, attracted to flashy covers, enough to flip to the descriptions.

"Read the first few pages," Malcolm suggests. "I can tell a lot from them—if the author is a sound writer and the story is one I want to spend time on."

One recent evening, he handed her a book of poetry. She pulled a yuck-face. "Me? Poems? Really, I—"

"Try it. Dare you." He added the book atop her growing pile. "If you don't like it, the burgers will be on me, next time."

To her astonishment, Danae adores Maya Angelou. The words sing, lifting her to a place where anything is possible. She reads everything by the woman, pulls up YouTube videos on the library's computers, to hear the music straight from the poet's lips. When Danae reads "Still I Rise," she feels more powerful than she's ever felt. The words *I Rise* become her new mantra. Danae worries when she learns the wonderful sage is over eighty. Some people, those so full of kindness and magic, should be allowed to live multiple lifespans, to subtract decades from people who are a complete waste of air, like her daddy.

"Mr. Sam. Our book for today is what the lady at the library calls," Danae scans her brain for the term, "a cozy mystery. That's one where there's no over-the-top violence."

The librarian always helps Danae select novels for Mr. Sam, and ones Danae might also enjoy. The best are stories where the main character ends up doing reasonably okay—hopeful, but not like fairy tale stuff.

"I'll go get the book. It's called *A is for Alibi*. The titles are like A is for this, B is for that." Danae revels in the fact the author has a string of them, all the way to Y.

Sue Grafton had died before she reached Z. Just wrong.

"Be back in a flash, Popsie." Danae turns toward the door.

"Cee-Cee?"

The voice is so low, Danae thinks she hears it only in her head. She pivots. Mr. Sam faces her, his eyes open and alert. She sets down the wash basin and crosses over to him. "Popsie, you're awake!"

"Cee-Cee?"

"Yes, Popsie. What is it?"

When she first accepted the ruse of being his daughter, picking out a pet name for Mr. Sam seemed right. The real Cecelia might have chosen Popsie. Mr. Sam's lips lift at the corners whenever he hears it.

"Cee-Cee, will you please say that Serenity Prayer I like so much?" He reaches out a thin, trembling hand and she grasps it, holding it with a soft grip.

Danae sits down. Sonny settles at her feet, looking up at them. In a calm, reverent voice, she recites the words she had often heard her mama speak at the request of failing patients. It was old, from the 1930s, Mama told her.

He gives her hand a tiny squeeze, smiles, nods, and closes his eyes. She watches, waiting until his breathing is slow and even.

For a few minutes, she sits beside his bed, still holding his limp hand. Her father would've never asked her to say a prayer. She's amazed she can remember the one from childhood.

One night, as she knelt beside her bed—she was little, maybe five or six?—her daddy stumbled into her room. "Get up off your knees!"

She fell backwards, then scrambled to tuck her body as close to the wall as possible.

He took a couple of lurching steps and plopped onto her bed. "You know what happens to people when they do all that church garbage, don't you?"

She moved her head slowly side to side.

"Lemme tell you about my baby brother. We was all forced to go to church. Got religion pumped into us like it was blood. I never bought into it, none of it. But Buddy did." Her daddy's eyes went glassy. "I was older. Smarter. Knew when to close off my ears.

"We come home from church that Sunday. The preacher'd gone on and on about how you should get rid of whatever caused you to sin." Her daddy swung his arms. "If your eye offends you, pluck it out. Better to lose that eye than burn in hellfire for eternity."

Her daddy leaned down. She smelled the odd, yet familiar smell, like fruit gone bad. "You know what he come home and did? Do you?"

She moved her head side to side again.

"He come home and took the machete in the barn and chopped off his hand! None of us seen him do it. I went looking for him, when Mama called us for dinner. Found him dead, sprawled on the dirt, blood all spilled around him. His eyes was open like he'd seen Lucifer hisself."

Danae hugged her knees to her chest and shivered.

"Know why he done that?" He spit a little with each word.

She shook her head.

"I heard that preacher tell my mama and daddy that Buddy said he'd been touching hisself in an improper way, and that God told Buddy what had to be done." Her daddy let out a snort that sounded a little like a laugh, with the humor sucked out. "My brother was barely old enough to start wondering why his pecker stood up and why it felt so good to rub it up and down. And he damn sure didn't deserve to die for it!"

Her daddy stood up, caught his balance on the wall. He snatched her by the arm and threw her into bed. "Go to sleep! Don't you ever let me catch you praying to no God that thinks that was a right thing to do."

Danae ducked beneath the sheet. She waited until she heard his bumbling footfalls thud down the hall, then the slam of the back door.

In a few minutes, she heard softer sounds. Her mama eased down to sit on the bed and reached to pet her hair. "You okay, baby girl?"

Danae nodded, though she wasn't, really.

"He's a little sad tonight, that's all. Yesterday would've been his brother's birthday. He didn't mean to scare you."

She smells her mama's scent: rose water and soap.

"Nobody can stop you from talking to God. Some days, it might be the only good talk you'll have. And He listens. I do believe He does."

**D**anae doubts there's anyone floating around up there. If so, why would bad things happen? Why would people drown, or run away, or have a stroke? Why would someone like Mr. Sam have to die in inches?

She stands, walks toward the door, and picks up the wash basin. "C'mon, Sonny. You need to go out." Her voice is just above a whisper.

The dog remains seated, looking up at her with sad eyes.

"I mean it. I refuse to come home and clean up your mess, and Miz Mevlyn surely doesn't need to either." She jerks her head sharply. "C'mon."

The terrier looks up toward the bed, then back at her.

"I am only asking you to walk outside and piss, for heaven's sake. He's sleeping. It's okay."

Danae can't believe how she talks to the dadgum dog like he can understand. Still, it works. Sonny stands and ambles behind her, goes outside for less than a minute, then scratches to be allowed in. He dashes back to Sam's room.

Such devotion. If she ever finds a guy, or girl, like him, she'll seize them up in a heartbeat.

After she rinses out the basin and puts away the dishes from the morning's meal, Danae picks up the Grafton novel and walks back into Sam's bedroom.

Sonny reclines on the bed. He turns his head and whimpers.

"Glad your mama isn't here. She'd beat your fuzzy little butt." Danae walks to the bed.

Sonny looks at her, to Sam, then back to her.

Mr. Sam's chest, it's still.

Must be the start of Cheyne Stokes, the place between shallow and deep breaths, when respiration pauses. She leans in, stares at him. Sonny whimpers. Danae holds two fingers to Mr. Sam's neck, probes to find no pulse. She checks his wrists to be sure. Rechecks his neck.

*Oh no.*

She sinks into the chair. Can't be. If she waits, he'll intake air. His heart will start up. It has to be stunned. That's all.

Minutes pass. She lowers her cheek to his mouth and feels no puff of moving air.

Death is stillness. She looks around, up, hoping to see something, feel his spirit.

Sonny's warm nose nudges her arm.

Danae fights through the numbness, looks first at the phone, then picks up the walkie-talkie. They've discussed this. Many times. No calling 911. No paramedics flying in. No CPR. When he still could make his wishes known, Mr. Sam had been adamant. And Mevlyn reinforced the same to Danae.

"Stay with your daddy," she whispers to Sonny.

Something reaches in and switches her to function. Danae doesn't feel her legs move her out the door, or take her for the few feet into the Wash-Away.

Mevlyn sees her enter and tilts her head, her eyebrows scrunched together.

All Danae can do is move her head from side to side. This time, it's not out of fear like it had been with her daddy.

It's because shock and sorrow hold her prisoner.

Mevlyn crosses the room, wraps one arm around her shoulder, and they both walk back to the house where Sonny stands guard.

## Nineteen

**P**lans for shadowing Mouse fall aside. Danae assumes the role of comforter, planner, housekeeper, coffee barista, and general organizer. *Like a daughter*, she overhears one woman say to Mevlyn.

Within two hours after Sam's death, Elvina Houston engages the casserole committee. The mortuary van has just pulled away with Mr. Sam's draped body when the first meal appears: a plate piled with crispy fried chicken, bowls of potato salad and coleslaw, green beans, and soft wheat rolls. A second woman drops off a still-warm sour cream pound cake and two gallons of sweet tea. A third pops by long enough to leave two bags filled with paper plates, napkins, plastic utensils, and hot and cold beverage cups, and a cooler filled with ice. It's as if the entire town has extra food stocked for death.

"Be sure to take down names and what each one brings," Mevlyn says. "Put a piece of masking tape on the bottom of the dishes, marked with the name, so we can get them back to the rightful owners."

Danae keeps the tape and a small spiral notebook and pen on the counter until the space is so filled with pots and platters, she moves the ongoing tally sheet to an end table next to the sofa. Plant dish gardens and cheery floral arrangements dot the house, most delivered by Jake from the Dragonfly Florist. Every time Danae answers the front door bell, someone hands over some form of comfort.

It wasn't like this after her mama died. A couple of neighbors stopped by, a handful of coworkers from the nursing home, one of the mechanics who worked with Daddy. Danae recalls a couple of cakes. One was dredged in whiskey, delivered by a busty woman with big orange hair and red lips that reminded Danae of a baboon's butt. The woman hung all over Daddy, weeping as if Mama had been her only friend. Though Danae had never seen the woman, her cloying, sweet cologne was familiar. It clung to everything it brushed past, including daddy's shirts. Laundry was Danae's chore, though she hated it and didn't do it very well, so she had spared her mama from the shadow mark of his infidelity. Had Mama ever detected the scent on Daddy? The smell might've spelled reprieve for Mama, Danae understands, now that she's old enough to fathom such. One less night of forced passion and grinding pain.

The folks who braved an audience with Big John didn't stay long; most came out of respect for Aunt Sylvia. Danae did her best to be the sorrowful and dutiful daughter. The sorrowful part she could pull off, as her chest felt as if someone had scooped out her heart with a grapefruit spoon. Dutiful proved difficult.

For three days, the house felt safe. Daddy wasn't around much, and didn't get rolling drunk. Aunt Sylvia camped out on the couch, making sure Danae ate, bathed, slept, and had proper funeral clothes. The refrigerator held adequate food. Mouse would've come home for the funeral, surely, had she known.

Though Estelle had regularly attended church when her work schedule allowed, Big John flat-out refused a sanctuary service. Someone drove Aunt Sylvia and Danae to the cemetery, where the plain pine coffin rested graveside, framed by two pitiful standing sprays of white carnations and ferns.

The flowers heaped on sadness and resentment. Mama had loved her garden, one of the few things that brought her joy, that she had any control over. Come spring and summer, Estelle's freshly-mulched beds bore blooms in every shade from eye-popping scarlet and yellow, to baby-blanket pink and lavender, and even pale blue.

But those plain, cheap white carnations. Dear God. Even in death, Daddy starved Mama of happiness.

Seated between Danae and Aunt Sylvia, Daddy acted the part of poor widower, even managed a few tears. When the preacher spoke about Mama's kind spirit and her work with the elderly and infirm, Daddy puffed up like he was solely responsible for molding Estelle Wilson Gray into one fine human.

For Danae, hatred bloomed full and crimson the day her Mama went into the ground.

"You gotta get me out of there," she whispered into Aunt Sylvia's ear on the way back to the car. "He'll kill me as surely as he killed Mama."

Firm words from a fourteen-year-old. Had Aunt Sylvia brushed them off as the effects of grief, Danae is certain the prediction would've become reality. As it was, Big John nearly managed it four years later.

*Daddy will never hurt me again*, Danae promises herself. She glances toward the den, where Miz Mevlyn holds court. She must be exhausted, too. Little sleep, mounds of decisions, operating on little more than sugar and adrenaline.

Danae misses the early morning run circuit and considers slipping away for a stolen minute or two for at least a half-mile loop.

What a horrible person she is, thinking of her own needs. Mr. Sam is dead. With him gone . . . The thought of having to ask Mr. Hal if she can shift back into the dank store room piles on worry. Mevlyn won't need her.

Time to move on.

Again.

Time to gather her sister and get started creating a life here, or somewhere, or anywhere.

Danae squirts a line of dish soap into the sink and turns on the faucet. Bubbles lift and scud. Like her, tossed to the currents, bouncing wherever the next puff of air takes them.

She scrubs a fine sheen of grease from a platter—someone had brought fried shrimp, one of the part-time servers from the Wild Rose. A warm hand clamps over her forearm and she jumps.

"I know what you're thinking, gal."

"Ma'am?"

"It's written all over your face." The hand pats now—one, two, three times. "I ain't about to ask you to move out."

"But."

Mevlyn's mouth smiles, though her eyes line with weariness. "Unless you got somewheres better you are burning to go, I'd be pleased if you'd stay a while."

Danae's eyes sting. Hard to fathom she has any tears left. "'kay."

"Settled." Mevlyn removes her hand. "Leave those dishes and go take yourself a little run." She leans over and lowers her voice, speaking into Danae's ear. "I'll have Elvina's troupe clean up this mess. Most of 'em are eating more than me and you put together."

The corners of Danae's lips lift. The old woman has a way about her.

"Better cut out of here before you get cornered." Mevlyn tips her head toward the kitchen door exit. "I can hold down this battered fort until you get home."

*Home.* The word worms past her ears and lodges next to her heart.

**W**hen she stands to move from the den to the kitchen, Mevlyn feels every muscle, every joint, every tendon. Aging not only requires strength, it requires superhuman effort. Losing Sam strips her usual steel, leaving behind weary stubbornness.

"You want some pie?" Danae asks, sweeping a hand over the generous offerings like a gameshow host presenting gifts. "Apple, blueberry, strawberry . . . umm . . . Oh, and pear."

"No. No pie. Thank you. I am about pie-d out." Mevlyn sinks into a chair at the kitchen table, glad it's there. Otherwise, her legs wouldn't have carried her even one more step. "I'm touched by the attention and food, but God as my witness, I'm relieved everyone's gone home."

"Tomorrow. The visitation," Danae states with as much enthusiasm as Mevlyn shares.

"Yes." Mevlyn sighs so hard she's amazed a lung doesn't shoot from her mouth. "And that means Sherman and Annabelle Leigh."

"Anna-who?"

Mevlyn laughs at Danae's bewilderment, shocked she has mirth left. "I know. Three names roped together, a mouthful. It suits my sister-in-law. She's a mouthful. At least Sam's brother has a normal name, though neither of that couple are anywhere near normal."

Danae pours mugs of decaf coffee, stirs in sweetener and milk, and carries both to the table. For two people who have only recently become acquainted, they share the ritual: cup of joe in the morning to jumpstart the day, cup of decaf joe in the evening to put the day to rest.

"Thank you, dearie." Mevlyn sips. "Lucky for me, and for Sam, he never got along with Sherman. Otherwise, I'd 've surely clobbered Annabelle Leigh."

Danae settles back into her chair, cradling her mug. "Fill me in."

"Where to start?" Mevlyn puffs out a breath. "Her hair is an unnatural shade of orange, more like an overripe peach—has been for as long as I've been in the family. She's about this big around." She demonstrates with an upheld pinky finger. "Because she feels one ounce of body fat is an honest to God sin, right up there with adultery and murder.

"She rarely shuts up unless she's asleep. Even then, I suspect she chatters in her dreams. A conversation with Annabelle Leigh is like pounding yourself on the head with a hammer. You can grow used to it, but it just feels so damned good when it stops."

Sonny waddles into the kitchen and sits at her feet, his eyes watery and forlorn. Poor pup. Sam's death affects him as bad as it does her. She kicks off one house shoe and pets him with her toes.

"Annabelle Leigh holds up the Ten Commandments like a political banner, yet she'll waltz into this house with her ferret eyes darting about for what she might be able to take away." Mevlyn jabs a different finger from the one she used to describe Annabelle Leigh's figure. "Which is not one single speck of dust or dog hair, if I catch her at it. You'll help me watch her?"

Danae bobs her head. "For sure."

"Sherman is as bad, but slick about it. Reminds me of an evangelist tent preacher. All smiles and *God-bless* and *how-can-I-help-you,* but with a motive stuffed behind every act of his notion of kindness."

"They sound like fun relatives," Danae says with a sarcastic tone.

"Sam stopped having anything to do with Sherman a few years ago. He and his brother got into it over something." Mevlyn taps her chin, "Mercy me, I can't recall what it was over now, or if I ever knew for sure. Sam came back from that visit with his lips pinched shut. He fished like a possessed man for a couple of weeks before his mood brightened. One thing about Sam: he was a forgiving sort, up to a point. He'd take a lot. But then, if one toenail finally slipped over that line, he was done with you. D-O-N-E, done."

"Must've been bad." Danae takes a turn toe-petting Sonny. "Mr. Sam seemed so even-tempered."

"And you met him at his worst. Wish you could've known my Sam before illness robbed him of his happy." Mevlyn feels her lips lift. Sam's laughter sings in her memory. "Didn't take much to make him pleased as a speckled pup."

Wait, that sounds wrong. It's *pleased as punch. Cute as a speckled pup.* She struggles with Southern comparisons. But not as bad as proper use of *bless your heart.*

"Did you notice those old buckets in his room?" Mevlyn asks.

"Yes."

"They're vintage. Some are cricket cages and the bigger ones are minnow buckets. Sam and his love of fishing and anything related to it. He loved finding those old things. The new ones are plastic, like everything else these days, including some people."

Danae chuckles. "Truth."

"I gave him some of them for Christmas, birthdays . . . The oldest one is from the early 1900s, beat up to hell and back, but you'd have thought I'd handed him a gold brick." Mevlyn spins the coffee mug on the tabletop, first one way, then reverses the direction for another spin. "Sam is a simple man," she pauses and swallows past a lump of emotion, "*was* a simple man. Never asked for much. A little lovin', a little time with a fishing pole, a decent meal, someone to sit with at the end of the day and talk about what all happened."

"Wish I could've had a daddy like him."

Mevlyn studies Danae, the sadness in her eyes, the look of Purtymuch Ruined that Mevlyn hadn't seen in a few weeks. No matter where this gal came from, or her history, she had seen some bad times.

"Sam thought you were our daughter. Far as I'm concerned, you can keep that title."

Danae lowers her eyes, but not before Mevlyn sees the tears gathering at the corners.

# Twenty

**D**anae follows Mevlyn from Elvina Houston's gold-toned Delta 88, a boat of a car in pristine condition, toward the Chattahoochee Woman's Club. From the curb, the white building with dark green shutters appears more a genteel family residence than clubhouse. On either side of the entrance, rows of azaleas and dogwood trees line the cement walkway. Their blooms are gone, but Danae figures they put on quite a show in the springtime.

Inside, the expansive hall teems with people. The blend of floor polish, air freshener, and a hint of cinnamon joins the scent of brewed coffee. Two tables contain cold drinks and a host of finger foods Mevlyn had preapproved. One area displays rows of floral arrangements, too many to count at one glance. Along the remaining two walls, easels hold pictures of Sam at various ages alongside Mevlyn; others show poses with fishing buddies or prize bass catches.

A hush falls over the room when they enter. Elvina steps ahead and parts the crowd, leading Danae and Mevlyn to a corner set up with a cushioned chair for the widow. Danae tucks herself to one side and tries to blend into the background. Because Mr. Sam knew so many people, his end-of-life mandates included holding the visitation at the Woman's Club. No casket—he dictated a no-frills cremation—so it's a time to gather and tell fish tales and have a laugh.

To Danae, it looks more like a party than the precursor to a funeral. The lack of a coffin with its lid propped open snatches center stage from a painted-up body to the loved one left behind. Danae admires Mr. Sam's decision on that basis alone.

Though Danae was too young to view her brother's lifeless body, she recalls every detail of her deceased mother. Hair stiff with spray.

Hands folded neatly across her chest. Thick makeup giving the illusion that Estelle had dressed to go out, then decided to take a little rest inside a pillowed box. The lips, painted slick red—something her mother would never abide.

Danae had touched Estelle Wilson Gray's hollow cheek, half-expecting a flush of warmth. Instead, the skin felt chilled and rubbery, like a dead fish. Danae vowed to never again look upon another corpse. Better to remember a person as they were in life.

Mevlyn falls into her role, accepting offered hands and hugs and shared tears. Danae eases from the group and wanders over to look at the photos. She reads a yellowed newspaper account of the official opening for the Jim Woodruff Dam and picks out a young Sam in the faded black and white group picture.

"Hey."

Danae jerks at the sound of the voice and spins to see Malcolm. "Oh. Hey."

"I'm sorry about Mr. Sam. He was a good guy." Malcolm leans forward, scanning a picture of Sam with several of his fishing buddies. Then, back to Danae. "I wanted to come by as soon as we heard, but my dad said it would be a zoo at Miz Mevlyn's house. Didn't want to add to it."

"Probably wise. It's been crazy for sure." Danae shifts her gaze from Malcolm to where Mevlyn holds court. "Neither of us have had much sleep."

"Understandable. When things calm down, maybe we can grab a burger."

"For sure." *Note to self: we still owe Gary a meal. Forget Rich. He can pay for his own dang burger, even if it was his boat that dragged us back to the landing.*

A disturbance at the Woman's Club entrance stalls their conversation. A couple brushes into the room. Instantly, Danae knows them from Mevlyn's description. The woman wears a charcoal gray skirt suit with black lace trim, and that hair! Danae mentally nicknames her *Peachy*. The man clutches her hand, ploughing through the people as if they're tall grass and he's a lawnmower. When they reach the corner, the woman flings herself over Mevlyn with a wail so loud and prolonged, Danae wishes for earplugs.

"She takes bereaved to a new level," Malcolm states. "Who *are* those people?"

Danae wants to rush over and shove them away from Mevlyn before she's contaminated. "That is Sherman and Annabelle Leigh." Before Malcolm can form a question, she adds, "later."

The bouffant-haired fellow—Danae decides to call Sherman *Preacher*—looks on with fixed benevolence, before dancing his gaze around the room. Danae notes how he takes in details, especially the elongated food and drink tables. Surely he won't try to secret brownies and those little salmon tarts into his suit pockets. If he does, she'll call him out as sure as she will if he comes into Miz Mevlyn's house looking for love in all the wrong places. He and Peachy are a perfect match.

Elvina Houston scoots across the room and rescues Mevlyn from Sam's kin. In minutes, Preacher and Peachy form their own pool of condolence. Danae catches the eyebrow twitch Elvina sends to Mevlyn and Mevlyn's subtle appreciative nod and smile.

Danae decides to like Elvina.


**"S**am promised the boat to Sherman. So, where is it?"

Danae compares Annabelle Leigh, aka Peachy, to a rooster cornered by a fox. Her orange hair puffs out beyond the limits of most hair products, short of shellac.

"News to me," Mevlyn says, her voice calm, as if she's discussing the weather or what fertilizer to use on the tomatoes.

"And his fishing gear, all of it," Sherman, the Preacher, adds. His face flushes as bright as his wife's hair.

Danae hovers in the kitchen, close enough to come to Mevlyn's rescue. She mentally tabs nearby weapons: a butcher's block filled with knives, a pair of dull scissors, a full can of wasp spray. She can aim that from several feet away and watch the foam lather Peachy's curls like sugar glaze on a pound cake. Should do it anyway, for the entertainment value alone, since Preacher and Peachy aren't making any signs of leaving. Bad enough they tagged us back to the house after the visitation. Isn't it enough that Mevlyn will have to deal with them again at the memorial service?

Peachy stands with her hands propped on her hips. "Have you taken my husband's boat off somewhere he can't find it, is that how you're playing this?"

Mevlyn doesn't answer.

"I'll get the police involved if necessary." Preacher postures beside his wife.

Sonny scrambles to all fours and spins, trying to decide who to bark at first.

Mevlyn's calm cracks. She slams both palms against the arms of her rocker. "Enough! You can both shut the hell up!"

Danae steadies herself against the kitchen counter and observes. Her muscles tense. Raised voices never work for her—too many years spent cowering behind chairs or secreted in a closet or, if she could creep to an exit, in the back corner of the yard where she and Mouse found safety.

Mevlyn lifts to her feet faster than Danae's ever witnessed. "First of all, *I* am the widow here. The sole beneficiary. The head cheese. I have the legal paperwork to back me up, too. Even if I didn't, Florida is a state where the spouse inherits if there's no will in place."

Preacher and Peachy grow mute, their eyes wide.

"Second," Mevlyn's tone evens out, "that boat is miles from here, with the new legal owner, one Adam Henry Wilson of Dixie county. A fine young man Sam found delightful."

Peachy's lips form an *O*. Before words can escape from the hussy's orange-painted mouth, Mevlyn sucks in a breath and continues, "if you'd been at all concerned about Sam, you'd know the reason he had to sell that boat he loved almost as much as he loved me. We had a mountain of medical bills from the surgery that did little good except to buy him a few months, and especially from chemotherapy that cost more than a room full of gold bullion."

Sherman tents his hands together. "We knew—"

"You didn't know shit, so don't crank up your line-up of lies. Neither of you has even bothered to pick up the damn phone, much less visit, in over four years!"

Danae's glad Mevlyn's on her side. She'd hate to have her as an enemy.

Mevlyn glares at Preacher and Peachy. They return the same. Sonny stands at Mevlyn's feet. A low growl rumbles his throat. The pup will get a good-boy treat later, for sure.

Preacher launches into an explanation so convoluted, Danae stops trying to connect the pieces. When he pauses, Sonny snorts, takes three steps, and lifts his leg to pee on Sherman's pants leg. Preacher's puffed-up hair jiggles when he stomps and curses. Sonny returns to his position by Mevlyn's feet.

Oh yes, Sonny will get an entire bag of bacon snaps. Danae pinches her lips tight to avoid a guffaw.

Mevlyn jabs a finger toward the couple. "Allow me to spell it out for you. Unless I decide to give you some small token that you clearly don't deserve, you get nada." She forms a zero with a thumb and middle finger. "Zippidy-do-dah-day."

If it was Danae's middle finger, she could put it to better symbolic use.

"Sam was *my* brother." Sherman's face pearls with sweat.

"And you were a flaming pain in his behind from the time you could toddle. Yes sir, I know all the stories, all the times he bailed you out of trouble, the times he handed over his hard-earned money because you gambled yourself into a Grand Canyon-sized hole." Now it's Mevlyn's time to snort. "I was the only woman you didn't try to snatch out from under his nose." She pivots toward Peachy. "Sam had too good of taste to look your way, so you're the exception."

Peachy spins toward the door. "We're leaving. Come on, Sherman."

"Wha—?"

"Now!" She stomps toward the kitchen door, throwing one last comment over her shoulder, "and we won't be back for the funeral!"

Preacher puffs out his chest. "This isn't over, Mevlyn. We know *who* you are, remember that."

Mevlyn curls one finger in a come-hither movement. Sherman steps closer. "And you have your own full set of demons, don't you? Make mine look like amateurs."

His eyes widen. The alarm disappears so quickly, Danae wonders if she imagined it.

"Now, Mevlyn, my dear one. You . . . you wouldn't."

Mevlyn's smile starts out slow and freezes into a malevolent smirk. "Maybe I would, if someone gave me good reason."

"Sherman Jenson!" Annabelle Leigh's screech makes her husband jerk like a tethered dog. He gives Mevlyn one last hard look. The door slams so hard in his wake, the dishes in the china cabinet rattle.

Mevlyn sinks into the chair. "At least Sam can be remembered in peace tomorrow." Sonny jumps into her lap and nudges her hand until she pets him.

Danae's chest hurts, seeing the old woman's battered sorrow. Why did she have to put up with Preacher and Peachy's crap on top of everything else?

"Can you do a quick check for me, Danae? Make sure nothing is missing, best you can. They weren't here long, but both of them took a turn in the bathroom."

"Sure." Danae darts down the hallway, roaming through the master bedroom and bath, into her bathroom, the small room where she sleeps, and finally into Mr. Sam's. Since his death, she's avoided this room.

It's barren now, the medical flotsam gone, and the rented hospital bed. One of the novels they never got to share sits alone on the narrow table. Nothing remains of the man she grew to cherish, except a lingering scent of stale sweat, his mounted fish, and the line of vintage buckets.

One spot is blank. She tears from the room and dashes through the den.

"What?" Mevlyn calls out.

"I gotta catch them! They stole one of the buckets!"

"Come back in here, gal!"

Danae screeches to a stop and steps back into the den.

"They didn't take it. I gave it to the funeral director."

Now Danae is completely flummoxed. Mevlyn noodles the soft spot between Sonny's ears. His mouth opens in a dog smile and his tongue lolls to one side. "It's his urn."

"But, you picked out a coffin."

"I did. A rental, for the memorial service."

Danae sits on the chair nearest Mevlyn. "A rental casket?"

"Sam couldn't abide the notion of being buried in a box, why he chose to be cremated. He's the one who picked out that banged-up old bucket to hold his cremains." Mevlyn moves her head side to side. "Odd word, cremains. Sounds like a fancy coffee creamer to me." Another head shake. "Anyway, Sam won't be inside that coffin tomorrow. It'll be closed with a blanket of flowers on top, like everyone expects. I'll get his minnow bucket urn back in a few days and I came up with the perfect way to send him off. I plan on talking to Jerome, see if he'll take us down the Apalachicola River so we can send his ashes floating toward the Gulf of Mexico."

Danae settles back into the chair. "Death is sure weirder than life."

**M**evlyn smiles. The gal is wise for one so young. She waits, sensing the questions bubbling behind Danae's eyes. Will the gal ask her about Sherman's comment? He's right. She *is* a fraud in the strict sense of the word. Pretending to be something you're not gains that title.

"Do you want a cup of that calming tea Miz Elvina bought over?" Danae asks.

"I'm not one much for hot tea, but I think right now, that would hit the spot. Yes."

Danae rises, takes one step, then turns to face Mevlyn. "That woman is an evil heifer."

Mevlyn agrees, though she's met female cows nicer than Annabelle Leigh. She watches Danae in the kitchen, putting the kettle on to boil, lining up the cups and saucers on a small tray, measuring the loose chamomile blend into ball tea infusers.

A person with secrets recognizes another person with things best kept hidden. For that, Mevlyn loves Danae even more.

Twenty-one

Danae sits beside Malcolm, across the booth from Gary. The Wild Rose Diner holds the lingering aura of the recent lunch rush.

"Good morning." Julie Nix flicks a quick glance toward her wrist. "Shoot fire. Make that good afternoon. Where has this day got off to?" She shakes her head. "Ah well. What for y'all today?"

"Cheeseburger, loaded. Fries," Danae says after both guys motion *ladies first.*

"Cheeseburger, catsup, mayo, pickles. No fries," Malcolm adds.

"And you, Mr. Gary?" The server pivots his way.

"Cheeseburger, all the way, except hold the onions. Yes to fries."

Julie flashes a set of deep dimples. "A burger kind of day, huh."

Servers who can sustain a cheerful attitude regardless of dealing with the public day after day deserve a national appreciation month.

"Three teas—one sweet, one unsweet, one half and half." The server's raised eyebrows ask for confirmation. They all nod and she leaves for the kitchen. In less than two minutes, the battered door swings open and Julie delivers their drinks before moving off to another set of diners.

"She's amazing," Malcolm states. Danae and Gary agree.

"What's up with no fries and unsweetened tea?" Danae asks Malcolm.

"Unlike you, I don't run every day. I'm trying to avoid piling on the *freshman fifteen* I hear everyone talk about." Malcolm pats his slightly bulging belly.

"You're taking online classes. Hardly think it counts unless you're on campus," Danae answers with an exaggerated eye roll, then shifts attention to Gary. "Sorry it's taken so long to buy you a rescue-burger." She takes a swig of tea so syrupy, she can almost feel her blood sugar elevate.

"No problem," Gary answers. "With Mr. Sam passing away, you've been a little frenzied."

An accurate statement. Death came with a boatload of paperwork and decisions, even with prearrangements in place. Poor Mevlyn. The activity kept grief from bubbling over, a smidge. Mevlyn had only missed two days at the Wash-Away, though Elvina had subs lined up for a solid week with others on standby.

The three of them fall into easy conversation. When Malcolm or Gary sense her confusion, they pause long enough to bring Danae up to speed. The last of the lunch crowd dwindles to their booth and one two-top where an elderly man dawdles over pie and coffee. Julie appears in a few minutes and deals out three loaded plates, a bottle of catsup, and extra napkins.

"Hey, by the way," Malcolm says after the server leaves, "my dad wants me to tell you how much he, we, appreciate you letting the dogs run with you. It has really settled them down. No more digging out."

"I like having them along," Danae replies around a mouthful of burger.

Too bad they're not bloodhounds. They could track Mouse.

"I have to get them in for their shots," Malcolm states. "Always such a joy."

"Let me take 'em. I go right by the clinic. Someone's generally there by that time."

"That would be fan-freaking-tastic." Malcolm beams. "I will gladly pay you in hamburgers."

"See? Works for us both."

The elderly gentleman finishes his pie and coffee, throws bills on the table, and leaves without summoning Julie.

Behind them, Danae hears the jingle of the bell hanging from the front door and assumes it accompanies the old man stepping outside. When Gary looks up from his plate, his expression shifts from pleasant to displeased. She tamps down the urge to swivel.

"Well, if it ain't the odd couple and their new groupie." The voice is familiar, not a person she wants to invite to join them.

Rich and Jack stop and hover by the end of the booth. Rich wears distaste like an overcoat. Jack looks bored.

"You sorta slummin', ain't cha?" Rich directs toward Gary.

Gary's eyes narrow. Beside her, Danae feels Malcolm tense.

Jack takes a step away. "Leave it alone, Rich."

Rich stares a beat longer before following Jack to a booth in the far corner.

Gary launches a discussion of the best fishing holes. Malcolm adds his thoughts. Since Danae has nothing to offer, she slips subtle glances toward the corner booth. Both Gary and Malcolm sit up straighter in their seats, and though their chatter is benign, their body language speaks of defensive wariness.

Danae finishes her burger in three bites. Neither Gary nor Malcolm tarry over their meals.

"We'll have to do this again soon." Gary leads the way to the checkout counter. "Only next time, I'll buy." When his eyes linger on her, Danae's skin warms.

Mr. Hal's given her a few days away from the shop, to be free to help Mevlyn. Though Danae assures Malcolm she's perfectly fine to walk by herself, he accompanies her the two blocks toward the Wash-Away before turning back toward his own street.

Inside, Mevlyn rests in her normal position. Instead of ledgers or some women's magazine, a stack of opened sympathy cards sit on her desk.

"Wish you'd let me bring you some lunch." Danae sits across from her. She takes several cards from the pile, grabs a handful of embossed thank-you cards, and settles into the mindless task of appreciating folks for food and flowers.

"I don't have much of an appetite. Besides, if I do, we still have a refrigerator full of food at the house."

"Ugh. Not to slam the cooks around here, but I had to have a break from all of that."

"I totally understand." Mevlyn bobs her head once. "Tell you what, when I do manage to get hungry, I'll call in an order and let you run pick it up."

"Deal."

Danae tries to keep her writing legible; never was one for pretty cursive. Mevlyn's handwriting looks like art. "What's up with Jack? He has a serious nasty attitude."

"Where'd you brush up against him?"

"He and Rich came into the café."

"Ah."

"It's like they have a case of hate, for me and for Malcolm."

"Their kind of mean goes way back." Mevlyn slips a folded card into its envelope and starts another. "Rich is just spoiled stinky. Bad guy wannabe with a bank account."

"I got that, but why does Jack look at me like he could gladly stick a knife in my gut?"

"That's more'n likely because of your affiliation with me and Sam."

Danae starts to lick-seal the stuffed envelope, recalls how god-awful the glue tastes, and reaches instead for the bowl next to Mevlyn, to dampen one fingertip on a wet sponge.

"How can anyone dislike y'all?" Danae asks.

"Goes way back to his grandpa. Sam helped put that no-good behind bars."

Danae settles and waits. This town yields a new story a minute.

"Local law enforcement folks have long called on fishermen like my Sam, people who know the Apalach so well, they could navigate it blindfolded on a moonless night."

Reserve dryer number one slows and halts. Mevlyn leans forward to stand. Danae halts her with a hand. "Let me get that."

Together, they fold the load of towels and sheets before returning to the thank-you notes and Mevlyn's story.

"Wasn't unusual back in the day, to call out for civilian help when someone was lost on the river, or if something illegal was in play. It was some of the state boys out of Tallahassee who came to the house one night, asking Sam to put his boat in the water and help them.

"Sam knew every turn, every spring, every private landing from here to Bristol. When the state boys told him a drug deal was going down somewhere between the second set of jetties and the sandbar before the Bluffs, Sam knew the most accessible spot for money and dope to change hands. Back then, it was mostly what they liked to call *square grouper*—bales of pot imported by small boats from farther south, brought up the river on some moonless night.

"My Sam figured out the one place they were likely to hit shore and led the authorities to a bend where they could watch and wait. Surely enough, well after midnight, two boats chugged upriver, their running lights off. The state boys gave them long enough to download the pot, then came up with floodlights and guns drawn, right as money was changing hands.

"Sam witnessed it all, even testified to get the smugglers put away. Jack's granddaddy was one of them."

Danae stops writing. "So Jack blames *your* family for messing up *his*."

"Something like that. Wouldn't trust none of that bunch as far as I could throw them."

"Where does Gary fit in?"

"Cousin, I believe. He didn't grow up here, so I don't know much about him."

Gary can't be a horrible person. Danae would've singled him out. Unless her danger hairs are losing their edge.

She's so lost in worrying, she licks the envelope seal. "Ugh!"

Mevlyn motions to the cooler. "Better grab you a cola, or that taste will ruin you for the rest of the day."

<h1 style="text-align:center">Twenty-two</h1>

$S$even days after Sam's passing, Mevlyn gets mad: white-hot, hair-pulling, rabid-skunk mad. It doesn't take that hospice pamphlet talking about the five levels of grief to tell her she's landed well above what *they* call level three, anger. She could bite the head off a rattlesnake.

She sits on the cushioned vanity bench and glares at the old woman in her mirror. The hag's cracked lips are drawn into a hard line. With no smile to lift those cheeks, the jowls droop like a bulldog's. And those eyes! Lord have mercy. She could cut you with those eyes.

"Sam would be so disappointed if he saw you like this," she admonishes her reflection. "Wasn't like he got plowed over by a bus. You've had ten months to get used to the idea of him not being around."

Rational thinking rarely replaces emotional distress. The harder Mevlyn tries to cheer up, the madder she becomes. The least she can do is smear on some rouge, a little lip color, and comb her hair. Forget the fake eyelashes and mascara. None of that can stand up to a steady stream of tears. If one of the falsies was to fail and lift at the edges, she might rip it off and take half her eyelid with it.

In one of their preparatory chats, Sam told her he'd figure a way to let her know he'd crossed over successfully and waited for her on the other side. Tossing around ideas on how he might go about it, they had both cranked up a case of teenaged giggles.

"Nothing corny, Sam," she says aloud to her reflection, replaying the scene. "Don't go turning into some butterfly and landing on my outstretched hand. That's way too much like a Hallmark movie."

Mevlyn lowers her voice to mimic Sam's. "Birds and butterflies are popular. Guess it signifies wings and flying off toward heaven."

"You could be a bat." She snaps her fingers as she had that day. "Nix that. If you ended up tangling in my hair I'd die right then and there."

At her feet, Sonny watches her with wide, bewildered eyes. "You best get used to me talking to myself," she aims in his direction. Sonny answers with a grunt.

That same afternoon, she and Sam went to the library and found a book on animal totems and what they meant.

"Here's one," Mevlyn mimics Sam's baritone, "cardinal. When a cardinal flies up, it means things will improve. If it flies down, trouble's coming. If it flies toward you . . ."

Mevlyn props her hands on her hips, like she'd done that day in the library. "Don't torment me, Sam. When a cardinal flies at you, what does it mean?"

She pretends to run her finger along a line of print, as he had. "It means . . . duck!"

Mevlyn drops her hands into her lap and stares toward the bathroom ceiling. "I wanted to slap you silly, but I couldn't help joining you with a laugh."

He'd told her to stop beating her head against the wall, that he'd find a particular way so she'd know it was him.

"Three days is what it should take for you to send me a sign, that's what all those other people say. Three days." She holds up the proper number of fingers. "I know. I know. You never did cotton to being on anyone else's schedule. You like to take your time."

Mevlyn recalls how Sam smiled slow after she said those same words, the way he did when he wanted to get frisky. And they had. And it was slow, and oh so good. That was the last time they made love, two days before the surgery, and six weeks before he started chemo. After that, he was either too sore or too weak to do little more than hug and kiss. At the very end, Sam could barely grip her hand.

Mevlyn stands up. Sonny pops to his feet. He follows her to the kitchen for seed to replenish the bird feeders. Coming down the hallway, she hears a repetitive hard *thunk, thunk, thunk* on the glass sliding door.

"What in the devil?" Nobody comes to that entrance. Friends enter through the kitchen. Strangers ring the front door bell.

She walks into the den and freezes when she notes the source of the sound: a cardinal hurling himself at the glass, a male judging by his bright coloration.

This happens in the spring, when the males grow defensive, attacking rivals and sometimes their own reflections. But it's almost the end of July—nearing the humid, god-awful dog days—not a time when birds are overly amorous.

Mevlyn slides open the door and steps onto the concrete slab. The black-crested scarlet bird flits to perch on a fence post. Sonny woofs. She holds a hand to quiet him.

"Sam, is that you?"

God help if anyone hears her. Good thing Danae's not home.

The bird eyes her. He takes to wing and flies directly at her. Mevlyn ducks, shielding her face. The bird lands on another post. Mevlyn opens her mouth to call him out. He zooms toward her again. She hunkers down. He passes so close, she hears the whoosh of wings.

The third time, Mevlyn's ready. She jumps aside as he passes.

"I got it, Sam! No need to kill your fool self, again."

The cardinal balances on a crape myrtle branch and sings out, "Chee-hoo! Chee-hoo! Chee-hoo!" His song lasts for a few sets. The scarlet bird extends his wings, lifts, and gives Mevlyn one final fly-by before disappearing into the tree canopy.

Mevlyn smiles for the first time in over a week. "Well-played, Sam. Well-played."

Inside her pocket, the cell phone vibrates. When she swipes the screen and answers, the funeral director says, "Good morning, Miz Mevlyn. Mr. Sam's come home to us. Is this a good time for me to bring him to you?"

"Surely. Bring him on to the Wash-Away. I'll set him by me at the desk so he can visit with the regulars."

When the funeral director replies, Mevlyn detects a hint of surprise before he rights himself. Imagine that, after all of the things he's probably been asked to do over the years of handling death, she manages to tip him off balance.

**W**hen Jerome sits, his gun belt leather creaks. Mevlyn finds the sound comforting. As long as folks like Jerome are on watch, safety is less of an illusion.

"Thanks for stopping by." She pats the battered cricket bucket and speaks in a voice too low for the patrons to hear. "When's your day off? Sam's come home. He kicked the bucket, now he's inside of one."

In spite of the serious nature of the subject, Jerome smiles at her presentation. "About that. We need to talk."

"If it's a hardship, I can get one of Sam's fishing buddies to handle this."

"No. Not that. I am all in. Danae's got the motor humming just fine. I'm off on Friday and of course, I want to help."

"Do I hear a *but?*"

"Something about sprinkling ashes in a river niggled me, so I did a little research. It's against the law to scatter cremains in any fresh flow waterway like the Apalachicola River. Even with the ocean, you have to be three miles off shore."

"Well, I'll be doggoned. There's a law about everything."

"Of course, I could get distracted and not actually witness you doing it."

"No sir. I'll be no party to the law *and* your ethics being stretched, not when it's your boat. Sam wouldn't stand for it either. Heck he probably knew all about that law, but I'd have no reason to know it. Until now."

Danae stands beside the desk now. "What is the big deal, anyway?"

"Fish pee and poop in that river, and birds, and gators." Mevlyn ticks off the count as she speaks.

"The official explanation is that no human cremains can be introduced into public drinking water. Lots of communities pull from that river."

"Someone could drink Sam," Mevlyn states. "Guess I understand that. Still . . ." Her face muscles feel too weary to lift her lips. "The thought of him being close to the thing he loved so appealed to me. Well, it is what it is."

"However," Jerome says, "I came up with an alternative plan."

"I'm all ears."

"Spreading ashes on private land is permitted, as long as one obtains permission from the landowner. If I'm thinking right, a couple of Sam's friends own property bordering the river."

Mevlyn sits up straight. "That is a pure fact. Let me make some calls."

Jerome stands. The gun belt creaks again. "You do that."

"If it works out, I can pack up a cooler and we'll make a day of it, picnic, run the river, even fish if we take a mind to. Really give Sam a solid send-off."

Jerome hooks his thumbs into the edge of his belt and rocks on his heels. "I am here to serve and protect."

"And that you do, sir. That you do."

Mevlyn and Danae watch him stride from the building and into his cruiser.

"That man is golden, for sure." Melvyn runs a hand across the top of the bucket.

In less than the time it takes for Danae to fold her clothes, Mevlyn gains a spot for Sam's final place of rest, close enough for his spirit to hear the lap of the Apalachicola. Even better, his longtime friend has an unused shallow landing where they can secure the boat and get off and on without taking an unintended swim.

Mevlyn settles the headset onto its cradle. "That's that. Sam's got waterfront real estate. Took dying to do it, but there you go."

Danae reaches into the cooler for two colas. She hands one to Mevlyn. "Better late than never." She pops open the top of her can and raises it in salute. Mevlyn does the same. They clink cans together and drink.

"In the end, all the real estate any of us can lay claim to is our final plot." Mevlyn lets out a belch that nearly parts Danae's hair. Sometimes she's so dang profound, Mevlyn surprises even herself.

# Twenty-three

**D**anae crouches on the dock and steadies the boat while Jerome and Malcolm help Mevlyn step on board. The sun is barely up, yet the temperature hovers in the mid-eighties. The air presses down, thick with humidity.

"It's gonna be a scorcher," Mevlyn comments. Her head tilts toward the bleached-out sky. "Not a cloud in sight, but hear me when I tell you, there'll be a thunderstorm coming in from Pete's mud hole by three. You can set a clock by it."

Malcolm flicks an amused grin toward Danae. Right. The worst storms come from the direction of Pete's mud hole, wherever that is.

Jerome fires up the outboard. The engine thrums with barely a missed beat. "Hasn't run this good since the day I bought it," he aims toward Danae. "Sure do appreciate you for that."

Danae's eyes burn. What is up with her tear ducts? Everything makes her weepy. Last night, she had to leave the den when a sappy burger commercial spurred her emotions.

Mevlyn settles into the cushioned seat adjacent to Jerome and sets Sam's bucket-turned-urn onto the floorboard between them. Malcolm nods to Danae. She unties the bow rope and steps from the dock onto the boat. He unfastens the stern, gives the boat a nudge away from the dock, then leaps on board. They sit side by side on the rear bench seat.

"Don't be in a hurry," Mevlyn says. "Sam would like to take the tour."

Jerome backs the vessel, aims downstream, and settles into an easy glide. The wind cools the sweat on Danae's brow. *Cadillac-ing along*, that's how her daddy used to refer to this leisurely pace. She shoves thoughts of her past aside. This day belongs to Mr. Sam, and to the woman he loved for so many years.

At first, Danae visually tags the spots Mevlyn points out: Sam's cherished glory holes. Each brings forth an explanation: the times he caught stringers of plate-sized bream in less than twenty minutes, "fast as he could pull 'em in." Other places bring forth longer tales of trips Mevlyn had shared with her husband. Most come with a tally of the sizes and numbers of the fish caught, too. Like most fish tales, Danae suspects the exaggeration that results from time and retelling.

"I cast my line into the limb that supported a huge hornet's nest over there." Mevlyn laughs. "I dang near crawled over Sam and the motor, trying to get the warning out of my mouth. That man of mine stepped up, sliced the line with his pocket knife, and managed to back the boat away real easy-like before the hive got agitated and caught scent of us. You don't want that kind of devils-on-the-wing tailing you. I've seen them chase a person, even swarm over the water waiting for that person's head to pop up in case they were dumb enough to think just dunking themselves might make a difference."

They share her laughter.

Danae stops trying to memorize details—the curve of the shore, how far from the jetties, whether it's the east or west bank. To do so seems disrespectful. These are Mr. Sam's spots. She'll find new places. And when she and Mouse move in together, they'll save up for a little skiff, nothing fancy, nothing designed for anything other than a lazy afternoon on the Apalach.

Today is a welcome change from the "official funeral," as she and Mevlyn call it. That day was filled with grays and black, somber, muted tones, voices kept low and mirthless. Per Mr. Sam's wishes, this day is a time for celebration and eye-popping shades. Mevlyn wears tan Capri pants, a daffodil-yellow shirt, and red sneakers; her lips are painted crimson with ear bobs to match. A silk daisy adorns the clip holding back her hair. Jerome sports a garnet and gold FSU shirt, his alma mater, plus matching the boat. Malcolm's polo is white and green-striped.

Danae looks down at her own contribution to the color parade: a sky blue T-shirt and shorts in a wild print of so many colors, no one shade dominates. The outfit is brand-spanking new. It still makes her uneasy, wearing something not secondhand.

For her first few years of life, Danae wore Mouse's hand-me-downs. Instead of feeling ashamed, Danae valued the connection to her older sister. The few times she sported something clearly crisp and unfaded, Daddy flew into a rage. "Wasting my hard-slaved money for something she ain't gonna wear for even a doggoned year!"

On occasion, Mama or Aunt Sylvia managed to slip an original into her closet. "The tags were still on it," she heard Mama say more than once. "I got it at the Goodwill on the rich side of Dothan. You know how those people are, John."

That would sidetrack Big John into a rant about wealthy folks and how they didn't appreciate anything, how they bought stuff just because they could, for the thrill. How they lived off the backs of working people like him.

At least Mama or Aunt Sylvia never had to worry about finding Danae fancy dresses. She didn't attend parties, or functions. Danae skipped the senior prom, though Antoine asked her to go as his date. Now, she wishes she had accepted. One happy memory, abandoned before it could happen. Antoine could dance circles around anybody at their school. And best of all, he was her friend and she didn't have to pretend to be who she wasn't.

"Do you know where this landing of Wyman's is?" Mevlyn asks Jerome. "I did my best to picture it in my mind."

"Not too much farther." Jerome motions toward the east bank. "You can reach it by Dolan Road, off the Greensboro Highway, but you'd need a jeep or four-wheel drive truck. Wyman said he let the access road go back to natural, said it keeps folks from trespassing on his property to get to the river."

"Understandable, what with drugs running amok," Mevlyn says.

"He said he'd leave a red bandana tied to a willow near the landing." Malcolm points. "As a matter of fact, there it is." He aims the bow toward shore and decreases speed, cutting the engine to idle as they coast into the shallows. Jerome moves to the front of the boat, hops out, and grabs the rope to guide the vessel to shore.

After Malcolm secures the bow rope to a stump, they step onto land. Mevlyn carries Sam's bucket. The hinges sing with her every step. They move close to the clearing's periphery.

"There!" Mevlyn points to a shady patch beneath a large ironwood tree. "That is it." She stands near the base of the tree and scratches out an X with the tip of her sneaker.

Malcolm digs a shallow trench with a garden trowel.

"Perfect. Not too deep. Not too shallow." Mevlyn looks from the hole to the three of them. "Are we ready?"

They nod.

"Seems like we should say something," Danae states.

"Good notion, gal. Why don't you start us off?" Mevlyn sets down the bucket near the trench.

Danae ponders for a beat before she speaks. "Mr. Sam, I didn't get to be around you for long. I wish I could've. You liked a good mystery and made me feel like I was important. I know I'm not your daughter really, but I sure loved pretending to be." She blinks back tears.

Mevlyn motions to Malcolm. He speaks, then his father. Mevlyn goes last. "Well, darlin', this here's your final resting place. You'll never be alone, I believe, what with the turtles sunning on that log. Looks like a good spot for wading birds to visit and I am sure, there's a gator lurking somewhere nearby." She looks out across the river. "All of your fishing buddies pass by here, so you'll get to see them, too. And one day, I'll join you, mixed in with the dirt. I love you. You are a part of me, no matter where you stay until I get to catch up with you."

The old woman lifts the bucket lid and removes the plastic bag. The average weight of human cremated remains is five pounds, Danae read online. Mevlyn unzips the bag and upends the open end over the trench.

Danae expects the cremains to send up a puffy cloud. They should lift, like angel wings carrying Mr. Sam to the heavens. A small amount is ash. The rest falls in a clump and reminds Danae of cat litter. Or, clay.

She stares at the trench and sees the top of her mother's coffin.

Her daddy stood on one side of her, her aunt on the other.

Daddy scratched up a handful of Alabama soil and flung it atop the casket. "Go ahead, Dannie."

Danae crouched down and scraped dirt into her palm. She froze, staring down at the coffin. "I . . . I can't."

"Do it," Daddy said.

"No. No. No."

"Do. It."

Aunt Sylvia put a hand on her daddy's forearm. "John, don't."

Anger flashed in her daddy's eyes. People stood around them—not many, but enough to keep him from showing out. "Take her to the car."

He scooped up more dirt, handful after handful. The sound echoed. *Thump. Thump. Thump.* Danae thought of the weight of dirt, how it would press down.

The nightmares began that night. Waking up, gasping, the vision of her mama under pounds of packed red clay, her hands clawing for escape. After that, Danae started to run. Aunt Sylvia bought Danae her first pair of good running shoes. Though her daddy protested, her aunt spent money for proper attire, and Danae joined the school track and field team. She's been running ever since.

Danae studies her hand. Instead of river mud, she sees the stain of Alabama clay painting her palm a dull orange. Her eyes lose focus.

"You all right, gal?" Mevlyn asks.

Profound sorrow seizes her chest. It rises up in cruel waves. Danae crumbles to her knees. She hears wailing and realizes the horrible sound emanates from her own mouth. She feels Mevlyn's hands on her shoulders and hears words, but they don't make sense. She sobs until nothing comes out but hoarse whooshes of air.

Danae is hot, then chilled. Her vision sparkles, as if hundreds of tiny fireworks explode behind her eyes.

Then, darkness.

When Danae opens her eyes, she's sprawled on the ground with her head cradled in Mevlyn's lap. Birds flit in the overhead tree canopy and she hears the music of the passing river.

"There you are," Mevlyn says. "You left us for a couple of minutes."

Jerome holds onto her wrist, taking her pulse. Malcolm hovers nearby, his face contorted with concern.

"Take your time getting up. You went down like a ton of bricks." Mevlyn smooths the damp hair from Danae's forehead.

Danae sits up. "I'm okay."

"I think we should get you back, maybe have you checked out." Jerome helps Danae to her feet.

"No." She refuses to wreck Mr. Sam's day. "I really *am* fine."

Malcolm steadies her and they walk to the boat where he helps her board. While the others smooth the dirt over Mr. Sam's trench and Mevlyn takes a few moments alone beneath the ironwood tree, Danae thinks again of her mama's funeral. Malcolm sits at her side, silent, holding her hand; his touch serves to anchor her to the present.

Jerome and Mevlyn climb aboard. Danae assures them once more, and Jerome cranks the motor. The rest of the trip downriver, nobody speaks. They beach on the same sandbar where she and Malcolm had enjoyed time. As the day continues, the mood lightens and the gloom surrounding Danae burns off like morning mist over water.


"**I** don't interfere with your life too much, gal. At least, I try not to." Mevlyn takes a chair beside her on the patio. The Tiki torches burn with citronella oil to chase away the mosquitoes. The last of the afternoon thunderstorm rumbles in the distance, moving on to share water with the next county. "I know you're carrying something hurtful inside of you. We all do."

"I'm sorry I ruined today."

"Sam was one who believed in letting bad out so it could bleach in the light of day. Seems to me, you did him an honor. Whatever you have trapped inside your heart can't be good for you. I think maybe you opened the floodgates today. And that's not a bad thing, gal. Sam would be happy about it."

Danae stares at the back yard with its whimsical chimes and metal art. Some might find Mevlyn's version of decoration gaudy. To Danae, the effect is magical.

"Another thing—I know you've been concentrating on Sam and me for some time now. I think you need to get out and have yourself some fun with folks your own age. Not that me and Sonny don't relish your company. We do. But I'm fine to be left alone a bit, and I want you to live your life. Agreed?"

Danae nods.

"How about I pour us both a nice tall glass of peppermint tea?" Mevlyn stands.

"Too hot for coffee."

"My thoughts exactly."

She watches the old woman shuffle inside. The fact Mevlyn cares, yet doesn't demand to know what fuels her demons makes Danae love her even more.

# Twenty-four

**M**evlyn spends a few minutes as she does every morning since Sam died—sitting in his favorite rocking chair on the back porch, looking out across the yard Danae now cares for as he once had. She pulls a life review. A detailed one.

The Wash-Away won't suffer for a few minutes. It'll be right there, waiting for her keys to jangle the lock.

People understand. They do. Grief deserves pause.

She has a good number of years to review. No need to rush.

Mevlyn's so honest with herself, she has to stop and apologize to Sam's spirit every now and again, especially for not telling him some of the secrets she's wedged so far back inside, she has to claw to get them to surface.

She wasn't what folks referred to as *pure* when she married Sam— not by some rash act meant to defy morality. But who would believe a teenager who'd been bounced from one kin's house to another until she was old enough to jump a southbound Greyhound?

Looking back, she should've been appreciative for a roof and food and clothing. She wasn't cast onto the streets after her mother died. Mevlyn never knew her father. Some said he was in the service, a fine and honorable man. Her mother didn't marry him—her wise choice or his lack of concern, who knew?

Mevlyn's extended family wouldn't answer her questions. She eventually stopped asking. What difference did it make? Her parents were erased from her life by the time she was seven. The only picture she has of her mother is the one saved inside her head: a dark-haired woman with a slight build and kind hands. She can't bring to mind her face.

Nobody deeply cared for Mevlyn after her mother died. She was fed and watered like a houseplant, and told to "put up or shut up" more times than she could count. No matter which family she joined for a while, she was relegated to secondhand clothes and cast-off affection, and mostly ignored.

Until she turned thirteen and sprouted breasts.

One cousin Mevlyn never thinks of by name took notice. Initially, he wooed her with small favors—a piece of chocolate, a pilfered slice of pound cake, daisies plucked from a neighbor's garden. Mevlyn craved his attention. She took time to groom her wild curls, pinked her cheeks with pinches, and snuck dabs of vanilla to perfume behind her ears. She smelled of baking cookies.

The first time he slipped into her bedroom, they cuddled. Her skin warmed as much as her spirit. He stroked her arms and face. He kissed her cheeks.

For several nights—Mevlyn can't recall how many—he made her feel cared for in ways she'd never experienced. He urged her to touch him, too. And she did. His hairless chest. The way his hips jutted below his ribcage. Other places foreign to her.

Early, before the house stirred, he left her bed, back to the room he shared with a much younger brother.

Mevlyn touches her lips with two fingers and can almost feel that first kiss. *This is love*, she must've thought, being a young girl who'd never had it offered so freely.

Sonny stirs at her feet, jumps to all fours, and rips across the grass toward a squirrel. Unlike the babies with their round, trusting eyes, this one's a veteran. The rodent freezes in place and waits until the dog is within a couple of feet before scampering up the nearest oak tree. Barely out of Sonny's reach, it hangs head-down, flipping its tail and chattering a taunt. An enraged Sonny circles the trunk, lunging and barking.

"Get back over here and leave that critter alone!" Mevlyn calls. "Sonny, now!"

The dog takes one last leap at the tree, hikes his leg and pees a few drops, then scruffs the grass with his back legs. The squirrel observes, unimpressed.

Sonny trots back to sit at her feet.

Mevlyn wonders where that boy cousin is now. Could be dead. He was five years her senior.

All these years, has she blamed him with stealing her innocence? Yes. She has. Time to get real before she has to answer to some higher judge.

She wanted his touch. Neither of them measured consequences. All they knew—speaking for herself, but he probably felt the same—is how damn good skin felt next to skin. How that heat warmed you from inside and burst out, nearly making you lose your sanity. It didn't hurt a soul. And life was bearable.

Until she got sick. Every morning, dry heaving, barely able to hold down a bite of toast. The boy worried about her, tried to help as best he could. Her monthly stopped. Her middle thickened.

The nightmare escalated when she awakened deep one night to her insides seizing up. Mevlyn crawled to the bathroom and curled up on the cold tile, shaking. Warm blood leaked from her insides. She was surely dying.

Her aunt found her there the next morning. Then, spirited her to the doctor where she endured the humiliation of his cold-hand probing and questions.

Back at the house, nobody spoke to her. The *thing* was past, but the punishment loomed. The boy cousin was sent to stay with a neighbor. Mevlyn took her meals in her room.

When she improved, her uncle and aunt packed Mevlyn's few belongings in a brown paper bag and shuffled her to the next house, to an old, widowed great-aunt with no humor and the wrath of the Almighty on her side.

Mevlyn never saw the boy cousin again.

Blamed for every Bible-scripted sin, and more her elders made up along the way, Mevlyn kept to herself. She attended the church where her kin practically lived and vowed to escape both the cold weather and a family that had shown her little warmth. Two goals fueled her days and nights: graduate high school, and work any odd job she could land to scrape together enough cash for bus fare and a cheap place to sleep.

Beyond that, she had landed in Alabama with no map, no compass, and no game plan.

Mevlyn clicks her tongue to Sonny and pats herself. He hops onto her lap.

She thinks about Danae. What had caused that gal to leap from her old life at the same age Mevlyn had fled her own? Someone had ruined her too.

Melvyn understands being Purty-much Ruined. Before Sam sat down in that booth and ordered up coffee and a ham biscuit with a special twinkle in his eyes, she had grown used to wearing ruination like a shroud.

Danae's shoes pop the pavement in a familiar rhythm. Now that her caretaking duties are past, she runs early, before the heat and humidity build to life-threatening proportions. Shoe soles melt in the Southern inferno. People die.

Girly and Levon flank her, their tongues hanging out. Both have peed and pooped so they're content to be running companions. With the two pit bulls at her side, she feels safe, though from what, she's not certain.

Mouse is foremost in Danae's thoughts. Maybe she's coming at this wrong. If she approaches her sister like the new girl in a town small enough to have limited choices, like she's looking for someone to hang with, Danae won't send off weird stalker vibes.

So. Common ground. How does she find such?

Her feet thump. Her heart pumps. Her breathing comes out even. Given enough training, her body adjusts to regular exercise and responds without conscious thought, leaving her free to scheme and dream. If only it wasn't so danged hot, this would be more enjoyable.

"Sometimes you have to think like a politician," Mevlyn said recently after watching the nightly news. "If something doesn't go as planned, you have to figure a different angle of approach. Eventually, a crack will open and you can slide right in, as if you always intended to go that way."

Girly and Levon need their yearly exam and vaccinations. Might as well swing by the clinic and set up an appointment. Jerome and Malcolm gave her the go-ahead.

Common ground: concern for animals. Danae bobs her head and smiles.

She rounds the corner of the narrow side street. Lights shine in the clinic's waiting room. Danae consults her watch: 7:40 a.m. Perfect. The early drop-offs will be done and Mouse won't be overwhelmed, if Danae can finagle a way to talk to her instead of the usual receptionist.

She slows her pace and eases into a fast walk. The dogs look to her with questioning eyes. Both drag against their leads, the closer they move to the clinic. She opens the door and urges them inside. Levon whines. Girly lowers to a sit. The place smells of disinfectant and blended animal scents. To the pups, it must reek of fear, bad memories, and being poked and prodded. Danae crouches and gives each dog ear rubs, speaking in a low, reassuring tone. Girly heaves a deep breath and stands, allowing all three of them to enter.

Instead of the usual receptionist, Mouse appears at the sliding glass window after Danae rings the buzzer. To Danae, she barely speaks, but the dogs get an enthusiastic *good morning*.

This is crazy. She should come out and say, "I'm Danae. Your sister. You can stop pretending. It's okay. I have found you, but that doesn't mean I've come to drag you back to that place."

The direct approach never works with Mouse. Danae's seen it before. How her sister curls into herself like a slug sprinkled with salt. Slow and subtle—that is the key.

"Hey, Carrie. I'm Danae. Remember, I met you when I brought in Miz Mevlyn's dog Sonny? These are Jerome's dogs. I run with them most days."

"Yes. I've seen you."

Danae makes an effort not to show shock. Mouse is aware of her. That has to mean something. "They need their annual exams. I told Jerome I'd take care of making an appointment and getting them in."

Mouse sits down and consults the computer screen. "We have time this Wednesday, if you can drop them off early."

"Perfect."

Danae watches Mouse for any slight give-away. Sure, Danae's not the little sister any more, and her voice has deepened, but surely Mouse can still detect how her own kin stands inches from her.

"Is there anything else?" Mouse stands, turning toward the back of the clinic before Danae can answer.

"No. See you Wednesday."

Her reply meets blank air. Mouse is gone; she's good at disappearing. Barks and feline yowls echo from deep in the clinic. Her sister talks to creatures better than she does humans.

Danae doesn't need to urge Girly and Levon to vacate the waiting room. As soon as she pivots toward the door, they bound to the end of their leads, dancing in place with their gazes trained on the exit.

<h1 style="text-align:center">Twenty-five</h1>

Two days later, Danae slogs the final half-mile, Girly huffing on one side, Levon puffing on the other. The dogs fare better than her. She may pass out before they reach the end-point, the veterinary clinic.

At least the pups will be less energetic for Mouse.

"Call her Carrie, call her Carrie," she reminds herself for the fifth time in less than a mile.

When they arrive at the clinic, Danae doesn't need to coax them inside, nor does she hesitate. Frigid air greets them. The dogs flop down on the cool tiled floor. Danae considers joining them, then decides to take a chair instead. If Carrie/Mouse saw her sprawled out on the floor, she might think more than twice about claiming her as kin.

Danae rests for a moment before she forces herself to rise on wobbly legs and pour both dogs water in the provided bowls. She helps herself to a cup of filtered water from the tall cooler. Have to admire a place with such basic amenities.

Ten minutes pass before the glass reception desk window slides open. Danae whirls, hoping to see Mouse. Instead, Dr. Johnson greets her. In a couple of minutes, he ushers all three of them back to exam room four. Has to be a good sign, her favorite number, the date of Mouse's birthday in May.

"Sorry nobody was here to check you in," the vet says. He gives Girly and Levon a treat each. "My front desk person has an appointment in Tallahassee and my vet tech is out sick."

Mouse, sick? She never gets sick.

"Does she have a cold? It's too early for the flu, I think." Danae tries to keep the over-the-top concern from her voice.

"Stomach bug, she said. That usually runs its course within forty-two hours."

Mouse could eat nails and not get nauseated. Danae wonders if her sister is avoiding her.

"Now, I see here I'm supposed to catch these two up on shots and blood work." The vet looks to the dogs. "Who's going first?"

As if they understand the commitment, neither twitch.

"Fine. Make me decide." Danae looks both in the eyes. "Guess it's you, dude." Levon hangs his blockish head.

"Let's go get you weighed and get our blood samples." Levon accompanies the doctor, casting one last pleading glance toward Danae on the way out.

"Don't look smug," she says to Girly. "You're next."

Danae eases into the only chair and Girly rests her head across Danae's thighs. All of her careful scheming, and Mouse isn't even here. The thought of her sister with nobody to care for her makes Danae crazy. This won't happen once they move in together. She'll cook soft-scrambled eggs and toast the way Mama used to when Danae had a sour stomach. Danae recalls the acronym: BART—bananas, apples, rice, and toast—the four bland foods perfect for digestive illness.

The veterinarian returns and swaps Levon for Girly. Twenty minutes later, she's out the door, back into the heat, with two vaccinated, healthy dogs.

If only she can get Mouse to make good eye contact with her the next time. She's bound to recognize the deep brown eyes Danae shares with Daddy and with J.J, though Danae can't truly recall his eyes, only what she's been told. Mouse has Mama's build and startling blue eyes, the kind that mesmerize people, when her sister manages to actually look at them full-on.

Mouse will see it's her. Danae. The baby sister. And everything will fall into place.


Sonny yips and bolts toward the kitchen entrance, the way he does every morning to greet the running gal. Mevlyn hears the refrigerator door open and close.

"Miz Mevlyn!" Danae's voice rings out. "Where are you?"

"Back here!" she answers. Danae appears at the bedroom threshold with Sonny twirling at her feet. "Goodness, gal. You need to get yourself into the shower. Your face is red as a ripe tomato. I can see the sweat dripping off your nose from clean across this room."

"I guess I need to start earlier. It is god-awful out there." She chugs bottled water then holds the chilled container to her forehead.

"How was the doctor visit?" Mevlyn asks.

"Uneventful. A lot easier with two pit bulls than with one terrier mutt, for sure." The gal roams her gaze across the piles of clothing surrounding Mevlyn—on the bed, on the floor, draped across every parallel surface. "What's up with all this?"

"Me sorting through Sam's clothes. I swore an oath to him that I'd not put it off."

"But the Wash-Away's open."

"Yes, it is." Mevlyn picks up a pair of men's briefs yellowed with age and tosses them onto the growing pile at her feet. "I took Elvina up on her offer of a fill-in. This may take me all day, or even a couple of days. I aim to see it through."

"Can I help?"

"It's your day off. Surely you want to do something more fascinating."

Danae uses her forearm to swipe perspiration from her eyes. "Oh yeah. Like I can find *anything* fascinating around this town." She winks, then adds, "besides, 'it's a smart person who knows to ask for help.'"

"Fine." Mevlyn waves her off with one hand. Is this what happens if you have a kid—they spout back your pearls of wisdom?

Sonny watches Danae leave, then curls up for a nap on one of the discard piles. The dog could sleep anywhere. For that, Mevlyn envies him. She hears the shower running. In a few minutes, the gal returns, wet hair combed, in clean clothes, and carrying two glasses of sweet tea.

"What do you want me to do?" Danae asks.

"Go get some garbage bags and a couple of boxes. Oh, and grab a pair of scissors. I want to strip up some of these undershirts for rags. We can throw out what can't be reused. This pile is to be packed up for charity."

She points to one tall mound at the end of the bed—a gently-used mattress set supplied by Elvina, so the room wouldn't look barren after the rental company took away the hospital gurney. Bless her. Sometimes that woman could be a pure pest, but she cared about her townsfolk.

Like the special spots on the river, some pieces of clothing spur a story: Sam's favored dress suit, the one he wore when he took Mevlyn out for their last anniversary; his lucky T-shirt that he swore helped the fish bite; those gaudy tropical-print Bermuda shorts he bought in Panama City Beach, the year they actually took a vacation.

"You're going to throw this out?" Danae holds up a plaid flannel shirt pocked with holes.

"Sam used it for yard work. Nobody would want it."

"May I keep it?" Danae hugs the ragged shirt to her chest.

"I can't imagine why, but yes, if you want."

"It looks like one my sister used to have, of my brother's. She slept in it."

The gal's expression is so forlorn, Mevlyn aches for her. The brother drowned, Jerome reported, and it had to have been horrible. And the sister, gone too. If only Danae would open that door a crack . . .

"I plan to go through Sam's fishing gear after this chore," Mevlyn says. "Figured I'd offer it to you, since you and Malcolm have taken to fishing regular."

Danae's face shifts from melancholia to glowing, just that fast. "Oh, heck yeah!"

"We can reward ourselves with some Chinese food when we take anything we don't need over to the Goodwill in Tallahassee."

"Why not give it away somewhere closer?" Danae stuffs socks and underwear into a trash bag.

"While I'm in favor of allowing someone to get use from Sam's clothes, I don't think I'd do well if I saw a man strolling down West Washington in one of his shirts."

"I get that."

In a couple of hours, the closets in Sam's room and the master bedroom are clear of his belongings. Five boxes hold shoes, suits, pants, belts, and shirts. Two bags bulge with discards. Mevlyn keeps one lined all-weather jacket and two pieces of jewelry—the cufflink set he had worn on the day they married and his gold wedding band.

Danae stands at the closet door. "There's one more box up here. Want me to get it?"

Mevlyn steps beside her. "Guess it's time for that to come down, too."

Danae stretches to reach the small box. She sets it down on the bed and Mevlyn unties the twine securing the lid. From inside, she pulls out a tiny white gown trimmed in yellow embroidered flowers, and a crocheted cap and pair of booties.

"This was my baby girl's first outfit, the one I planned to dress her in when we brought her home. Only, she never got to wear it." Mevlyn doesn't try to staunch the flow of tears. "I sewed the gown. My mother-in-law did the embroidery and crocheted the cap and booties. They're so tiny, like our Cecilia was."

Danae reaches over and holds Mevlyn's hand.

"Sam and I wanted so badly to be parents. I'd had three miscarriages, all before I carried the babies less than a couple of months. The first one hit me hard, but the doctor assured me it wasn't unusual for a woman's body to repel that first baby. Soon as I felt up to it, we tried again. I got pregnant right off and was over-the-top happy. I miscarried in eight weeks.

"By the third time, I was not encouraged. I didn't share news of my pregnancy with anyone except Sam until I was showing so much, I had to. Didn't buy any clothes or start up a nursery either. Then I knew when months went by, this time was the charm. I was going to be someone's mama!" In spite of her tears, Mevlyn beams. "I went crazy, sewing up little outfits—of course, I didn't make any of them pink, in case the baby turned out to be a boy. People didn't find out about the sex ahead of time, back then."

Mevlyn trills her fingertips across the delicate stitching. "After it happened, my mother-in-law saw how hard I was taking it. She cleaned out all of the baby clothes and supplies we'd gathered, all except this outfit. She packed it up and shoved it way back in that closet. I didn't find it until some years later, when I got a wild hair one spring and cleaned out every closet in the house. If not for her, I would have nothing but a little grave marker to remember my Cecelia." She folds the gown and tucks it back into the box. "Guess it's time to let it go too."

"Why not keep it?"

Mevlyn closes the lid and wipes the glaze of tears from beneath her eyes. "The one thing that you'll come to understand as you get older—when a person leaves this earth, all of the material things he or she used during their stay will be picked over and either passed on or thrown in the trash. Who will want this? Nobody. Might as well be me who decides to move it along."

Danae reaches over and slides the box toward her. "I have an idea."

Mevlyn tilts her head.

"My mama used to make these things for some of the women she took care of, back in the nursing home. Like a frame, but not for pictures, and it was deeper."

"A shadow box?"

"That's it. That way, it can be displayed."

"I like that notion."

"Mama got them in the Walmart, I think."

"Your mother sounds like a good person."

"Yes. She was." Danae shifts her gaze away from Mevlyn. The set of her jaw tells Mevlyn not to pry.

Mevlyn changes the subject. "I think of how I would've been a grandmother by now, even a great-grandmother. Imagine."

Danae appears to shake off the reference to her family. "Why didn't you adopt?"

Mevlyn had often asked herself that. Why hadn't they? Because she worried about too many questions, about her upbringing. Yes, she could tell everyone the lies she had invented, but what if the adoption agency looked into her past? No, she hadn't killed anyone, but the way she'd been jerked from one home to the next might throw shadows on her ability to be a mother. Sam had assured her they wouldn't dig that deep, and that she was looking for boogers behind every bush.

Instead, Mevlyn became *Mama Mevlyn*. Every child that set foot in the Wash-Away became her instant family. She made herself content with that.

"Reckon I didn't think it out too well." Mevlyn motions for Danae to take the box. "I'd love it if you would make me one of those display frames."

"Trade you for a pot of chicken 'n' dumplings?"

"Help me get this mess loaded into the trunk of the car and I'll throw in a sour cream pound cake."

## Twenty-six

Danae wipes sweat from her eyes and imagines how wonderful it might be to live in Alaska or Oregon. She's seen pictures of both. Either would beat this. Summer in the Deep South is as close to hell as she wants to get.

To tease her mind from hot thoughts, she switches to her next dominant topic: Mouse. Is she afraid of Danae, and if so, why? Sure, Mouse must've hardened to survive since leaving Ala-dang-bamer, but a person can't overhaul their personality.

Without the thin fiber binding Danae to her sister, where will she go next? Another town. Another random job. Another dead end.

Nope, there's no time for that kind of thinking.

She attaches a new oil filter to the car on the lift and tightens just enough.

Mouse is her sister, her blood, and their future is limitless. Has to be. To believe otherwise would crush her. Danae swerves back to her plan, since the last vet visit hadn't gained ground. The other common tie—Jack Dixon. She needs to find the creep and somehow fall in with his troupe. Rich is a pampered moron, she knows little about Taylor, and then there's Gary. He's the only sweet spot, the good guy who doesn't fit into that clan.

Mr. Sam is gone. Mevlyn is sad, but strong. Her job with Mr. Hal is sound—he gives her more responsibility every week.

It's past high time to lasso Mouse into the decent life Danae has managed to cobble together.

The city sedan on the rack is an older Crown Vic, a classic police cruiser. Some of the officers she's overheard rag on the newer cars. They're cramped, slow on the uptake, and hard to get in and out of quickly with gun belts and gear. This vehicle belongs to the chief, and by golly, he swears he won't give it up until the wheels fall off.

With the car on the lift and her mind engaged in the standard oil change and lube, Danae doesn't pick up on the presence of another person at first. Mr. Hal discourages customers from hanging out in the pits because of liability. Some ignore the rules. If something lands on this idiot—a wrench, expelled fluids, or the whole dang car—don't come pointing fingers at her. On this point, she agrees with something her daddy used to say: there are more idiots than regular Joes anymore.

From her viewpoint, Danae can see from knees down on a pair of male legs, not bad-shaped, tanned, and toned. When the legs don't make a sign of moving clear to find someone better to annoy, Danae ducks from beneath the Crown Vic's chassis.

"What can I do for you—" Her automatic customer-pleasant chatter stalls.

"I'da know. What *can* you do for me?"

Danae feels the heft of the wrench in her palm. She could plant it between his eyes. The local Po-Po might consider that excessive. "Hello, Jack. What do you need?" She slips the wrench into her leather waist belt and wipes grease from her hands, then quickly adds, "Wait, let me rephrase that. Do you have a car to schedule in?"

"I got a slow leak in my front driver's side tire. Damn warning light keeps coming on."

"Those sensors can be a bit touchy." The newer models crammed in more and more techno prompts. Whatever happened to using common sense? Pick up a tire gauge and check the pressure every now and then, for Pete's sake. If it's low, air it up. Though, Danae admits, the back-up camera feature is great. Not like she needs one on her cycle, but they sure make backing a vehicle in a parking lot less risky. People had grown so accustomed to them, they'd step behind your bumper, dependent on the car to save their ass from getting flattened.

"Can you leave the truck with us?" she asks. "I have two ahead of you, but I can work it in afterwards. Could be a bad sensor. If that's the case, I'll have to order the part, then remove the tire from the rim to replace it."

If Danae ever moves from a cycle to an automobile, she vows to locate an older model without all the electrical handholding. One less complex thing in her life.

Jack jangles keys in his pocket. "Couple of hours, maybe?"

"At least."

"Well. Okay. I can borrow a car, I reckon. I gotta get over to Tallahassee."

"Leave your keys at the front with Mr. Hal." Danae watches him turn toward the office. "Hey, Jack, before you go . . ."

He swivels to face her.

"Y'all still getting together a group up at the lake to—"

"Socialize?" he adds. "Yeah. We pitch a little campfire and pass around a beer or two and . . . other things."

The way he eyes her when he says *other things* creeps her out. "I might like to join up."

"Town's closing in on you, huh."

"I can only watch so many *Gunsmoke* reruns."

"Lemme toss these keys to Mr. Hal and I'll get some paper, draw you a map. The landing where we meet isn't easy to find."

His gaze runs up and down Danae until she is tempted to check that she's still clothed. "Be good to have a little fresh blood with us. Oh, and don't forget to hose down with bug spray. We have the fire going, but the gnats and skeeters are legend."

Jack oozes across the shop and enters the office. He thinks he's hot, which makes him *not*.

Danae ducks beneath the Crown Vic and rechecks the oil drain plug and the oil filter. Jack rattles her so much she can barely think, but being a sloppy mechanic is not an option.

Mevlyn glares down the line of dryers. Three on the fritz. Just like that. Amazing how a thing can be perfectly fine one moment and perfectly *not* the next. Number six and four of the regular dryers and her own number one reserved dryer, blowing with no heat. If she could rig up a pump to send the outside air into the drums, that would work. It's another ninety-five degree day with air soggy enough to wilt a beauty queen's hairdo the second she steps out the front door.

"Lord help!"

She snatches up the phone and her number-file box, grumbling. It's as if every dadgum thing is trying to break at once. Even back at the house, where the kitchen sink faucet drips, one of the stove elements is out, and the drapery rod in her bedroom hangs by two stripped screws.

Add to that, Danae's acting stranger than usual the past few days. Staying out to all hours. Smelling of stale alcohol. Keeping Mevlyn at arm's length. Sure, she wants the gal to have some fun, hang with young folks, and make friends. But what sort of friends is she making?

Mevlyn's so accustomed to worrying, she plugs in Danae where Sam used to be, and ramps up her anxiety until she imagines all manner of terrible scenarios. What it's like to be a parent, she supposes. No wonder most of them turn prematurely gray and look like they've been beaten senseless.

This keeps up and she'll be the one with loose screws and even more gray hair.

She presses numbers and waits. Third ring. "Hey, Butch. Mevlyn. Again. I got three dryers wonky and a washer with a slow leak."

Mevlyn waits while the repairman explains his already-packed work schedule.

"Next Monday?"

He stammers through a complex apology, having to do with his wife's aunt's surgery or some such, plus one of his best workers with a second DUI. Her ears shut down after that.

Bottom line: things will be bumpy at the Wash-Away. People, including her, will just have to deal with it.

One of her regulars stands at the counter. His sheepish expression tells her he might have some aggravation to add into her day. She firms up the repair date and returns the handset to its base.

"What cha need, Carl?"

"Miz Mevlyn. I hate to be the one to tell you . . ."

Her one last nerve gives up. "Spit it out. I'm aging by the second."

"The air conditioner is making a strange noise." He offers up sympathy with raised eyebrows and his hands tented together as if he might break out in prayer. "It doesn't seem to be putting out cool air."

"Good God Almighty." Mevlyn rounds the counter, barreling down the same path she's walked so many times, she's worn a dull rut. Sonny trots in her wake. "Like I have time for this."

She discovers the error of careless speed the second her balance fails in front of washer four, where the water draining from washer five rivers the tile.

One second she's upright, pissed, and on a mission. The next, she's staring up at the stained acoustic ceiling tile. Sonny barks and circles, then launches into the high-pitched keen he uses for complete disaster.

"Oh my goodness! Miz Mevlyn!" Carl hovers over her. "Are you hurt?"

"Let me take stock." Everything moves when she sends the signals. Her left leg throbs.

"I should call 911. That's what I'll do."

"No. You will do no such thing. Help me sit up."

By now, other patrons surround her, a moat of concern. With assistance, Mevlyn rises to a sitting position. She reaches up and pats her head, amazed that she didn't crack her skull on the hard tile.

"I want to stand up."

The group pulls in different directions, ineffective. "Wait. Just a couple of you, one on either side. I feel like a rope in a tug-of-war."

With their help, Mevlyn rises to her feet.

"Can you walk?" Carl, who's appointed himself the chairman of the aid committee, clutches one arm.

When she moves, sharp pain shoots through her lower left leg. "Well, ain't this a fine fare-thee-well. I think I've sprained my ankle."

"I can drive you around to the clinic." Carl shoves his hand into his pocket and brings forth a ring of keys.

"I reckon that's a good notion, if you don't mind. Only, I need to tend to the shop."

The two women regulars agree to watch the business.

"And will someone step over to Mr. Hal's and let Danae know? Don't scare the bejabbers out of her. She can come over after she gets off and close up here."

Sonny whines.

"And if one of you will take Sonny to my house, I'd greatly appreciate it. The back door is not locked."

Leaning on Carl, Mevlyn manages a slow hopping pace. She gathers her purse and they move to the parking lot where he settles her into the passenger side of his subcompact and hurries to get behind the wheel.

"Don't get us killed getting there, Carl. It's not a wide-screaming emergency."

When Mevlyn looks down, her left ankle is deep red and twice times its normal size. She eases the shoe from that foot, praying to every angel on the docket: *Please, please, don't let it be broken.*


"**M**evlyn. Mevlyn Jenson." Danae sucks in a breath. "Where is she?"

"And you are . . .?" The clinic front desk lady gazes at Danae with uplifted brows.

"Uh. I live with her." Danae grapples for a title to get her past the battleax gatekeeper. Yeah, she's a large woman, but Danae can take her if necessary. But no, resorting to blows is her daddy's first line, not hers.

"I can't give out information on a patient if you are not a family member. HIPPA regulations."

Danae girds for a full-on verbal battle. Before she can speak, a nurse steps up to the front desk and smiles. "Danae, right? Miz Mevlyn's been asking for you." She tips her head to the left. "Go to the door. I'll buzz you inside."

Just that fast, she's in. And nobody had to bleed.

The nurse in light blue scrubs motions to her. "This way."

Danae trails the nurse down a short hall and into Exam Room Four. Four, her favorite number, her mother's, too. Bound to mean everything's okay.

In the room, Mevlyn reclines on a paper-covered, padded table. Her features scrunch with pain, then shift to relief when she sees Danae. Resisting the urge to cry out, Danae scuttles to stand beside the table. Mevlyn holds up her arms and Danae leans down for a hug.

"Shore glad you're here. They're threatening me with all manner of bodily harm."

Danae spins, searching for whoever *they* are.

"Relax, gal. I was just attempting to lighten up this mess I've tripped myself into."

"They said you fell and it was bad."

"Bad. Not fatal. Take a breath. You look like you're about to pass out."

Danae wills her shoulders to lower.

"Seems I busted my leg above the ankle."

"Ah, jeez."

Mevlyn shifts on the table. The paper crackles. "Danged if my butt don't hurt worse than the leg. This ain't the most comfortable bed."

Danae backs up and sits on the edge of a vinyl chair. She reaches to clasp Mevlyn's outstretched hand.

"Now that you're here, they'll let me go home with an air cast and ice bags, probably a prescription for pain medication." Mevlyn pauses, frowns, and adds, "I hate to take that stuff. Binds up my bowels."

"Air cast. Does that mean no plaster one?"

"They'll be calling me up from the Orthopedic Hospital over in Tallahassee, the doc says. I'll have to get over there for a regular cast. Used to be, it was one-stop shopping. Not nowadays. Nope. Every dadgum body part has its own doctor." The old woman shrugs. "Guess I need to thank the Good Lord I didn't bust up my bad hip. I'd be getting a replacement sooner than I want."

Danae thinks. "Okay, so I can—"

"All I need you to do is get to the house and fetch my car. Elvina's already called up here to let them know she's on task with everything else."

This Elvina lady is like a fairy godmother, a nosy one.

"By now, Elvina's lined up folks to hold down the business, probably has a casserole or two on the way." Mevlyn smiles. "By tonight, you and me both will be on the prayer lists from here to Indonesia. Before the internet, Elvina was confined by geography."

Danae's mind races. What to do first, next, then . . .

"One step at a time. You fetch the car. I'll be waiting right here. I imagine they'll round me up a set of crutches."

"Oh no they won't." The familiar authoritative voice causes them to turn toward the door where Elvina Houston stands, her arms crossed. "I got you a wheelchair lined up to start off. We'll see what you need after that."

Heaven help anyone who crosses that woman. Yet, Danae's glad Elvina's on their team.

"I got the Olds parked outside the door with the ramp. I'll carry both of y'all to the house. My friend Piddie used to say my back seat's big enough for a rugby team."

# Twenty-seven

**August 6, 2010**

Danae hesitates beside Elvina Houston's kitchen door.

"Go on now. I'm fine." Mevlyn flips a shoo-hand in her direction. "Spend some time with your friends."

"I'm here with her, dear. I have Netflix DVDs, popcorn, and junk food." Elvina Houston sits in a chair near Mevlyn's, holding the TV remote like a magic wand. "Y'all need a break from each other."

Danae opens her mouth to offer a rebuttal, then decides against it. Elvina's assessment is true. For the past two weeks, Danae's done nothing outside of working at the shop, watching over the Wash-Away volunteer staff, cleaning house, cooking, taking care of Sonny, and helping Mevlyn bathe, dress, grocery shop, and visit doctors' offices. Usually good-humored, Mevlyn snaps often and issues orders. After dealing with her own mother's illness, Danae grasps the frustration and keeps her comments and backtalk at bay. Still, their relationship tugs at its tethers. Mevlyn's worn out. So is Danae.

Danae holds up her hands in surrender. "I have the phone with me in case you need me. You'll call, right?"

Elvina's lips lift. "I have you on my contact list, m'dear."

Good to know she rates with the official head of Chattahoochee. If anything were to happen to Mevlyn . . . Danae stalls the worry train before it can build steam.

When Danae steps outside, the stubborn humidity and heat slam her. How she wishes it was September, a time when some folks up north anticipate hot chocolate and colored leaves. But it's not. It's August and the Deep South clings to summer like it does Confederate flags and pig lard. For sure, when the day comes when she can afford to leave, she'll go somewhere it never peaks the eighties.

Right. With what she makes, she has more of a chance of chilling inside a Walmart.

The sun streaks orange across the sky by the time she steps from the convenience store Mevlyn calls the Stop-N-Rob. Showing up at the party spot with brewskies in hand has to win her points. Does Mouse drink? Danae thinks not. More so than her, Mouse would veer from intoxication.

She straps the six pack to the cycle with a bungie cord and pulls out the updated map Gary had sketched for her a couple of days back. The meeting spot shifts periodically to keep local law enforcement from crashing the party. This one is across the river near Sneads, a small town west of Chattahoochee. The abandoned power plant hosts some of the best, and worst, throw downs.

Danae carries a multi-tool, its one thin blade sharpened to a shine. Not as lethal as a gun, but she can at least slow down anyone stupid enough to come at her.

A couple of miles past the Victory Bridge, Danae turns south onto Florida Power Road, closely paralleling the winding route of the Apalachicola River. As she approaches the site of the Florida Power Plant, she slows. From the road, she sees no cars, but Gary filled her in on this point: everyone pulls into the woods to avoid easy detection. She drives as far as the terrain will allow, then dismounts and pushes the cycle into a stand of small oaks and pines. The musky smell of dead, freshwater mussels floating like popcorn in the overwarm river water hits her nostrils. Danae removes her helmet and wipes sweat from her face and neck with a dampened bandana; Antoine used to give her shit about wearing it, said it made her look like an outlaw cowgirl.

She unlashes the six pack and stands on the periphery of the property, ears tuned to the early evening opera of crickets, frogs, and a few remaining cicadas. How she detests those dang insects, with their keening *see-see-see* call—enough to drive a person insane. Yet another plus for cooler temperatures. The infernal cicadas will pitch to the earth with fading death rattles, silenced until the next generation emerges to torment human ears.

Beyond the cracked asphalt parking lot, she spots the shadowed outlines of trucks and a low slung sports car. Curious, she checks them out. The dark, older truck belongs to Gary. The other pickups, she doesn't recognize. She shakes her head over the corvette. What kind of show-off idiot would drive such a fancy piece of metal to a backwoods party? Easy answer. Hey, if you're not paying for the insurance and body work, who cares if tree branches spoil the paint job?

"Rich, you asshole," Danae mumbles. "It's handed to you on a silver platter, and you don't appreciate it."

Barely a three-quarter moon tonight. She flips on the cell phone's flashlight. To the far right of one listing tin outbuilding, Danae follows a narrow path that leads toward the river's edge. In a few minutes, the low flicker of a campfire shows through the underbrush. Danae halts, sounds three short whistles, waits for Gary's whistled reply, then continues until she steps into a small clearing.

Gary greets her and motions her to a vacant spot on his ground cloth. "Wondered if you'd show."

"Told you I would if I could." Danae scissors to a sitting position and swings her head to take in the group.

Rich half reclines, his arms slung around a petite girl with hair so bleached, it glows white in the campfire light. Taylor sits with head hung low, his body rocking side to side—drunk or high, hard to tell. Three more guys hunker with their arm candy. No Mouse. No Jack either. One disappointment, one blessing.

Danae breathes out a sigh and snaps a beer from its plastic ring-tether. She hands the rest of the six to Gary. The pop-hiss of opened cans joins the snap from the kindling fire. Someone passes a lit joint. Not a great idea to drive a cycle after too many beers. Danae decides to sip one slowly and take a couple of tokes to hone down her edge. By the time she gets ready to drift home, the buzz will fade to a safe level. She hopes. Gotta fit in with the group if she expects to get close to Mouse. If she's not at this particular powwow, she may attend the next. Better chance of talking to her here than at the vet's office. That's clear, even if nothing else is. Besides, what more is there to do around here other than watch reruns of old westerns?

"Where's your boy?" Rich's words slur.

The dude's toasted. Only a matter of time until that shiny corvette fishtails into a twisted hunk of useless metal and plastic. Shame. If she owned it, she wouldn't even crank it after a sip of alcohol.

"My *boy*?" Danae can't resist the volley. She accepts the joint Gary passes her way.

"You got a thing for that dark meat, don't cha?" Rich chuckles low.

"Give it a rest, Rich," Gary says.

Taylor makes a weird mooing sound. Nobody seems to notice, or care.

The blonde giggles. Was she Rich's cheerleader squeeze in high school? Probably. Danae knows her type. A plastic-doll cutie. Dressed in the latest fashion-disaster knock-off. Barely a hundred pounds if that. She doesn't shine with the aura of someone born into wealth—good reason to glom onto a male who does. Sad. Like so many others, she'll learn the hard way. Those titled boys rarely settle down to one woman—and if they do, it's to a porcelain doll from their own social stratum. For now, this girl has her sights set to Absurd High, level 10.

Danae takes a deep drag from the joint before passing it to the couple next to her. It's a mystery why Gary hangs out with these goons. Then again, choices are limited in this town.

"Here." Gary hands her a can of bug repellant. "Better hose down. You'll be okay next to the fire, but the second you step away, the mosquitoes will sound the dinner bell."

Danae starts to remind him how she's from the South and has provided a feast for every kind of biting insect imaginable, but decides instead to take the offered spray and leave off the side order of snark. Rich will feel the necessity to chime in and she's not in the mood for his crap. Feel good and relax—her goals for this evening, since catching up with Mouse tanked. That, and make it back to Miz Mevlyn's alive with the cycle intact.

The beer and pot steer emphasis away from her arrival. The guys swap fish and hunting stories. The females manage to insert a benign comment here and there, and giggle-hang on the males' every word. Danae remains silent, content to stare into the orange flames. Around them, night creatures stir in scuttles and snaps. Danae doesn't fear slithering creatures, or the hairy varieties on all fours. Two-legged mammals pose more of a threat. Her body uncrimps. Nobody in this little social club alerts her danger hairs.

Sometime later, Danae's bladder nudges and she lifts to her feet.

"You're not leaving, are ya?" Gary asks.

"Gotta whiz."

With her eyes now accustomed to the low light, Danae wobbles through the willows until she's well away from the clearing, drops her shorts and underwear, and hunkers over the sand. For once, she manages not to pee in her shoes. She redresses, relieved and jubilant.

The low rumble of flowing water draws her. She finds a narrow slip of dirt beyond the tree line and settles to listen.

Mouse, Miz Mevlyn, her old life back in Ala-dang-bamer—she holds each thought long enough to acknowledge it, then allows it to drift. Does it ever feel good to just sit and not stress, if only for a moment.

The brush stirs behind her. Danae jerks and instinctively reaches into her pocket for the multi-tool.

"Mind if I join you?"

Danae withdraws her hand and uses it to pat the ground beside her. "Saved you a spot."

Gary lowers himself. "Thanks."

They share the solitude. Only Mouse had this same ability to simply be with her, not expecting jabber to fill the space. Even Antoine—friend and confidant—felt the necessity to talk. Turning slightly, Danae studies the dim silhouette of Gary's face. Strong jaw, the suggestion of full lips. His scent joins the river's, easing into her mouth and nose—the smell of line-dried clean clothing touched with wood smoke and his distinctive male musk, perfumed with bug spray. His arm brushes hers. Her skin hums low.

"Gary?"

He turns at the sound of her throaty voice. "Huh?"

Danae leans toward him and their lips meet. She pushes him down; her mouth explores his. She pulls back long enough to shuck her shirt and sports bra, then lies beside him. Her fingers fumble with his shirt buttons while her mouth explores his neck.

"Wait. Danae, wait."

She levers away. How stupid, to assume. But he's a guy, right? What male wouldn't . . . "I'm sorry. I'm so sorry. I didn't know you were—"

"Were?"

"You know, not into girls."

His laughter comes out full. "Nope. Not the issue."

Danae sits up and brushes sand from her skin.

"No protection," he states.

"Seriously?"

"Not like I carry something with me at all times, in case." Gary pauses. "I didn't invite you out here so you'd have sex with me."

"Right."

Gary sits up and reaches for her hand. "God, Danae. Is that what you think, for real?"

"Guess I did."

"Don't get me wrong. I'd like it, I really, really would."

"So why not?" Danae doesn't wait for his answer. "Unless you have some disease. Do you?"

"No, as far as I know."

It's been so long since anyone touched her, besides a hug from Mevlyn. "Please."

This time, Gary moves first. Danae expects the usual rush to glory. Kiss. Fondle the boobs. *Slam. Bam. Thank you, ma'am.*

Gary eases her to her back with a gentle touch. He traces her face and neck with two fingertips, kissing the whisper trail left behind. By the time he removes his shirt, her every cell screams. Hormones cloud her brain.

Gary takes his leisure, kissing and exploring. He enters her in fractions, so slow she's tempted to grab him and speed things along. Those other times, she had taken the lead. Get it in, get to the climax, get off me. Suppose when it comes down to it, she's just as slam-bam.

Now, she allows Gary to strum her body in time with the river music.

Afterwards, Danae slips back to sit beside the fire ring first. Gary joins a few minutes later. Only Blondie takes note with a knowing smile and the flick of one perfectly painted eyebrow. The rest are either too high, too drunk, or too involved in their own hopeful foreplay to give two cares about anyone else's outdoor escapades.

Blondie leans over to Danae. "What was it like?"

"Excuse me?"

The blonde leans in and mouths into Danae's ear, "with that, you know, his fake leg."

What the hell kind of question is that? Danae tamps down the urge to set Blondie straight, but it's her first time with this group of misfits, not the point to openly insult one of them, if she plans to wiggle in far enough to get real with Mouse.

"It was, um, kinky." It wasn't. At all. Gary's leg, or lack of it, was the last thing she had thought about. Danae figures Blondie will enjoy the tease.

"O.M.G." Blondie's bloodshot eyes widen. She sneaks a glance toward Gary before snapping it back to focus on Danae. "Like, as in, how?"

Best to nip her new BFF before she wants a blow-by-blow. Danae holds one index fingertip to her lips. Blondie's lips make an *O*. She nods.

Danae may be a lot of things. Loose-lipped about her private matters is not one of them. In her family, she learned early: secrets are vital. But she's no part of that clan now. The realization causes an odd, untethered sensation, as if part of her has been amputated, yet still sends ghosted signals of what once existed.

Good riddance to bad rubbish, Aunt Sylvia used to say. Danae can hear her aunt's voice in her head; she must be the lingering, attached tendon.

Gary bumps her arm. She accepts the stub of a joint, considers, then passes it along. Where his fingers touch hers, Danae's skin reacts.

No. No. So *not* happening!

Attachments lead to entrapment. A casual friendship's okay. Beyond that, messy. Can't have ties here. She and Mouse will probably move to a new town, to start fresh. These people—even Malcolm, Miz Mevlyn, and Mr. Hal—are temporary players. Right?

The blend of pot and endorphins nudge her thoughts to wander deep into what-ifs. She and Mouse will have a small house, no larger than Miz Mevlyn's. A dog rescued from some shelter. Jobs that provide food, a roof overhead, and a few extras. They'll have a decent car. And travel. She's always wanted to see Maine, Oregon, Colorado, even Canada and Alaska.

Like dandelions seeds whooshed to the breeze, she and her sister will fly the highways. No crazy-drunk daddy. No worries. Just two sisters and a faithful pup, on the road.

Danae's so deep into the fantastical future, she fails to register the thump of footsteps and the others shifting to clear space for someone.

The ground vibrates with a heavy thunk. Danae jerks. Calls out, "Yah!"

"Wassamatter, dyke? Scare ya?" Jack leers from across the circle. The stack of logs he dropped sit at his feet. "You ain't much of a she-man if that's all it takes."

"Shut up, Jack." Gary's words ring with contempt and unmasked warning.

Blondie speaks up. "She ain't no dyke. She just *did it* with Gary." Danae's fresh ally glances from Jack and fixes on her.

Nobody speaks for a beat. The others watch, waiting. She must be the entertainment for the evening. Pitiful.

Danae can rip Jack's face off. Right now. She's taken on guys far bigger. Heck, she once laid Antoine out and he's twice the size of this redneck rooster. Instead, she palms the last beer of her six pack and holds it up to him. Hot beer now. At least she's not squandering an icy brewski on the blowhard.

Jack eyes her offering then snaps it up. He clicks open the pop top and slugs it all, crumples the spent can, pitches it into the shadows, and belches. One of the other guys—what was his name?—passes him a lit joint. Jack settles in across from Danae. The fire throws hateful shadows across his features.

Danae recognizes a fellow damaged soul. Not one to mess with. Like her.

The joint makes the rounds again. When Gary offers it to her, she passes it along. Time to let the buzz wane. No need to become a head injury stat.

The group falls back into boasts, belches, drinking, smoking, and the occasional fart accompanied by guffaws and high-fives.

Left to her thoughts, Danae wonders why she reacted so strongly when Jack dropped the logs. Something about that particular sound stirred her. But what? She's had a similar reaction before. Each time, Danae picks to uncover the reason behind the blind terror it elicits.

Loud sounds usually don't disturb her, thanks to years of tinkering with engines, and living with Big John. Yet, faced with this sharp noise, it took everything not to jump up and haul ass in any direction.

Her animal brain must've sent off adrenalin. Fight or flight.

No. That wasn't it. The sound reminded her of something vague—a melon colliding with a brick wall. Cracking, its soft pink insides scattering in glistening chunks. Some book she'd read suggested that traumatic events experienced before age eight caused the brain to store the memory in a way different from how it might in maturity. The underlying truth of those strange phobias, the ones you can't reason aside, lie deep and hard to exorcise. Hours of some expensive touchy-feely therapy and an opened checkbook—all it takes to reach the core event.

Maybe she's just high. That's it. Easy to imagine monsters.

Danae picks up a dead leaf and plucks at the brown webbing until only the skeletal veins remain. Who needs to imagine a monster, when a real one had haunted her life for eighteen years?


Mevlyn wobbles, then thanks the heavens she has her trusty walker. With God as her witness, she surely doesn't want to tip over and break another bone. Just a few days before getting the nasty, sweat-sponging cast cut off and a fresh walking cast put in its place, and she's tempting it to happen again. That Elvina and her hard lemonade! But it's Hades-hot and the chilled drink went down easy. Still, she should know better.

"You are a lightweight, Mevlyn. Never suspected such from you." Elvina steadies Mevlyn on one side.

"I seldom imbibe. And I can't recall the last time I was up after midnight, unless it was because I ate spicy food for dinner."

"We simply must get you out more." Elvina holds open Mevlyn's kitchen door and guides her inside. "I'd fix you some coffee, but it's too late for caffeine. Besides the fact I endorse green tea for its health benefits for us senior citizens."

"Who you calling a senior citizen?" When Mevlyn laughs, the wobbles hit her again. "Woo. I'd best sit down."

Elvina guides her to the den and onto the recliner. "Sit. I'll stay with you until you get sleepy."

Between the sugar and that generous splash of vodka Elvina poured in what she called a *sissified hard lemonade*, Mevlyn figures it will take more than counting sheep to help her. Elvina claimed she and the late, beloved head of the Little Old Lady Hotline, Piddie Longman, used to drink two or three of the benign-tasting concoctions during every FSU football telecast. By the time the contest reached halftime, the two were barely able to see the famous Marching Chiefs band on Elvina's big screen TV. Elvina claimed the libations made collegiate football much more than a spectator sport.

"I see your boarder isn't home yet." Elvina sets two tall glasses of iced water on the end table and settles down onto the couch. "Who's she run with, do you know?"

"She spends a great deal of time with Malcolm, Jerome's son. But they're out of town for a few days, up somewhere in South Carolina visiting someone Jerome used to work with." Mevlyn sips her water. Not a gut-bomb like that lemonade, but more her speed. "I try not to pry."

"Malcolm is a good kid, for sure. Still, I hear tell your girl hangs with some of those Dixon boys. Not the best company."

"Who Danae spends her time with is not my concern. She's over eighteen."

"Should concern you, Mevlyn. She lives under your roof. Why she still does is a mystery to me."

"Because I choose to let her stay, is why."

"I like Danae, don't get me wrong. She did a lot to help with Sam, and you. Still …"

"Listen to me, Elvina. Everyone deserves a second chance, or a third, or a fourth."

Elvina sniffs disapproval. She motions toward the shadowbox hanging near the couch. "When did you get that?"

"Danae made it for me."

"Those your baby girl's clothes?" Elvina shifts her gaze from the frame to Mevlyn.

"Yes. Our Cecelia."

"I didn't know you then. A bit before I moved to town. Piddie told me about the child. Such a heartbreak." Elvina looks toward the shadowbox again. "Nice of Danae to do that for you."

"Yes. She's a good gal."

"Bet her people would like to know she's alive and well." Elvina taps her painted fingernails—a shade she calls *Saturday Night Special*—on the frosted water glass with a distinct irritated rhythm.

"Don't you go sticking your nose where it doesn't belong."

Before Elvina winds up for a roster of reasons why Mevlyn should or shouldn't stress over Danae, the rumble of a motorcycle engine sounds outside, then the kitchen door opens. In a minute, the gal steps in.

"Hey, youngun. Glad you made it home safely. Hope you had a good time with your friends." Mevlyn watches the way Danae walks, as if her every step lands on egg shells.

"Y'all are up late." Danae pulls a cola from the refrigerator and joins them. A distinct sweet scent wafts Mevlyn's way, and the whites of the gal's eyes look like a roadmap of New York. Mevlyn's never been to the city, but supposes the comparison is accurate.

"Elvina treated me to a Netflix marathon. The best was about a fellow named Ben and his buttons."

"The *Curious Case of Benjamin Button*," Elvina supplies.

"Yeah. That's it. We've decided to get together once a week and watch a DVD. Just for something fun to do." She doesn't add the part about the hard lemonade.

Elvina leans forward, her gaze spearing Danae. "Where does someone of your age go for fun?"

"Here and there." Danae picks up her cola and stands. "Gotta head to bed. Opening for Mr. Hal tomorrow. Y'all don't stay up too late."

The gal breaks into a full case of the snorting giggles, though Mevlyn finds her statement only somewhat clever.

Mevlyn hears the flush of a toilet, then the snick of Danae's door. Elvina points down the hall. "You best keep an eye on her. Something isn't right."

Mevlyn agrees, but doesn't voice it. No need to set Elvina's tracking dogs lose. Not yet, anyway.

# Twenty-eight

**"S**o, how was your trip?" Danae shoves a catsup-loaded fry into her mouth. Around the table she and Malcolm share, the lunch bunch finishes up before heading back to work.

"Good. Sad. But good."

"Sad?"

"The guy we went to see has end-stage cancer. My dad's torn up about it. Think it brought up bad memories of what happened with my grandma."

Danae makes a *hmm* noise and waits for Malcolm to continue.

"Nana died of breast cancer when I was a little boy. I don't remember her all that well, but from what Daddy tells me, she worked three jobs to put him through college and the police academy."

Danae drags another fry through catsup.

"She couldn't afford health insurance. She died a few days shy of President Obama's inauguration—the guy who helped make that happen for a lot of people. One of the last things Nana said was how she wished she could see Barack Obama sworn in. My daddy assured her he would watch for the both of them."

"I'm sorry, Malcolm."

He nods and drops his gaze to the half-eaten French Dip sandwich on his plate. "Nana was caught up in the perfect storm. Bad disease, expensive meds, and no insurance. And she worked so hard."

Danae wishes she could pull a few comforting words from the air. Nobody found them to ease her pain after Mama died. She gets how impossible it is.

Malcolm picks up his sandwich and takes a huge bite. "Anything momentous happen in the 'Hooch while I was gone?"

Someone approaches their booth. Malcolm spots the person first, then Danae.

"Hey." Gary steps to the end of their table.

"Hey." Danae wipes catsup from her lips. Inside, her emotions play tug-of-war.

Gary and Malcolm exchange banter.

"Okay. So. See you around," Gary says. He walks off, toward a table where Jack Dixon sits opposite of Taylor.

"What's up with that, Danae?"

Her cheeks burn. "With what?"

"C'mon. Gary's a fairly benign guy. I mean, he did help us out when the boat broke down. Otherwise, I can count on exactly two fingers the times he's said more than a sentence to me." Malcolm dunks the edge of the sandwich into a bowl of meat juice and holds it to drain before biting down.

"He's okay. I guess."

"Your face is red as that moat of catsup." He drops the sandwich. "Oh my dear God in heaven. You and Gary? Wow. I go away for a few days and the earth tilts on its axis."

Malcolm sees through her like Antoine used to. Crap, crap, crap.

"Give it up, Danae. I'm all ears and no big mouth."

"So we screwed. What's the big deal."

When Malcolm lets out a hoot, others turn in their direction.

"Keep it down, will ya?" She sneaks a glance toward Jack Dixon's booth. Good. Gary is facing away from them.

"Your torrid affair is our little delight." Malcolm gnaws another hunk of French Dip. "Any sordid details you wish to share will be greatly appreciated and closely guarded, girlfriend."

"Nope. Some things are best left to the imagination." If he asks her about sex with a one-legged guy, she'll throw a fry at him, catsup and all.

Instead, he backs off. "We never hang out like this anymore, Nae."

Danae smiles. Malcolm is one of the few people who has given her a nickname. Antoine calls her by the first syllable of her name, though it comes out more like *Duh*.

"I get it. I do." Malcolm bites into an onion ring. His lips shine with grease. "I'm busy with classes and you're busy with work and Miz Mevlyn. Getting older is not as much fun as I thought it might be."

Danae doodles with her fry, twirling it in a pool of catsup. "I hear ya. It does have some perks." Like being able to leave Ala-dang-bamer.

"Do you ever think about having kids, Nae?"

Malcolm's question wallops her. "Didn't see that coming."

"Not, as in, *now*. I mean, some day."

"Never given it much thought." Actually, she had, but only in broad sweeps—she'll be the cool aunt to Mouse's children. Never for her own. No telling how many ways she might totally screw up a kid.

"I want a family, at least three, or five, or six." Malcolm's eyes take on the misty shimmer of tears.

"That's cool, I guess. Only, how? I mean, you don't have the necessary parts, and I assume, neither will your partner."

"Adoption, Nae. Of course." He studies her with a puzzled expression. "You don't approve of two guys raising children?"

"I think it's great. I just don't want any of my own. Before you start, allow me to emphatically state, I am not a maternal type. I missed out on that gene."

"Debatable. I've seen the way you coddle Miz Mevlyn, the way you take time to explain technical car issues to people. You are deep-down kind and patient."

"Gosh, Malcolm." Danae holds a hand over her heart, fingers splayed like a high-society lady's fan. "I appreciate your vote, but no kid's coming out of this girl. Nope. Though, I do enjoy the warm-up exercises."

Malcolm makes a show of astonished amazement. "Why Miz Danae, I nevah . . ."

The exaggerated plantation accent sends Danae into guffaws. Fellow diners turn in their direction. For a moment, she and Gary lock gazes.

Danae jerks her eyes back to look at Malcolm. She stretches for a deep, sultry tone. "The practice is like tasting silky dark chocolate, the kind you pay five times the amount you would at the Dollar Store. Oh my, how it ripples across your tongue and makes your heart go piddy-pat."

"Dear Lord. Stop. I'll have to sit in this booth until supper before I can walk out without a bulge announcing my smutty thoughts."

"I can dump my ice water on your lap. I would do that for you."

"Don't even."

They share another hearty laugh. How good it is to kid around, to talk to someone who makes her feel safe and accepted. On impulse, Danae grabs Malcolm's hand and kisses it lightly across the knuckles. He draws back, staring at his hand, then glances up to her.

Rich passes by their booth, Blondie on his arm. Perfect timing, naturally. He doesn't stop and speak, but his glare says it all. When they reach the table shared by Jack, Taylor, and Gary, Jack motions for Taylor to move. He shifts to a two-top nearby and stares down at his hands.

"You got to be careful, Nae," Malcolm says in a low voice. "Times have changed, but black and white still live in different worlds."

"Screw it." Danae wads up her napkin and casts it onto her plate. "I'll show affection when and where I wish. Nobody's running my life but me."

"You are a force, for sure." He tilts his head, studying her, then taps one thumb on his chest. "Whereas *I* am chicken-shit to the core. I don't want to bring down that bucket of hate over my head."

"Aw, c'mon. Not like someone's gonna jump from the bushes and toast a cross on your front lawn."

"You'd be surprised."

All Danae can do is stare and blink.

"The South may be covered with a drape of civility, but the hate is there, waiting for a good enough reason to pop out. I am no crusader. I don't plan on providing that reason."

# Twenty-nine

**"I**'m heading into the home stretch and this is *not* my real hair," Mevlyn confesses to her own reflection.

Sure do need to pick up a new mirror for the Wash-Away bathroom. This one's fogged and webbed with cracks. The misty surface acts like a soft-focus filter—these days, they would compare it to a Photoshopped image, whatever the heck that is. Good Lord, she guesses she might have to break down and learn to work a computer. Maybe she won't live long enough to be forced into techno-literacy. Danae kids her about struggling to answer the infernal cell phone.

"Nope. I'll stick to this worn-slap-out mirror. Thank you very much."

Age has a few perks. The way everyone hangs on your words as if you're oozing wisdom. The way she can embrace being "old school." How she can pull on her styled hair and paste on lashes. All, in the win column.

The only person who knows for sure about her crowning glory is Mandy Andrews, head stylist for the Triple C Day Spa and Salon. Like Mevlyn, Mandy holds a treasure ship full of info on many townsfolk, and she grasps the importance of discretion. Mandy might share some tidbit passed along by Mevlyn, but she won't tell a soul about the three wigs Mevlyn drops off for *freshening up* any more than Mevlyn would reveal secrets of Mandy's laundry. Now Elvina Houston? That woman could learn a thing or two about zipped lips.

Mevlyn uses a comb tiny enough for a fairy to cultivate her bushy eyebrows. When she was Danae's age, women plucked the hair thin and penciled in any blank spots. These days, fashion shines on eyebrows resembling twin wooly caterpillars, so thick and dark, they could be used to predict a hard winter.

A patch of stiff wolf hairs jut from her chin. Dear Judas on a pogo stick! She snatches a razor from the cabinet over the sink and mows over them. Hair sprouts from every dang place besides her head. Good thing sex is in the rearview. Her privates are as bald as the day she got pushed from her mama's womb. Then again, the young folks wax their nether hairs so she's in fashion in that respect, too.

Sonny waits on the other side of the door. Mevlyn bends and gives him a pat. What would she do without the little mutt? Dogs are the closest thing to angels. Unlike angels, they won't scare the bejabbers out of a person by popping up unannounced, glowing like the holy firmament. Him being a street dog, there's no clear way to predict his true age, or how much longer he'll be here to follow her every step. She pets him again. Sonny licks her hand, then putters behind her to the front desk and his nest of freshly-laundered rags.

The latter part of summer is a busy time at the Wash-Away. The heat won't break until end of September, or as late as November. Still, the optimist in some folks makes them drag out stored quilts, blankets, and comforters way too heavy for most machines, and here they come to the Wash-Away to refresh their winter bedding.

Mevlyn can launder the devil and half of his dark minions in her triple front-loader. By golly, by Jove.

"Well, there's my favorite officer." Mevlyn consults her faux-bejeweled wristwatch. Even if she wasn't near a time piece, she'd know it's two-thirty on the nose-tip. Jerome's on evening shift for six weeks, bless his heart. Even on his day off, he looks like he's been pitched in a washer and set on a fast spin.

"Hi, Miz Mevlyn." His voice echoes with lack of sleep and a wealth of aggravation.

Mevlyn waits until he fills his favored washer before commenting with her usual level of concern.

"I know. I know." Jerome holds up twin palms. "I look like forty miles of bad road."

"I don't know how you do it, switching from working days to nights then back again. Wears me out just thinking about it."

"Comes with the job." He settles into the chair opposite of hers.

"Anything you need to catch me up on?"

"Two more break-ins since last week. Nothing of worth stolen, mostly vandalism. It's as if the perp's getting jollies from outsmarting us."

"Your fancy video surveillance hasn't caught anyone in the act?"

"Hoodies." Jerome puffs out a breath. "Hoodies are the bane of my existence. Keeps us from seeing faces and hair color. Still, it's only a matter of time and luck until we snag the perps."

"No clue on who might be up to no good?"

"Sound ideas. But we have to snag them in the act or have proof. Law seems to side more and more with the offenders and not the enforcers."

They switch to casual banter. Jerome hears enough about the underbelly of humanity. Mevlyn figures interjecting a little harmless gossip helps in some small way. Her leg sends a nervy jolt and she jerks.

"You okay?"

"Fine and dandy, for the most part. Still a few healing pains. Can't wait to finally get this walking cast off, though it's a sight better than the first one. It takes me forty years just to cross my yard to this place. Speedy, I'm not."

"Festive sock you got there, Miz Mevlyn." Jerome motions to her knee high.

She tugs at the snug top band. The first time she pulled on the compression sock, Mevlyn felt like a trussed-up rotisserie chicken. Danae vetoed the bland tan, said it made Mevlyn look like a ghost granny, and insisted on painting patterns on it with different colors of permanent markers. The sock feels so dang good and her leg doesn't swell by the end of the day. Bound to help the other leg too, once she gets it free of plaster.

"I bought several pairs, found them in black, to go with my uniforms. I swear by 'em." Jerome smiles. "Don't make the mistake of putting them into the dryer. Ruins the elastic."

"Me in this business for over fifty years, and you don't think I read the how-to-care labels?"

Jerome stands and helps himself to a cup of coffee. "Sorry. I yield. You *are* the expert." He returns to his seat. "And I am the expert when it comes to keeping an eye out for this place and for you. Will you allow me and Malcolm to install that video equipment we talked about?"

"I reckon. But it'll have to wait a couple of weeks. Danae's decided to paint this building and I gave her the all-clear. We rode over to Tallahassee and got the paint already. Soon as that's done, you can hang enough cameras around the outside to turn the Wash-Away into one of them reality TV shows."

The days fall into a rhythm for Danae: run with the dogs, work, yard and house chores, shower, read a few pages of some novel, and drop dead-out asleep. Repeat, adding in a meal here and there, or some TV show at Mevlyn's urging. Saturdays offer a highpoint, sometimes starting as early as the wee hours of Friday for those others who don't work on weekends.

Painting the concrete-block outside of the Wash-Away building takes up the majority of recent days between the regular line-up time slots. Mevlyn chose the color after they looked at the corresponding sample card. *Fairy Dust*—one of the high-end paint company's Magic Series— appeared serene on paper but in reality, it comes out more like Oaf-nose Red with a solid punch of Pepto-Bismol. No matter. Mevlyn purchased five gallons of the custom-mixed special order; the original buyers must have seen the true shade and decided the fairies had gotten a bit heavy-handed with their dust. Danae grasps why those five gallons had been on extreme sale.

"The color is, um, eye-catching," Gary remarks at the week's movable party.

Around her, the air is heavy with smoke from a small fire and an abundance of shared joints. With the gosh-awful humidity still hanging in the air and radiant warmth stored by the dirt, Danae figures they could forgo a campfire that spits out even more heat. But at least it keeps the mosquitoes at bay.

Danae stares into the flames, noticing every spark and flicker, analyzing each flame tip for height. Her brain buzzes in a pleasant way after a beer and a couple of hits of homegrown weed. The dull ache between her shoulder blades subsides. Maybe if she made a serious enough case, Miz Mevlyn would allow Danae to sow a few pot seeds at the back of the vegetable garden. It could help the old woman's arthritis and improve her outlook on life at the same time. A case can certainly be made for medicinal purposes, to ease the pain from her ankle.

"Earth to Danae. Earth to Danae. Come in, Danae."

She blinks and gives up a delayed laugh. "Huh?"

Why doesn't Gary make up some nickname for her, like Antoine did? Dude is getting his sexual needs met a couple of times a week. If you like somebody enough to do all of that, you should at least get a *honey* or a *babe*.

Gary gives her shoulder a gentle nudge. "We were talking about that paint, remember?"

"Paint?"

"The one you're slapping on the laundromat."

"Oh. Right. It is—" The speck of her brain still functioning searches and lands on a suitable adjective, "intense."

Gary chuckles. Danae can't fathom the reason why, but she joins him until both crumble into rolling guffaws. They jostle on the leaves, colliding like uncontrolled bumper cars. Their laughter spreads to the others.

Across the circle, Blondie giggles once, then clips a clamp on it when she looks at Rich, who is busy *not* being amused. Typical. Blondie hangs on every sound coming from Rich. She gazes at him in a way that reminds Danae of Sonny mongering a chewy treat. Exception: Sonny gets the treat and Blondie probably will not, long-term.

Danae wipes belly-laugh tears from her eyes. Rich glares at her. Seriously, dude, what *is* your problem? Oh yeah, if he's not the center of attention, Little Lord takes offense.

*Little Lord.* Oh, that is a good one. Danae decides Little Lord will be her pet name for Rich, going forward. The nickname issue surfaces and her thoughts go wherever they take her. Okay, so if you like, or love, someone enough to give them a special name, does that also apply to someone or something you loathe?

"I'm going for a whiz," Gary says into her ear. He stands, brushes dirt from his cutoffs, and disappears into the darkness.

Wait.

Did he say *whiz?*

Danae corrals her thoughts.

Yessiree Bob, he did.

Hey, she and Gary might not call each other sappy, lovey-dovey names, but they do have a party-sex signal word. Danae does her best to allow a few minutes to pass before standing and leaving the fire circle.

Five steps into the quest, her bladder informs her, she really does need to whiz before she meets up with Gary. Danae angles away from the banks of the narrow cove and hustles several steps into the woods. Got to make this quick. No way she'll miss the best part of her day, heck her week.

She peels off her shorts and crouches before warning bells about poisonous ivy or lurking snakes have a chance to sound. Only thing she misses is toilet paper. Dripping dry, she hates it, but what else is there to do. She teeters, her ears tuned to the hum of insects and darker things.

Is that something crunching through the trees, a Florida panther, or a bear? Oh dear God. This might be one of those horror movie scenes, where flesh-eating bugs wait in the shadows, hordes of them, twenty times the size of normal.

*Paranoid much?* Danae scolds the stoned-stupid section of her brain.

Before actual swamp mosquitoes can zero in on her unprotected skin, Danae stands, inching up her shorts, though why bother when she'll be taking them off as soon as she finds Gary. A large moving object slams her chest. She loses balance. She lands with a thud. Weight grinds her into the dirt. Strong hands—Danae can feel them now—tug and rip her top and shorts.

She offers no resistance at first. Makes no sense. Gary's not into this kind of thing. He'd never force her, nor would he need to.

Now, Danae struggles against the hands. She's strong, but the attacker holds the advantage. Danae hard-arches her back. The movement dismounts the guy long enough for her to grapple for the multi-tool she'd slipped into her shirt before leaving the house. Normally, she stores it in her pants, but this pair of shorts has two blown-out pockets she hasn't bothered to mend.

The buttons are missing halfway and her shirt gaps open, but Danae locates the edges of the metal in its pocket.

She grunts when the man once again pins her. *Go limp.* That's it. Danae stops moving. That scent—that musky, insanely-expensive cologne—she recognizes it. *Think!* Jerome says so often when schooling her and Malcolm, *make yourself remember little details.* Those tidbits could mean life or death, and help authorities if you survive to relay them.

A knee shoves her legs apart. She feels his fingers fumble. Is he inside of her now? *Oh hell no!* She exhales, inhales deep, blows it out, then arches her back with doubled force. The guy wrestles to stay atop, but falters. In that instant, Danae nabs the tool, flips it open, shoves her hand toward the hard thing pressing against her thigh, and clamps down on one of the soft fleshy bulbs behind it.

"Ahhhhh!"

Danae holds firm. The multi-tool's pliers resist each jerk. She and the guy pitch and roll.

One last full-body shove and she's free. Her grip releases his privates with a sickening flesh-rending noise. His body makes full ground contact and curls into a ball. Danae listens. Animal whimpering, heavy sucks for breath, cursing. She picks out *dyke, bitch, slut.*

"You moronic ass-wipe," Danae leans down and spits into one of his ears, "you ever touch me again and I swear I will fucking kill you."

Danae runs, wild. Not like the guy can get up and haul ass after her. He's going to pull off a miracle just to stagger. Leftover adrenalin cranks up her pulse; her heartbeat pounds in her ears. Low vines rip dotted lines across her shins. Once, she stumbles and manages to catch her balance.

In a pool of moonlight at water's edge, Gary waits. Danae stops short. Only then, does she allow herself to fully react.

"What's wrong?" Gary wraps his arms around her and Danae leans in, sobbing, sucking in breaths.

"Get me out of here. Now!"

Without firing questions, Gary grasps her hand and they weave a roundabout path well out of sight of the campfire, to a thick copse of trees where his pick-up and her cycle wait. He motions her toward the pick-up and rolls her bike into a thicket, and they both jump into the truck.

"I'll come back later with a ramp and get your cycle." Gary cranks up and pushes the old truck hard. They bounce over downed sticks and washed-out dirt potholes until they reach the paved county highway.

As soon as he slams the truck into the highest gear, he says, "tell me what happened."

Danae hugs her arms across her chest. In spite of the balmy temperature, she shivers.

"C'mon, babe. Please."

"I was . . . he came at me, it was . . ." Danae chokes out a clipped sob. "Rich."

The engine whines. The mechanic in her worries about it being able to take the strain.

"What *about* Rich?" She barely recognizes Gary's voice. Dead-calm anger, white-hot. The kind that makes an easy-going person into a murderer.

Danae leans onto the door and allows the night air to rush over her face and neck. Bits of leaves and thorns poke through her shirt into her skin. She opens her mouth to speak, then clamps her lips together. Fresh tears flow.

They ride in silence for the three miles it takes to reach the Florida/Georgia line. Gary turns next to the Wash-Away, onto the driveway leading toward Miz Mevlyn's yard.

"Can we ride around a while, let me calm down before I go inside?"

"Sure." Gary stops and throws the truck into reverse.

They cruise from one end of Chattahoochee to the other, then take three more laps before Gary speaks. "You ready to go home yet? If not, I can—"

"I'm good."

This time, Gary makes it up the driveway and parks by the house.

Danae can't bring herself to kiss him, even touch his hand. All she wants is to go inside and scrub her skin until it turns red. "We'll talk. Gary, I promise. I just can't right now."

"Whatever you need, babe." His tone returns to its usual even tone. The ride has soothed him, too. "Call me. I'll come. No matter what time."

And he will. Danae owns the feeling wafting from him, and the matching one budding inside of her own heart.

Gary loves her. He actually *loves* her.

She leans hard into the old pick-up's handle and the door swings open. The hinges screech the way she wishes she could.

# Thirty

"Get up, gal." Mevlyn stands at Danae's bedroom door.

Danae groans, opens one eye. She covers her face with a sheet.

"Something bad has gone down at the Wash-Away. Get up out of that bed. I need you."

The sheet flips off and Danae rolls off the mattress. Her hair sticks up in wallowed spikes and her eyes are so puffy, the eyes show through narrow slits.

"You look rough."

"Ugh."

"Get dressed. I have coffee brewing." Mevlyn turns and clumps toward the kitchen. Hopefully, caffeine will help her understand what she just saw outside on her building. She hears the bathroom door open and close, a flush, water running, then off, and the door opening. Danae slouches into the kitchen.

"Must've been a wild night. Your face is pure torn up." Mevlyn looks Danae up and down. "And look at your legs and arms! Good Lawd, did you tangle with a briar patch?"

"Something like that." Danae pours herself a cup, adds sugar and cream, and sucks it down like life depends on coffee. Mevlyn is in that same state of mind, though she suspects, for different reasons.

"I made us both a ham biscuit. We need to eat a bite before we face the hot mess."

Danae squints her swollen eyes. "Huh?"

"Sit." Mevlyn points to the kitchen table. Danae grabs up the plate of ham biscuits and her coffee, then slides into one chair. Mevlyn picks up her cup and joins her. "Soon as we eat, we got to call Jerome."

The events of last night—whatever they were—paint concern on the gal's face. Like she knows what's coming, but how could she, unless she was somehow involved. Hurts Mevlyn's soul to even consider such.

They eat and drink without talking. In less than ten minutes, Mevlyn and Danae head toward the Wash-Away. Sonny pads beside them. As soon as Danae spots the side of the pink building, she stalls, wide-eyed and open-mouthed.

"Think that's bad? Wait until you see the wall facing the street." Mevlyn gives Danae a nudge.

This early on a Sunday morning, few people stir. Thank goodness. Still, there won't be time to cover up the vulgar drawings and obscenities sprayed across the fresh paint. When folks pass on their way to Sunday school and church . . . Mevlyn halts the chain of concerns. Yes, it will be the talk of the town, probably even make the *Twin City News* front page.

"What the—" Danae starts when they reach the curb and get the full view.

"Exactly. I found this when I let Sonny out for a little stroll. You were snoring, so I didn't want to wake you up to take him." Mevlyn turns from her scrutiny of the building to face Danae. "What time did you drag in last night?"

"Wait. You think *I* had something to do with this?"

"I can't fathom why you would. But I need a time frame. Did you see anything then?"

Danae shades her eyes from the lemony morning sun. "Probably after one. I'da know exactly. Gary drove me home."

"And everything was okay then?"

"I know we would've noticed this. I mean, the streetlight's a beacon."

The words scrawled across the blocks shout out in oversized letters: *Dike, Niger-lover, Ho.* "Whoever it was can't spell worth a damn," Mevlyn says.

The drawings are elementary. Several appear to be erect male body parts and one is an elongated diamond-shaped slit with curly lines radiating from the edges, the artist's crude female representation. The ones that scare and anger Mevlyn more than the others combined are several large, bold swastikas, the universal sign for bigotry. While most people can identify the hateful slashes, Mevlyn lived through the years stained by Hitler's madness.

"All of the windows are broken." Danae's tone switches from incredulous to flat.

"Why would anyone do this?" Mevlyn pulls the cell phone from her apron pocket and hits one of the speed dial icons. "Hey, Jerome. Sorry to bother you, but you need to come to the laundromat soon as you can."

She taps to end the call after a brief conversation. "Wish I'da listened to him earlier, about those security cameras. I was going to let him install the system soon as you finished the trim work."

"I think I have enough paint left to fix this," Danae says. "I'll start on it right away."

"Not until Jerome takes evidence photos," Mevlyn states. "The person, or people, who did this gonna pay." She puffs out a sigh.

Danae's lips set in a firm line. Mevlyn's seen the gal determined, frustrated, and stone-drunk. She's never seen her so angry.

A patrol car pulls alongside the curb and Jerome jumps out. "Woo-wee." He strides to stand beside them, leaning down to give Sonny a quick pat. "Who in the world would want to do this?"

"That's what we're gonna figure out." Mevlyn plants her hands on her hips. "And you best catch them before me or Danae do." If she had spurs, she'd clank them together.

"Let me grab my camera. Promise me you won't take things into your own hands, Miz Mevlyn."

Mevlyn doesn't answer. Seems wrong to outright lie to a policeman.

The *Twin City News* editor pulls her SUV to the curb behind the cruiser. She emerges with a camera lashed around her neck.

"That didn't take long." Mevlyn forces a neutral expression and does her best to keep her eyebrows from doing a dance. Have to feel sorry for the journalist. She'll be hard-pressed to take one shot that's clean enough for a family-oriented, small-town paper.

"Come on back." Jerome meets Danae and Mevlyn at the secured door leading to the inside of police headquarters. They step past the threshold and follow him down a long hallway.

Danae takes it in: the gray walls, shiny tile floors, everything ordered and industrial. Weird, being on the right side of the law instead of being kin to a man who ended up in a building similar to this on more times than she can count.

"Did one of your other cameras point in the direction of my place?" Mevlyn asks.

"No. But what we did capture might help us." Jerome steps into a room with a long table surrounded by chairs and motions for them to take seats. He sits nearby and enters a code into an opened laptop. A grainy black and white image appears on the flat screen monitor attached to one wall.

"We best make this snappy. I left Elvina in charge at the Wash-Away." Mevlyn gives Jerome a stern look. "Heaven only knows what I might go back to."

"I'll keep that in mind," Jerome says with a nod. "The same night the Wash-Away was vandalized, two other businesses got hit. We think, by the same perp."

"I have never been one to believe in coincidence," Mevlyn states.

"Nor have I." Jerome forwards the video and freezes the frame when a hooded figure appears. "Same height and build as the person who tore up the four other stores a few weeks back. Figured you could review this with me, see if something stands out. Look for mannerisms, anything distinctive that catches your attention." He taps a key and the hooded figure moves.

Danae focuses on the person. Tall. Broad shoulders. Football player build. Especially, the shuffling walk. Hesitant, lurching as if in pain. "Huh."

Jerome pauses the video clip and glances in her direction.

It all fits, like the teeth of a closed zipper. The drawings, the hatred. Someone mean enough to use the words *nigger* and *dyke* and *whore*, and ignorant enough to misspell them.

"Got something?" Jerome asks.

Danae uncrosses her arms. "Yes." Means she will have to share at least part of what happened. She looks to Mevlyn.

"Go on, gal. You got anything to say, do it. It's me and Jerome here. Nobody else needs to know."

"No reason to be afraid." Jerome watches her. "You have my word, Danae. What is said in this room will go no farther."

Danae holds off, as if one more minute will make a difference. No matter about her own bruised feelings, but Miz Mevlyn, her opinion matters.

Mevlyn reaches over and rests a warm hand on her shoulder.

"I think it's Rich."

"Reason?" Jerome prompts.

"That person in the video is walking like he's hurt."

"Yes, I took note of that."

"And Rich *would* be."

Mevlyn gives her shoulder a gentle squeeze. "Go on, gal. Speak up."

"I know because about an hour before that time stamp, I practically wrenched off one of his balls."

Jerome doesn't speak. Mevlyn sits, her mouth agape.

"Will you tell us what happened?" Jerome says.

His tone registers with Danae; Jerome's in full cop mode. She outlines the encounter with Rich, glazing over in spots.

Jerome drums a pencil on the table. "You can press assault charges, Danae."

"My word against his. Nobody saw what went down. Everyone was pretty high."

"This is going to sound rough, no matter how I put it." Jerome leans forward, his face grim. "Did Rich—"

"He didn't get inside of me long enough to . . . If that's what you're reaching for."

"So a rape kit won't provide evidence," Mevlyn says.

The word *rape* hangs in the room, as hateful as the act itself.

Danae could open her shirt, reveal the reddened smudges that promise to bloom into bruises. What's the point. His father's a lawyer, Rich is a fine, upstanding son, and she's a lowlife slut, right? A person with money and power always triumphs.

"What now?" Danae asks.

"I'm going to call the paper, get them to hold off on publishing that picture or any write-up about it." Jerome picks up his cell phone. He speaks, listens, and taps to end the call.

"Why did you do that?" Mevlyn says.

"When someone craves attention, you don't give it up." Jerome's lips curl up at the ends. "Assuming it *is* Rich, he's jonesing for a reaction. I want you to get busy painting over his masterful artwork."

"Won't be able to do anything about those windows until my insurance man comes by," Mevlyn states.

"That's ok. Just keep any talk or speculation to a minimum."

"I don't get it." Danae frowns.

"Ladies, we're going to set bait and wait for Rich, or whoever has been terrorizing this town, to take it."

"Like a rat trap. What makes you think that will work? He's gotten away with it so far." Danae wishes she could meet the creep in a back alley, her multi-tool in hand, and assure Little Lord will never pass his genes along to some innocent child. Killing him wouldn't be sufficient. Plus, he's the one who needs to end up in prison, not her.

"When we don't play up his latest handiwork, he will provide us with more." Jerome closes the laptop.

Mevlyn snorts. "How you figure, Jerome?"

"I know his type. Protected by class position and daddy's money. Sure nothing can touch him and daring anyone to try. This isn't the first time we've had issues with him. His bad behavior is escalating."

"Suppose the 'black person' in question is either you or Malcolm, since we both hang tight with you." Mevlyn's lips ooze into a malevolent smile. "Sitting right here is the number one 'nigger-lover'"—she pulls air quotes— "who's gonna bring him down. Though, I detest that term and would never use it to stab anyone. Infuriating."

"I am also a fan of differently-shaded people." Danae thumps her chest. "I suppose I'm the *dyke*? Though, I'm not."

"Guess that makes you the Po-Po *Ho*," Mevlyn directs toward Jerome.

Jerome leans back in his chair and chuckles. "Been called a lot of things. That's not one of them."

After Danae leaves the station, Mevlyn lags behind.

"Something else on your mind, Miz Mevlyn?" Jerome asks.

"I got something to say to you in particular."

Jerome motions toward a cubicle barely large enough for a desk and two chairs. Mevlyn sits. Jerome closes the hallway door and takes the rolling chair next to his desk.

"That business about the hate words. It really gets you down," Mevlyn says, "and I want you to know it cuts me to my core seeing you that way."

His gaze falls to his folded hands. "It's okay. Really."

"You got anything to drink in this joint?"

The offhand question makes Jerome raise his head. "Nothing hard, but I might be able to rustle up a cola."

"Do that, then. One for both of us. I can feel the sweat pouring off me, even under my walking cast. And you're bound to be hotter than a three-peckered billy goat in that bulletproof vest and uniform."

Jerome chuckles and leaves the office, returning shortly with two aluminum cans. He hands one to Mevlyn, then pops the top on his.

"Talk to me, Jerome. You and me go way back. Something has crawled up under your skin and festered."

Jerome sighs. "There are times when this job gets me down. And it isn't only kids like Rich, or men like his father."

The best gifts Mevlyn can give her friend are an open heart and closed lips. She downs the cola and waits for him to corral his concerns and herd them her way.

"I get dejected about myself." His lips form a thin line.

"Well now. That caught me between the eyes. You're the good guy in this play. You wear a badge that puts a target on you the minute you step out your door, and drive around in that patrol car until your back near'bout breaks. Up against all kinds of folks—some off-track, others downright evil. Never short-sell yourself, Jerome. If nothing else, Sam taught me that."

"I'm not, Miz Mevlyn." He punctuates the statement with a clipped laugh. "You won't let me." His smile fades. "I'm sad because, after so many years of doing this job—I love it, don't misunderstand me—I find human nature sadly predictable. I hope for the best out of folks, I do. But I no longer expect it. More and more, I'm not even surprised."

"You and me—" Mevlyn indicates herself with a thump to her chest and him with a pointed finger "—are what I call *bruised optimists.*"

Jerome drains the last of his cola and pitches the can into a cardboard box labeled for recyclables. "You, maybe. I don't know about me. I think I'm more of a pessimist."

"Nope. I have to disagree with you on this point, Officer." Mevlyn feels her eyebrows twitch the way they do when she's onto some marvelous revelation. "We are optimists with a few scrapes. Battered, but not broken." She gazes into space as if the grayed walls hold truth. "There's always somebody out there who's just as bruised and banged up." Mevlyn returns attention to Jerome. "Neither you nor I can save 'em all. But every now and then, the gods shine down on one in particular. Our job is to keep our eyes open for the beacon."

Jerome holds up his palms.

Mevlyn finishes her own cola and slam dunks it into the cardboard box. "Two points! I should've been a basketball player." She pushes herself upright with a grunt and balances with the cane. "I left Elvina in charge of the Wash-Away. I best get on back before she wreaks havoc."


Mr. Hal gives Danae the rest of the day off to finish painting. Minutes after she coats over the first male body parts' drawing, a truck pulls up.

Danae turns to see Jack, Taylor, Gary, and Carrie stepping from the crew cab carrying supplies. In the crazy spin of the past few hours, thoughts of pursuing Mouse evaporated. Now, here she is.

"Figured you might need some help." Jack picks up a paint roller, loads it, and moves to stand beside her. Taylor and Gary provide their own brushes. Mouse lifts her gaze long enough to offer a shy smile, then takes a brush, dips it into the paint tray, and applies the gosh-awful pink in slow, even strokes. Danae doesn't engage, only returns to her task. Two hours later, the Wash-Away once again looks like a huge pastel slab of saltwater taffy.

"Thanks." Danae throws the paint brushes into a bucket of soapy water. "That would've taken me all day."

Mouse scampers back to the truck. Jack wipes his hands, motions to Taylor, and they follow. Gary remains.

"Danae?"

She makes eye contact with Gary for the first time since he dropped her off the night before. Her cycle sits in its usual spot by Mevlyn's. Her mind wraps around the fact he took time to go get it so soon.

"Can we talk?" he asks.

"Sure. But not now. I gotta get cleaned up, get onto work, since this is done."

"Okay, so when can we—"

"I'da know. One day, after I get off. I'll text you."

She's aware of him standing, waiting for her to make a move. She has no energy to reassure him, or whatever it is he requires. Small wonder anyone ever gets involved with another person. Too much trouble.

Maybe if she hadn't been wasting time with Gary, she'd be closer to Mouse by now. Maybe the attack would never have happened.

"Ok. So. See you then." He turns toward the truck.

"Gary?"

He turns.

"Thanks for bringing my cycle back."

"Sure. No problem." He waits a moment. When she doesn't speak, he once again turns to leave.

Danae wallows the brushes in water pink as baby shower punch. She doesn't look up to watch him walk away. The truck's engine sputters, catches. She hears it pull away and accelerate, and feels like a big fat jerk for casting blame toward Gary. She curses under her breath, slings the excess water from the cleaned brushes, and empties the bucket.

**T**wo days later, Jerome enters the Wash-Away. Mevlyn grabs the remote and mutes the television. Y and R can wait.

"We got him. Guess you've heard."

Mevlyn points him toward the cooler for colas. He hands one to her before sitting down with his own.

"Nothing much slips by me, Jerome. But I'd like the inside scoop."

"Rich painted obscenities on the backside of the post office. I watched him move down the alley to a defunct insurance business and empty two more spray paint cans. When he turned from his mastery, I popped on my headlights."

"Bet that scared the bejabbers from him."

"Boy took off like a scalded dog with a bum leg." Jerome takes a swig of cola. "I didn't bother going after him, not that he was able to gain any speed, given the injury to his private parts. One of my squad mates waited on the other side of the gap between the buildings."

"There you go." Mevlyn salutes Jerome with a cola-can toast.

"Don't think he'll slither out of this easily. I can give my eyewitness account, and I have video from four cameras to back me up. His hoodie slipped off when he took off, and one of the angles clearly shows his face."

"His daddy will find a way to get him off."

"I'm sure he'll cut some deal. That's what attorneys do. Best we can hope for is a hefty fine, a slap on the wrist, and maybe community service." Jerome slumps into the seat.

"I know you feel like you fight a hopeless battle, Jerome. Want you to know, I appreciate everything you do. At least it might ratchet that delinquent down a gear or two."

"His daddy won't like his good name smeared around town. I bet he makes arrangements to send Rich off to school somewhere besides FSU."

"Hopefully in another state."

"The part that gets me, even after all the years I've been in law enforcement, is that guys like Rich don't learn. It's only a matter of time until he starts up his nasty business somewhere else. Add a degree and a high-paying occupation to his column, and he'll abuse the same power his daddy does." Jerome takes a deep breath and lets it out. His gun belt leather creaks.

"Been the same ole story since Eve ate the apple, Jerome. Don't go letting yourself feel responsible. Ain't a thing you, or me, can do to make folks behave."

When Jerome's eyes focus on Mevlyn, they mirror exhaustion and hopelessness. She would hug him until he gasped for air, if she figured that would do any good.

"Miz, Mevlyn. It's a losing battle."

"At least we're still swinging, baby."

# Thirty-one

**D**anae parks the cycle on a section of cracked pavement a few feet from the main river landing, in what was once an important road. Now, it leads nowhere. Mevlyn encouraged her not to venture onto what remains of the Old Victory Bridge. Rules can be broken or at least stretched. Heck, if Mevlyn had her way, Danae wouldn't step one toe out of the city limits.

The handful of times Danae's been here since Malcolm shared the spot with her, she has never bumped into anyone. The end of the demolished bridge is sacred space for a number of people, she suspects, even if they have to climb a padlocked chain link fence.

The setting sun tips the trees and spills onto the deteriorating concrete. Danae walks around the barricades and scales the fence, then navigates past clumps of brush that have sprung up between the cracks.

The scent of marshy soil drapes over her: the river's distinctive perfume. She strolls, taking in lungsful of air. Her shoulder muscles uncrimp more with every step. From here, Danae hears the low, liquid rumble of the Apalachicola. Air wisps through the river willows. A bullfrog thumps his bass love song in the wetland beneath the pilings. Crickets tune up for their night concert in places the sun seldom reaches. Thoughts of Rich's hands, of her father's rage, of her own sister's distance: all dim.

The ruined bridge curves for a quarter mile above a thick stand of hardwoods and a palmetto swamp. The span ends abruptly, with a chain-link fence stretched across the severed edge. Beyond, a drop-off leads to the roiling river. She walks to the fence and curls her hands over the steel horizontal bar.

Upriver, the Jim Woodruff Dam funnels the waters collected from the Flint and Chattahoochee rivers by Lake Seminole, then selectively spews that water through its gates. The section of the Apalachicola sweeping beneath the jagged edge of the old bridge boils with swift eddies. Danae thinks this would be a perfect spot for someone planning suicide. At times in the past, after Mama died, she considered it. So far, her good sense has outweighed her despair.

She backs up to sit upon one of the concrete side rails. Looking out across the river, she thinks about God and creation. It's easy to forget such when surrounded by asphalt and buildings. Danae believes in the idea of God, of some kind, benevolent overseer. Religion? Nope. She no longer holds to humans' interpretation of things.

The sun sinks behind the tree line. Soon, the waning moon provides enough light to make out silhouettes.

Danae recalls the time when mainstream religion fell from her favor. It had nothing to do with Daddy and his opinions.

Before her mother fell ill, the place her mama smiled and laughed was in church. There, Danae witnessed joy in her mother's expression—not an emotion Estelle Gray showed beneath their family's roof. Outside of the sanctuary, Danae saw her mama happy only in her garden. The fresh faces of black-eyed susans, tomatoes shifting from lime green to deep orange, the heady scent of confederate jasmine and tea roses: all pleased Mama.

Since Daddy seldom ventured into the garden, Mama reigned. Plants responded to her touch. Stems withered to sticks sent forth tender shoots. Even the weeds warranted Mama's love, especially the flowering varieties. Daddy tried to shame Mama into pulling them up. Danae witnessed Estelle Gray standing firm on the matter. Weeds deserved credit for surviving, too.

Other than the one time Daddy came in stumbling drunk, face-planted into the dandelions, and got so angry he had ripped up handfuls, Big John reserved his finest rage for better uses, hitting his wife with such force, she limped for weeks. And keeping his children scared spitless.

Danae watches the moon glitter on the water and shifts her thoughts from her daddy to remember the moment she decided church had nothing to do with God. Mevlyn calls such memories *pivotal*: those times when the senses store each second, ready to recreate the scene at a moment's notice. Danae replays the clip now.

Mama decided it was a fine idea for Danae to join the youth choir, a small ensemble of six to no more than ten teenagers who bumbled their way through time-worn hymns once or twice a month, and at the yearly cantatas before Easter and Christmas.

The notion of a loving being with a long white beard and kindly expression appealed to Danae. Love your fellow man, treat people like you want to be treated, use this life to secure a spot in the one that followed: the requirements and promises seemed wondrous and forthright.

Added to the charm, church was the one place both she and her mama could rest assured Big John would not invade. He would hair-lip Hades before setting one toe inside a sanctuary. Heck, he vowed not to enter even following death. "Don't you roll my coffin into no damn church building, Estelle. I'll haunt you the rest of your days and meet you in hell later." Danae heard some version of that threat more times than she could count, usually after someone in the community passed away and Mama dressed for the memorial service. Big John wanted no part in religion. Period. The only time he mentioned God or Jesus was when he spewed out a string of curses.

That Christmas, three months after Danae turned thirteen, Mama sewed up a deep red velvet jumper and embroidered poinsettias across the yoke, and along the collar and cuffs of the thrift store white shirt to be worn underneath. It was the prettiest outfit Danae had ever seen.

Danae's voice didn't fit in with the sopranos. She managed a solid alto. The minister of music, a wormy little man, lavished praise even when one of his choir members was stone-cold tone deaf. Still, he taught Danae how to harmonize. Danae could hear a tune and instantly set her voice to complement and blend. She never learned to read music, but could pick up on any melody after hearing it once. Chalk that up in her winner's column, along with running and a knack for tinkering with engines.

She stood in her position, second row, center, next to another alto and the four boys who provided tenor and bass. The front row held five sopranos. The small sanctuary with two sections of pews could seat sixty, if they scrunched up cozy, and another fifteen in folding metal chairs during special occasions or in case someone beloved died young. Tonight promised to be a full audience, with more standing at the back.

On that night, ten days before Christmas, the space glowed with the flicker of five standing candelabras and the illumination of dimmed overhead lights. Poinsettias and holly festooned the end of pews and circled the podium. Danae thought this was how the original holy night must've felt: family, love, angels hovering above, and hope.

"Invite your friends!" the pastor had urged for weeks ahead of the event. "We shall raise our blended voices to the Lord's glory!"

Mama sat close to the front, three pews back, as near to the center as she could manage. Danae caught her eye and Mama beamed, so proud. Mama looked tired, as she had a lot lately. Too many long shifts, coworkers out with the flu or with sick children, or laying off work because of the demands of the season.

How had Daddy put his opinion of that night? Just another chance to *troll for souls*. Yes, Big John had called that out as she and Mama walked from the house. Mama had laughed to defuse him, then hustled Danae to the car.

It was true, what Daddy said. At the end, the preacher would issue a call for redemption. The pianist would play at least ten verses of *Just As I Am*, the old hymn meant to snag new converts and drag those who had backslid into the fold. The cantata was timed at forty minutes. The preacher's plea might add twenty, depending on how many repentant souls trudged to the front. Same as every Sunday, only more fervent because of the celebration of Jesus' birth.

People shuffled inside, greeting others, smiling, taking seats. The pianist played low. Around Danae, the young choir vibrated with readiness. They'd practiced for nearly six months until they shone as much as the reflected light on the butt-worn wooden pews.

Her best friend in the universe stood at the rear entrance. Danae lifted her hand in a tiny wave. Antoine's young sister cowered beside him. Heads pivoted toward the two. Danae watched one of the church elders—a man about Daddy's age—stride purposely to where her friend and his sister waited. After an exchange of words and gestures, two more elders joined the group. Antione held up his palms as if he surrendered. Then, they were gone.

Why had they decided to leave? Had the sight of so many white faces turned them around? She wanted to run after them, convince them to stay. Danae shot her mama a questioning look. Mama shook her head with two fingertips pressed to her lips, looking dejected.

Danae sang as if God tapped her, every note a perfect pitch. Antoine should've been there to hear how well she performed.

Only later, after the cantata and call for souls, when she climbed into the car still reveling in praises, did she learn the truth: Antoine and his sister had been told to leave.

"Why, Mama?"

"They're black, dear. It might seem fine in my and your eyes, but others find it inappropriate for them to mix with us."

Even now, Danae recalls how her pulse had quickened, the flush of resentment mixed with shame.

She turned to her mama and said, "Jesus loved the little children. 'Red or yellow. Black or white.' That's in the song, right? But hey, *not* okay for my best friend and his sister to come inside a church to hear me sing?"

Mama could not explain in any way Danae would accept.

That night, Danae split ways with the church.


She still likes the idea of God, even prays in spite of her daddy's disregard for the practice. And skin makes no difference in choosing friends.

Her phone's text alert chimes, a sound foreign and invasive in this natural place. Danae hopes it's not Mevlyn. Again. She loves the old woman, but for Pete's sake, why did Danae ever school her on texting? Now that both she and Mevlyn have cell phones, they're connected wherever, whenever. Comforting and annoying at once.

It's Malcolm. **On bridge B there in 2**

Even if she didn't know the identity of the person, the brevity is a give-away. Mevlyn composes epistles with full sentences, correct spelling, and precise punctuation.

Danae hears twin huffs behind her and slips her phone into her shirt pocket. The other holds the trusted multi-tool, a required companion since the incident with Rich. Levon and Girly reach her first, their tails whisking the heavy air, rearing up to snuffle her neck and face, then licking a slobbery greeting. Levon leaves behind a pool in her left ear. Girly assures the right side equal lubrication. Danae hugs and pets them until their excitement diminishes.

She should get a dog of her own, something big and protective. Danae wonders if Mevlyn and Sonny will warm to the idea. She can buy the pup goggles and a helmet, teach her how to be a proper motorcycle babe.

Danae noodles the dogs' ears and coos love words. Yes, she can rescue a dog—a mixed-breed mutt someone has cast aside, not a good fit for their family. She identifies with that.

Malcolm materializes from the shadows. Good thing he texted and the dogs let her know he was not far behind. The dude is a true stealth. He lowers to sit beside her.

"You seriously need to think about joining up with special forces, Malcolm."

"My dad says the same thing. But the whole gay/ *don't ask, don't tell* thing is too much for me. Bad enough I'd always be on guard for my military career, I'd have to constantly monitor every indication of my sexuality every minute. So, not."

"Life sucks."

Malcolm palms her shoulder. "You're a breath of stale air this fine evening. What gives?" Before she can answer, he adds, "forget that. The whole hate-talk paint job at the Wash-Away. I get it."

"Everyone's heard by now. No matter that your dad squelched the front page write-up."

"Chattahoochee's small, Nae. Word was probably around before you and Mevlyn laid eyes on it."

"Guess so." A light breeze stirs the hairs on her forearms. Her skin echoes with Rich's touch, pressing, groping. She shudders.

"Hey. Are you all right?"

How she wishes she could tell him about the assault. Every detail, the ones she glazed over when she talked with Jerome. "Just a case of the willies, I guess."

"You, afraid of anything? Since when?"

Danae's defenses rise. "Like you've never felt fear?"

"Girl, you are smart about engines, but sometimes clueless about people. I'm scared every time I step from the house, out of my car . . . I have three strikes against me: I'm black, I'm male, and I'm gay. Add in a bigot and a swig of whiskey, and any one of those becomes a good enough reason to pound me to a pulp."

Danae rakes clumps of sweaty hair from her face. "I hate it. I hate it all, so much."

"As do I. But it's reality, especially in the Heart of Dixie."

She turns away before he reads her expression in the low light. Malcolm can sense her turmoil as well as Antoine could. Though she detests hiding anything from him, Danae can't bring herself to tell him about the revulsion she feels when she looks at her breasts in the mirror. The bruises will fade, but not the memory of them. Doubt niggles. Did Rich penetrate her? Parts of that night are foggy, as if her internal editor decided to overwrite them.

*What if Rich . . . and what if I get . . . What if?*

Danae shudders again.

"You must be getting sick. It is not cold out here at all."

"I'm good. Really."

Malcolm doesn't push.

Her thoughts shift to Gary. What about him? Danae promises her worn brain, she'll catch up with him soon. The way he had looked at her earlier confirmed he won't be shocked by anything she has to say about Rich. And like Malcolm, Mevlyn, and Jerome, Gary will believe her.

It's saying it out loud that stalls her. And the certainty she'll have to live with the aftereffects—memories and other, physical repercussions.

"You ever feel like . . . like all this stuff is swirling around you and you have no control at all?" Her voice quivers.

His reply comes out tender. "Only, all the time."

"I figured I'd have a solid grip the minute I turned eighteen, you know, an adult."

Malcolm pivots to face her. "My dad says the older he gets, the less he understands."

"Encouraging."

"Isn't it?"

Danae steers to lighter subjects. Within minutes, Malcolm makes her laugh. With the two dogs lounging at her feet and her best friend seated beside her, Danae relaxes for the first time since the assault.

# Thirty-two

**M**evlyn eases the vintage sedan from the driveway, stopping long enough to wave at Danae. It took every argument Mevlyn could create to get the gal to allow her to drive herself to the grocery store. Sure, her balance is that of a twelve-pack drunk and her leg is weak since the cast came off, but if she doesn't do something independent soon, she'll run screaming naked to Georgia, or at least to the end of West Washington Street, walking as fast as her current level of mobility allows.

She comes to a full, legal stop, turns east, and abides by all speed signs until she reaches the city limits. A half-mile later, Mevlyn zooms along at seventy miles an hour. If she gets nabbed by the Gadsden County Po-Po, she can charm her way out of a ticket. Being old and clever are as important as good insurance.

Twenty minutes later, she hits Quincy city limits and returns to only eight miles over the posted limit. The car's old, stands to reason the speedometer might be a bit off.

This early, the Winn Dixie parking lot is nearly empty. She takes her pick of prime handicapped parking spots. Coffee's on sale, a plus. And she needs some big bottles of Sprite at the house. No perishables to worry about. Danae and Malcolm drove over to the IGA in Sneads just two days ago for the rest of her list.

So much of getting through advanced age revolves around other people. They mean well, they do. But let her have one incident, break one little bone, and all of a sudden, everyone jockeys to rule her life.

Mevlyn's been in charge of herself for years, even before Sam died, and by golly, she will fight like a cornered junkyard dog to keep control.

A small man walks across the parking lot, armed with a sawed-off mop handle. Mevlyn slows to watch him pass. Turquoise camo-printed top, black spandex shorts with lingerie lace trim, two anklets, and a multicolor tattoo on one calf; he takes no notice of Mevlyn.

Goodness. It pays to get out and view the world.

The icy air hits her as soon as she steps through the automatic doors. Summer is the season that makes entrances and exits come with a sound track. She says *Sweet Jesus* when the artificial chill relieves her on the way in and *Good God Almighty* when the heat slams her on the way out.

For a beat, she considers an electric scooter cart, then chooses a push buggy. The whole point of this expedition is to *not* feel like an invalid. She rests the cane across the top and uses the shopping cart like a glorified walker. Gathering the items on her list takes less than twenty minutes, even with the addition of browsing the bakery display. And, would you look at that, the 2.5 liter Sprites are on sale, buy two, get two! Life is surely sweet when you least expect it.

She reaches the row of registers. Only two are open, with no line at either. She chooses aisle #4—Danae's favorite number—and steps in front of the shopping cart to guide it into the chute. The young black woman cashier looks downtrodden. Mevlyn unloads her order, one item at a time, with the four soft drink plastic bottles laying side down on the conveyor belt. No need to add one of those divider bars. Nobody stands behind her. That done, she grabs the cane, inches to the pay station, and proceeds to find something funny to make the young woman crack a smile.

A loud thud sounds, followed by a hiss. She and the cashier turn toward the commotion. One of the bottles bounces on the tile, spewing soda pop like Old Faithful.

"Oh—" Mevlyn starts. Before she can speak another word, the second bottle rolls off the belt and hits the floor. This one lands on its side, bursts open, and spins like a whirling dervish. The whole thing is a slow motion disaster. She leans, stretching the cane to catch the third bottle before . . . It takes a rolling dive, hits the tile next to the first bottle, and erupts. Twin towers of soda cascade over the tiered display rack filled with candy bars and gum.

A small group of fellow shoppers gather, their mouths hanging open, eyes round. It's like the Fourth of July, rendered in carbonation. In less than a minute, all three bottles are empty.

"Well. Goodness gracious." Mevlyn surveys the moat of Sprite. "I am *so* sorry."

"Everyone has a bad day," the cashier says. "It's okay."

"I'll pay."

"Oh no. No need. It was an accident." The woman looks a little less haggard, and certainly more amused than she did when Mevlyn first stepped up to her station.

"I won't be able to set foot into this store, ever," Mevlyn says.

"Oh now, please don't say that. Come visit us again." The cashier reads out the total as if half the storefront gets drenched with Sprite every morning.

The manager appears and casts white powder over the spilled soft drink. Her fellow shoppers wander off to check out elsewhere.

"Those soda pops were such a good price, too." Mevlyn hands over her cash.

"I can send someone to get you more if—"

"Oh no." Mevlyn holds up a palm. "Put the one that didn't fling itself over the edge back on the shelf. I've lost my desire for any today."

"Let me get you another buggy." The cashier hands over Mevlyn's change and leaves her station.

The drenched shopping cart, like everything within a four-feet radius, rains Sprite. Mevlyn's hair and clothes are soaked on one side, as are her shoes. Good thing it was the sugar-free variety. At least everything won't be sticky. For sure, she'll be cool on the way to the car.

When she pushes the cart to the double door, Mevlyn takes one last look back. Two checkout aisles are closed, the display racks rolled aside. Four workers push mops while the manager stands, shaking his head. The cashier gives Mevlyn a faint smile and wave.

As she makes her way to the car, still incredulous, Mevlyn takes note of the four other shoppers who exited at the same time. All angle in long arcs away from her, heading to their own vehicles with furtive glances her way.

She loads the three plastic bags into the front seat, returns the shopping cart to its corral, and slides into the driver's seat.

If that wasn't one huge lesson in not always being in control, nothing is. Mevlyn replays the scene, wishing someone would've caught it on camera. Authors make up crazy incidents to add in for comic relief. Mevlyn reckons the Good Lord squeezes a few into her life, too. This last one fits up there with the time she walked down the aisle at church with her dress hung up in the top of her pantyhose and thought she must be looking pretty good for all of those people to be smiling so wide at her.

She's still chuckling when she pulls onto the highway heading toward Chattahoochee. She'll get Danae to Google nearby locations of the chain store, for the next time coffee goes on sale. And Elvina will stop by the Dollar Store for Sprite, if Mevlyn decides she can't live without it for the next few days.

# Thirty-three

The moment the woman enters the Wash-Away, Mevlyn sizes her up, as she does all newcomers. Looks to be late sixties, petite, but with a determined walk. Something about her seems familiar.

The woman stands in front of Mevlyn's desk. No laundry basket. No leaflets for sales, or church. Way she's standing, she's out for some purpose.

"Good morning. You must be Mevlyn. I'm looking for Danae Gray."

Mevlyn crosses her arms over her chest and gives the woman her blankest expression, willing her eyebrows to remain still. "Who's askin'?" Sonny emerges from his bed and gives the lady the sniff-over.

"I'm Sylvia Franklin, her aunt from Alabama."

Good lord. Bound to be because of Elvina and her meddling. Mevlyn surely didn't go seeking out any of that bunch. Danae had her reasons for taking off, and it was up to her if she wanted to tiptoe back across that border.

The woman's face softens. Her eyes hold the same kind of weary sadness, that P.R. look Danae had the first time Mevlyn spotted her. What's ruined this woman?

"Please," she says after it's clear Mevlyn's gone mute, "may we talk?"

"I got coffee."

"That sounds good."

"Pull up one of those chairs."

If anyone can send this here woman hauling buggy to the Florida/ Alabama line, Mevlyn figures it's her. "How do you take yours?"

"Not choosy. But a little sugar and creamer would be nice if you have them."

Mevlyn pours two mugs, adds in sweetener and a packet of instant creamer per cup, and returns to the desk. Two patrons share the Wash-

Away. Both are so engrossed in their phones, Godzilla could be sitting at the counter and they wouldn't notice.

"So, tell me why you're here." Mevlyn settles into her chair and shoves one filled mug toward Sylvia Franklin.

"It's important that I locate my niece. Do you know where I can find her?"

"I might. Up to me to decide if I *want* to."

Thirty minutes later, Mevlyn knows more about Danae than she's managed to piece together with Jerome's background information and Elvina's deep diving. Certainly, much more than Danae has ever revealed.

"I'll call her." Mevlyn slides the ancient pushbutton phone toward herself. Could use the cell phone and text, but then the woman will know Danae has one, too.

"Tell me where my niece is, and I will go to her."

"Nope. I plan to be right here when y'all talk."

"I see." Sylvia Franklin manages a trembling smile. "The woman I spoke with told me you were a force to be reckoned with." The lip curves wilt into a firm line. "But so am I."

Mevlyn picks up the business phone and taps in a number. In less than five minutes, Danae rushes through the door and starts to fire off questions, then the identity of the woman in the flowery dress hits her. Danae's mouth forms an O. All that comes out is a *wh-wh-wha* noise.

"Sit yourself down. Your aunt's come with some news she wants you to hear." Mevlyn stands. "I'll take Sonny out for a pee." She rests one hand on Danae's shoulder as she passes. "I won't be far, gal. Call out if you need me."

Danae watches Mevlyn and the dog leave. Sonny glances back at her once. Mevlyn doesn't.

She can run out of here this second, jump on her cycle and find the next place to hide. If there's one thing she's learned, there's always an option.

"I'm *so* glad you're safe," her aunt says. "I've been worried sick."

Danae looks down to her clasped hands. "I was planning on calling you." She lifts her head and meets her aunt's direct gaze. "I *was*."

"I understand why you took off. I know about your run-in. Your daddy is a piece of shit." Her aunt spits out the last word with a crisp *T* at the end.

Danae clips short a startled chuckle. Aunt Sylvia doesn't cuss. Ever. Not even *damnation* and it's in the Bible.

"I'll get to the point. Why I'm here. How I found you is no nevermind, only that I did. Your daddy is dying."

Danae stares, unblinking. Is she supposed to feel bad?

"If you want to see him . . ."

Still, Danae has no words.

"Regardless, I'd like for you and me to stay connected, if that's what you wish."

Danae nods.

The woman stands and hand-presses the wrinkles from her dress. "That's all I came to say. I got him at my house. Done called in hospice to help me. His liver is bad. No chance of a transplant, even if the money was there. Not with his drinking." She leans down and gives Danae a quick hug. "It won't be long."

After Aunt Sylvia leaves, Mevlyn and Sonny walk into the Wash-Away. Sonny sits at Danae's feet. Mevlyn rounds the desk and reclaims her chair.

"You heard?" Danae asks, her voice low.

"Why do you think I propped that door open a crack? You know I'd never waste cool air for nothing."

"What should I do?"

"I can't dictate that." Mevlyn lets out a breath that whistles at the end. "Way I see it, the only good thing about getting a heads-up is being able to say what you want to say, what you *need* to say, before you no longer can. There's not a day passes, I don't miss Sam and wish I could talk to him. Oh, I speak to the sky and like to imagine he's listening. But there's no way to be certain of it.

"Your aunt offered you a chance to say what's on your mind. Whatever that is. It's up to you whether or not you choose to take it. No do-overs." Mevlyn stops to make change for one patron without either of them speaking. "You know I support you, no matter your decision. I'll even ride over with you if you need me to."

Danae rises. "I have to get back to the shop. I'm in the middle of a full-service."

## Thirty-four

When Danae pulls up in front of her aunt's white wooden-frame house, emotions scramble over each other, fighting to surface. She kills the cycles' engine, dismounts, and secures the kickstand. She removes her helmet and rests it on the seat, then freezes in place, staring at the place she had called home for nearly four years after Mama died.

Aunt Sylvia loves her flowers, same as her own sister Estelle had. Though summer has yet to yield its grip, beds on either side of the steps grow thick with fall chrysanthemums. On the shady front porch, pots suspend from the overhead rafters, offering up oranges and yellows, and the lush greens of her aunt's cherished Boston ferns.

Danae stalls, taking time to recall evenings when she, Uncle Bully, and Aunt Sylvia would languish in the rockers, talking over the day's high and low points, with the background music of crickets and tiny frogs her aunt called peepers. Even on the hottest evenings of August, they made it onto the porch, iced tea glasses in hand.

Bad memories surface, too. The time after Mama died, when Aunt Sylvia had first managed to gain guardianship and Big John pitched such a drunken fit, the law had been summoned. And that wasn't the only instance. Uncle Bully managed to keep most of the bad out of her sight, until he passed away. Left to her own to defend her house and her niece, Aunt Sylvia could wield a fierce iron frying pan if pushed hard enough.


That last night, when Danae stopped by Aunt Sylvia's house to change out of her graduation gown, Big John had been lying in wait. He must've parked the truck somewhere else. Danae spotted him only after she got off the cycle and he stepped from the shadows.

"Thought you'd get off without saying a word to your daddy, didn't you, Dannie?"

With her aunt still back at the gymnasium making her way around to everyone, wishing the kids Danae had grown up with a good life and congratulations to them and their families, nothing stood between Danae and Big John. She can't recall the precise conversation, and how it went from bad to really bad.

"You think you gonna shame me by hanging out with them filthy niggers? Do you?"

Same thing he used to rant to Mama, about Mouse. Never stopped her sister from being kind to anyone.

"They're my friends. Don't call them that."

"I saw you hugging up on that one big black buck. You his whore?"

How her liking the kids in her class makes her a whore . . . "You said I was a dyke, just last week. Which is it, Daddy? Don't seem I would be screwing a *man* if I'm a lesbian."

That sent him coming at her, rage coloring his face red, his rheumy eyes wide. He grabbed her by the hair, snatched back her head. She elbowed him in the gut.

It had felt like forever that they tussled. He outweighed her, but Danae was as tall, quick, and wiry strong. The alcohol threw off his timing just enough.

Danae's fist found his head. He dropped to his knees, then thudded in a full face plant.

She remembers looking down, stunned. What had just happened? She had cold-cocked her own daddy! The tiny shred of elation fled when she realized: if he comes to, he'll kill me.

Inside the house, she tore off the commencement gown, snatched on a pair of jeans and the first T-shirt she could lay her hands on. She stuffed a thin roll of graduation cash into a backpack, along with underwear and a couple more shirts.

In the yard, Daddy lay prone, his face caulked with red-clay dirt.

Danae pulled on the helmet, cranked the cycle, and fishtailed from the unpaved drive. At the highway, she idled. *Which way?* She thought of how she and Mouse used to decide direction. She spit in one open palm, then sliced the puddle with the side of the other hand. The majority of the mass splashed to the left. She aimed the bike south toward the Florida border. Later, she used the same method to send her cruising east on Highway 90 toward the Atlantic coast, only she hadn't made it nearly that far.

**A**unt Sylvia appears at the front entrance. The hinges sing out when she swings open the screened door. "You coming inside?"

Danae takes a deep breath and takes the four steps in twos. At the top, she hugs her aunt.

"He's in the front bedroom."

Danae nods.

"I don't know if he'll respond to you. He generally worsens in the early evening. He hasn't reacted to anything for the past day or two." Her aunt blows out a weary breath. "I'll be in the kitchen."

Danae inches into the darkened room. The odor gags her. Like ruined flowers, leaves pressed to powdered mold: sulfurous, the tang of ammonia. Reminds Danae of Mr. Sam. Only far worse. Do evil and hatred mark a person's final smell? Danae mouth-breathes to tamp down the nausea. Puking up the pimento cheese sandwich Miz Mevlyn urged her to eat before she left Chattahoochee won't make the air improve.

Daddy lies in a hospital bed propped with pillows, his head and shoulders elevated. Danae observes for movement. Is she too late?

She forces herself to inch to the edge of the gurney. His breathing is shallow and quick, barely displacing the wrinkles in the sheet over his distended belly. Jaundiced skin stretched tight by fluid retention looks as if it might burst if touched. He takes a loud, raspy inhalation. The next few breaths are deep, as if the demons shadowing his life review have him cornered. Then he stops altogether. Danae leans down. He's still again. The barely detectible puffs of air resume.

The Death Rattle. What Mr. Sam's hospice nurse had tagged as Cheyne Stokes respirations—the abnormal pattern indicating the body's imminent shut down, that part of death dubbed *active dying*. Her daddy has three days, tops. Danae thinks back to Mr. Sam, how his last hours hadn't been overly horrible.

"Daddy?" Danae says in a low voice. "It's me. Dannie."

No response. She fights the urge to flee. Reminds herself he can't hurt her now. At least, not physically.

The years of drinking. The rage. The fists. Lashing out at everything.

For the first time, Danae wonders what had set him up to be the way he was. He never talked about his past. Mama only said he left Mississippi when he was fourteen and never looked back. Danae knows nothing of that side of her extended family. Doesn't want to know, if Daddy was a product of them.

Danae glances around, then scoots a small wooden stool beside the bed and lowers herself. She picks up his hand. It's cold, as if that part of him has already given up.

"I am sorry I hit you." Tears burn her eyes. "I don't want to be like you, Daddy."

Does she feel a slight flick of one finger?

Her daddy's lips part. They open, close, open, close. Danae thinks of a fish snatched from the river, reflexively searching for a way to stay alive.

Strained sounds come from his mouth. The smell of ammonia chokes her. She girds herself and leans closer to his face.

"Mouse. Mouse."

"Yes, Daddy. What about Mouse?"

"Mouse failed."

*Failed?* "I don't get it, Daddy. She failed at what?"

"Failed. Failed." He lifts his head with a groan. Then his head sinks back into the pillows. His face goes slack. Drool pools at one corner of his lips.

Danae squeezes his hand. Nothing. She relaxes her grip, holding him this way for a few minutes, hoping. His breathing falls back into the pattern dictated by death.

The hospice nurse walks into the room. How anyone can be in this part of the profession defies Danae. Watching people die. Seeing families grieve.

Danae stands, gives her daddy one last, long look. She grabs a tissue and dabs the spittle from his chin.

"You'll be here, right?" she asks the nurse.

"Yes."

"And you'll let me and Aunt Sylvia know if, when . . ."

"Yes. Of course." The nurse has a soft voice Danae could listen to forever. "Do you wish to remain beside him tonight? I can bring in a cot."

Danae shakes her head. "I got a room in town." Thanks to Mevlyn. Clean sheets, quiet, comfortable bed, and near enough to get here fast. Even Aunt Sylvia agrees it's best for Danae. Seems she and Mevlyn discussed it.

"I'll be back first thing in the morning."


Daddy dies at four a.m. The cell phone buzzes. Danae fights her way back from fitful sleep.

"He's gone," are her aunt's only words.

The next two days pass in a blur. Danae checks out of the hotel and moves into Aunt Sylvia's spare room, not the one where her father had died. That door remains shut, the curtains drawn.

Using an old address book Aunt Sylvia had slipped from the house after mama died, Danae manages to locate one of her daddy's brothers living near Jackson, Mississippi. He listens, but hangs up without committing one way or the other. Danae doesn't blame him. Why would he or any of them ride several hours to pay final tribute to someone they barely know. All that remains are small details: picking out the coffin, setting a time, and shelling out money for the funeral home's services, thanks to her aunt. Some preacher Aunt Sylvia knows will say a few words, not many. It's the respectable thing, her aunt says.

Danae peels back the sheets and rolls out of bed, then dons the same T-shirt and jeans she'd worn the day before. She stops by the bathroom long enough to pee and splash water on her face.

"Someone's here to see you." Aunt Sylvia hands Danae a cup of coffee. "I'll go with you to the funeral home when you're ready."

Danae opens the front door, carrying her mug. A guy sits in one of the porch rockers and stands when he spots her.

"Oh my God." Danae meets Antoine halfway, hugging, crying, and trying not to spill her coffee at once.

"Hey, Duh."

She leads him to the rockers and they sit. Danae swipes tears from her eyes. First time she's actually let loose with anyone, more from the relieved joy of seeing her friend than any sadness over losing her daddy. "You want coffee?"

"Nah. I'm good. Just came to see you."

"Pay your respects?"

"Don't mean this to sound bad, Duh, but I didn't have any of that for your daddy."

"Makes two of us."

"We all thought he run you off like he did Mouse, or killed you and threw your body to the buzzards."

Nerves crackle up her spine. Had she not gotten that good swing in, with her daddy too stone-drunk to retaliate, it could have ended much differently. "I had to leave. I didn't . . . I'm sorry . . ."

"Hey," Antoine holds one hand over her forearm. "It's me you talkin' to. More than anyone, I get having to remove yourself from a screwed-up situation. I'm just happy to see you."

"I've missed you, too." Danae gives Antoine the condensed version of her life for the past few months, leaving out the details of why she fled after graduation, and how she's shadowing the person she believes to be her sister. As long as she doesn't say it to anyone, it could be true. As to the final battle with Big John, Antoine doesn't deserve to hear her daddy's racist rants against their friendship. For sure, she won't tell him about Rich.

   

"I *am* sorry for you, Duh. No matter you and your daddy didn't get along, he was still your blood kin." Antoine rocks, silent for a minute. "You coming back to stay now?"

"I don't know. I haven't thought that far yet." If Mouse will come with her, they could live with Aunt Sylvia until they figure out what to do next. But what about Miz Mevlyn and Mr. Hal and Malcolm and Gary? Does she ditch them the way she did her aunt and best friend?

Being an adult is a pain in the ass. Though, truthfully, the years before it hadn't been a pleasure cruise.

"Chattahoochee ain't so far. I could come see you." Antoine offers up one of his beaming smiles. "Long as you don't have me locked up while I'm there."

"You lost me." Then, before he can elaborate, she snaps her fingers and adds, "Oh, you mean the mental institution. I know the town's famous for that, but honestly, I forgot about it a few weeks after I landed there." She returns his smile with a wink. "Besides, I don't think they'd take you."

"Reckon I should go." Antoine rocks forward and lifts from the seat. "I'll be around if you need me. I won't be coming to the old man's funeral. Sorry." He gathers her into a tight hug.

"No apology necessary. I get it."


The coffin is the least expensive in the showroom. No flower drape covers the top, only a plastic lily arrangement on either side, sent from the guys Big John worked with, and his drinking and hunting buddies. Aunt Sylvia and Danae sit in folding aluminum chairs three feet from where her daddy lies, in a suit Danae doesn't recall him owning. A handful of people stand at the edge of the tent shade. No one looks particularly sad, not even the first woman he had moved into the house shortly after Mama died. Guess she wised up fast. The rent-a-preacher says the usual things. One of the funeral directors cues up a CD tune. *Amazing Grace.*

Early afternoon, supposed to be edging toward fall by now, and the temperature still tips mid-eighty. Sweat runs between Danae's breasts and soaks the band of her bra. She conceded to wearing one, but hell no to a dress. Black pants and a simple shirt. Let them say she looks like a boy. Who cares? Mouse is the one with flowers and ruffles, and she's not here. What did Daddy expect? He never gave Mouse credit for anything, no matter how hard she tried. From the time J.J. drowned, Danae became what Daddy wanted: a stand-in he called Dannie, someone to hunt, fish, tinker on cars, and later, beat on.

"They'll bring food to the house." Aunt Sylvia stands by her car at the edge of the cemetery plot. Danae's motorcycle is parked behind it. "You coming by the house?"

"Maybe later."

Her aunt turns to open the car door, then swivels to face Danae. "You always have a place with me."

Danae leans into a hug. "I know."

Her aunt reaches over and touches Danae's face. "Wish things could've been different."

Danae huffs out a breath. "Miz Mevlyn says 'wish in one hand and poop in the other and see which one fills up the fastest.'"

Aunt Sylvia's lips curl at the edges. "She seems like a good lady." Her aunt opens the car door and slides behind the wheel. "Don't be a stranger, baby. And please, please stop by and eat a little bite or two. I don't know what I'm going to do with all the food folks have brought over."

## Thirty-five

**W**hen Danae pulls the cycle in front of the house where she grew up, the hair at the base of her skull prickles. Houses look sad when nobody cares about them, her Mama used to say about any deserted structure they passed by. Houses need love, too.

Mama had tried to love this house. Insisted on a fresh coat of white paint every four years, planted flowers, sewed cushions for the rockers on the porch, hoping it would invite folks to visit and chat.

Danae shuts off the engine, removes her helmet, and secures the bike.

She pauses on the porch of the family home. With her daddy dead, it's her house now, crappy as it is—and Mouse's too, if she comes back. Clapboard and wood frame, probably roost to scores of termites. She unlocks the front door and passes through before she can give in to the tiny inside voice screaming, *Go! Get away as fast as the cycle will take you!*

The rooms smell of stale grease, cheap perfume, spilled booze, and dust. She moves quickly to the rear of the house. If she hesitates, every corner will prompt memories of raised voices, whimpering, glass shattering, bones breaking. Only one thing interests her.

When she opens the door to the bedroom that was once hers, Danae sees blank walls, a bed with no covers, and barren floors. Two steps bring her to the single dresser. She pulls open each drawer. Nothing remains, not even the faded liners her mama had put inside. None of her clothes hang in the tiny closet. Five wire hangers suspend from the wooden rod, one bent nearly flat by the force of someone snatching off whatever once took up space. She glances down. Dust bunnies. No shoes. She peers up. The shelves, too, are empty, save for a couple of shoe boxes, shoved far back into the shadows.

Danae jets to the kitchen and returns with a chair, climbs onto the seat, and sweeps down both of the boxes. She steps down from the chair.

One box holds crumpled paper and a sleeve of desiccant. She throws it aside and cradles the second in her arms, her eyes closed in a silent prayer.

She opens the lid. Mouse's sleep gown, folded and yellowed, rests in a nest of white tissue.

She walks to the bed and sits down on the edge, the gown grasped in her hands.

Danae remembers the day Mouse moved. The week before Christmas, ten years ago. A cold, bitter day, gray with low clouds. The year her sister disappeared and everything changed.

Her jumbled thoughts fade from chopping down a scraggly, short-needled north Florida pine to suffice for a Christmas tree, to a morning so typical it could've been any time of year.

It was the last day of school before a few days of what should have been fun. But fun in this house with her parents was not the Norman Rockwell vision of the holidays. Her daddy hunkered over breakfast, wearing resentment and a hangover like a permanent overcoat.

"Notice anything about my eggs, Estelle?"

The tone of her daddy's voice froze Danae's hand in midair. A drop of milk slipped from the shaking spoon, missed her cereal bowl, landed on the table. Her gaze flicked down, then up to her daddy's ruddy face.

Danae sensed her older sister Maria—"Mouse" to everyone, for obvious reasons—shivering in the chair next to his. Her knee bumped Danae's. *Shut up*, the knee said.

Her mama moved from the stove where she forked bacon crisp-done in an iron skillet. The apron covering her institution-green nursing scrubs was printed with cheerful fruit and flowers: yellow, orange, red. Tiny plastic Santa Claus figures dangled from her earlobes.

Danae's daddy hooked one large finger in her direction. "Get over here."

Estelle Gray placed the fork just so on the aluminum spoon rest and stepped to the Formica-topped table. John James Gray, Big John, stabbed the center of one of the eggs resting in a glistening pool of grease. Beside the eggs laid clumps of grits the dark yellow of too-much butter, strips of fat-rippled bacon, and four biscuits. Always four. Two to sop up the excess yolk and grease. Two for syrup.

"How am I supposed to eat this shit, Estelle?"

Danae noticed the thick sheen of that tan goop her mama painted on her face each morning. Beneath one eye, a greenish-yellow bruise showed through. Mama told anyone who asked: *I could fall over thin air.* The only air Estelle Gray fell over was the dead space before Daddy's clenched fist. Air before seeing those circling rings of stars, like on the cartoons, Danae thought.

Mouse drew in a breath, as if she was starved for oxygen. Big John's red-rimmed eyes slid from his wife to his fourteen-year-old daughter. "You got something smart-ass to say?"

"No sir." Mouse's voice barely made it past a squeak; her knee once again sought Danae's, as if her baby sister could offer protection. Danae felt it quiver like a trapped rodent.

"I'll deal with *you* later." Daddy pitched a soiled crumpled napkin in Mouse's direction, then pushed away from the table so violently Danae and Mouse's orange juice glasses trembled.

"Guess I'll have to go uptown to eat since MY WIFE— " A line of saliva shot from one side of his mouth as he spit out the words. "—can't seem to cook an egg without the got-damned yellow turning to rubber."

Big John picked up the dish—Grandma Wilson's chipped china—and hurled it. Somehow her mama managed to avoid a direct hit. This time. The sound of shattering glass hung in the grease-soured air.

The back door slammed so hard the house shook. A visit-Florida commemorative plate crashed to the linoleum floor. Porcelain pieces of The Sunshine State joined spilled grits and eggs. Their mutt dog belly-crawled from his hidey hole beneath the table and licked the remains of breakfast, avoiding the glass shards.

Mama returned to the bacon slabs—now ruined and black. She pitched them into the trash, added three fresh pieces. Stared at the strips that jittered in the hot grease like angry tethered rattlesnakes.

Danae glanced at Mouse. Then down to her bowl. Gross. Milk-bloated cereal. She put  down the spoon. Mouse resumed eating pinches of dry biscuit. No butter. No syrup.

Mouse amazed Danae. Nothing ever seemed to bother her for long.


Danae holds up the gown and presses it to her nose. If only some faint scent of Mouse remains, she can ferret out some detail she's missing. The body stores memory in forms other than visual, she had read somewhere. Touch. Smells. Sounds. The gown gives up no secrets.

What's left? She could run her fingers across every surface in the house. Or go with asking her brain to bring up what she heard. Worth a try. Then, she is the hell out of here.

Danae shuts her eyes. It takes a few minutes to calm the monkeys swinging through her brain. She coaxes her breathing to slow, deep and even. Her adult-self tells her how dang corny this is. She does it anyway— asks her child-self to guide her back to that time. It's live-time, not like a long-past memory, and she experiences it as if she is there. Now.


It's bedtime. Mama's car cranks. Then Daddy bangs out of the house.

Mouse's cool hands tuck and smooth the covers around Danae's shoulders. "Sleep tight. Don't let the bed bugs bite."

They giggle. Danae likes bugs as good as her sister and neither of them would mind sharing a bed with them.

Her bedroom door closes with a soft snick. Mouse tiptoes down the hall. Another door closes.

A sharp breeze rattles the window and fingers of chilled air tap her exposed skin. Danae feels the bed soft beneath her. She burrows into the warmth of quilted layers and falls asleep.

Raised voices nudge her awake: a man's deep shouts, a girl's feeble replies. Danae pulls the covers over her head, with only one ear sticking out. She and Mouse know—when sounds scare you, don't move. Don't open your door, or go to where the voices are, or try to hear the words. The sounds will stop, eventually.

The wall vibrates with a loud thwack, like something hitting the wall separating Danae from the voices.

Then stillness.

She lies awake for a while longer. Whatever happened, it's okay now. She pulls the quilt down so both ears can work. Footfalls pass her room, a door opens and closes. In a short while, the same foot noises go the opposite way. A thump-thump sound. Something shushing outside her door. The feet take different kinds of steps, heavy and slow. A door bangs shut.

A long time passes. No more house sounds. Then, she hears the crank and rumble of Daddy's truck engine. It roars past her window and fades.

She breathes out. Mouse is nearby. Daddy's not. The bad things are over.

Mouse is gone by the next morning. Left, like it mattered not one hair to Danae or anyone.

**D**anae opens her eyes. The gown crimps where her palms have sweated. She hand presses it smooth.

Something niggles. *What?*

She reviews the days that followed. The policemen who came to ask questions. Mama crying and crying. Neighbors stopping by, bringing food like someone had died.

Danae remembers hiding from the adults in the secret fort where she and Mouse often went to escape—a patch of briars and overgrown brush at the back corner of the property.

The recall shifts once more, playing back as if she's once again in that moment.

**H**er younger self sobs so hard no sounds come out, then she notices something odd. The bed of pine straw and leaves she and Mouse raked into their spot has been disturbed. The ground shows in places, pressed down.

She barrels to the carport storage shelves, looking for the sleeping bags Uncle Billy and Aunt Sylvia gave them last Christmas. Her blue bedroll is there, tucked tight in its drawstring bag. Mouse's pink sleeping bag is missing. Her sister didn't run off! She's been camping out here, close by, waiting for Daddy to calm down. Things will get better as they always do, before they get bad again.

For the next two days, Danae slips food and water to the secret spot. Mouse won't have to sneak into the house if she has enough to eat. On day three, Daddy snatches Danae from bed, questions her about the paper plate of wrapped ham biscuits he had found, and tells her it *will* stop. If he catches her anywhere near that corner, he will tear up her behind so bad she won't walk for a month. He'll know if she defies him. She's too scared to try.

By the end of January, Daddy has cleaned out all of Mouse's clothes. Thrown her writing pads in the trash. Torn up all of the pictures, everything that proved Mouse ever existed. Gone.

Except for one gown Danae manages to shove into a shoebox.


Now, Danae's grown-up self hears her daddy's final words repeat in her mind until she chants them out loud. "Mouse failed. Mouse failed. Mouse failed."

*Failed. Failed. Failed.*

Her eyes pop open wide.

*Failed, or Fell?*

"Fell! Oh dear God, *fell!*"

Danae's mouth goes dry. She jumps to her feet, takes a few stumbling steps at first, then breaks into a run after she exits the back door. At the corner of the yard, she weaves through the thicket to her and Mouse's secret spot. Through thorny vines and weeds, she can barely make out the oval patch where no trees grow. She falls to her knees and sweeps layers of deadfall and leaves aside until the dirt shows.

She plows her fingers into the earth, heaving up the layers softened by a recent shower. The dirt grows dense, packed hard. Her nails chip and the cuticles tear. Blood taints the disturbed clumps Danae pitches to the side. When the ground fails to yield further, Danae jumps up and runs to her mama's old tool shed, returning with a rust-pocked trowel.

Layer upon layer of heavy soil give way.

She's wrong. Has to be. Crazy to even think what she's considering. How could anyone, even someone like her daddy—

A rotten piece of hot-pink material snags on the tip of the trowel. The dark-stained image of a butterfly rips asunder when Danae pulls back.

Two more scoops reveal the round, blanched white of a skull. The trowel falls and catches on the briars. Danae stares at the edge of Mouse's sleeping bag. She brushes away more soil, feels hard lumps beneath the cloth. She stumbles back a few feet, falls to all fours, and vomits until nothing comes out, save for strings of bile.


**D**anae listens for the sound of sirens and wonders if they will screech into the driveway, lights flashing. The neighbors will get a kick out of that. Then again, they probably won't take particular notice since the authorities have visited this house, and her aunt's, so often.

But no, there'll be no need for sirens. The real emergency happened so long ago, only the bones and tattered physical evidence remain, as lifeless and faded as the plastic, flowered wreath on the front door.

The late morning is gray, reminiscent of the day Mouse moved. Fogged, like Danae's brain. Random thoughts come and go: the porch needs a fresh coat of paint; a shutter hangs askew; a broken oak limb pins down one of Mama's spindly rose bushes. She studies the blood clotted around her torn cuticles and the caked dirt beneath her fingernails.

She feels nothing. Not sadness. Not amazement. Not even the need for a drink.

## Thirty-six

Danae sits on the front step. A changeling wind blows from the north, crisp and dry, a welcome shift for this part of the Deep South. As if Daddy died and took the devil's heat with him.

A cardinal flits to a branch next to an empty birdfeeder, eyes Danae, and flies off. She thinks of the story Miz Mevlyn told her, about her encounter with a similar bird after Mr. Sam died. If this one brings love-filled greetings from beyond, are they dictated by Mouse?

She's tired in every corner of her body and soul. Aunt Sylvia offered her assistance with the final cleanout, but Danae politely refused. Her aunt had more than paid her dues.

Piles of trash wait by the roadside. Thank goodness for Antoine and his cousin's help. The furniture, dishes, and her daddy's best clothing went to charity. She signed over the hunting truck, fishing boat, and trailer to Antoine. Aunt Sylvia found a buyer for the F150 pick-up. Could've kept either, or both, of her daddy's vehicles, but merely looking at that shiny Ford F150 and beat-up Ranger gave her a sick feeling. A couple of her father's work cronies took tools and whatever else they could tote. Beyond a trifling of items, Danae scraped the rest into garbage bags.

Two cardboard boxes hold the few things Danae plans to store at Aunt Sylvia's: pieces of Grandma Wilson's china, Mama's battered watering can, a metal box of fishing tackle, and a hammer that had belonged to her maternal grandfather. She found nothing else of J.J., Mouse, Mama, or herself: Big John had swept all of them aside like they had never existed.

Sad, years of life in this house, and only a small fraction is worth passing along. The remainder will languish in the county landfill.

Danae hears the asthmatic rumble of the engine before she sees the car. Mevlyn pulls into the dirt drive and parks; Danae feels something besides weary gloom for the first time in days.

The old woman carries a wicker basket in one hand and uses her cane with the other. Sonny bounds from the back seat and slams his nose to the ground. The tip of his tail quivers like a reed sticking from swift water.

"Don't you go running off," Mevlyn calls to him. "I'm not of a mind to chase your sorry ass across Alabama."

Danae watches the old woman trundle toward the house.

"Figured I'd find you inside, sorting things out," Mevlyn says when she reaches the steps.

"Air's fresher out here." Danae descends, gives her a hug, then helps her ascend. "How'd you find me? Did Aunt Sylvia call you about . . . ?"

"She did." Mevlyn shuffles to a porch rocker and sits with a grunt. "Besides, it's hit the news."

Danae's shoulders tighten.

"Surprised you don't have a passel of reporters and such camped out in the yard. They'll come, you know. Won't be a'tall amazed if they don't do one of those true crime TV shows about it."

"Probably."

Mevlyn gives the porch and house an appraising look. "This is all yours now, reckon."

"Yep."

"I brought you crispy chicken, biscuits, and some of my potato salad you like so much. Figured you wouldn't be cooking, what with cleaning things out."

"Thanks Miz Mevlyn." The scent of fried food sifts from the basket and reminds Danae how hungry she is. When was the last time she ate? Had to be day before yesterday, leftover funeral food. Her stomach roils a bit, as it has for the past few days. And she's so exhausted, breathing requires effort. Daddy's in the ground. Suppose what's left of Mouse will be soon, once the authorities release the remains.

Mevlyn opens the basket lid and pulls out a thermos, pours two Styrofoam cups of coffee, and hands her one. Danae takes a deep draw of the creamy brown liquid, perfectly sugared. Every cell feels as if it goes *ahhhhh*.

Mevlyn gives her a long look. "This mess coming out is bound to help you, after a fashion. No more wondering."

Wondering. She'll always do that. The only person who knew exactly what happened that night is in a box with six feet of fresh red clay weighing him down. Was her daddy a murderer? She'll never know for sure, until she's on the same side as Mouse. Not like the movies, where everything is tied up with a neat bow at the end—who done it, why, when, and how it went down.

Danae runs her hands through her hair and feels it thick with oil. Good thing the weather's shifted a bit, or she'd stink to high heaven. The water and power are on inside, but she hasn't been able to bring herself to shower in *that* house.

"Everyone will know my family's awful secret."

"The new will wear off, eventually. Something else will happen and that pack of wolves will stalk different prey. Besides, everyone has secrets, m'dear." Mevlyn's eyes narrow to slits. "I'm gonna tell you mine." Mevlyn pauses. "I'm a Yankee. A *Damn* Yankee. From Ohio."

Danae's mouth hangs open.

"Everyone believes I'm from south Georgia, by way of Alabama."

"How the heck did you manage that?"

"When I first stepped off the bus in Montgomery, I saw right off that I would have to find ways to blend. Otherwise I'd always be a misfit. Back then, a Yankee was as welcome down here as a full-blown case of the clap. By the time I married Sam and we decided Chattahoochee was where we would settle, I was already well on my way to being a bona fide Southern belle. After all of these years, I even *think* in Southern."

Danae laughs. Mevlyn is the one person who always finds ways to surprise. "Is that the huge *sin* Sherman referred to?"

"Yes."

"Curious, if you don't mind me asking, what do you have on Sherman?"

"Sam and I talked a great deal after he first got his diagnosis. He worried his brother might be a thorn in my side if he ever figured out my charade. Now, my husband wasn't one to hold anything over anyone's head. I promised I would take Sherman's list of no-good deeds to my own grave, unless I needed leverage."

"Must be one heck of a list."

Mevlyn tilts her head. "We all had lapses in judgement when we were too young and ignorant to care about consequences." She hesitates. "Suffice it to say that Sherman Jenson is not the elevated saint he wants everyone to believe he is, nor is his wife. Annabelle Leigh would lop off his man-parts and deep fry them if she learned even a fraction of the things Sam shared with me."

Danae burns to know, but it's Mevlyn's tale to tell. Or not. Danae waits.

"I wrote it all down, every word Sam and I shared before he died, from his brother's ne'er-do-wells to more intimate things between me and my husband." Mevlyn turns to face her. "I've set up certain papers, Danae. No matter what your future holds, what you decide to do with the rest of it, you're family—to me, and to Sam."

Mevlyn pivots to stare out into the yard where Sonny continues to nose-root for anything that moves. "Read my scribblings, if you've a mind to, after I'm gone. Most of them are a sure-fire cure for insomnia. Others are better than a trashy novel."

Danae watches the old woman's features harden. "If Sherman and Annabelle Leigh haven't busted Hades wide open by the time I 'shuffle off this mortal coil'—that's die, in case you aren't a fan of Shakespeare—you can commit his, and her, transgressions to memory, to give you the same leverage I have now. I assure you, if I drop onto the Wash-Away's linoleum tomorrow and do more than break a bone, those two will burn ruts in the pavement getting to Chattahoochee to lay claim to anything not tied down." She huffs. "But you'll have the law on your side. Send them wheeling back in the direction they came from. Promise?"

"Yes ma'am."

"I trust you to keep *my* secret." The old woman gives Danae the stern eyes, the same expression she reserves for errant children and annoying traveling salesmen.

Danae crosses her heart. "What secret?"

Secrets fester. They have a way of exploding. Or become so much a part of a person, they burr beneath the skin.

Bordering the porch, the woody skeleton of heat-scorched lantana bushes sit like tethered tumbleweeds. Carcasses of perennials litter the flowerbed around it, a moat of brown. Purple cornflower, zinnia, and coreopsis: the names come to Danae in a flash. A hazy memory paints over the long summer heat's kill and she sees purples, oranges, yellows, and hot pinks, and Mama bending over the blooms, an uncharacteristic pleasant expression on her features. The little plants lean their petal-ringed faces toward her.

Other bits float into Danae's reminiscence. How Mama snipped flowers and scattered bouquets through the house, her small way of interjecting beauty into ugly. Light into dark.

A faint sensation brushes her cheek like the wings of a trapped moth. Danae blinks and looks at the dormant lantana. No clusters of pink and yellow. No fuzzy serrated leaves. Only brown. Dried up. She senses the house behind her, as barren as the flower garden. Somewhere, shoveled beneath the layers of sadness and misery, do a few bright memories remain in this place? If she waits long enough, will they fight to surface?

Sonny circles and dances around a pine tree, eyeing a squirrel. Danae and Mevlyn sit in comfortable silence for a bit, rocking, listening to the country quiet.

"First time I laid eyes on you, I pegged you as a PR person," Mevlyn says after a few minutes.

"Huh?"

"I never told you that story?"

Danae shakes her head.

Mevlyn chuckles. "Means *Purty-Much Ruined.* You looked like you'd been run over by a log truck and nothing was left save a flattened husk."

"Describes me."

"It may have then. Not now."

Danae turns to face her. "What am I supposed to do, Miz Mevlyn?"

"It's up to you. I *made* my home. You can make yours where you choose. Here, or in Chattahoochee, or anywhere. You'll always have a place with me. And I can tell you for certain, you got friends that love you, and don't even get me started on Mr. Hal. He's lost without you at the shop. You even won over Elvina Houston and that is no small feat." She rocks back for momentum, pushes up with both arms, stands. "Reckon I best get on back."

Fresh sadness squeezes Danae's chest. "So soon? You just got here."

"I got responsibilities." Mevlyn looks into the distance, as if she can see Chattahoochee and the Wash-Away Laundromat from miles away. "You got that cell phone. We can talk from time to time." She clutches her cane and balances, gathers Danae for a warm hug. Then, she whistles and Sonny appears. "Get to the car, dog." The old woman grabs the basket and Danae helps her descend to the yard.

Mevlyn gives her arm a squeeze and walks toward the car. Sonny runs past her and waits by the passenger side door.

Danae glances behind her. She takes a deep breath and lets it out.

"Hold up, Miz Mevlyn."

The old woman pauses.

"You have room for a couple of boxes?"

Mevlyn nods.

"Let me grab them and lock up. I'm coming with you."

# Thirty-seven

**M**evlyn watches Danae cram in two bananas and a cinnamon roll, chewing as fast as possible. "When you gonna own it, gal?"

Danae lops off a thick slice of cheddar cheese and shoves it into her mouth. "What?"

"Don't talk with your mouth full. You'll choke." Mevlyn wills her eyebrows to stillness. Now is not the time for an excited ripple. "You know exactly what I mean."

The gal avoids eye contact and pushes another chunk of cinnamon roll into her mouth. Her cheeks bulge. Sugar crusts the corners of her lips.

"Chew that up and swallow before I have to call 911. Meet me out on the patio. I got the skeeter torches already lit." Mevlyn turns and walks away before Danae has a chance to invent forty reasons why she can't join her. Sonny prances side to side, looking from Mevlyn to Danae and back, then trails behind Mevlyn.

Outside, lightning bugs flit in the hedges. Yard fairies, Mevlyn likes to think of them that way. Like everything in nature, their show is about attracting mates, procreation, and the survival of a species. Comes right down to it, isn't everything about surviving? If it wasn't for the next generations, what would be the point of it all?

Mevlyn settles into a butt-worn chair cushion. Behind her, the sliding glass door opens and closes. Danae lowers into the chair beside hers and sets a tall glass of milk and a saucer loaded with four cinnamon rolls onto a side table the gal had recently repurposed from a downed tree trunk. Clever, Mevlyn thinks. City folks would pay a pretty penny for what they now refer to as *rustic chic.*

Three citronella torches cast arcs of amber light and scented air, a barricade to mosquitoes. Though the evening temperatures are tolerable now, it will take a solid frost to kill off the blood-suckers. Everyone with good sense longs for the crisp weather of fall, though the season arrives later and later. Just last year, it had been after Thanksgiving before Mevlyn unpacked a light jacket, and she wore a short-sleeved shirt to a Christmas party. Mother Earth is unsettled. So are its inhabitants.

"You planning on eating all of those rolls?"

"Maybe," Danae says.

"Lot of sugar to dump in your system this late of the evening."

"So?"

Mevlyn reaches for a slick way to steer the conversation. "So, there's more now to consider than just yourself."

"Not catching your drift."

"Like I asked you inside, when you gonna come clean about it, Danae?"

"What?"

Back from his pee-sprinkle rounds, Sonny whines at Mevlyn's feet. She pats her lap and the terrier jumps aboard. "Denial is a wonderful thing. I admit to being darn good at it. But what you're shrugging aside won't keep hidden much longer."

"Miz Mevlyn, I don't—"

"Listen here, missy. I may be older than moon dust, but I am still a woman. And I might not have been successful at the thing only a woman is capable of doing, but I do recall the signs."

Cravings. Yes, she had her share. Not sweets. Bacon had been Mevlyn's prenatal focus. Every morning. On sandwiches later in the day. Two or three slices before bedtime. Eaten sizzling-hot from the skillet or days-old cold, it didn't matter. She chopped it up and mixed it into her biscuits, her omelets, and her pimento cheese and egg salad. Sam kidded her about consuming a pig a week, but didn't dare stand in her way.

Those first few weeks, she would wolf it down and puke it back up. Thank goodness that stopped after month four. Until the reason for her cravings ceased, Mevlyn had swallowed enough lard to last her the rest of her life. After she and Sam lost little Cecilia, years passed before Mevlyn could stand the smell or sight of bacon.

Mevlyn waits for the gal to speak. When she doesn't, she decides to tackle it straight-on. "You're pregnant. If I sensed it, you most certainly have."

After they returned from Alabama, Mevlyn and Danae had settled into a restful routine. Danae worked at the shop, Mevlyn held court at the Wash-Away, and things only happened to other people. Elvina kept her abreast of the town's drama and picked out DVDs for the two of them. Mevlyn watched her soap opera to fill in the gaps.

Aside from intuition, Mevlyn found confirmation in the sticks Danae had peed on, trussed in toilet paper in the bathroom garbage. Four of them, as if the first three told lies the gal hoped the final would rebut.

Mevlyn knows one fact: no matter if it's on one of her shows or part of reality, life is a series of squalls with patches of sunshine slipped in between.

In the low light, Danae's features don't give away her reaction. "What'll I do." The words come out flat, a statement of resolve, not a question.

"Ain't like times past. Nowadays, you have options. It's not my decision. And I won't sit in judgement. But no matter what you settle on, I will be right here to help you through it." Mevlyn reaches for Danae's hand and gives it a tiny squeeze. "Do you know the father?"

Danae hesitates, then says, "Gary Dixon."

A nice boy, in spite of his kin. Mevlyn worries a bit about the subtle uptick in the gal's voice, the uncertainty behind the name.

"In the morning, we can call up and make you an appointment with a doctor over in Tallahassee. Got to start somewhere, and a doc out of town will slow the tongues that are bound to wag, for a while." Mevlyn nudges Sonny from her lap, then stands. "But for now, we need to rest our spirits and calm our brains. I'm gonna brew us both a cup of chamomile tea."

## Thirty-eight

**D**anae bolts into the kitchen after work, talking loud to Mevlyn, wherever she is. "Pimento cheese! I *must* have pimento cheese, that yummy kind you make with the bacon!"

She opens the refrigerator and paws past bottles and plastic tubs of leftovers. "Oh, please, please, please, tell me you made some more." She spies the margarine tub with an X marked on the top and lets out a squeal. "Yes!"

Can't wait on bread or crackers. Danae pulls out a drawer and grabs a tablespoon to dig into the creamy cheese mixture. "Swear to you, Miz Mevlyn, I have never really liked this stuff that much before, but yours is . . . Ohmygah . . . So good! This baby's gonna come out with red dashes on his or her skin—no, I'm thinking it's a girl, definitely. I—"

Danae stalls and blinks. Two figures sit in the dimly lit den. The blue light from the television flickers. Miz Mevlyn and who is—? *Oh crap.*

For a beat, no one speaks. Danae swallows the last glob of pimento cheese. She walks into the den with the tub and spoon still in hand.

"Funny coincidence," Elvina Houston says. "I came over to beg Mevlyn's secret recipe for pimento cheese for a women's club meeting. Try as I may, I can never get the same taste to mine."

"It's the Greek yogurt I add," Mevlyn says.

"Did you . . . tell her . . . about. . .?" Danae's hand lowers to cup a small mound at her midsection.

"Dear girl, I believe you just accomplished that." Mevlyn blows out a breath. "It was bound to come out soon anyway. Pregnancy is a secret with a short shelf life."

Danae shovels pimento cheese into her mouth.

"I don't reckon that tub of cheese spread will have to concern itself with shelf life," Elvina states.

Tension evaporates with their shared laughter.

"Elvina, now—" Mevlyn says.

Elvina holds up a hand. "I swear on a stack of Bibles, I will keep my mouth sealed shut." She motions toward Danae. "Your belly's gonna make the announcement. All I ask, when it comes out, is that you let me handle the baby shower. I've collected ideas for games, over the years. Best one I ever heard is where you smear different brands of melted chocolate bars inside disposable newborn diapers, then everyone takes turns opening them up and smelling them to guess what they are."

Mevlyn and Danae say *yuck!* at the same time.

"You are a shoe-in for the shower organizer, but we may need to discuss the games," Mevlyn says. "If you can help us keep this under wraps, at least until Danae makes a solid plan, we'll let you go with us to the first ultrasound. They're in 3-D now."

"So, I gather you're keeping this baby?" Elvina directs toward Danae.

"I want to. She's mine." Danae eats more cheese, licks the spoon. "I have no clue how I will pay for any of it, or how I will be able to raise her."

Elvina tips her head and smiles at Mevlyn. "I reckon between the three of us, we can figure it out, eh Mevlyn?"

"Reckon we can."

"Amazon will deliver every single thing we need to get started. I can have the orders sent to my address. People are used to seeing delivery trucks pull up to my curb." Elvina taps on her smartphone. "We can set up gift registries for the rest."

Danae rushes to where Mevlyn and Elvina sit, their heads bent together. She smushes them into a hug.

Elvina smooths the front of her dress. "You best ease up a bit now. You're dealing with two old women with spun sugar for bones." Her tone might fuss, but her face shows she's touched by the affection.

"Speak for yourself." Mevlyn shoulder-bumps Elvina. "I'm made out of pure concrete."

"Says the woman who just got over a broken ankle."

Before the two can devolve into a one-up insult contest, Danae spins and returns to the kitchen.

After Danae leaves for her room, loaded with a bag of pita chips, a plate piled high with chopped veggies, and a tall glass of decaf iced tea, Elvina turns to Mevlyn.

"Give it up. What's got you so tied in knots?"

"You just heard it. Danae's pregnant, unwed, and barely employed."

Elvina whisks the statement aside. "Surface cuts. All, manageable." The head of the Little Old Lady Hotline leans in and squeezes her eyelids into slits. Mevlyn's seen this before—those narrowed, zeroed-in, truth daggers. As much a part of Elvina Houston's persona as Mevlyn's bouncing brows.

Mevlyn wrings her hands. She used to think the affectation was an invented cliché for the state she's in. Nobody wrings hands. Now, she's perfected it to the point the webbing between her fingers are rosy. "Worry is about to chew me up and spit me out."

"I realize I have a rep in this town." Elvina purses her lips, then they straighten and twist to one side. "I've worked hard to build that reputation."

Mevlyn's hands stall mid-wring. "You have jumped the rails. We are discussing *me* and *my* worry."

"If you'll let me finish," Elvina says, her voice stern. "I know close to a hundred percent of what goes down in Chattahoochee and about eighty-five in Gadsden County. Now, as for Sneads," she motions in the general direction of west, "across the river is not my jurisdiction. I never overstep. Not professional."

Amusement tamps down Mevlyn's anxiety.

"Point is, I know a *lot*, but I only share *some*. My dear departed friend Piddie Longman taught me well. Even *she* took some secrets to her final rest."

Elvina sits with her back straight and her hands resting prim in her lap, like a queen after an important declaration. When Mevlyn doesn't offer clarification on her end, Elvina sucks in air and huffs it out in a sigh so exaggerated, Mevlyn's surprised she doesn't blow an artery.

"I am worried about everything, Elvina," Mevlyn says. "I've put legal papers into place, but the what-ifs are keeping me up nights. What if something happens to me? Say, I drop one morning when I take Sonny for a walk . . . ?"

At the mention of his name and *walk* in the same sentence, Sonny raises his head, thumps his tail and whines. When no walk seems imminent, he lowers his head and closes his eyes.

Mevlyn presses on. "What if Sam's degenerate brother and that fat-lipped tart he's married to bowl into town and try to kick Danae and the baby out onto the street? What then?"

Elvina's lips part. Mevlyn barrels ahead. "And there's the birth. Even with modern medicine, women still die in labor. That innocent baby will be cast to the wind." Mevlyn ponders. "There's the aunt, Sylvia, but she's no spring chicken herself. If she can't take the youngun in as the next of kin, that child will be snatched away and pitched into the system. All, with me standing here with my arms spread wide and my heart breaking, and not a damn thing I can do about it!" Mevlyn's voice cracks. "I've lost Sam. If I lose Danae, or the baby, I don't think I can pull myself together enough to draw another breath."

"It would be simpler if Danae was your daughter. Grandmothers raise children all the time."

"But I am not, Elvina. I. Am. Not." Mevlyn doesn't try to staunch the tears. "I'm nobody's mama, as much as I have always wanted to be."

Elvina digs in her purse and hands over an embroidered handkerchief. "Adoption could be the answer."

Mevlyn blows her nose with a honk. "Thanks for taking me seriously."

"Not, as in adopting the infant. Adopt *Danae*."

"She's an adult."

"Still. It's done. I know for a fact. Adult adoption." Elvina whips out her smartphone with such a snap, she reminds Mevlyn of a gunslinger. "Let's consult Google." Her fingers tap, then she leans in and reads,

"'Depending on how quickly a person conducts the filing and the case load of the court, adult adoptions may take between sixty and ninety days. Both parties must agree to the adoption.'"

Mevlyn nurtures a flicker of hope. "Has to be expensive, and it would need to happen pretty fast."

Elvina stores her phone with a practiced flourish. "I know people, and people who know people."

"You do this for us, Elvina Houston, and I'll clean your quilts for no charge for the next couple of years."

"Only a couple?"

"I'd say ten, but who knows how long I can keep going."

Elvina shifts to barter mode, another gear Mevlyn recognizes from watching the woman negotiate with the city commission over whatever issue she's supporting, the most heated being the argument against moving *all* large holiday celebrations to the river landing, which Elvina's side had won. "How about, if you clean up to three quilts and/or comforters per year, for as long as you operate the Wash-Away?"

"You damn sure got yourself a deal." Mevlyn extends a hand and they seal with a shake.

"Bears to mention, dear—if you're going to have a baby around, you have to curb your cussing."

"I know. I know. But you've said it yourself, Elvina. Sometimes *shoot* and *darn* don't cut it."

"True. I'll see what I can find out about filing the papers and such. Only thing is, Danae has to agree to this."

"She will." Mevlyn hopes. Tomorrow and the day after that shine brighter. Finally, she will have the daughter she's always wanted. And, God willing, a healthy grandchild.

Elvina secures her purse in the crook of one arm. "I best go and get started on my inquiries. And you best get busy securing that girl's permission."

Mevlyn grabs her cane and stands. Elvina leaves, giving a thumbs-up before she steps from the kitchen door.

She squares her shoulders. "Come with me, Sonny." The terrier pops to all fours and trails her down the hall. She raps on Danae's door. Music lowers on the other side. Danae opens the door.

"I got something to propose."

"Is this a patio talk or a house talk?" Danae tilts her head.

"Whatever will put you at ease."

The gal's face shifts away from amusement.

"Nothing bad. Wipe that ranch dip off your lips and let's sit outside."

Mevlyn moves to her rocker. Danae joins her in a few moments. Sonny makes the pee rounds and returns to sit at their feet.

"What's up?" Danae asks.

"How would you feel about being my daughter?"

"Huh?"

Mevlyn lays out the plan doing her best to keep her tone neutral.

She really wants to plead.

Malcolm brushes aside leaves and settles onto one of the three cement picnic tables facing the river. "Okay, why this emergency meeting of the advisement council?"

"I can't just *want* to talk to my friend?" Danae slides in beside him.

The sound of the river calms her. If she waded into that brown water, she could float for miles, past the jetties, past the Apalachicola River Bluffs, to the places where the river widens to lakes then blends with the Gulf. Then, to the Gulf Stream, tugged to touch other shores. By that time, she wouldn't be Danae with child, she'd be just one organic mass, supporting the scavenger fish.

Must be the hormones. Online articles say how they make a pregnant woman bat-shit crazy.

"You know you can tell me anything, Nae."

"Brace yourself."

Malcolm makes a flamboyant show of making himself as stalwart as possible. "Ready. Go."

Danae pauses before she blows her best friend's ever-loving mind. Malcolm probably thinks this is about her other family drama, the one where her sister ended up rotting in the briars. She doesn't want to talk about that anymore. To anyone. Besides, the gory details are all over the internet and Jerome has access to the police report.

"I'm pregnant. I think it's Gary's. I can't be sure. Because I got high and drunk and Rich attacked me and I am really not a hundred percent positive he didn't full-on rape me."

"Sweet Jesus wept."

"And Mevlyn wants to adopt me."

"I don't drink to excess and I don't get high. I may have to start doing both."

Danae snorts out breath. "Don't recommend it."

"There's so much . . . I don't know where to start." She takes a breath, closes her eyes, and listens to the river. She releases her air to join the gentle breeze whispering through the willow branches. "Let me lay it all out. Hold questions to the end, please."

Malcolm cups his hands behind his ears first, then indicates full visual attention with two fingers held in a V, pointing toward his eyes, then toward Danae's.

The telling takes a half-hour, counting intermissions for Danae to stare across the Apalach, cry, or cover her face with her palms. Malcolm remains silent. Finally, she turns to him and asks, "What do you think?"

"It is a boatload to absorb."

"Try living it."

"My first impulse is to find Rich and strangle him. But then I'd end up in prison for life, and not be of any use to you or your baby."

"I had dark thoughts too, not only of killing him, but that he'd get locked up and gang-raped in prison." Danae stretches, cracks her knuckles. "Since he'll never spend even an overnight incarcerated, that won't happen either."

"Does Mevlyn know?"

"Most of it. I haven't told her that I can't actually say if Rich . . ." She shivers.

"I am not being judgey, but why didn't you go to my dad, have the creep arrested?"

"Mevlyn and I did, because of what happened to her building. But at that time, I felt pretty sure there was nothing I could prove. No physical aftermath, if you get my meaning. My word against his, and you know how that would've flown. And by the way, don't go getting all pissed at your daddy. He promised not to tell anyone, not even you."

"Fits with his ethics, it being a police matter." Malcolm scooches over and drapes an arm around Danae. "What about Gary?"

"Been sort of avoiding him. I know he wonders why. He's texted me a few times."

"You'll have to tell him, eventually."

"I know. I will. Can we just drop it for now?"

Malcolm gives her shoulder a squeeze. "Sure. Now, as to this adoption? What's up with that?"

"Mevlyn's way of looking after me and," she pats her stomach, "the bug."

"It sounds reasonable."

"What should I do?"

"Your call, Nae. My dad always tells me to 'sit with it' when I have to figure out some heavy question." It's Malcolm's turn to stare out across the river. "When does Miz Mevlyn need an answer?"

"Fairly soon."

"Guess you have some sitting to do." He drops his arm from her shoulder and reaches for her hand. "I only have one tiny request."

Danae faces him.

"Let Uncle Mal be in the delivery room."

"Oh, that's creepy."

"Nothing creepy about it, Nae. I'd really like to be there with you. I could even be your labor coach."

"And, *Uncle* Mal? Really?"

"What, you don't want me to be a huge part of this kid's life?"

"You absolutely can."

"Be Uncle Mal, or be there for the delivery?"

A version of the upcoming scene plays out in her mind. Some stark hospital room with buzzers and beeps and starched sheets. Her legs strung up in stirrups. Her face streaming sweat and snot. And her best friend watching a head emerge from her hoo-hoo. There'll be blood and yucky excretions. Mevlyn will be there, of course. And the doctor and a nurse.

"The uncle part is a go. I'll have to sit with the question of whether or not you get a front row seat."

# Thirty-nine

The Tuesday morning crowd at the Wash-Away is thin. Danae snaps on Sonny's leash.

"I appreciate you taking him to the vet. That ear's been dealing him a fit again. Nothing I do seems to help." Mevlyn looks down at Sonny with her brows crimped together. "Go ahead and get them to give him a bath and clip those talons. I'd rather be slapped with a mildew-sour towel than do them myself."

"Don't mind taking him at all." Danae gives the dog her *poor-baby* look. "Bet he has ear mites again."

Mevlyn cases the room before she says in a low voice, "you given that other thing we talked about any thought?"

"Matter of fact, I have."

"When you and Sonny get back, I'll have us some sandwiches ready." She holds up a hand before Danae can speak. "Pimento cheese with bacon and jalapenos."

"Oh, yes!" Water gathers in Danae's mouth. If she wasn't pregnant, she'd worry about the strange cravings one minute and nausea the next. Early mornings are especially hard. A few more weeks and the retching will ease up. She hopes.

Not that she's against a woman's power to choose what happens to her own body, but abortion had never entered her mind. After learning the truth about Mouse, the glob growing inside of her is the only thing keeping Danae from folding in on herself. Bug is less than an inch long, according to the charts she's studied online, and the bag of cells and chromosomes makes her feel less alone.

"Get on your way before it gets hotter." Mevlyn waves them toward the door. "I don't like the idea of you running every morning. I've been pondering on ways you can get your exercise without having a heat stroke."

"I'll just run earlier." Danae inches toward the exit. "Promise."

"That won't work. You could get run over, the way people pay no mind to their driving. Too much rushing to get to work and looking at their phones."

"Okay, Okay. Later." Danae hustles Sonny to the door before Mevlyn can drum up more concerns. Though Danae hasn't shared her decision about adult adoption, Mevlyn's already acting like a fretful parent.

She's eighteen. She doesn't need a mother.

It dawns on Danae: Yes, she does. Especially now.

If only her own mama were alive. Estelle Gray loved babies as much as she did the elderly. Aunt Sylvia pops to mind. Her aunt was the one who kept her afloat after Mama died. She deserves to know about Bug.

Danae envisions how her aunt and her mama would carry on and on about a baby on the way, scouring the Dollar Stores and garage sales for clothes and supplies. Aunt Sylvia never had kids and always wanted them so badly. Yet another *if only*—Mama and Aunt Sylvia, taking turns cradling Bug in their arms, cooing and humming lullabies. Danae wishes ...

"Wish in one hand and shit in the other and see which one fills up fastest." one of her daddy's bits of wisdom. Mevlyn says it too, only her version makes Danae smile.

Danae and Sonny turn from West Washington Street and traverse the block to the veterinarian's office. A few short days ago, seeing Carrie would have thrilled Danae, back when she was Mouse hiding out as a meek vet tech. Now, Danae counts a trip to that building as just another errand. The truth took away the pressure of planning every action, longing for a crack she might find to get Carrie to open up.

When she and Sonny enter, one other patient waits, an unsettled feline in a gray carrier. Danae nods good morning to the cat's owner, then signs the check-in sheet. She grabs up a pet-lover's magazine and leads Sonny toward the padded chairs farthest from the yowling cat.

The lady looks familiar. Danae searches memory. She must be suffering pregnancy brain, Normally, things pop up the second she summons. Ah, yes. Now she recalls. Red Chevy sedan, front brake pads, tire rotation.

"How are those new brakes working out?" Danae asks.

"Wonderful. A relief, actually. I had begun to worry about running into someone."

They discuss cars and traffic for a few minutes before the front desk woman motions the lady and the complaining cat to the back. Danae distracts Sonny with the bacon bit treats she has stuffed in one pocket. The door opens and Carrie indicates it's their turn.

Danae's chest squeezes at the sight of the person she thought to be her sister. The flash of seeing the place Mouse had lain for years brings fresh tears. Mouse is gone. Not hiding in Chattahoochee. Just gone. Forever. She takes a breath and forces her mind off that sad reality. Carrie leads them to Room Four, then closes the door behind them.

"I'm glad you came in today." Carrie makes full eye contact. "Gary's concerned about you. Me and Jack are, too. And Taylor, as much as Tay can be concerned about anything."

Danae lowers onto the plastic chair, stunned. Did that long string of words come from the woman who barely acknowledged her presence before? All she can utter is, "Oh."

Carrie crouches to pet Sonny's head. "Poor boy. It's that naughty ear again, huh?" She looks back to Danae. "The humidity sets some dogs up for yeast infections. They're hard to cure."

Danae and Carrie stare at each other for a bit before Carrie speaks again. "We know what Rich did to you."

"Oh?" Is that the only word in her blank brain? Jeez.

"Gary figured something bad had gone down. But we didn't fit it together for sure until Jack and Rich got into it about something else." She flips one hand. "Can't remember what, now. Anyway, Gary stepped in to back up Jack, and Rich let loose on him, said some awful things about you. Gary punched him, broke his nose and busted his lip. Bled like a busted pipe. That's after Rich went on his last vandalism raid and before his daddy swept him out of town."

Danae leans back and crosses her arms over her midsection, as if she needs to spare Bug from hearing anything disturbing.

"Gary's tore up about it all. What happened to you, how he feels like it's his fault." Carrie halts, her lips still moving like the words are there, unwilling to leave. "Rich said something that let us know exactly what happened that night."

"Oh."

"When Gary stepped into the fight, Rich said," Carrie dropped her gaze, "'You think you're so special. Well, you ain't the only one that plugged the hole in that dyke. I done her and I done her better than you ever could. She done gone straight because of me.'"

Danae tightens the embrace of her middle.

"I thought Gary was gonna kill him. Jack finally got them pulled apart, but I can tell you, Rich got the worst of it. Horrible thing is, we all know Rich will never answer for what he did to you." Carrie glances at the wall clock, then adds, "the whole thing set Taylor back. He hasn't spoken a word since."

"What's up with Taylor, exactly?" Danae grabs the excuse to shift the talk away from Rich and that night. Finally, she has more to say than *oh*.

"Tay is special needs. Autistic. As long as he's with Jack, he manages all right. Raw emotions, yelling, fighting: they can send Tay deep inside himself to a place none of us can reach, even Jack." Her hair drapes over her eyes when she lowers her head. "I couldn't shield him. Sometimes, you can't keep bad away."

Danae leans over and rubs one hand across Sonny's back and waits.

"Sometimes Jack acts like a complete jerk, but he's not deep-down bad. And he loves his little brother, Tay, like I love mine. When I see Gary hurting, I hurt with him."

"Wait. Gary is your . . . brother?"

Carrie smiles for the first time since the conversation began. "Yes. Half-brother, actually. I didn't grow up with him or even spend much time around him until he was around twelve. Jack and Taylor are our cousins. Our family is," she shrugs, "sort of mixed up."

"I can identify." Danae observes Carrie as she offers dog biscuits to Sonny. How her hands soothe the dog's shaking and her voice comes out slow and even.

It strikes her as profoundly ironic: Carrie isn't her biological sister, but if Gary is Bug's daddy—she sends up a silent plea he is—she and Carrie will be connected by biology. All of the months she chased after Carrie hoping to draw her in, and now the universe presents the woman she used to think of as Mouse as part of a package deal.

Carrie stands, brushing her hands free of hair and crumbs. "You want to hang out and wait, or leave Sonny with us?"

"I'll come back by and get him later, if that's okay by you."

"Sure."

"Is . . . Is Gary around, do you know?"

Carrie consults the wall clock. "Let's see. He's off work by now, should be home. No, wait. He said he'd stop by the Dollar Store for a bag of Meow Mix." She smiles. "We're feeding a little family of feral cats that live in the woods behind the house, a mama and three kittens. Soon as I can gain their trust, I'll bring them in for check-ups and shots, and get the mama cat spayed."

Carrie urges Sonny to walk with her. The way he gazes up at her, the mutt would follow her to Neptune if she asked him to. "You might be able to catch him now, or I can text him to come by here."

"That's okay." Danae stands and tucks her hands into her pockets. "I'm heading there anyway."

"I'm so glad you're going to see him. He's been a wreck." Carrie depresses the door lever.

Danae reaches out and rests a hand on her forearm. "Carrie. Thanks. For talking."

"Sure."

Danae spots Gary in the Dollar Store minutes later, standing in front of the dental supply display, a bag of cat food in hand. His face lights up with a broad smile when he sees her. Danae's lips respond in kind before she can tamp them down. Love is like that, the romance novels say, where the room fades away and all two people can see is each other. Danae holds one palm over her stomach.

"Hey," Gary says.

"Hey."

Gary breaks the moon-eyed contest and looks back to the shelves. "Ever notice how many there are? I mean, whitening, tartar control, enamel repair, cavity protection, mouthwash added. How does a person decide?" He returns attention to her. "Do we really need so many choices of toothpaste, for God's sake?"

Danae picks up a box and hands it to him. "I use this one. Plain, simple. The least amount of extras, Miz Mevlyn says, the better. Same thing with laundry soap."

"Ah."

"It's good to see you, Gary."

"Good to see you, Danae."

How is it, that she made love with this guy—the kind where they sweated and scratched, or rocked sweet and easy—yet she can't seem to piece together a conversation? She opens her mouth, reconsiders, and closes it.

No way will she tell the (hopefully) father of her little bug the BIG NEWS in the toothpaste aisle of the dang Dollar Store. Though, it would make a funny redneck story to tell the kiddo later.

Danae decides to keep it simple, like the choice of toothpaste or soap powder. "We need to talk. Can we go somewhere?"

Gary nods. "Sure. Lemme pay for the cat food and this *simple* toothpaste."

<h1 style="text-align:center">Forty</h1>

Danae plucks at the leg elastic of her bathing suit. "I can't believe I let you two talk me into this."

"Relax, Sparky." Malcolm slathers sunscreen on her back. "You look fabulous. And water aerobics never killed anyone."

The maternity one-piece isn't horrid, roomy enough to accommodate Bug for as long as the weather holds onto summer temperatures. Actually, it's the first bathing suit she's ever owned. Nobody around her part of the Ala-dang-bamer backwoods had a pool, other than the five-inch-deep, round kiddie variety from the Dollar Store. Cut-off jeans and a T-shirt worked fine for creeks, rivers, and ponds. The focus was on avoiding water moccasins and gators, not fashion.

A petite woman tanned to the shade of coffee ice cream greets the three of them. "Don't believe I've met you." She extends a hand. "I'm Willa."

Mevlyn directs the introductions. "I'm Mevlyn, this is Malcolm and Danae. She's expecting, due in early May."

The aerobics instructor turns to Danae. "As long as you have clearance from your doctor, this is a great way to exercise without overheating. You can avoid some of the abdominal crunches if they're uncomfortable, otherwise it's all good."

Mevlyn nods, winks at Danae. "Told you. This'll beat jogging on hot pavement all to pieces."

They stash the beach bag beside a row of lounge chairs and stand, watching the other attendees file by with clear purpose. "You'll need a pool noodle and a set of dumbbells apiece," one hat-clad senior advises on her way past. "Your first time?"

All three nod.

"Stick with the narrow noodles and the dumbbells that have only one ring on either end. It'll be easier until you get the hang of it."

Danae notes the rows of flotation exercise tools already stacked by the edge of the pool. Many are marked with initials.

"Stay put," Malcolm says. "I'll fetch our stuff." He crosses to a wire cube filled with the long pool noodles in every color, then to plastic shelves piled high with dumbbells made of the same light foam material.

"Don't be shy." A tall woman with short-clipped gray hair motions to the steps. "You can't do this wrong. Just keep moving. That's the main thing."

The shallow end of the Olympic-sized facility fills with over thirty people. The majority are women; most appear closer to Mevlyn's age than to Danae's.

"Surely wish we had a pool like this closer to us." Mevlyn stands on the edge, her hands propped on her hips. "Still, we ought to be able to make it over once a week."

"My dad knows a couple of guys on the squad who have pools. We can learn the routine, then do some days back home."

"It will work out." Mevlyn descends the stairs, using the bar to balance. "Oh my, this is delicious."

Danae eases in behind her, making sucking noises through her teeth when the tender parts meet the chilled water.

"Wieners." Malcolm bounds in and ducks under, then pops up dripping and grinning.

They step and paddle their way to the center of the shallow end. Long floating lap lines separate the area from the lanes where serious swimmers pull lap after lap without pausing. This early, most of the children romp in the adjacent activity pool with its sprays and slides. Danae hears their delighted squeals and laughter. Bug will love this when she's out in the world; for now, she'll have to experience it through her human carriage.

"You'll like Willa," the sweet-faced black woman next to Mevlyn states. "She gives us quite a workout." She leans over and says in a lowered voice, "we call her *Switch*."

"Why's that?"

"You'll find out." The woman smiles, then joins the others who are already water-jogging lengthwise of the area designated for the class.

"Okay, all! Let's move!" Willa calls out. "Get those knees up! Pump those arms!"

The buoyancy is marvelous. Danae imagines Bug in her suspended cocoon, bobbing like a cork. Running in water is easy, and Danae doesn't have to wipe stinging perspiration from her eyes. She feels guilty for shirking her responsibility with the two pit bulls; Malcolm promises to walk them early, before he leaves for class. Too bad Girly and Levon can't come to water aerobics.

Willa takes them through ski-hops and sideways bounces and frog kicks.

"This one, I want you to put one foot down, then kick the other stretched-out leg and paddle your hands to turn yourself in a circle," Willa says.

Beside her, Mevlyn laughs. "This one reminds me of a sprayed cockroach."

Several ladies around them chuckle and agree. The steps become more challenging—hoping and kicking in one direction until Willa calls out *Switch!* They lunge in the opposite direction.

"Line dancing in swim trunks," Malcolm dubs it.

Given the frequent changeups, Mevlyn struggles to keep pace. "See where she gets that nickname."

"Heard that." Danae smiles. The water makes her happy. Being cool adds to it.

Since the BIG REVEAL, Danae is seldom alone. Gary, Malcolm, Elvina, and Mevlyn hover like brood hens. Even Jack and Carrie turn up at the oddest moments, once Danae gave Gary permission to let them in on her condition. As soon as Bug debuts, they'll be family. Her insides clench, as they do anytime she considers an even remote possibility that Rich could be Bug's father.

*No! Gary is Bug's daddy.* End of discussion! She muscles the thoughts aside. Willa shows them how to cross-country ski in the water. Danae swooshes her arms and legs. Who knows, one day she may take Bug somewhere with snow and learn to actually ski. Wouldn't that be something.

*I need to tell Aunt Sylvia*, Danae scolds herself for the third time in a few days. Willa changes the move to side karate kicks. Danae stretches one leg out to the side and narrowly misses a collision with an older gentleman who carries himself like a British aristocrat.

Danae takes in the people around her—jogging, hopping, switching. Every shape, height, size, and level of ability. Getting along. Laughing. How often does that happen in any group, these days? Danae is the youngest, but it doesn't matter.

Willa bounces to the edge of the pool. Everyone follows her example, picking up pool noodles for a few rounds, then swapping for dumbbells to work the arms and shoulders.

"It is purely hard to push and shove these dumbbells under the water when they don't weigh nothing at all," Mevlyn comments. "I keep this up and I'll lose my underarm flaps. How will I move around in heaven without my wings?"

"Float like everyone else, I suppose," Danae answers. She attempts Willa's next exercise, a balancing feat with the dumbbells behind her back and both legs in front, slicing together then apart. Reminds Danae of a huge pair of garden sheers.

"Now, bend your legs at the knees, keep them out in front, and spread your legs out, then in, out then in. This stretches your inner thighs." Willa makes the movement look effortless.

"This one will get you ready for being up in those stirrups, come April," Mevlyn says to Danae in a loud voice.

The instructor and several of the ladies chuckle.

Danae flashes Mevlyn a lip twitch. No telling what the old woman will say next.

An hour passes. The class breaks up and clutches of women move to the building housing the showers and restrooms. Others head for the parking lot.

Danae wraps her towel around her. "That was big fun!" Her mouth hurts from so much smiling. Feels amazing, being this happy.

"Agreed." Malcolm motions to the door to the men's room. "I'll change clothes and meet you back here." He digs a small stack of dry clothes from the bag.

"We'll pick out a good place to grab some lunch before we head home," Mevlyn says.

"I adore that part of a workout, getting to pig out later." Danae walks beside Mevlyn with the beach bag slung over one shoulder. One of the cell phones vibrates. She stops, sets the bag onto a lounge, and checks all three of the phones in the Ziploc baggie. "It's yours."

Mevlyn takes the phone. "It's Elvina. Now, she knows we're busy with your doctor's appointment and this class. What in the world?"

"You going to answer it?"

"Let it go to voicemail. She'll leave a message. I could eat a bull moose, I'm so hungry. Elvina can wait."

A couple of hours later, after Italian food and a stop by the Dairy Queen for soft-freeze ice cream, Malcolm steers Mevlyn's car back toward Gadsden County. Mevlyn's phone trills, a text message from Elvina.

"Is she okay? That's the fourth time she's tried to reach you." Malcolm takes his eyes off the Interstate traffic for a second, then resumes being the best driver ever.

"I don't know what's gotten into her." Mevlyn reads the text. "She's got some news she's about to bust to share. Says to call her as soon as we get home so she can come right over."

Danae swivels to look at Mevlyn. The old woman lounges on the sedan's back seat, with her legs propped up. "Must be hot gossip if she wants to deliver it in person," Danae says.

"No telling with that woman." Mevlyn pitches the phone into her purse. "One of her cat videos probably got over a thousand hits on Facebook."

**M**evlyn hears the kitchen door open and bang shut.

"Where are y'all?" Elvina's voice. "Yoo hoo!"

Mevlyn drapes her wet towel over the shower curtain bar and moves from her bathroom and down the hall. She passes Danae's bathroom, hears the toilet flush.

"Elvina, I swear to whoever wants to listen, it is true that you have eyes and ears all over this town. We ain't no more stepped in the door and—" The expression on Elvina's face stalls her sermon. "Come sit down. You look like you're about to pass out."

Elvina crosses the room and settles onto the couch. Her eyes are red-rimmed. She clutches a handkerchief in one hand.

"What in the world has you so upset?"

"Where's Danae? I *must* talk to her."

As if on cue, the gal rushes into the den, her mouth going ninety to nothing. "I want the biggest bowl of ice cream in the history of the world! I don't care if we just had some less than an hour ago, I gotta have—" She stops. "Oh, hi Miz Elvina."

"Danae, Sugar. Please come here." Elvina's voice quivers.

"Okay. Sure. But ice cream—" Danae aims toward the kitchen.

"Please. It's important."

Danae shrugs, moves back into the den.

"You might want to sit down."

Mevlyn's concerns multiply. "Elvina, what in the world?"

Danae slides into a chair. "Sitting. What's up?"

"I don't know how to say this." Elvina dabs her eyes. She pulls her shoulders back. "No easy way. Guess I'll just do my best." She looks at first Mevlyn, then Danae. "Your aunt passed away last night."

Mevlyn notes how Danae flits one hand to rest on her belly. She reaches across and clutches the gal's free hand.

"No. That's not right." Danae frowns. "I just spoke to her day before yesterday. I'm going to see her. She has some stuff to talk to me about and I have things to tell her, too. She's making dumplings and a pear pie."

"I am so sorry, Sugar. My friend that knows your aunt called me this morning. When Sylvia didn't show up for some church social, one of the ladies went to check on her. Your aunt never misses a function, and is never late for anything, especially since your daddy passed."

Mevlyn watches Danae's face, how a wave of shocked sadness washes over her features. That same wave laps over Mevlyn.

"Your aunt passed in her sleep," Elvina says. "A stroke, they believe."

"Why would they call you instead of me, or Danae?" Mevlyn says. "Sylvia had our numbers."

"My friend said they looked everywhere. They found Sylvia's cell phone, but it was locked with no way to know the passcode. The numbers are most likely in there. The lady who found her knew that my friend was the one who connected me to Sylvia to start with, so she contacted her and she phoned me up. I suppose they could've located Danae through the police, but calling me was fast and sure."

"The services. I have to go over there. Aunt Sylvia has nobody to—"

"That is all taken care of," Elvina says. "Your aunt set it all up and paid for everything after your daddy died. Sylvia told her friend, then, that she didn't want anyone to be saddled with any of it."

"She always takes care of everyone." Danae lifts the hand from her belly and holds up a finger count. "That's three. Daddy, Mouse, now Aunt Sylvia. Though, Mouse died years ago. But for me, she left the day I found her."

Death comes in three's: the old saying. Odd, how that often works out. Mevlyn figures it's a way for folks to explain random things that often make no sense. Maybe if they reach that magic number three, they can rest easy. They and their loved ones are spared, this go-'round.

"When is," Danae chokes out a sob, "the funeral?"

"Your aunt will be cremated. The memorial service is set for this Friday at that little country church she and your mother attended."

"Like that. She's just . . . gone." The gal stares, her eyes dry now. The comfort-hand rests on her stomach again.

"We can all go over with you," Elvina offers. "My car will hold five in comfort. She may be an antique and folks poke fun, but she's dependable and cradles whoever's riding inside."

Three days later, two vehicles caravan to Alabama. Elvina drives the Olds. Mevlyn rides shotgun, with Danae in the back seat, flanked by Gary and Carrie. Taylor remains in Chattahoochee, being unable to tolerate such emotion. Behind them, Malcolm and Jack follow in Jack's truck. Necessity makes for strange bedfellows, another old saying Mevlyn holds up as truth. A gay black man and a redneck white man cooped up in the same space. Their mutual love for the gal sets aside differences. Still, Mevlyn would pay good money to eavesdrop on the conversation in that truck.

The church is small and filled to capacity. The preacher keeps the eulogy brief—Sylvia's request, from what Elvina had heard—with two hymns, one being the obligatory *Amazing Grace*. Mevlyn anticipates the usual tiresome invitation for souls at the end, until Elvina whispers: "Only two verses. Sylvia specified that, too."

After the service, the ladies of the church bereavement committee have casseroles, desserts, and sweet tea ready in the fellowship hall beside the sanctuary. Many approach Danae to offer condolences and stories about her aunt, and her mama. No one mentions the rest of the family, or the row of tragedies.

Some things are best kept buried, Mevlyn thinks.

A lady introduces herself to Mevlyn and Elvina. "I'm Belinda. I found Sylvia." The woman shifts her gaze to where Danae sits, a platter of dessert in her lap, the only thing the gal has touched of the meal. Gary stands behind her chair on one side, Carrie on the other. Jack and Malcolm hover nearby. Being the only person of color in the room, Malcolm must feel a bit uncomfortable. He doesn't show it. After the incident Danae had shared with her from not that long ago, Mevlyn's relieved he was allowed in the church. Maybe there's hope for mankind yet.

"I went with Sylvia to the lawyer, to draw up her papers, after *he* died." The way the woman doesn't acknowledge Danae's father by name lets Mevlyn know how she and probably the rest of this congregation felt about him. "It's almost as if Sylvia knew." She dabs her eyes with a wadded tissue. "There's a will in place. She left the house and land to the church, but she packed up several boxes for Danae about a week back. I kept telling her, 'now Sylvia, why're you doing that? She's coming soon and you can sort through things together.' But she insisted."

Another pause to snuffle and dab. "She specified that anything in the house Danae might want—furniture, dishes, whatever—she could take. The church will either sell or donate the rest." The woman taps her temple. "There's something else, what is it? Oh. Yes. She was adamant y'all should take up paying for the health insurance she's carried on Danae. I know where she keeps the policy, so you can take it and call the agent about where to send the bills. Sylvia wanted to assure that her niece had proper coverage, no matter what."

Mevlyn feels deep respect for Sylvia. Even when Danae took off. Even when she didn't let her aunt know where she was, or if she was alive. Even when she didn't make it back to see her after her daddy died. With all of that, Sylvia watched out for her niece. And thank God for it, with Danae's doctor and hospital bills coming their way.

Three hours later, Elvina points the Olds toward Florida. Three boxes packed by Sylvia rest in the trunk. In Jack's truck, a single bed and chest of drawers complete the sum of what Danae selected.

Mevlyn had watched Danae when the gal exited the small frame house and shut the door. She never once glanced back.

Behind her, Danae sits in the Old's cushy seat, her eyes trained on the road ahead, arms held crossed over her belly.

Nobody speaks until they hit the Alabama/Florida border.

"Can we stop for ice cream?"

Mevlyn smiles. Elvina glances in the rearview mirror and says, "Danae, I was just now thinking how much I'd enjoy a soft-serve cone."

Mevlyn picks up her phone. "I'll text the guys."

# Forty-one

**December 21, 2010**

**D**anae sits at the shop's desk. Mounds of receipts teeter on one side of the laptop, queued up to join the accounting software files. As Malcolm has suggested many times, Mr. Hal really, really, *really* needs to convert completely to a digital system and ditch the paper trail. This old way is double the work—correction: double *her* work.

"I'm leaving, Danae. You and Jack make sure to lock up," Mr. Hal calls out.

"Will do."

Since Mevlyn insisted Danae spend more time off her feet, Mr. Hal hired Jack Dixon to train. Strange how things work out. Jack's natural talent blended with instruction from both Mr. Hal and herself bring out a self-confidence and respectability Elvina says the boy's not shown before. Hard to fathom he and Danae had ever been at odds. The more they work together, the more she likes Jack. Underneath the bluster, he's a decent person who got dumped with the muck of his family. Since Rich's dad relocated his son to another part of the country, Jack's started hanging out with Blondie. Brittany's not a bad person, for sure not the sharpest knife in the drawer, but Danae's warmed to her. Taylor hangs out at the shop some afternoons, so stealthy he often startles Danae. Tay's gentle and sweet, and has a knack for organizing the shop supplies and tools, which greatly helps with inventory and ordering.

Knowing Jack's close-by makes staying past dark to catch up the year's end paperwork less daunting. Danae admits it, to herself if to no one else: she often feels afraid. Has to be the hormones and the fact there's more now to protect than herself. She hears Mr. Hal call out goodbye to Jack, who toils in the shop, completing tune-ups on two city trucks. Everything crams into the final days of the year, so Mr. Hal says. If there's a dime left in a budget—personal or business—folks rush to get things completed before December 31st.

Everyone's bustling about, shopping, cooking, cleaning, or adding last-minute decorations. The whole dang town's gone mad. The Wash-Away's infested with holiday cheer. The reds and greens clash with the pink paint job. Mevlyn doesn't care. She is unusually festive this year, with the baby on the way. Since she saw Bug on the last ultrasound, Danae's freshly-minted, court-approved relative is buying up girl-baby clothes and décor, even things in readiness for this time next year, when Bug will celebrate her first Christmas.

Danae's thrilled, too. Still, she holds back. Maybe she doesn't deserve Bug and the happiness the baby will bring. As long as Danae doesn't overly celebrate, those life-altering demons won't take note and destroy the future's promises.

Thanks to Mevlyn, the Wash-Away's cheer oozed across West Washington, and the office around Danae looks like drunken elves have partied hard for days straight. Tinsel loops the walls, blinking lights strobe red, blue, green, and yellow, and angels fight for space with Santa figurines and reindeer. Still, Danae can't complain. The weather's cool now and the heaviness she's felt since Aunt Sylvia died lifts more each day.

She slips the black and white ultrasound image from beneath the papers and smiles down at her daughter—yes, her *daughter*, Bug—confirmed by the 20-week ultrasound.

Her phone text alert chimes: Carrie. Got lemon bars 4 U. C U soon.

Lemon bars! Oh heck yeah! Anything lemon: the craving of the week, not only in food. Next week, it could shift. Early in the second trimester, Mevlyn had thrown up her hands trying to keep Danae's most recent obsession stocked and enlisted help to supply the urgent needs. Someone is always available and willing to make a food run.

From pimento cheese, Danae shifted to sugary treats, then broccoli with ranch dressing. On to tacos and fish sticks and cabbage slaw chocked full with mayonnaise. Then Italian food, Chinese, and shrimp and grits thick with heavy cream and cheese. The weirdest combo—this one had made even Mevlyn gag—was hot buttered popcorn smothered in condensed cream of mushroom soup, straight from the can. Lucky for everyone, that strange craving lasted only a few days.

Now, it's the week before Christmas. Danae can't get enough of the taste or smell of lemons. Elvina heard and brought by a basket of lemon verbena soaps and skin products she found in some fancy store in Tallahassee. Since Mevlyn always keeps fresh lemons in a basket on the kitchen counter, the old woman revels in the fact she is, for once, ahead of the game.

Danae pours lemon juice in her hair after she washes it, makes lemonade by the gallon, and searches out recipes of any kind using the juice or zest. The fruit brings to mind summer sun and the scrubbed-clean scent after a thunderstorm. Even the color yellow brightens her life. Elvina theorizes, it's because Bug's conception fell during the high part of the hot season. That woman has a theory for everything, and can find supporting evidence on one of her many social media forums.

Lemon oil is good for the relief of anxiety, so Elvina tells Danae and Mevlyn. In that case, Danae should dip herself in the stuff once an hour. *Is the baby ok? What if, what if, what if?* Malcolm brings her reference books from the library, but Mevlyn forbids her from reading endless online articles about everything that can go wrong during pregnancy and childbirth.

Then, there're still a few lingering thoughts about Rich. He's up north, ensconced in some high-falutin' college; nobody seems to know where, not even Elvina. Each time the slime ball pops to mind, Danae shoves him down. Bug will not be tainted by that night! Not if *she* has a say. Or if Mevlyn is ever involved, for that matter. Though she chose to retain her birth name, Danae is officially a Jenson; as of November 15th, they have the court dictate to prove it. Rich will have to get past Mevlyn, and Elvina, and Gary, and Malcolm, and Mr. Hal, and Jack, and Carrie . . . One heck of a clan.

Danae lifts her chin and clenches her teeth. If Rich dares to show his face, the creep will have to stand against this protective mama bear.

Will she tell Bug about Rich, and about her family of origin? Probably. It will come out, and she'd rather be the one to relay it. To deny any of it would be a negation of J.J., Mouse, Aunt Sylvia, and Mama, and of the trials Danae endured to find her own way. Good or bad, the history is hers, and by rights, Bug's.

Danae stretches her legs. Have to go for a walk tomorrow, for sure. The water aerobics classes won't resume until the second week of the new year. Two of Tallahassee's city pools hold the classes during the cold months; her group favors the facility with a heated air dome enclosure. Though Danae's steadily expanding belly makes the ab crunches impossible, she plans on trekking to the capital city every week until that last ride to Tallahassee Memorial Hospital.

Willa is on a long vacation break and Danae misses the teacher's fast pace, but Robert, the older gentleman who leads the classes, is well-loved. Most of the regulars have nicknames now: Floppy (after her hat), Sparkles (her pink visor sports rhinestones), Perky, Coach, Teacher's Pet, Poodle (her hair), and Burger (what she gets after every class), among others. They call Danae *Lil' Mama* and Mevlyn *Brows* for obvious reasons. Malcolm dubbed himself *Crash*, because of his tendency to bump into folks at least once a class. Robert usually goes by the nickname *Style*—the instructor likes his poses executed with flair—but lately, some of the women have dubbed him *Nutcracker*, as many of his moves are named after parts of the traditional Christmas ballet.

Last week, after the ultrasound visit, Bug moved for the first time, in aerobics class, during the Dance of the Sugar-Plum Fairies. Danae had squealed and held her rounded stomach. The instructor swished over to check on her, as did Mevlyn and the rest of the women. When they figured out she wasn't in danger, everyone asked permission to feel Bug twitch. Bug rewarded a couple with kicks. Mevlyn held out that the kiddo was doing her own water aerobics. After that class, many of the ladies and the Nutcracker insisted on providing cell phone numbers so Mevlyn could text them with updates. Bug hasn't even made it out yet, and she has many anxious fans.

When the shop's front door opens, Danae doesn't bother looking up at first. "Oh, thank God. I am so ready for those lem—"

Rich stands in front of the desk. Danae's pulse picks up. Inside her body, Bug thumps.

"Hey there." Menace oozes from him.

"What are you doing here." Her reply comes out flat, with no uptick at the end. Danae pushes back the rolling chair and stands, the desk a barrier between them.

"Christmas break. A time to reconnect." He diddles one of the angel figurines, hovering over the carved female's chest in a motion so lewd, Danae flinches. His lips curl up. "Thought I'd drop by and say hello to a *friend*."

The word sounds harsh and foreign. Danae edges toward the door leading to the inner shop. "Guess you're out of luck then. Nobody here meets *that* description." She regrets the taunt the second it leaves her lips. *Never dance with Crazy*, her daddy used to say. *Crazy always leads.*

She lunges toward the doorway. Rich intercepts, shoving her hard against one wall. A pegboard of keys jangles behind her head. The spoiled odor of liquor hits her nose. She turns her face away. Her stomach lurches. If only she could vomit as readily as she had those first three months.

"You ain't going nowhere with *my* baby," he hisses into her ear. "It's mine. You know it is. And I ain't gonna have no white trash bitch raising it."

Danae inches down one hand for the multi-tool, but finds empty pockets. She flicks her gaze to the part of the office she can see. If she can just get to the doorway . . .

When she moves, Rich pins her neck with one forearm and she can barely suck in air. She feels his other hand slide down her stomach, then lower, under the stretchy panel of her maternity jeans. She sucks in air, arches her back.

"Oh no. No you don't. Not this time." Rich flattens against her.

*Oh dear God. It's happening again.*

"Back off." The male voice comes from the shadows. Jack Dixon steps from the shop into the office.

The groping hand retreats, moving up. Danae feels the edge of something hard against her stomach.

"I'll get rid of this little problem right now." Rich spits the words.

"Drop it, Rich." A female voice echoes behind Jack. Carrie steps forward. One hand holds a white paper sack. It crinkles when the opposite hand eases into the cloth hobo bag looped across Carrie's shoulder.

Rich's attention shifts to Danae. The sharp thing stings her belly skin. She feels warmth flow. Danae holds complete stillness, something she had perfected as a child.

The next sound is the paper bag thumping the concrete floor.

Carrie holds a handgun in her clutched hands. "I will send you straight to Hell."

"I'll slice her wide open before you can pull the trigger, bitch."

Danae closes her eyes. *Please, please, please, NO!*

"You've seen me shoot. Really want to take that chance?" Carrie's eyes glitter in the strobe of Christmas lights.

The cold metal edge lifts from her skin. Rich doesn't step back for the longest couple of minutes Danae has ever experienced. Even longer than the night Mouse left.

Rich gives her neck one last hard shove, then steps away. "This ain't over." He sidesteps until he reaches the front door. Then gone.

Carrie lowers the gun, sets the safety, and slides it back into her bag.

## Forty-two

**May 4, 2011**

**D**anae cleans. The closets, the walls, the floors, the tubs, the toilets, Sonny. Anything she can reach past the part of her that's swollen to twenty times its size.

The fact it's still spring break for some universities wedges in her mind. She *must* have this baby before Rich comes blowing into town again. And then what? Then what?

"When are you coming out of there?" she directs to the baby-barnacle. "I know it's cozy. And it's scary as hell out here, but hey, you can't stay in there for-flippin'-ever. You're running out of room."

The baby has dropped into position. Danae's nipples leak colostrum, the pre-milk that will nourish Bug for the first few days. She's two days beyond what the dang doctor swore to be her delivery date. Bug must be operating on a different calendar. Danae's ankles remind her of old socks with blown-out elastic. Stretch marks spiral from her middle like she's been clawed by ghost dragons. And she has to pee every five minutes, no matter if she's drunk anything or not. Danae has fresh respect for mothers everywhere. To think, Estelle Gray had done this three times! And lost two of those children. How did her mama's heart keep from falling from her chest?

If Danae lives through this pregnancy, she promises herself it will *not* happen again. Sex, maybe. This, no. The thought of someone touching her intimately right now makes her want to pick up a meat cleaver and lop off anything resembling a penis.

Bubbles scud the air. She scrubs the last of the pots, then goes after the hard water crust around the kitchen faucet with a toothbrush, dipping it repeatedly into the basin of suds. Something douses her lower legs and ankles. She curses herself for being clumsy. Now she'll have to mop the floor again!

Out of habit, she looks straight down. Bug blocks her view. She makes an exasperated noise, pivots her head, and leans over enough to view the vinyl. A watery puddle surrounds her feet. It's not soapy. And it never touched a dish.

"Um, Mevlyn?" When she hears no response from the den, she pumps up the volume. "Mevlyn! Mevlyn! Mevvvvv-lyn!"

The old woman scuttles into the kitchen. "I was in the bathroom. I heard you screeching from way back there. What is—" Mevlyn stares at the puddle. "Is that—?"

"Yes. It *is*."

"Oh Jesus, Mary, and Joseph!"

Three biblical references in one breath. And the way Mevlyn's brows dance. Wow.

"You, uh, you go sit down." Mevlyn makes scoot motions with both hands. "I'll make the call."

"I will sit, but first I am going to pee, then change into something dry." Danae surprises herself, all calm and adult-like. She's halfway down the hall when the first hard pain hits. She grabs at the bathroom threshold for balance. What is it that she's supposed to do? Oh, yeah. Count the minutes between contractions.

In the bathroom, she lowers onto the toilet, pees while stripping off the soaked underwear and pants and strapping on her watch. First babies take a while, according to the books she's read. It's a good hour to Tallahassee Memorial. She and Mevlyn have it timed.

Less than five minutes later, Danae is clean and wearing fresh clothes, with a thick pad lining her undies in case more grossness oozes out. She hears Elvina's excited voice. Good. The plan is set in place. No way will she let Mevlyn drive. She gets too nervous behind the wheel under normal circumstances.

Mevlyn grabs up the bag that's been on-the-ready for over three weeks, then gets her phone and handbag. Gary rushes through the door. The scenario is rehearsed. Elvina driving her big, comfy Oldsmobile, with Mevlyn navigating. Gary will sit with Danae in the back bench seat, him being her second official labor coach. No way she'd kick Malcolm from the role, since he was there from the start.

"Did you reach Malcolm?" Danae asks Gary.

"Yep. I texted everyone as soon as I got the word from Mevlyn. He's in Jack's truck with Carrie. They're parked behind Elvina, engine running. Let's go!" Gary helps her stand and holds her by one forearm. The other cradles her shoulders.

"What about Taylor?" Danae asks.

"He's with us, too. He wanted to come along and Carrie thinks he's in a good enough place to handle it."

Sonny tap dances at Mevlyn's feet. "You have to stay here, Mister." His ears droop. "Don't worry. I got someone on standby to take care of you, too."

In no time flat, Gary settles Danae into the back seat. Elvina motions to Mevlyn to hurry up and get herself buckled in. Elvina swivels her head right and left to assure nobody will get in her way and pulls out of the driveway. Jack's truck follows.

Elvina takes it easy over several traffic-calming bumps, mumbling under her breath. As soon as she gains smooth pavement, she exceeds the speed limit. By the time she hits the Interstate four miles from the city limits, she launches from the on ramp and busts it wide open.

"You're gonna get the whole dang lot of us pulled over, Elvina!" Mevlyn looks up from her phone. God only knows who she's texting now.

"If I do, we'll pick up a police escort. We are officially an emergency vehicle motorcade."

Danae can't concern herself with Elvina and whether or not some highway patrol cruiser lurks between Gadsden and Leon counties. A contraction sends her into a separate orbit.

"Breathe." Gary sits beside her, rubbing the small of her back.

The contraction eases. His hands feel warm and steady.

"How close between contractions that last time?" Gary asks.

"A little over twenty minutes. I think."

"Ah."

And these are supposed to be the mild ones? Danae does her level best to breathe and remain calm.

Less than two contractions later, Elvina pulls into the emergency room drive. Mevlyn and Gary hop out and help Danae stand. They move toward the double sliding doors, waving Elvina off to park. Malcolm jumps from Jack's truck and runs inside to procure a wheelchair.

Inside, it gets real.


For reasons that now seem utterly insane, Danae had opted for the no-drug approach to delivery. "What in the hell was I thinking?" she asks Mevlyn for the fifth time in less than a half hour.

Malcolm coaches from one side of the gurney; Gary pants, encourages, and massages on the other. Danae alternates between praising both and cussing Gary for every sperm cell he owns, has owned, and will ever own. She strings together profanity in such creative ways, she wishes someone would jot them down.

People come and go. They offer up *atta girl* and *you got this* and *hang tough*. Elvina and Carrie shuttle cups of ice chips and refresh the damp washrag on her forehead. Jack paces a rut in the floor until Gary suggests he might do that in the adjoining delivery waiting area. Taylor slips in and out once, handing over a hand-drawn picture of flowers with butterflies.

Machines beep and buzz. Everyone short of the Governor of Florida himself takes a look and comments on her private parts, which are obviously no longer private, but open for the entire freaking public.

She dilates more, then more, then more.

The pain rolls over her. Each interval, she's amazed to be alive. Bug must have a head the size of a volleyball.

Nothing lasts forever. Except labor.

Mevlyn remains in the room, along with her trusty labor coaches. Ten hours have dragged past. Bug *needs* to make her appearance. The

old woman looks worn out. Please, Bug, c'mon! You can do it—
"OWWWWW! Jesus, God, *some*body!"

Through the pained fog, Danae sees *him*. Rich looms at the end of the gurney. His stare, toxic. He's come for her, no, for Bug!

"HELLL NOOOOO!" she yells.

Rich isn't there. He *was*, right? Sweat stings her eyes. Another contraction pushes any conscious thought aside.

Finally, the doctor comes in. Has to be a good sign. Please, please, please, let it be a good sign.

"Going to ask you to push now, Danae." His voice is practiced and calm.

Sure, easy for him to be all chill—"OWWW. Sweet Jesus wept!"

Gary's fingers are blue-tinged in her grip. She swivels to see Malcolm's hand. Paler than his usual shade. They're going to hate her later. She'll buy them something nice. Maybe—"OWWWWWW! Good Lord Almighty! Help me!"

"One more, Danae. Push, push, push!"

Danae raises her head and shoulders to meet the pain full-on, then falls back onto the bunched, sweaty pillows.

She hears Bug's voice for the first time. Strong. Loud. More than a bit pissed off.

"She's a mouthy one." Mevlyn's face shines with tears. "Like her mama."

Malcolm cries.

Gary passes out. Cold.


Later, in the hospital room, Danae wears a fresh, dry gown. Malcolm and Gary plump the pillows behind her until she urges them to settle before she takes a swing. Mevlyn sleeps in the vinyl recliner in a way that promises a stiff neck when she awakens. Elvina occupies the other chair, her fingers flying on the cell phone screen. By now, everyone in Chattahoochee, heck, in the universe, knows Bug has arrived. The prayer circles take a breather. The water aerobics team rejoices.

Malcolm rambles on and on about how Levon and Girlie are now dog cousins and reassures Danae how much they love kids, how gentle and protective they are, so no worries even though they are pit bulls. Sonny will be a best friend to Bug. Mevlyn's coached up the terrier every day since Danae admitted to being pregnant.

People will come soon, bearing gifts and later, food: well-wishers anxious to set eyes on Bug. Others will drop by once they arrive back in Chattahoochee. As fits her Head Little Old Lady status, Elvina is the gatekeeper.

Nobody from Ala-dang-bamer. Only those Danae count as family now.

"They can do that blood test now, if you want," Gary says to Danae. His gaze never leaves the baby.

It doesn't matter who's the biological father. Gary is the father, the one who stood by her and Bug.

Danae looks up from gazing at her daughter to cheese another pose for Malcolm. He's glowing for reasons beyond becoming a new *uncle* to Bug. Someone sparkles his smile. As soon as she can think clearly—if she ever does again—she'll corner him and get the scoop. No matter if he's found a special person to share his life, and in spite of Danae's time being absorbed by motherhood, she will cordon off a special space for him and he'll save one for her. Piling love atop love doesn't have to smother it.

Must be the endorphins and mommy hormones. Her thoughts run so deep, Danae feels her brain pulse.

"Oh my goodness. Just read on my news feed," Elvina says in a low voice. "Rich has gotten himself into some bad trouble. This time, I don't know if even his daddy can get him out of it."

Malcolm stops taking pictures long enough to consult his own cell phone. "Wow." He gives Danae a loaded look. "He's going to be tied up for quite a while, with this one."

A small part of Danae registers relief. Most of her is consumed with falling deeply in love with the swaddled, rosy newborn she holds to her chest.

Bug is here. May 4. She shares a birthday with Mouse. She's magic.
Stella Marie Gray.
Seven pounds, four ounces, and twenty inches long.
That is all that matters.

# Afterword

**Ala-dang-bamer, Summer of 2018**

I tag along with the realtor. She jabbers on and on about the land and the mature trees at the back of the property. How someone might want to restore the structure, it being one of the few old cracker-style farmsteads left standing. Barely.

I half-listen to her. Besides getting rid of this connection to my first eighteen years on the planet, I have other loose ends to tie up. Those are part of my *now*, not my *then*. A hell of a lot more important.

I ask myself why I've hung onto this place for so long. A clear answer never surfaces. Living in the past will make you stumble into the future, according to Miz Mevlyn.

I smile, shake my head. Should've figured from the way her eyebrows rippled, that old woman was up to something. After dinner last night, Mama Mevlyn dropped the fizz bomb. She had used most of Mr. Sam's life insurance money to buy Mr. Hal's business, building and equipment, down to the last spark plug wrench. He and his wife will set off on an Alaskan cruise adventure at the end of the season. That fact alone brings me joy.

Mevlyn handed over the keys, said the business was now mine to run. Over dessert of banana pudding, Gary, Mevlyn, and I tossed silly names back and forth until she offered, "How about the Roll-Away?"

I replied how that sounded too much like a car being towed off for junk metal. I countered with *Zoom-Away*.

We all laughed. Sonny barked. Stella asked for seconds on the pudding. Neither Mevlyn nor I liked the idea of sugar at her night meal, but we were celebrating. I let Stella dish up three heaping spoonsful. Gary took seconds, too.

The Zoom-Away Automotive Shop across the street from the Wash-Away Laundromat. Where I started and where I ended up. I like the circular nature of it.

Jack Dixon has had his own redemption. Married for five years to Brittany, with a toddler son and a daughter due any day, Gary's cousin is overcoming his mangled past. After Jack and Brittany's wedding, Carrie and Taylor moved into an inexpensive, two-bedroom apartment Elvina helped them find. Carrie's now the office manager for Dr. Johnson. She slaved to get her Associate Degree from Chipola Junior College and takes evening classes at FSU.

Malcolm lives in Atlanta with his partner, employed by a prestigious accounting firm. We see both of them every few months, and Bug Skypes with Unc' Mal and Unc' Chad at least once a week. Jerome's Chattahoochee's new Chief of Police. Elvina reports he's been seeing some nice woman from Sneads and it looks promising.

With the cash from the sale of this piece of haunted dirt in a forgotten corner of Ala-dang-bamer, I can upgrade the shop with high-end diagnostic equipment, and send both Jack and myself through the coursework and exam to become ASA certified mechanics. I can set money aside for Stella's college education, maybe even help Carrie attend veterinary school. Good coming from bad. Happens all the time, so I've heard.

Back in Chattahoochee, Gary and Mevlyn will be waiting for Stella and me. My heart warms. Stella opened up something inside of me, and I'll be damned if I can slam the lid shut. More and more, I realize I don't want to.

It's taken me this long to seriously consider marrying Gary. It's not him that's the issue. It's me. I've not seen marriage and love looped together, other than glimpses of Miz Mevlyn and Mr. Sam before he passed, and a few dim images from my time with Aunt Sylvia and Uncle Bully. I won't magically turn into my mama, and Gary won't wake up some morning and be my daddy. I've had a few years to figure that out.

But there's Mevlyn to consider. Since her hip replacement, she's not as fast or steady. No way will I leave her old and alone, or take away the child she refers to as her *sugar-plum grandbaby*, not after all she's done for me and Stella. Mevlyn's our family now, in heart and in the eyes of the law. She teaches me and Stella new things all the time, about cooking, gardening, and living a good life in spite of things that aim to keep you from it. I pitch in my knowledge of anything mechanical. Stella puts both of us to shame with computer and phone tricks. When all three of us work together, we're a force.

Because of my daughter, I will stand up taller. When I falter, her father and her Mama Mevlyn—heck, half the town of Chattahoochee—will be there to take up the slack. It's like Mevlyn says: *sometimes you come into a family and sometimes a family comes to you.*

"You best marry that man," Mevlyn told me. "I ain't known you to be a fool, save for that little stretch of time you headed down the wrong track with Jack and his boys. Don't make me go to my grave a' worryin' about you. Everyone needs some piece of family to call her own. I had Sam. I got you and the sugar-plum. And you got me and her. But Gary needs you and Stella. And he loves you to pieces. I believe you love him, too."

She's right. As soon as I get business settled in Ala-dang-bamer, I'm heading home to tell him yes, and hope he hasn't given up on me.

Being Mevlyn, she's put together a proposal for "when I wise up and take her advice." Gary and I can take the big bedroom. She'll move herself and the dog into Mr. Sam's old room, the one Stella and I have shared since she was born. Stella can settle into the little study where I used to bunk. Having her own room will light that child up.

Mevlyn has big plans to get my daughter involved in picking out new paint and décor for her own space, no doubt splashes of color, and images of flowers, butterflies, and bugs. When I point out how cramped the house will be, Mevlyn says none of us take up much room, and that she needs less and less as time marches on. She doesn't admit it, but I know Mevlyn's thinking ahead to the time her ashes will join Mr. Sam's on the bank of the Apalachicola River. I hope fate gifts Stella and me a few more years with her.

Sonny's arthritic and white in the face. Most days, he curls up in his bed, content to stay in the house rather than chase squirrels or take the short walk to the Wash-Away. He adores Stella, has from the first time he gave her the sniff-over. He put his seal of endorsement on Gary, too. Other than one incident early on when he went to barking like a crazy fool over Gary's prosthetic leg, the mutt's been smack dab in the middle of our cobbled-together family, happy as a seagull with a French fry.

There's the matter of Rich, too. I despise the guy, still. His first year of college, he and three of his rabid cronies—rich, entitled, "superior gene pool"—gang-raped two freshmen coeds at a frat house party. Unlike me, those young women pressed charges against their attackers, despite open threats, public media shaming, and limited monetary resources. Rich and his gang are serving year six of fifteen-year sentences, with a chance of parole in two more.

People like Rich don't learn. I hope I have. I've been a coward in so many ways. I can blame some of it on being young and ignorant. Rich's assault that night by the river happened before the "Me Too" movement, before accountability became fashionable. Still, I carry back-bending guilt. Had I stood up to Rich and his father, those two girls might not have paid the price for my failure.

*Forgive yourself,* Mevlyn often reminds me. None of us can judge the decisions we made before life taught us better. Wisdom extracts a price.

I have no doubt Rich will haunt my dreams *and* my waking life, showing up to lay claim on Stella. I'll get the paternity test, for sure. I know Stella is Gary's daughter, even without clinical proof. The way her lips crimp when she's tickled, her thoughtfulness, the gentle way she has with babies, animals, and the elderly. Stella reminds me of Mouse, and she holds the best pieces of me and Gary. I will fight for her in ways I never fought for myself. And Gary? He claims someone will have to murder him to get to Stella, Mevlyn, or me.

Yesterday, I watched Stella and Mama Mevlyn in the kitchen mixing a batch of cathead biscuits. Flour dusted their arms and dough caked their hands. You should've heard the giggling and animated conversation. How

I wish I could've grown up with someone like Mevlyn in my life. Thank God I have them now.

If God is a real thing—I've come to hope He, or She, is—and heaven is a place where souls mingle, I believe Mouse sits with Maya Angelou, talking deep. The two are kindred spirits. Maybe I will see both of them one day. Won't Mouse be surprised, how her baby sister can talk books and authors and plotlines and favorite bits? There's a folded piece of paper in the car. It's *Still I Rise*, my favorite Maya Angelou poem. I'll read it to Mouse today, before me and the kid leave this state.

Sometimes, I think maybe I read too much. Mevlyn would slap me on the arm for even thinking that. The more you read, the more your mind opens up, she believes. Otherwise, your brain spoils like an overripe melon left to rot in the field: her words.

I picked up a self-help book last month, one of those feel-good, awareness things. The writer—a doctor with so many letters after her name it looked like alphabet soup—claimed it was never too late to have a happy childhood.

What a total load of crap.

Someone who believes that has either deluded themselves blind or has no clue just how bad a childhood can be.

I can't rewind and live charmed. Can't swap recipes with Mouse, hug my brother at holidays, or share laughter over the silly things our children get themselves into. I can't hear my mama humming in her flower garden.

I halt next to one of mama's overgrown flower beds. The realtor walks on ahead, still babbling about relative land values and closing costs and such. Stella dashes from one clump of wiregrass to the next, capturing and releasing more grasshoppers. Perhaps she chases fairies and dragons or whatever her imagination picks as the moment's activity.

By any standards, I've had a strange life. Ain't even out of my twenties and I've endured more shit storms than most have in eighty. "You don't *get* life," Mevlyn says, "you *make* one."

Thanks to Mevlyn, Gary, Malcolm, and Mr. Hal—and yes, even Elvina Houston—I have managed to make mine.

It's too late for me to have an idyllic childhood. But not so late for my adult self, or for Stella. I can't promise Bug unending bliss, nor can the others who adore her as much as I do; I can surely stretch for a reasonable level of happiness.

Mama called me a ditch weed. If she could see my daughter, she'd figure her for one, too.

Ditch weeds get ripped up, poisoned, and mown over. Their leaves wilt in the summer sun and curl brown with the first hard frost. Given a basic shift—some earth to put down new roots, a little water, a bit of time and space—a ditch weed can flourish again.

Even flower.

## Miz Mevlyn's Best Pimento Cheese Spread

Ingredients:
- 1 cup freshly-shredded sharp cheddar cheese
- 1 cup freshly-shredded Monterey Jack cheese
- 1 cup freshly-shredded mozzarella cheese
- ½ cup mayonnaise
- ½ cup plain Greek yogurt
- Two dashes cumin
- Dash garlic powder
- Dash onion powder
- 1, 2-ounce jar pimentos, with a smidge of the liquid

Mix all ingredients together well. You may add more mayo and yogurt if mixture appears too dry, as long as you keep proportions 1:1.

Allow the spread to refrigerate overnight for the best blend of flavors.

Always shred your own cheese—the packaged version will make the spread less creamy. Trust me on this—don't be lazy.

For variety, add either three slices of crispy cooked bacon, crumbled, or one jalapeno pepper, finely diced, after removing the seeds and fleshy insides.

This recipe is a no-brainer as long as you use equal parts of all three cheeses and a 1:1 ratio with your mayo and yogurt. I make mine by sight and feel, and of course, taste.

## Miz Mevlyn's Oatmeal Butterscotch Cookies

Ingredients:
- 3/4 cup butter or margarine, softened
- 3/4 cup white sugar
- 3/4 cup packed brown sugar
- 2 eggs
- 1 teaspoon vanilla extract
- 1 1/4 cups all-purpose flour
- 1 teaspoon baking soda
- 1/2 teaspoon ground cinnamon
- 1/2 teaspoon salt
- 3 cups rolled oats
- 1 cup butterscotch chips
- 1 cup chopped pecans (optional)

Preheat oven to 375° F (190° C).

In a large bowl cream together the butter or margarine, white sugar, and brown sugar. Add the eggs and vanilla, beating until the batter is smooth.

Stir together the flour, baking soda, cinnamon, and salt. Gradually add the flour mixture to the butter mixture and stir until blended. Stir in the oats, the butterscotch chips, and pecans. Drop by rounded teaspoonfuls onto a cookie sheet lined with that wonderful baking parchment paper. (I like to flour my hands and roll each dollop of batter into a ball, on account of this makes the cookies turn out round and pretty, but you can use a spoon if you don't like to get your hands gooey.)

Bake for 8 to 10 minutes, until the edges begin to brown. Allow to rest for a few minutes on the pan before transferring to a plate or rack to completely cool. Store in an airtight container.

## Miz Mevlyn's Red Potato Salad

Ingredients:
- Red potatoes—8-10, depending on size—scrubbed and cut into bite-sized hunks (leave skins on!) *
- ¾ cup plain Greek yogurt
- ¼ cup light sour cream
- 3-4 Tbsp. mayonnaise
- ¼ cup red onions, finely diced
- ¼ tsp dried parsley
- ¼ tsp. garlic powder
- 4 Tbsp. bacon bits, or cook about 4 bacon strips crisp, drain, and chop
- Salt and pepper to taste

Boil potatoes in lightly-salted water until fork-done (soft, not mushy), drain and allow to cool.

Mix together all other ingredients except the potatoes. Add cooled, cooked potatoes and fold them in until everything is combined.

This salad is best after overnight refrigeration, so the flavors will get acquainted and blend.

* Red potatoes differ in size, according to how soon they're harvested.

If the salad appears to be too dry, you may add a few more tablespoons of yogurt and mayonnaise.

# About the Author

Rhett DeVane is the author of seven published mainstream fiction novels, two coauthored novels, short stories, flash fiction, middle grade chapter books, and poetry. Her short fiction pieces have appeared in five anthologies.

She has won numerous awards for her fiction from the Tallahassee Writers Association, Florida Authors and Publishers Association, and the Florida Writers Association.

For the past forty-plus years, Rhett has made her home in Tallahassee, located in Florida's Big Bend area, where she splits her time between writing and thinking about writing. She is currently working on the next novel in line, as well as a series of middle grade and young adult fiction, because her muses refuse to contain her in a single box.

Author photo by Lance Oliver Photography